Libby Page wrote her debut novel, *The Lido*, while working in marketing and moonlighting as a writer. She graduated from the London College of Fashion with a BA in Fashion Journalism before going on to work as a journalist at the *Guardian*, and later as a Brand Executive at a retailer and then a charity. *The Lido* was a *Sunday Times* bestseller, has sold in over twenty territories around the world, and film rights have been sold to Catalyst Global Media.

Libby lives in London where she enjoys finding new swimming spots and pockets of community within the city.

Follow Libby on Twitter @libbypagewrites

Also by Libby Page

The Lido

'A quirky tale of powerful friendships, flaws and fallouts. Get your tissues ready!'   *OK Magazine*

'A feel-good and lovely read. It makes us want to step inside the café!'   *Closer*

'A feel-good novel *par excellence*'   *Daily Express*

THE

24-Hour

CAFÉ

LIBBY PAGE

ORION

An Orion paperback

First published in Great Britain in 2020 by Orion Fiction
This paperback edition published in 2021 by Orion Fiction,
an imprint of The Orion Publishing Group Ltd
Carmelite House, 50 Victoria Embankment
London EC4Y 0DZ

An Hachette UK Company

1 3 5 7 9 10 8 6 4 2

A CIP catalogue record for this book
is available from the British Library.

ISBN (Mass Market Paperback) 978 1 4091 75261
ISBN (eBook) 978 1 4091 7527 8

Typeset by Deltatype Ltd, Birkenhead, Merseyside

Printed in Great Britain by Clays Ltd, Elcograf, S.p.A.

www.orionbooks.co.uk

FOR MY FRIENDS

12.00 A.M.

The city never sleeps, and neither does Stella's. A glowing red sign marks out the café that serves fish and chips, bangers and mash and American pancakes to Londoners and visitors at any time of day or night. While buses pull up and drift away outside the window, the coffee machine hisses and administers caffeine to the sleepless.

The diner occupies the ground floor of a tall building opposite Liverpool Street station, during the day one of the busiest stations in London, at night a waiting ground for holidaymakers catching the coach to Stansted airport, drunk students heading home from a night out in Shoreditch, and those with nowhere else to go huddling beneath the awning of the Starbucks concession.

Inside, the café is a gaudy mash-up of British and American nostalgia – nostalgia for a time and place that perhaps never existed on either side of the Atlantic. Every wall is covered in

1

pictures. A pop-art style portrait of the Queen hangs next to a red plastic Coca Cola sign. Framed beer coasters below an old London Underground plaque that reads 'Liverpool Street' in huge letters. A lending library housed in a red wooden telephone box and a frumpy fringed lampshade hanging from the ceiling. Black and white checked linoleum lines the floor. Old wooden school chairs with space to slot books at the back sit opposite Formica tables and banks of fake leather seats. There are high tables with stools on either side, as well as diner-style booths where lamps hang low in the middle. Small packets of sauces sit in Oxo tins on the tables, red paper napkins stuffed beside them.

In the middle of the café, at the back, is an antique Cadbury's cabinet filled with cakes and smoothies in glass milk bottles. On a counter beside it is a shining silver coffee machine that glints with the reflection of the café and the faces of its lost souls. Behind the coffee bar is an enormous painted Union Jack, taking up the whole length and height of the back wall. Right in the centre, leaping from a wooden mount, is a stuffed brown bear. Its paws are outstretched, permanently frozen in 'attack'. The bear is wearing a top hat.

HANNAH AND MONA

The bear is called Ernest. At least that's how Hannah addresses him as she pushes open the door to Stella's, a rainbow striped scarf wrapped tightly around her neck, flame-red hair poking out beneath. It is mid-September but chilly at this time of night and she is glad for the warmth of her scarf and her bright red woollen coat. Hannah steps into the café, the smell of fried food and the sound of Johnny Cash singing 'I Walk the Line' greeting her.

'Good evening Ernest,' she says, nodding up to the bear, who looks back through glassy eyes, but says nothing. 'Or should I say good morning,' she adds.

The clock above the counter, its round face painted with a 1950s Kellogg's advert, reads 12.05. She is five minutes late for her shift, which for Hannah is early. Lateness is just part of who she is, like the tattoo on her ankle, her aversion to conflict and the colourful clothes she wears like a uniform. The night has technically turned to morning, but it didn't feel that way as she rode the bus earlier, loud groups heading home from nights out as she sat quietly with her earphones in, on her way to work.

Beneath the bear, a tall woman is stood at the counter, a loose, dark plait falling over one shoulder and her eyebrows meeting in a frown as she reads. She has skin the colour of well-done toast and her face is enviably free of any blemishes or marks other than a small, dark mole just beneath her left earlobe. She looks up as Hannah enters and their eyes meet; they share a smile of familiarity. Mona.

'Hi,' Mona says, at the same time that Aleksander, the chef on duty, shouts from the kitchen, 'That bear is very dead!' in his strong Polish accent.

'Don't listen to him, Ernest,' says Hannah as Mona slips her book, a play, into the pocket of the red and black apron that is tied around her waist. She reaches behind the coffee bar for a second matching apron, which she throws at Hannah.

'Give me a minute!' says Hannah, catching the apron and placing her coat and scarf on the back of one of the many empty chairs.

'I'm sorry,' replies Mona, with a sigh, 'I'm just knackered. I've been on my feet for twelve hours.'

Today both Hannah and Mona are working double shifts. Stella, the café's owner and their boss, knows they both care more about their wages than the legalities of sensible working hours.

Mona stretches, extending her arms in an elegant way that another dancer would immediately recognise as a sign of a shared passion. She reaches a hand to the base of her neck and rubs firmly.

'I know,' replies Hannah, bundling her layers in a box under the counter and tying the apron, 'My turn now.'

'Lucky you.'

Mona has been here since 12 p.m. the day before when the sun was high above the buildings and the café was busy with people taking an early lunch. Back then she wore a neat plait and her apron was clean; now her hair is in disarray and her apron is smeared with stains – tomato ketchup, coffee, spilt milk. Despite this and it being the end of her shift, she won't leave immediately. Instead, this quiet moment between night and day is a chance for her and Hannah to catch up. Not that they don't often see each other. As well as working together, they also live together.

They share a one bed ex-council flat in Haggerston, Hannah using what is supposed to be the living room as her bedroom.

It's not where either of them pictured still living, aged thirty. They imagined flats that they would own and perhaps small gardens fit for a BBQ and a dog. But then many things about their lives are different to how they imagined when they were younger.

The flat is on the third floor of a horseshoe-shaped building that looks down on a communal garden where raised beds house a mix of messy fruit bushes, neat rows of vegetables, and bare, empty dirt that the local cats use as litter trays. Inside the flat, Mona's room is fastidiously tidy. The only things on show are a yoga mat and weights propped by the door, novels and hardback biographies of famous dancers stacked neatly on the bookshelves and one large frame above her bed filled with a grid of photographs. The bed is covered with crisp white ironed sheets, an extravagance that Hannah laughs at Mona for whenever she sees her at the ironing board, struggling with the large duvet cover. Hannah hasn't used the ironing board once since they moved in four years ago.

Hannah's room is more chaotic but more personal too. Clothes are constantly strewn on the floor and abandoned shoes mark a path to the bed, obscuring a colourful rug that covers the worn carpet. A crumpled, floral duvet and a scattering of cushions crown the bed. Sentimental knick-knacks gather dust on the windowsill, lights twist around the headboard of the bed and a jug of flowers, Hannah's weekly indulgence, bloom on the bedside table.

Most days there is a drying rack propped in the hallway of the flat, draped in colourful shades (Hannah's) and an array of cropped trousers and over-sized shirts in muted tones (Mona's).

The walls of the flat are covered with pictures of Frida Kahlo, Katharine Hepburn, Virginia Woolf and posters from their favourite shows.

But the pictures are attached with sticky tabs that are designed specially not to leave a mark on the rented walls, which are painted a slightly greyish shade of magnolia that neither of them would have chosen themselves. At Christmas they decorate the flat with handmade paper chains and invite their friends over for mulled wine and pigs in blankets, but they never bother buying a Christmas tree as they both spend the holiday out of London and hate the thought of returning to skeletal branches, pine needles shed like an unwanted coat on the floor. It is a transient, temporary sort of home that nonetheless feels like their own corner of London.

Hannah grew up in a small village in South Wales where she stayed while studying for a performing arts degree in Cardiff. After graduating she headed to London. She was one of a convoy of performers arriving in the big city, some of whom she still sees, others who drifted across the city and disappeared from her life, slotting into someone else's instead. She has lived in London for nine years and still remembers when she first started referring to London as 'home', her parents' house in Wales becoming 'home home' and later 'my parents' house'. After a failed two-year relationship, at twenty-five she found herself moving out of the flat she rented with her boyfriend and into shared accommodation again. She left with half a set of kitchen equipment, her guitar and a collection of records, suddenly in need of somewhere to live. It was in that house in Bounds Green shared by other artists and performers that she met Mona. It had been a relief when, a year later, they decided to move in together – sharing with just one other person felt at least slightly better than the hectic house share that had been depressingly similar to her first flats in London.

Mona has the almost-but-not-quite American accent of a former international school student. With a German mother and an Argentinian father, she grew up in Singapore, attending an international school while her parents both worked at the city's university. When she was fourteen her parents divorced, her father returning to Argentina where he shortly remarried. Mona's half-brother Matías was born when she was seventeen. At eighteen Mona left Singapore for London (a city she had dreamed of but never visited) and a degree in dance. Now, her friends and family are scattered across the world, her mother and father on separate continents and some school friends still in Singapore but others in America, Australia or Europe. On her worst days, Mona feels like she belongs nowhere. On her best days, she belongs everywhere.

For both women, waitressing is just one part of their lives. When they fill out forms that require them to list an occupation, both of them struggle to find a succinct answer. Hannah: Singer/Waitress. Mona: Dancer/Waitress. Their lives are constantly shifting: a daily balancing act of interests and the need to earn a living. Unfortunately, over the years the two have not overlapped as much as either of them would have liked. It's not just their living situation that they imagined would be different at this stage in their lives: neither of them expected to still be working as waitresses. Yet the job facilitates the pursuit of the dream that they both still chase, despite it all. Both women are driven by a fierce ambition that sometimes bubbles up in an uncontrollable feeling similar to nostalgia: nostalgia for a life they imagined but have never quite realised. It gnaws at them, making them feel at once empty and full of an energy that has no outlet, a force with no direction. Many of their friends have flats, husbands, babies and pets. They have each other, and this ambition.

The song in the café switches and the fast-paced intro to 'Tutti Frutti' plays loudly through the speakers. Hannah drops the tea towel she had been carrying.

'Come on!' she says, suddenly swaying her hips and waving her hands above her head.

'I don't know if I can, I'm knackered!' says Mona with a groan.

'You're never too tired for dancing,' Hannah replies.

Mona pauses and then surrenders to this silly tradition, her hips starting to move and then her arms. It's their rule – if they are on a shift together and this song comes on, they have to dance. She can't quite remember who started the rule – probably Hannah, back when they had both just started working at the café and thought it would only be a temporary thing to fit around auditions. It seems a very long time ago now, but the tradition has stuck, perhaps because it reminds them both of what it felt like to be so full of hope and ambition that you just have to dance.

Luckily, this time the café is empty. Mona might be classically trained but when she is off stage she dances like a wild thing. Hannah follows her lead and shakes and wriggles and waves her limbs as though they want to separate themselves from her body, her hair fanning around her face like a bright red mane.

'We're too old for this,' says Mona as she swings enthusiastically.

'Definitely!' says Hannah in reply. But neither of them stops dancing.

Hannah is half-aware of movement outside the café window – the buses and cars and the few people on the street – and the sound of Aleksander groaning 'Not that fucking song again' from the kitchen, but the other half of her is absorbed by the music and the feeling of her friend's body moving beside hers. She suddenly feels filled with the memories of all the many times before in her life when music has overwhelmed her: the early singing lessons at school, her first performance at the village hall, and more recent gigs in underground bars where her feet stick to the floor but it doesn't matter because everything is song. For Mona, it's the feeling of her body stretching and swaying that hooks her. Even after hours on her feet her body still knows how to dance.

When the music stops they both look around as if dazed, suddenly remembering where they are. The smell of frying wafts from the kitchen and the lights seem to throw a suddenly harsh glare on the café. They catch each other's eyes, both thinking the same thing but not saying it. *What are we still doing here?*

Hannah shakes off the thought and instead reaches for a cloth and starts absent-mindedly wiping the coffee counter.

'So tell me, what's been going on today?' she asks.

This is a ritual of theirs too – sharing their observations

of the customers who have visited the café, some witnessed, others imagined. As waitresses, they can melt into the surroundings – they are as much a fixture of Stella's as Ernest the bear and the gaudy pictures on the walls. It allows them the perfect opportunity to watch and listen.

'Well, unhappy soya latte woman is finally getting a divorce,' says Mona as she wanders between tables, rearranging paper napkins and wiping surfaces, 'and about bloody time, according to her friend. She's been secretly saving up for her own apartment – now she has found one in Limehouse that she loves, so she can finally admit she knows about the affair and move out. She's taking the cat.'

'Good for her,' replies Hannah, knowing whom Mona is referring to immediately. Hannah pictures the scene: the customer sitting on the sofa with a suitcase at her feet and a cat on her lap as her husband arrives home, calling him in to the living room and calmly telling him it's over, that she knows about the other woman and she wishes them the best – her lawyers will be in touch soon and she doesn't expect it to end well for him. Her mind turns suddenly to Jaheim, her most recent boyfriend. It's been three weeks since they broke up and the pain is still raw. She wonders for a moment whether Mona has noticed her sudden intake of breath and guessed where her thoughts have wandered, but she doesn't seem to, as she continues talking.

'There was a hell of an argument in the afternoon too,' says Mona, 'A mother and teenage daughter. They were speaking a language I didn't recognise so I obviously couldn't work out exactly what they were saying, but I did notice a new-looking eyebrow piercing on the girl so maybe it had something to do with that.'

Hannah smiles; she remembers her own mother getting angry when she got her tattoo, a small string of musical notes on her left ankle, when she turned twenty-two. She was home for a week during the summer, some time off between temp jobs, and was stretched out on a deckchair in the garden enjoying a rare day of sunshine as her father struggled with the sun umbrella. Her mother had been furious. Hannah had resisted an argument – she usually did anything possible to avoid a confrontation – but inside she seethed. It was her body, it always had been, and she was a grown woman.

Mona pauses for a moment.

'I've got something to tell you,' she says eventually.

'Go on?' says Hannah, putting down the cloth she'd been using to clean the counter and turning towards Mona to indicate she is listening, that her friend has her full attention.

'I got a call-back!' Mona says, smiling, her cheeks flushed.

There is a brief moment when Hannah says nothing and her face rests in a blank expression. She feels her heart pounding inside her chest and a sudden drop of her stomach as though she is falling. But in an instant, she has found her smile, pulling it out like a pair of keys dug out of the bottom of a handbag. She steps forward, enveloping her friend in a hug.

'Mona, that's amazing,' she says.

'It probably won't come to anything,' says Mona, pessimism being her usual defence strategy. 'It's just a call-back, not a definite offer.' But she is smiling, and Hannah can read her smile.

She isn't sure which audition this one is – they both attend so many that they long ago stopped sharing all the exact details – but she certainly knows the significance of a call back. When they first started living together, Hannah's and Mona's careers felt at similar stages, but in the last few years Hannah knows this has changed. Recently she has felt as though she is falling far behind. She leans against the coffee counter to hide the fact that her hands are shaking.

Hannah doesn't want to admit to herself or to Mona that she is tired. But she is. Last week there was an audition for a singing role narrating a well-known modern circus show. Hannah knew that it was a great opportunity and that she should go for it. But she also knew she would be joining queues and queues of other hopefuls at the audition, all wonderful singers, most probably several years younger than her. And suddenly, she just couldn't face it. When the day arrived, Hannah regretted having told Mona about it – she was so enthusiastic and wished her luck as she always did, but Hannah really just wanted to stay in bed. She knew she couldn't though. Since knowing each other, and particularly since living together, it has been their thing to spur each other on. They are in it together and have always made a point of pushing each other to be the best they can be. Mona would tell her to go to the audition and would be disappointed if she didn't. So, Hannah dressed and left the flat but at the last minute changed her mind and went to a local café for brunch instead. That night she told Mona she hadn't got the part and Mona opened a bottle of wine in commiseration. Hannah still hasn't told her the truth.

As Hannah watches Mona's smiling face she thinks back

to her last serious gig, several months ago now and held in a theatre in Islington. It was an evening she had to self-fund and after renting the space and paying the other musicians she didn't manage to break even, despite the fact that the room was packed with friends and family who had bought tickets and come along to support. Despite the lost money, one good thing had come out of the gig. A friend of a friend who had attended the show works at a central London hotel and recommended her to the manager. She has been offered a couple of trial shifts for October, singing in the cocktail bar. Hannah holds tightly onto the thought of those gigs – just three weeks away now – wondering if it could finally mean the start of something bigger, and the chance to give up the café job for good.

They have both had breaks before – jobs they have both adored – but shows finish and tastes change. And each year a new swathe of eager, bouncy, fame-hungry young performers heads for London and turns up to the same auditions as Hannah and Mona. They can all sing, they can all dance. But most of them are now ten years younger than Hannah and Mona, and some are just that little *more,* that 'more' being impossible to pin down or describe. Hannah thinks of it as 'sparkle'. Some people just sparkle. They are the ones your eyes are drawn to in a dance chorus on the stage, the voice you single out in a choir – the people who have the ability to become a shining individual in a crowd of sequins and jazz hands.

'When is the second audition then?' asks Hannah, focusing on keeping her smile firmly on her face.

'It's tomorrow. Well, technically *today*. 9.30 a.m.,' replies Mona.

'Ouch – will you be OK?'

'I'll have to be. I'm going to sleep as soon as I get home; hopefully I'll get enough to be at least vaguely co-ordinated. And then there's coffee.'

'Text me to let me know how it goes, OK?'

'Of course.'

Mona pauses.

'I really, really want this one, Hannah,' she says, more quietly this time and looking down at her hands. Mona is usually so composed, keeping any anxieties about her career much more carefully hidden than Hannah. She never usually expresses nerves before an audition; instead she pours her energy into practising, often refusing to talk about her feelings if Hannah presses her.

'I've just got to get this bit right,' she would often reply to a question from Hannah about whether she was nervous, her feet tapping out her anxieties in a perfectly mastered piece of choreography.

In the café, Hannah watches her friend, her face lined with a frown for once.

'I know you do,' she replies. And she does. Looking at Mona she feels it – that well-known feeling in her stomach, a yearning that, despite her exhaustion, hasn't diminished over the years. She takes a deep breath.

'You'll be great, you're amazing,' she says, and instead of wishing Mona luck – they have grown to believe the stage superstition – she adds, 'Break a leg.'

Hannah glances at the clock: it is nearly 12.30.

'What are you still doing here?' she says suddenly, 'You

14

should have mentioned your audition straight away, I wouldn't have kept you here so long dancing to stupid songs and making you talk to me.'

She laughs, but the truth is these are some of her favourite moments with her friend. Night turning slowly into day, the café nearly empty, quiet enough to talk and to make themselves milkshakes without anyone noticing. It feels special, secret, and entirely theirs.

Mona glances at the clock.

'That's OK. But you're right, I should probably go.'

She retrieves her belongings from beneath the counter and swaps her apron for her black coat, giving a wave once she is ready. Hannah lifts the cloth and waves back as Mona heads for the door. And then she is gone, stepping out into the light of the street lamps and away down the road. For a moment Hannah stands in her friend's absence, filling the space where she was just now, her head full of the things she meant to tell her. Unsaid words rattle inside of her like the wings of moths brushing a bulb.

After a moment of staring out the window, following Mona long after she has disappeared down the street, Hannah turns her attention back to the café. When her mind wanders and her worries about her career and her future threaten to overwhelm her, she finds it helps to ground herself with this view, on the details of the everyday. She returns to cleaning, this time focusing on the coffee machine, wiping the silver surface, the café looking back at her in the reflection.

Once the coffee machine is clean she pulls up a chair and sits, waiting to serve whoever wanders in from the city outside.

1.00 A.M.

HANNAH

The door opens and a boy who looks in his late teens or early twenties steps into the café. He is wearing a green hooded jumper and pale jeans that look too big for him and he has a large backpack on his shoulders. He nods at her, making eye contact only for a brief moment before looking down at his feet. As he tilts his head, sandy blond hair falls in front of his face and dangles in strands beside his chin. Hannah notices the shadow of a few-days-old beard on his chin.

'Hi!' she says, looking up from the counter, 'Sit wherever you like.'

She watches as the customer eyes up the tables and chooses one on the edge of the café – a table, not a booth. He places his rucksack on the chair next to him and rolls his shoulders, tilting his neck slowly from one side to the other. He sits down and opens the bag, pulling out a pile of books that look like university textbooks. They have a certain academic-sounding thud as they are placed on the table. The boy lays them out neatly and then examines the menu. After a few seconds he puts it back, zipping his hooded jumper all the way up to his chin and sinking slightly lower in his chair. Hannah takes hold of her notepad and pen and stands up.

'What can I get you?' she asks when she reaches his table. He looks up from a book. Hannah catches a glimpse at the page – lots of diagrams and numbers.

'Can I have a cappuccino, please,' says the boy, his voice softer than Hannah imagined.

'With chocolate?'

'Does that cost extra?'

Hannah laughs, but then stops herself when she sees his face.

'No, of course not.'

The boy's cheeks turn bright red.

'Yes please,' he says quietly.

'And anything to eat?'

The boy glances at the menu again then at the counter where Mona had just laid out a fresh selection of cakes supplied by Aleksander – the last job on his shift.

'I'd recommend the carrot cake,' says Hannah, following the boy's eyes, 'or the pancakes. The pancakes are always good.'

The boy pauses, then shakes his head and turns back to his books.

'Just the coffee, thanks,' he says, flicking his eyes quickly up to meet hers, before turning them back down to the page he is reading.

'No problem.'

As she leaves the table she notices a sleeping bag poking out the top of the boy's rucksack. Before bringing him his coffee, she adds a large chocolate biscuit to the saucer at the last minute. He smiles at her, then returns to his books.

'Good morning!' comes a cheerful voice from the doorway. It's a voice Hannah recognises immediately, with its Spanish accent and a smile that clings to the words.

She smiles too and says a 'good morning' in reply as Pablo, the other full-time chef, bustles into the café, removing a leather jacket to reveal his chef's whites beneath. They are slightly off-white, like sheets that have been washed many times. Pablo is a short, stocky man who Hannah has guessed is in his late fifties, with a thick head of curly, dark grey hair and a permanent smile on his rosy-cheeked face. He is a stark contrast to Aleksander, who often talks to himself in Polish but rarely talks to others. And yet the two chefs seem to have a silent understanding with one another – a bond that is perhaps formed by their shared profession, or maybe simply because they support the same football team.

'So, she's started walking!' Pablo says as he heads through the café towards the kitchen.

Hannah is used to this habit of Pablo's: he never seems to start a conversation, instead he simply continues where he left off the last time he saw you. 'She' is Rosa, his granddaughter. She holds a tie with Arsenal football club as the love of Pablo's life.

'Last week she was just holding on to that little trolley with the bricks, pushing herself around,' he continues, 'But yesterday she was up on those little legs all by herself. She's going to be running before we know it. I've already bought her a football, get her into it early I figure. Here, look.'

He reaches for his phone and scrolls through several photos, holding them up so Hannah can see. He is clearly in no rush to get into the kitchen, but Hannah doesn't mind. She is always happy to see photos of Rosa. Pablo's cheeks glow a bright shade of proud as Hannah nods and coos at the photographs.

Pablo brushes an eye and shakes his head.

'You should'a seen it,' he says. He lets out a deep, happy sigh then waves at Hannah and heads into the kitchen. She listens to the short conversation as Pablo greets Aleksander, who offers a few 'hmm's and 'yeah's in reply. And then Aleksander is heading out into the café, shrugging his coat onto his shoulders.

'Are you off?' asks Hannah. Aleksander nods, looking at his feet.

'Have a good day then,' she adds. He nods again and heads for the door.

Once Aleksander has left, Hannah glances over at the young man with the rucksack. His eyes look heavy and he leans his head in his hands as he flicks through the book on the table. Every now and then his head nods and then jolts back up again.

The door opens again – this time a man in his fifties with grey hair that sticks out in tufts. He runs a hand through it as he enters and it flattens slightly, apart from one spike that seems reluctant to go down. He is carrying a faded bookshop book bag over one shoulder and Hannah notices a couple of pens clipped to the front pocket of his navy shirt. He heads immediately for a seat in the middle of the café, leaving one empty table between

19

him and the other customer. He settles himself and draws a notepad and a crossword book from his bag. His seat is facing the window and Hannah follows his gaze outside.

A man wearing one shoe staggers past, a can held tightly in his fist. Hannah notices his hands, bright pink until the tips of the fingers, which are tinged blue as though they have been dipped in ink. She knows it is not ink that has left those marks, though, but cold, and she feels suddenly grateful for the warmth of the café and her room that she knows will be waiting for her at the end of her shift. A small queue of people flanked by suit-cases has gathered on the other side of the road. Some are in couples or small groups, huddled together, others stand alone and look down at their phones, the screens illuminating their faces in an eerie glow. Above them tower office blocks: some are completely dark, a few are bright, revealing rows and rows of empty desks. Beside them, on the top of the brick tower at the entrance to Liverpool Street station, sit four pigeons, their heads tucked inside the puffed ball of their feathers.

The view of the city makes Hannah think of Mona – she wonders if she caught the night bus and got home OK and whether the audition will go well for her. Maybe she will be too tired from her long shift to really do her best. Maybe her height will be a problem, like it has been many times in the past. The thoughts enter Hannah's mind without her control, as quick as a blink. As soon as she notices them there she shakes herself. Mona will be great. She is her closest friend and she deserves a break.

Pushing the thought from her mind, she picks up her note-pad.

'What can I get you?' she says to the man with the crossword book, the line she will repeat until it loses any sense of meaning and she has become sick of the smell of coffee and chips.

DAN

The smell of pancakes wakes him up. At first, he feels groggy and disorientated. But then he remembers where he is – in the 24-hour café with his university books spread around him and his rucksack on the chair. A taxidermy bear in a top hat stares down at him from its mount on the café wall, claws extended, mouth curled in a snarl. If he were a child, that bear would terrify him. Lucky, then, that he is a grown man. A shudder runs through him as he turns away from the staring glass eyes.

He looks around him quickly, checking to see if anyone had noticed him sleeping. The café is nearly empty apart from a middle-aged man on a table just across from him who is writing in a crossword puzzle book, and the waitress who stands at the counter and looks absent-mindedly out the window. She is pretty: her skin so pale it's almost translucent, and a shock of red, wavy hair framing her round face and falling over her shoulders. She wears a lot of make-up (a flick of black eyeliner and coral lipstick that clashes with her hair) and he guesses she is in her late twenties or early thirties. He hopes she didn't see him sleeping. He particularly hopes he didn't snore.

Sitting straighter in his chair he reaches for the textbook in front of him and opens it near the middle. He picks up the pen that he must have dropped on the table when he fell asleep, and the notebook resting by his now cold cup of coffee. Then he tries to read but the smell of pancakes and an ache in his stomach and somewhere closer to his ribs distracts him.

He looks at his watch, counting the hours until the university library opens (eight) and until his first lecture (ten).

The door opens and the sound of laughter and voices invades the café. Dan looks up as a group walks in. There are three girls and two boys of around his age. The girls wear brightly coloured dresses that are wrapped around their bodies like bandages and stop just below their thighs. Despite summer being over, their legs are bare. The boys are in jeans and checked shirts that are buttoned to the neck. He can immediately tell they are all drunk – they walk with hesitant, wobbly steps like toddlers. The girls have their arms linked together and are giggling, holding each other for support as they teeter on their platform heels.

Carefully he reaches for his rucksack, takes it off the chair next to him and tucks it under the table.

The waitress takes their orders and they sit down, girls on one side of a booth, their bodies close to each other and their arms still linked, and the boys piled on the other side, leaning back heavily against the fake leather seats. Dan tries to focus back on his work, pushing out the sound of carefree laughter and conversation coming from the other side of the café.

But then the sound of shouting draws him out from his books.

'Shots! Shots! Shots!' shouts one of the guys. Dan looks up again and sees him pulling sachets of ketchup, mayonnaise and brown sauce from the tin in the middle of the table and lining them up in front of his friend. The girls are shrieking now and one has her phone out, holding it up as though she is filming – maybe she is.

Dan notices the man with the crossword looking across at the group and then turning back to his puzzle, shaking his head.

'No, mate, no way!' says one of the guys, waving his arms across his body.

'Shots! Shots! Shots!' continues his friend, the girls joining in now too. They thump their hands on the table and Dan catches the waitress looking over at them too. She opens her mouth, perhaps as though about to shout at them, but then stops and returns to preparing the drinks orders. Dan can hear noises from the kitchen, and they reignite his hunger.

After a moment, the guy stops his protesting and stands up. He rolls up his sleeves and mock flexes his muscles. Then he picks up the packets, ripping them open with his teeth and spitting the plastic onto the table. One by one he squeezes them into his mouth, ketchup, mayonnaise, then brown sauce.

Watching them, Dan's stomach turns, imagining the taste of ketchup and brown sauce in his mouth. But despite the revulsion the laughter of the student's friends hits him hard in his gut, piercing him with its casualness, its ease.

Their food arrives and the group tuck in greedily. Dan half reads and half watches as the girls laugh and take their shoes off under the table, their bare feet making them look younger despite the dresses. They sip their milkshakes and rub their tired feet, occasionally nudging each other affectionately or resting a head on each other's shoulders. He thinks about where they might live; perhaps in one of the nicer student halls, and what their parents do, whether they have any siblings. Watching them he suddenly hopes that they never have to learn what he has learnt: that life is a bitch and that one day you'll find yourself entirely on your own. He wishes they could stay in the café all night drinking milkshakes and laughing at nothing, even finding the gross inanity of the boys hilarious. That time could pause and keep them right here with no worries other than the hangover and blisters that await them tomorrow.

HANNAH

She has served hundreds of other kids like them before. That's how she thinks of them now – kids – even though in reality they are probably in their twenties – not that much younger than her really. The distance between them seems vast, though. Hannah tries to remember the last time she was out at 1 a.m. for any other reason than work. If she doesn't have a late shift at the café or a gig she prefers a quiet night at home, watching Netflix and relishing being in bed early. Her teenage-self would have been ashamed of her for favouring unflattering pyjamas instead of going out clothes. She can't remember the last time she went '*out* out'. The thought of a club filled with sweating bodies and music that is not for listening to, but only for drowning out drunken voices, makes her shudder.

As she watches the group she remembers moving to the city for the first time nine years ago. Suddenly the exhaustion, the disillusion and all the years fall away and she is twenty-one again and Life with a capital L is just about to start.

*

She drags a suitcase behind her down the station platform, filled with as many clothes, books and records as she can carry. One wheel is broken and juts out in a different direction to the others (she recalls her mother's words: 'If you fill that suitcase any more you're going to break it'). Together, Hannah and the bag make a swift but wobbly path through the crowds, as though drunk.

'Let me take that for you, Hannah,' says her father, reaching for the suitcase, but she pulls her arm away.

'I've got it, Dad, stop worrying.'

He throws a glance at her mother that Hannah tries to ignore. She doesn't need to look at her mother to know her face is pink and swollen. It has been that way since last night – their last meal together as a family. Hannah's father reaches for her mother's hand. They walk like that, hand-in-hand behind her as she makes her way to the train. As usual, Hannah took longer to get ready than she thought, so she takes quick, long strides down the platform, listening to the tapping of her mother's heels as her parents struggle to keep up with her.

Across Hannah's shoulders is slung her purple guitar case, its solid weight knocking against her back with the pace of her strides, reminding her of the years of singing lessons and drama classes that have led her to this point.

'Knock 'em dead': she recalls the words of Josephine Wagner, the director of the performance arts degree in Cardiff that

25

Hannah finished just over a month ago. It was their final day and Hannah remembers looking across the hall of young women and a handful of men as Josephine said, 'You are all going to be stars.'

For the first time Hannah had wondered whether there was enough space out there for all these newly fledged stars. Standing among the brilliance of her course mates and friends, she felt her own brightness dull to a faint imperceptible glow. Perhaps she should have thought about it before – the reality of her future – but somehow she never had. Not really, not with any clarity. Her judgement was clouded by well-worn clichés and inspirational phrases that she lived off as though they were food. It would all work out. Hard work would pay off. If she wanted it enough, she would make it as a singer, just like she had decided when she was nine years old. Everything would be OK.

The image of Josephine Wagner crosses her mind again as her phone buzzes in her pocket. It's a notification from the WhatsApp group of the seven other friends from her course who are heading to London. Four are already there; three are on the same train as Hannah. Clara, Becky and Amy are her closest friends and will be her new flatmates when she arrives in London. A month ago they spent a weekend in London visiting endless flats until they found one they could afford and that wasn't too damp or dark or above a chicken shop. It is tiny, but it will be Hannah's first flat in London so she doesn't care.

'Where are you?' *the message says,* 'We've saved you a seat! Don't miss the train! And we've got cava! London, here we come!'

She feels her confidence returning. It's like a surging force that flows through her body and fills her up, making her stand taller. It's the same feeling she gets when she is on stage or perched on a stool with her guitar on her lap, her lips parted in the second before she starts to sing. It's a confidence instilled by years of stage school, then a drama degree, countless gigs in pubs and village halls, and endless instructions from Josephine and others to 'smile' and 'own your own space'.

She readjusts her guitar on her back as she reaches coach C.

'This is my coach,' she says, stopping and turning back to her parents.

'We could have driven you, you know,' her mother says, 'You could have taken more of your things that way. And we would have been able to help you settle in.'

'I know,' replies Hannah, 'But it's a long way, you didn't need to do that. And besides, my room is tiny, I'm not going to have space for that much stuff.'

Hannah agreed to the smallest room in the flat on the basis that she would pay less rent. It only fits a single bed, a wardrobe and a chest of drawers but she doesn't care. She doesn't think she will spend much time in it anyway: she pictures herself exploring the city, attending shows, singing at the gigs she is confident she will line up, and partying with her friends in the clubs she imagines will be a million times better than those in Cardiff.

Her phone buzzes again and an overhead announcement calls out her train and its departure time – two minutes from now.

'I have to get on, the train's about to leave.'

She looks at her parents. Her father still holds her mother's hand. Hannah notices for the first time that they have dressed up: her mother in a navy A-line dress with white polka dots and a pair of court shoes, and her father (who usually prefers jeans when he is home from work) in chinos and a blue shirt beneath his grey coat. There is one straight crease in her father's shirt, across his chest; he has a way of ironing creases into his shirts, rather than smoothing them out. Both of her parents are flushed from the dash along the platform and her mother's neat ponytail has come loose. Watching her parents standing there in their smart clothes waiting to see her off, their fingers locked together, Hannah feels her eyes begin to sting. She had been so excited to leave that she hadn't really thought about saying goodbye. She had stayed at home during university, choosing to save the money and drive to Cardiff each day instead, so this is her first time leaving home.

For the past three months Hannah's bedroom wall has held a large calendar on which she has crossed out the days leading up to today – the day that she leaves. Last night her mother had come in to her room to help her pack and had stared for a long time at the calendar, a large circle drawn around today's date. Hannah pictures the calendar still pinned to the wall, her bed neatly made and her wardrobe filled with empty clothes hangers.

She puts down her guitar and reaches for her parents. They wrap their arms around her and the three of them stay like that for a moment, their small family held tightly in each other's warmth and the smell of each other's hair and the same washing powder they all use. Hannah realises she can't remember the brand – she had never thought to properly look. With a sudden feeling of panic, she realises she won't be able to pick it out in the supermarket (she would be too embarrassed to ask her mother *for the name) when she shops for herself in her new home. Her clothes will take on a new smell. She puts her face closer against her mother's shoulder and breathes deeply.*

'OK, I really have to go now,' she says, pulling herself away from them. Her mother sniffs and pulls a tissue from her sleeve. Her father puts an arm around her shoulder.

'Go get 'em,' he says, his voice falsely cheerful.

Hannah picks up her guitar and suitcase and steps onto the train. She doesn't look out the window as the train pulls away and she heads through the carriage, following the sound of laughter and loud chatter.

She would never admit it to the girls she is about to share cava with on the train, but right now this beginning feels like an ending.

'Hannah!' shouts a voice and Hannah waves, spotting her friends sitting around a table, suitcases stacked in the racks above them. They are noisy and giggly, and as she walks closer Hannah tries to ignore the sighs of a man in a suit sat just in front of them. There is an empty space waiting for her and this is her tribe. She smiles and Clara, Becky and Amy smile back, no hint of worry or sadness on any of their faces. They spend the journey drinking and talking about what they are going to do in London – the stages they will conquer, the things they will create. Hannah feels herself settle into the optimistic timbre of their voices. Everything will be OK. As the train clatters away from Cardiff they spill cava but don't care – they barely even notice. There will be more to drink tomorrow. There will be more of everything tomorrow.

*

Hannah thinks back to her first few months in London. It had been hard to adjust, but she tried to keep her difficulties hidden. Hers was the faux confidence of a performer; she treated her own life like a show and found that her act of self-assuredness and optimism often convinced even herself that the feelings were real.

She found a job at the Odeon on Tottenham Court Road, spending her days off attending auditions and trailing around bars handing out CDs of her music, asking if they had slots for a new singer. She banked the 'no's like an investment in her future: the more times people said 'no', the closer she must be getting to a 'yes'.

At first, she relished living in a flat with three of her friends, all performers like her. They ate when they wanted and went out most evenings when they weren't working. They left dishes piled in the sink for days, enjoying the fact that there were no parents to tell them to wash up. But eventually the care-free lifestyle began to grow tedious. Hannah wanted to cook a proper meal and know there would be clean saucepans for her to use. Although her room was always a mess, she was surprisingly tidy when it came to the communal spaces. She started to resent the fact no one else ever seemed to empty the bins or clean the bathroom. When she brought it up the others said they did do their share, she just never noticed, or that she was being uptight. They started to argue frequently about stupid things. Who last bought toilet roll, who came in late and forgot to lock the front door. But at the time they didn't seem insignificant and things became so fraught that

Clara, Amy and Becky didn't even feel like friends any more, just annoying people whom she lived with.

Hannah tries to remember the last time she saw her first flatmates but finds she can't. After she moved out she kept in touch with them for a while but something in their friendship had been fundamentally altered since living together. She and Becky stayed in touch for the longest – she'd always been particularly fond of the flamboyant, funny actor. But even they drifted in the end, their lives stretching further and further apart until the link between them broke entirely. Facebook informs Hannah that Clara is now married and living in America, Becky is teaching performing arts at a stage school outside of London, and Amy still lives in London, works in marketing and has a one-year-old daughter.

She'd stayed with the Cardiff girls for a year, then spent the next two years bouncing between places she found on SpareRoom, sharing flats and houses with strangers. Over the years she mastered house sharing, learning to keep her best kitchen supplies and stashes of chocolate in her bedroom and to cook dinner late in the evening so she would have the kitchen to herself. She made the life-changing discovery of earplugs.

Hannah became friends with a few people in those house shares but also encountered many she was happy to leave behind, like the drummer who practised early in the morning before his day job at a telesales firm, the compulsive liar who convinced her flatmates she was a twin despite being an only child, and the young woman who kept a pet mouse in a cage under her bed (Hannah has had a lifelong phobia of mice).

And then she'd met Sam. Hannah flinches at the thought of

her first serious boyfriend, back when she was twenty-three. She'd dated other guys before, but there had been no one like Sam. No one who'd left quite such an impact. She had never lived with another boyfriend and hasn't since. That has been one bittersweet consolation in the recent painful break-up with Jaheim. At least she still has her flat, she still has Mona. A fresh stab of pain pierces her as she thinks about Jaheim and wonders what he is doing now. Sleeping, of course, she thinks to herself. She knows she shouldn't care and shouldn't let herself think about him at all, but she does.

'What is it?' asks Pablo, whom Hannah hadn't noticed leaving the kitchen. He carries a tray of chocolate brownies, fresh from the oven. These early hours can be quiet and Pablo usually fills them by baking, partly in preparation for the day ahead and partly because he loves to bake. If you saw him in the street you might not guess that he can make a chocolate ganache so shiny that you can see your face in it, but over the years Hannah has learnt that the one thing you can rely upon is people's ability to surprise you.

Before placing the brownies inside the counter Pablo tears one off and hands it to Hannah.

She smiles at the simple gesture.

'It's nothing,' she says, trying to hide the shake in her voice. He looks at her, his sympathetic face scrunched into a frown. She finds herself talking without meaning to – it's hard not to when he smiles like that. He makes her think of her father; although they look nothing alike she feels almost as at ease with this Spanish chef as she does with her dad.

'I don't know why but I was just thinking about my first

boyfriend,' she finds herself saying. Pablo has worked at the café even longer than Hannah and Mona and with his chatty, inquiring nature he knows the ins and outs of their lives almost as if they were his own family. Pablo shakes his head as Hannah continues.

'I haven't thought about him in ages, but I guess since Jaheim and I broke up, it's brought it all back really.'

She finds herself gulping back tears. Even mentioning Jaheim's name is hard. The pain is mixed with something else, too – embarrassment at another failed relationship. She can't help but think about all her married friends and the seemingly endless wedding invitations that she receives every year now. Jaheim is gone and she is alone again. To stop her eyes from overflowing she takes a large bite of the chocolate brownie instead. It is delicious and holds back the tears.

Pablo is nodding now, clutching the brownie tray and shifting his weight from foot to foot.

'You're better off without them,' he says in his gentle voice.

Hannah hasn't spoken much about Sam to Pablo, and she certainly can't bring herself to tell him the truth about Jaheim and why they broke up, so it heartens her slightly to know he is on her side without needing to know any of the details.

'My Rosa is never going to have a boyfriend,' he says fiercely, 'All trouble. I'll fight them if I have to.'

Hannah pictures an aged Pablo fighting off Rosa's prospective boyfriends and can't help but laugh – she just can't imagine the curly-haired baker who wells up over photos of his granddaughter involved in a fight. She then stops herself, remembering suddenly the little she knows about Pablo's life before he started working in the café. It is so easy to forget that when he started here it was the only job he could find – no one else wanted to hire an ex-convict. Despite his usual openness, he has never told Hannah or Mona what he was in prison for, only that he spent eighteen months there and that it was hell on earth. He is a wonderful chef; Hannah sometimes wonders whether he has stayed here so long because no one else will have him, or out of loyalty to Stella.

'You finish that brownie, *chiquita*,' Pablo says, 'Brownies help everything.'

Hannah smiles at 'chiquita' – she feels far from a young girl – but it's what he always calls her and Mona. She eats the brownie as instructed and Pablo nods and returns to the kitchen.

Eventually the group of students finish their food and get up to leave, reading the name of their Uber driver and the licence plate out loud. The girls carry their shoes as they head to the door. They walk close to the table of the young man with the rucksack, looking to Hannah as though they might bump into his chair. But they skirt around him and then they are gone, the sound of their carefree young voices ringing in her ears.

2.00 A.M.

DAN

The café is quiet again, the only sign the group were there the half-empty plates and milkshake glasses on the table in the booth that the waitress is currently clearing away. She nearly drops the tray she is carrying but steadies herself against one of the chairs, taking a deep breath before she continues clearing. He notices that her make-up has already started to smudge and that she looks tired in a dazed sort of way.

One of the girls at the table has left two pancakes and Dan's stomach roars at him. He looks up at the menu and fumbles in his pocket – the pancakes cost £4.50 but he only has a fiver on him, and that has to last him for breakfast tomorrow too.

'They certainly had some lungs on them,' comes a quiet voice.

Dan looks up. The man with the crossword book at the

nearby table is looking at him, a pen poised in his hand. He wears round tortoiseshell glasses and a navy corduroy shirt open over a Pink Floyd T-shirt. An additional pen is clipped to his shirt pocket and Dan notices that one of the buttons is different to all the others, bright red instead of white. He has the start of a beard and Dan guesses he is in his fifties. He has the kind of face that looks meant for smiling – there are creases around the corners of his eyes – but is clouded by something. Worry, tiredness, illness perhaps.

'Yeah, I guess they did,' says Dan, offering a small, polite smile. The man continues watching him and Dan thinks he sees his eyes glancing to his rucksack under the table and back again.

'Are you a student?' asks the man, gesturing towards the books on the table. Dan nods and the man asks him what he is studying.

'I want to be an engineer,' Dan replies, holding up the book in his hand.

'*Materials Science and Engineering: an Introduction*,' reads the man out loud, 'Wow, impressive stuff.'

Dan shrugs.

'I'm not sure I understand all of it just yet.'

'But still, you must have done well at school to get on to a course like that. They don't let just anyone design our bridges and whatnot.'

Dan smiles. He *did* do well at school. His mum always encouraged him to study, to work hard. She wanted him to have a better life than they had – even if he'd never once complained about their lot, not the charity-shop clothes nor the beans on toast for dinner three nights a week. Their mantelpiece was like a shrine to his education: school photos and every prize he had ever won, however small (one was a certificate for just entering the school's Maths Challenge, but his mum still framed it and put it up there).

'I flunked my exams myself,' continues the man, 'I was a bit rebellious at school – far more interested in girls.'

He smiles at Dan, and Dan can tell that the man is willing him to smile back, so he does, this time digging out one that he hopes looks a little more genuine.

'I'm getting another coffee,' the man says, 'Do you want anything? Something to eat maybe?'

Dan's stomach grumbles again, but he shakes his head. He promised himself he wouldn't rely on charity.

'Are you sure?' the man says, rising and heading to the bar. The waitress looks up from the book resting on the counter.

'I'm sure,' says Dan.

While the man is at the bar Dan returns to his textbooks, but his mind is elsewhere. He's thinking about his mum. The lingering smell of pancakes in the café takes him back to being seven or eight years old and sitting on the worktop in their small kitchen as his mum pours the pancake mix into the pan. He watches it sizzle, bubbles appearing as though a sea creature is trapped beneath the doughy mix, trying to get out. The thought unnerves him, but then he breathes in the sweet smell and his mind turns to golden syrup and Nutella. They are having pancakes for dinner. It's not even Pancake Day. Dan is delighted. But later, as they sit together in front of the TV, Dan with his favourite Power Rangers plate that he knows he should have grown out of by now, his mum starts to cry. Dan can't understand it, and he shuffles closer and tries to wrap an arm around her shoulder but can't reach all the way.

'I'm sorry, buddy,' she says, sniffing.

He doesn't know what she is sorry for, or what to say, so he rests his head on her arm.

'These are the best pancakes I've ever eaten,' he says, and he feels her body softening as she smiles.

The man returns to the table just as Dan swallows hard.

'God, I need another coffee,' says the man, sitting down, 'That's one of the problems with being an insomniac – I'm constantly knackered but can never sleep. Funny, isn't it?'

Dan doesn't think it sounds very funny but doesn't say so. The man rubs his forehead and tilts his neck from side to side, stretching. Outside the café a bus pulls up and two men throw cigarette butts in the gutter and step on.

'What, so you just can't sleep at all?' Dan asks, turning back to the man. Dan doesn't have any problem sleeping. At the moment his issue is staying awake.

'I get *some* sleep,' the man replies, 'I'd be a medical marvel if I got none at all and was still standing. But it doesn't come easily.'

'Is there anything you can do about it? Aren't there pills you can take?'

'I've tried them all – pills, meditation, counting, listening to music,' says the man. 'Sometimes I drift off for a bit, but then I'm wide awake again, just staring. I get so sick of looking at the same cracks in the ceiling that I come here instead. Nearest place that's open all night. Handy, isn't it?'

The man is looking at him, but Dan wants to avoid the subject of the café and why he is here at two in the morning with his university books around him and a sleeping bag beneath the table.

'So what do you do when you're not trying to sleep?' he asks.

'I'm a script writer.'

The man points at the crossword, 'When I can't sleep I do these. I really should make the most of the sleepless nights and write instead – I'd be far more productive.'

'What do you write?' asks Dan, looking closely at the man. He hasn't met a writer before. He tries to imagine what it would be like – designing with words rather than physical materials every day. The thought makes his head swim. He likes solid, tangible things you can hold on to, like equations, steel and brick.

'Nothing you'd watch,' he replies with a laugh, 'The stuff your mum or auntie would watch. Murder mysteries, daytime dramas …'

He mentions a few names, and one causes a spark of recognition.

'Oh yeah, my mum used to watch that one,' says Dan, '*Dan! Switch over, no more car programmes, it's time for* Midsomer Murders!' He imitates her voice, enjoying the smile that spreads over the man's face as he does. Dan's mum liked the old-fashioned murder mysteries that were set on riverboats or steam trains; it was her lifelong dream to go on the Orient Express. She had a glass jar on the mantelpiece where they both put spare coins. It had 'Orient Express' written in her handwriting on a sticky label. Dan once looked it up and found out how much it would actually cost – he wanted to know how far away they were. When he found out he didn't tell her. He realised that the coins would never get his mother on the Orient Express but he still dropped his spare ones in there anyway. In the programmes his mum liked the characters wore chic suits and drank cocktails from trolleys. She had bought a glass and metal trolley from a charity shop once and it stood in their living room next to the TV, holding the TV guide and her library books, tins of beer and her ashtray. She had wheeled it all the way home from Bethnal Green to Stepney.

'Used to?' says the man with a laugh, 'Did she switch shows when my writing got worse? I think it has recently, lack of sleep really messes with the imagination.'

'Mum died a few months ago,' says Dan.

The man's face turns pale. He rubs at his beard and shakes his head. Dan almost feels sorry – he doesn't like seeing other people uncomfortable. It makes him squirm too. But he doesn't know any way to soften the truth. He can't bring himself to say the well-worn euphemisms like 'passed away' or the worst: 'we lost her', as though he was in some way to blame for his carelessness, or there was hope that she might one day be found.

'Shit,' the man says, making the word sound much longer than its four letters. It helps, a bit. Sometimes Dan would like to say that word himself, over and over. Yell it in fact. Scream it until he has no breath left for shouting. He's never been much of a swearer – it used to upset him when his mum did it when he was younger, when she dropped something or stubbed her toe or sometimes when she spoke loudly on the phone to

40

someone (she never told him who – 'Just a bastard you don't need to know', she'd say).

'God, I wouldn't wish that on anyone,' says the man.

After she died, Dan had been determined to start university despite it all. He knew his mum would want him to go – they'd both worked so hard for him to get there. But they didn't own their home, and she had debts. He couldn't stay in the flat and he knew it wasn't sensible to enrol in halls of residence. He didn't know how he'd meet every payment – his student loan wouldn't cover both the accommodation and his living expenses, and he had no one to ask for help. He didn't want to tell his course mates or his lecturers what had happened – he didn't want to be treated differently. So instead he asked friends if it was OK to crash with them for a while until he sorted things out, telling them there'd been a problem with his halls and his room wasn't ready yet. He stayed with different friends for a few days at a time. Rob, a guy who'd been a few years above him in school and now lived with two friends in a basement apartment in Stratford, let him stay for four weeks. He gave Dan his own towel and pumped up an airbed in the living room, where marijuana grew in heated glass houses and a soppy Ragdoll cat called Pumpkin shared his bed, falling asleep on his feet. Dan grew fond of the cat, and would sneak her Wotsits (his favourite snack, since he was a child) when the others weren't looking. Dan helped with the cooking and made sure his bed was packed away neatly each morning. He got on well with Rob and his flatmates Matt and Jared – some evenings they'd play *World of Warcraft* together and share beers. It was a good month, considering.

But one evening Rob mentioned that his flatmates had been asking him when Dan would be moving on. Dan couldn't help but feel disappointed – he thought Matt and Jared had liked him. But then he'd stopped himself. It wasn't personal, this was their home. Of course he couldn't stay forever. It was ridiculous to think that, to have let himself forget for four weeks and feel almost settled.

'No problem mate,' Dan said that evening, 'I'll be out of your hair tomorrow morning – is that OK?'

'That's great – did you get your halls sorted out then?'

'Yeah, it's all sorted.'

'That's wicked, you're going to have the best time at uni, trust me bro.'

Except it wasn't sorted.

'I don't know what to say,' says the man and Dan looks up, remembering that at this particular moment, he is not alone. 'My dad went just over a year ago. It's when the insomnia started. I just suddenly found I couldn't sleep any more.'

'Yeah, the first few nights I didn't get much sleep either,' admits Dan.

'Fuck, those first nights are the worst,' replies the man, shaking his head again. 'But then it hits you again a bit later doesn't it? About a month afterwards when things have sort of settled down and people have stopped checking up on you – just that realisation that they're really gone.'

Dan has never heard anyone else talk like this. Not many of his friends know about his mum. The ones who do try to understand but just can't. Some offer stories of grandparents' funerals and he wants to tell them it isn't the same, it's not nearly the same and how could they possibly think it would be, but he doesn't want to be unkind.

It hit him hardest the week after her funeral. He was walking back to the flat from Tesco; he was still living in the flat back then. The shopping bags were heavy and cut into the skin on his hands and he was worried that he hadn't bought the right food – that he'd spent too much money by giving in to his craving for Wotsits and pancake mix. It started to rain and the pavement was slippery and he looked up at the grey sky and it suddenly hit him that the world no longer held his mum in it.

The waitress brings a cappuccino and a steaming pile of pancakes to the table and sets them down in front of the man.

'Thanks,' he says. The waitress smiles and looks at them both.

'Let me know if you need anything else.'

Dan tries not to stare at the pancakes (they are drizzled in maple syrup, crispy slices of bacon resting on the side), and covers his stomach with a hand under the table, attempting somehow to stifle the gurgles that to him sound loud enough to fill the café, but that he knows are probably quieter.

The man takes a few bites of the pancakes and pushes them away.

'I'm not hungry after all,' he says, 'I think I'll just stick to the coffee. I wouldn't want them to go to waste, though …'

Dan thinks about it. The pancakes will just be thrown away otherwise and unlike the leftovers he'd observed throughout the night at other tables, these are right in front of him and being offered to him.

'If you don't want them …' he says eventually. The man

43

passes the plate over and after a moment's hesitation, Dan begins to eat.

The pancakes are delicious. They are freshly made, he can tell, and dripping with butter and maple syrup. The saltiness of the bacon goes perfectly with them – unlikely, but ultimately well-suited partners. His stomach gives a satisfying rumble as he eats. They're still not as good as his mum's packet-made ones, though.

'I know what you mean about trying to write,' says Dan between mouthfuls, the sugar reviving him and creating a sudden urge to steer the conversation away from his mum, 'I've been trying to study but it's not going well.'

'You should try a crossword,' says the man, sipping his cappuccino. 'They're a good distraction, I find.'

He tears several pages out of his book and passes them to Dan, along with a pen from his shirt pocket. The man picks up his own pen and returns his focus to the crossword, so Dan does the same. For a while they sit in silence, doing the crosswords.

Every now and then Dan looks up and is reassured to see the man still sat nearby, absorbed in his puzzle, his pen resting between his teeth. It is nice not to be alone, especially at this hour.

Doing something different instead of trying desperately to absorb the information in his textbooks makes Dan feel more awake. The pancakes might have helped, too. He feels more positive about making it through the night to the opening of the university library, where he will wait until his first lecture.

After a while he goes to the bathroom and washes his hands

and splashes water on his face. He looks at himself in the mirror. His blond hair is in need of a cut and he forgot his shaving things at Rob's and needs to stop by to pick them up. But he likes his eyes – they're green, just like his mum's. They match the green hoody that he wears with the fleecy lining, zipped up to his chin even though it's warm in the café.

On the wall next to the mirror someone has written 'Nick is gay' in permanent marker. Underneath is a pencil arrow pointing back up to the writing and a note that says, 'No, you're gay'. Next to it is a crudely drawn penis, scratched into the paintwork. Without realising exactly what he's doing, Dan takes the borrowed pen from his hoody pocket and starts work on the drawing, adding ears, a face, two legs, a tail. The drawing has become a cat. He adds a collar and writes 'Pumpkin' on it.

Then he heads back into the café, sits down opposite the man and returns to his crossword.

HANNAH

Hannah cleans the Cadbury's cabinet and rearranges the cakes and smoothies inside, wiping the glass. She has a feeling she already cleaned the case but can't seem to remember doing it.

The boy in the green hoody and the older man with the tortoiseshell glasses and the scruffy hair are now sat at the same table. For a while they talk and Hannah catches snippets of the conversation over the music, too small to piece together. But now they are silent, both focusing on a crossword.

Once she is finished with the cabinet she checks the

customers are still intently looking at their crosswords and then reaches for her phone. She scrolls through the calendar, looking at the week ahead, checking her shifts. Another double shift on Saturday, then a single on Sunday and Monday, a break on Tuesday ... At Wednesday she stops. The phone feels hot in her hand as she stares at Wednesday's date and realises its significance. It would have been her and Jaheim's first anniversary. They had planned to go to Honey & Co., their favourite middle-eastern restaurant, near Warren Street. She had even eagerly booked a table a couple of months ago and suddenly remembers that she has forgotten to cancel it. She will have to call them later and wonders what she will say – whether she will find the energy to make up an excuse.

As she writes a note on her phone to remind herself to call the restaurant, she has an idea. Why should she not get to enjoy her favourite restaurant just because she no longer has a boyfriend? She pictures her favourite dish, pomegranate chicken with a fragrant salad, and finds her mouth watering despite the strange hour. She will keep the reservation and ask Mona to come with her instead. Perhaps it can be a celebration if Mona's audition goes well. She finds herself smiling at the idea and changing the note to remind her to invite Mona to dinner instead – she is pretty sure she isn't working that evening either.

Because that's a big difference between this break up and the one before. When she and Sam split up she was suddenly entirely on her own. She had friends back then, but when she moved in with Sam she found that she saw them less and less. At the time she hadn't minded – she was happy spending her evenings in their flat together, cooking and watching television and building a life fit for two. But when they split up she came out of the relationship as though coming up from being underground, only to realise that everyone she knew had moved on.

*

She sits on the living room floor surrounded by boxes, an empty wine glass held in her hand. From where she sits she can see the bottle resting on the table just a few steps away, but the effort of standing and walking to retrieve it seems suddenly too much to manage. Scraps of newspaper and bubble wrap litter the carpet but the boxes are all empty, waiting to be filled. Hannah looks again at the bottle. If Sam were home he would top up her glass without her even having to ask, planting a kiss on the top of her head at the same time.

And then she starts to cry. Because Sam is not here. And if he were and he tried to kiss her she would flinch and pull away, her stomach twisting and her mind filled with one huge thought: does he kiss her like that too?

She found out about his affair by discovering an Ann Summers receipt in the hoover a week ago. She hadn't been looking for clues – she had no idea she needed to. They'd been happy. They were talking about getting a cat. The hoover wasn't working and she pulled out a clump of hair and paper and the name caught her eye. He'd never bought her anything from there. Dislodging the blockage didn't work – she was left with a broken hoover and a broken heart.

After several denials he finally admitted to it, saying she was an ex-girlfriend whom he had bumped into a few months ago – they'd both found there was something left there that they couldn't let go of and that they needed to explore. He hadn't wanted to tell Hannah because he wasn't sure if it would lead anywhere. But it had.

His confession was worse than she could have imagined – not only had he had an affair, but he had fallen back in love with the ex whom he'd complained about to Hannah several times over the past two years. It seems strange to call it an affair – Hannah always used to think of that word in connection to married couples in their forties and fifties who stray with secretaries or nannies. It's not something she ever imagined experiencing at twenty-five.

Sat on the floor with hot tears streaming down her face, Hannah thinks she finally understands the true meaning of the word 'cheat'. She fell in love and followed the guidelines, letting her guard down and committing to Sam and to their life together. But he didn't. He wanted to win but ignore all the rules.

They have a month left in the flat contract but Hannah cannot bear to stay there until then. Instead, Sam has been staying at his brother's house (at least that is what he said – Hannah suspects he is with her but tries to pretend he isn't) and she has spent the past week scouring SpareRoom and Facebook trying to find somewhere to live and trying to summon the energy to pack her things. Two days ago, she found somewhere – a spare room in a house in Bounds Green occupied by other creatives in their mid-twenties. She managed to find a van at the last minute and it is booked to collect her and her belongings tomorrow morning.

But so far all she has is an empty wine glass and twenty empty boxes.

She places the glass on the floor and wipes her face with her sleeve. She has to make a start. Looking around the room she takes in all the details of their shared life. On the walls, the framed travel posters from the holidays they have been on together – a weekend in Venice, a summer holiday to Sam's parents' house in the South of France. On the sofa, the cushions they bought together at IKEA when they first moved in and the blanket her mum gave to them both as a house-warming present. Everything she looks at is linked somehow to him. The bottle opener resting on the table – hers, but used to open the nice bottle of red they treated themselves to when they moved in and all the other bottles they have shared together since. The pile of magazines on the coffee table that she loved to read with her legs flung over his on the sofa in the evenings when she had the night off work. A vase on the mantelpiece, empty now but bought specially to hold the huge bunch of sunflowers he bought for her twenty-fifth birthday.

When Sam left, he said she could choose what she wanted to keep, that she could have whatever she wanted. But looking around the living room and the kitchen, she finds she doesn't want any of it. Instead, she drags the empty boxes into the bedroom. Stepping inside, her breath catches again. Since Sam left she has been sleeping on the sofa. She is much too tall for it and wakes up stiff from curling into a ball. But she can't bring herself to sleep in their bed alone and knowing what she now knows.

The room feels very still and she pauses for a moment on the edge of the mattress, feeling her hand pass tentatively over the sheets. They haven't been washed since he left, since they last shared the bed together, her unknowing and huddled up against the warmth of his chest. She slips a hand under the duvet, wondering if the bed would still smell like him if she were to crawl inside. She knows that she should feel angry, that she should want to shred his shirts with a pair of scissors and take all the nicest crockery from the kitchen with her to the new flat. She knows it, and yet she feels too exhausted by sadness to feel angry.

With great effort she rises from the bed and opens the wardrobe doors. Her clothes hang like a rainbow on one side of the rail, nudging up against his shirts in shades of grey and blue on the other side. Beneath his clothes are neat rows of his shoes; hers lie in a haphazard pile at the bottom of her side of the wardrobe. She stares at the wardrobe for a moment and then reaches for her clothes, still on their hangers, and lifts them in armfuls off the rail and into the boxes. She doesn't bother folding them, instead she heaps them into a box until it is full and she starts on the next one. Once the rail is empty she makes a start on her shoes. She works quickly and when she is finished she stands back for a moment and looks at his shirts hanging neatly in the now half-empty wardrobe. As she closes the doors, one of his shirt sleeves catches in the gap between them. She opens the door, pushes the sleeve carefully back in, smoothes the shirt and closes the door again.

Apart from her clothes, the only things she packs are her records and books, her laptop and her guitar, which she props by the front door ready to carry by hand to the new house. Once the boxes are packed she returns to the living room and lies down on the sofa, wrapping herself in the blanket that was a gift from her mother. She stares at the ceiling, trying to sleep but instead simply counting down the hours until the van arrives and she will leave this flat forever. It had been their home, but as she shuffles and tries to get comfortable on the sofa she realises it is now just a flat. Just walls and doors and windows and belongings that she no longer wants or needs. When Sam cheated, he didn't just end their relationship, he cheated her out of her home. By the time she falls asleep the sun has started to rise, peeking in through the gap between the curtains.

*

When Hannah left that little flat in Stoke Newington for the last time, her parents couldn't get to London at such short notice to help her so she did the move on her own. She'd only paid for the van and driver, not for help with lifting (she couldn't afford it) but in the end the driver helped her carry her boxes from the second-floor flat down to the van, perhaps because he was tired of waiting while she struggled one box at a time, or perhaps because he could tell she was close to crying.

She had help at least at the other end, from her new house-mates. There were five of them in the house, including her. Poppy was the young woman whom she had met when she'd viewed the house a couple of days before. She was a dancer and actress and immediately chatty and friendly, despite Hannah's sombre attitude. She shared the top floor of the house with Lily, a quiet, slim woman who introduced herself as an artist but who also worked as a part-time sales assistant in a shop. On the middle floor was Bemi, an acrobat/events organiser

51

with a pet lizard called Maud, and Sophie, a Scottish musician/marketing executive with a double bass called Betty. Hannah's room was on the ground floor, which was a relief when it came to moving in. There was another bedroom on the same floor but it was currently empty – Poppy told her they were still looking for someone to move into that room and that for now they all shared it as a practice/arts/yoga space.

Once the housemates had helped her unload the van and Hannah had paid the driver, the others left her to unpack. She remembers standing among the boxes and listening to the quiet chat of her new housemates in the living room down the corridor, feeling somehow even more alone than she had felt in the flat. It seemed to her like the housemates were all friends and she felt like an intruder. And however helpful they'd been carrying her boxes from the van into the flat, she couldn't help but feel bitter disappointment at being back at that point again, with just a room of her own after sharing a whole apartment with Sam. It felt like starting all over again and that filled her with a sense of loneliness unlike anything she'd felt before.

But she hadn't met Mona yet, Hannah thinks in the café, who over the course of just a few years has come to feel more like a sister to her than a friend. She smiles at the thought. This time she is not alone and she doesn't have to start all over again after her break-up. She can just continue her life with Mona, in their flat with the posters on the walls, clothes drying in the hallway and wine always in the fridge. Hannah puts the phone back in her pocket, already looking forward to their dinner together next week.

3.00 A.M.

DAN

'You know,' says the man after a while, not looking up from his crossword, 'You seem a lot better than those kids who were in here earlier.'

Dan pauses, his hand hovering above the crossword page. He is aware of the song playing from the speakers – Elvis Presley singing 'Heartbreak Hotel' – and the shape of the waitress sitting at the counter, staring out the café window. Headlamps flash past outside, brightening the room in quick bursts. Dan pictures the university library, dark and empty at this hour. He thinks about the students who were in here earlier – imagines them sleeping soundly now, half-drunk glasses of water and open packets of paracetamol next to their beds. He thinks about his mum, and the mantelpiece topped by his school awards.

'It might not seem like it now,' continues the man, 'But I'm sure everything will work out for you.'

The black and white boxes of the crossword swim into one another as Dan gulps hard.

'I've met some really horrible kids your age,' the man adds, looking up this time and finding Dan's quickly blinking eyes, 'My son included.'

The man laughs, and Dan raises his eyebrows. He didn't picture the man as a father – somehow it is hard to imagine his life outside of this café. He seems to Dan as a kind of apparition, existing only in a world of insomnia and crosswords. But of course, that is silly – he has a life to return to, a family, his own problems, a home.

'I love him, of course I do,' the man continues, 'It just happens when you have a child. You love them and always will. But he can be a mean bastard. A foolish one too. You don't seem like that. I bet your mum was proud of you.'

Dan is silenced, his head spinning, his heart beating hard beneath his jumper. He doesn't know this man but his words cut through his clothes, through his skin, right inside.

Dan nods slightly, the only acknowledgement of the man's words that he can manage. The man nods back, and they return their attention to the crosswords.

After a while the man stands up.

'It's time for me to go,' he says, 'I'd better get back if there's any chance of me doing any work tomorrow. Good luck with your studies. And everything.'

'Good luck with your writing,' replies Dan.

The man reaches out to shake Dan's hand and he takes it,

enjoying the warmth of another person's hand in his.

'Your crossword book,' says Dan, pointing to where it sits on the table.

'You keep it,' he replies.

The man heads to the counter, says something to the waitress, pays and then leaves, waving at Dan before he goes.

Dan is on his own again, left with an empty plate and a half-completed crossword.

After a few moments, the waitress comes over, carrying a tall glass filled with strawberry milkshake, an extravagant swirl of cream and a strawberry resting on the top.

'The customer who just left asked me to make this for you,' she says.

As she says the words, Dan realises he never asked the man his name. The milkshake sits on the table, ice cold and the colour of kindness.

HANNAH

At the small table the young man finishes his strawberry milkshake, using the long spoon she gave him to scoop the last droplets of pink from the bottom. He is smiling and it makes Hannah smile too. She is just wondering at the young man's story when a gorilla and Marilyn Monroe step into the café. Hannah can't help but stare at the new customers. Once they are inside, the gorilla tugs at his mask, pulling it off to reveal a flushed but very much human face. Hannah lets out a sigh of relief.

'God, I was burning up in that,' the man says. He holds the mask by his side, the rest of his body entirely covered in a hairy gorilla suit.

'You could have taken it off ages ago,' snaps Marilyn Monroe while attempting to smooth her white dress, which is looking somewhat crumpled.

'Yeah, but wasn't it great seeing the face of that bus driver?' the man laughs. Marilyn Monroe sighs and adjusts her blonde wig.

'Two Americanos please,' she says to Hannah, before moving to a booth at the back of the café. The gorilla follows and slumps himself in a seat opposite. He pulls a phone from somewhere inside his suit and starts scrolling. Marilyn Monroe stares out the window, her arms crossed firmly over her chest.

The couple in their fancy dress costumes make Hannah think about the night she and Mona first met. It was a few weeks after she'd moved in to the house in Bounds Green. She was still feeling shaken from the break-up with Sam and the adjustment to shared living, but the housemates seemed friendly and there was a warm atmosphere in the slightly chaotic house. Hannah particularly liked Poppy but she was often out, rushing to keep up with her busy work and social lives. When she was home she was sometimes distracted, checking her phone as she received endless notifications from endless WhatsApp groups. The other housemates were busy too, pursuing their individual passions while juggling part-time jobs that paid the bills, like her. They still hadn't found a new housemate to fill the spare room and they were all starting to feel tense, noticing the squeeze of the extra rent they were each having to pay to cover the cost of the empty room.

Halloween was approaching and Poppy decided to throw a party, partly as a chance to catch up with her wide social group, partly because there was nothing she loved more than fancy dress, and partly because she suggested it might be a good way to find someone who was looking for a room. If they told enough of their friends that they had a spare room to fill, surely something would come up. The others agreed and soon set about preparing costumes and decorations.

There were many parties throughout the year Hannah spent in the Bounds Green house, but she always remembers that Halloween party in particular as the night she met Mona. Except she wasn't Mona that night – she was Harley Quinn.

*

Hannah dabs paint gently onto her face. She is dressed as Sally from The Nightmare Before Christmas, *wearing a handmade patchwork dress. Her body is covered in green paint with seams drawn in black eyeliner on top. Every few minutes the doorbell rings and Hannah listens as someone answers it, usually Poppy (she recognises her voice as she tells guest after guest how fabulous their costumes are), and conversations head past the closed bedroom door and down the corridor to the living room, where the music and the drinks are. Loud bursts of laughter rise over the sound of the music. It sounds exactly how fun should sound, but Hannah is very conscious of the fact she knows none of the* voices and no one at the party, apart from the housemates she has only lived with for a few weeks.

On her green face she paints a few more seams and extends her mouth into a wide smile. She knows this party is her opportunity to make new friends and to start over again after her break-up. And yet she pauses in her bedroom with the door closed, blinking at herself in the mirror.

It has been a hard week. A bar where she made connections and had been offered a singing gig called her yesterday to tell her the space has gone to a more experienced musician and that there won't be a spot for her any more. She had been visiting the bar every Thursday for three months, reminding them of her face and trying to chat to the manager about singing there. She now feels foolish, thinking also of the money she spent on cocktails there – money she doesn't have to waste. She is also still reeling from her break-up with Sam.

But tonight it's a party and the house is full. She takes a deep breath, pushing her feelings deeper inside her and adding the final touch to her make-up. She pauses for a moment at the door then leaves the bedroom, stepping out into the corridor.

The music hits her as she makes her way through the house, decorated tonight with strips of toilet roll and torn scraps of bin bags, fake cobwebs dangling from the doorways. On the stairs, a female grim reaper holds her scythe in one hand and a plastic cup of wine in the other, talking intently to Wonder Woman. Ahead of her in the corridor are a slim man in a skeleton outfit and a petite woman in white tights, a giant papier-mâché pumpkin covering her body from her chest to her thighs. Hannah follows them towards the living room, the pumpkin *bashing slightly against the doorway. Inside, a huddle of vampires dance beneath a disco ball suspended from the ceiling. Shards of silver light skitter around the dark room, falling on the ceiling, walls and many unfamiliar faces before darting away again.*

Hannah's eyes scan the busy room, seeking out her housemates and someone to talk to. Poppy, tonight Cruella de Vil, is laughing in the middle of a group, gesturing animatedly with her hands as she talks. In the semi-darkness Hannah can just make out Bemi and her girlfriend Anya too, talking with Sophie and a couple of other people Hannah doesn't recognise. She can't see Lily and wonders if she is still getting ready. Everyone in the living room looks deep in conversation or dancing and laughing so happily that Hannah would feel like an interloper joining their group. Instead she makes her way into the kitchen, deciding a drink is a good place to start. As she steps inside she bumps straight into a woman dressed as Harley Quinn, a blonde, red and blue wig tied in bunches.

'I'm so sorry!' says Hannah, steadying herself on the kitchen table and stepping back from Harley Quinn, who she notices is holding a plastic cup which has spilt onto the floor.

'No, it's my fault,' replies Harley Quinn, 'I'm sorry!'

'I really wasn't looking where I was going,' says Hannah, reaching for some kitchen roll from the top of the fridge and padding it on the floor. Inside she chastises herself for her clumsiness and for making such a bad start at fitting in to this party. Perhaps she should have just stayed in her room.

'Thanks,' says Harley Quinn, 'It really was my fault though, I should have moved out of your way.'

'Wow,' says Hannah, standing up again, 'We don't really make great evil characters, do we?'

The woman dressed as Harley Quinn looks down at her costume, her painted face breaking into a smile. It's a warm smile that immediately makes Hannah feel slightly less on edge. She feels herself relaxing a little, not having realised that her whole body had been tense as she surveyed the living room, trying to find a way in to the party.

'No, I guess we don't,' says the woman, 'I'm Mona by the way, the rest of the time.'

'I'm Hannah.'

Hannah properly takes in the woman who shares the small kitchen space with her. Mona is a similar height to Hannah and has the physique of a dancer. She guesses she is around the same age as her, but it's hard to tell her natural complexion or hair colour beneath the wig and make-up. Sounds of the party flow in through the door to the kitchen and Hannah wonders whether she should head back out again and make another attempt to meet people and chat with her housemates, but she finds she doesn't want to. She wants to stay exactly where she is.

'So, are you a housemate or guest?' Mona says. Hannah notices an accent but cannot place it.

'Housemate – I only moved in three weeks ago. So I know you're a guest.'

Wilma Flinstone walks into the kitchen and Hannah and Mona step aside, waiting until Wilma has found a still half-full bottle of wine and carried it back into the living room.

'I'm an old friend of Poppy's,' says Mona when they are alone again, 'We went to dance school together. She's great, but I haven't seen her in a little while – I think she's invited our whole graduate year group tonight.'

Hannah hears another burst of laughter and swell of voices rising from the living room and the spare room, where guests have now started to congregate too, and thinks Mona might be right. The house is heaving.

'Yeah, I get the sense she likes a party,' Hannah says.

Mona laughs.

'Yeah, that's Poppy. We had some crazy ones when we were students.'

'She's also got this plan to try and find someone who's in need of a room – the room opposite mine has been empty since I moved in.'

'You've got a room going?' asks Mona, looking interested. Hannah nods and Mona looks as though she is going to ask something else, but instead she pauses and takes another sip of her drink.

'So what are you then?' she asks brightly, 'An actor, dancer, artist?'

Hannah raises an eyebrow and they both find themselves laughing. Hannah feels suddenly aware of the strange bubble that this house, and her life, exists in. Most of the guests at the party are women and from what she knows of her housemates so far, she guesses most of them are 'creative' in some way like they are: young people balancing individual passions with day or night jobs. Hannah guesses that the proportion of people who can tap dance in this house compared to those who can't would be way above the national average. Hannah thinks about the bizarreness of that fact – the strange skills of the people assembled *under this roof. She wonders how many other 'bubbles' there are spread across London – villages within a city, villages with their own tribes, their own traditions, their own language even.*

She tells Mona her usual story, about moving from Wales and her struggle to find work after graduating, a struggle that she paints in a positive light, like they all do. A knack for positive spin is essential in their world.

'At the moment I'm working as a part-time receptionist, but it's great that it gives me the flexibility to do gigs,' she says, ignoring the fact that she has just had a series of gigs cancelled and doesn't know when her next one will be, and that she hates her job. She very briefly summarises her history with Sam, saying only that they were together for two years and have just broken up, and that's why she is living here. She doesn't give any more detail and Mona doesn't ask. Instead she listens intently, nodding and smiling, silently topping up Hannah's cup of wine while she talks. Then Mona tells her story too, how she grew up in Singapore but left for a dance school in London at eighteen. Other than a year dancing on a cruise ship she has been in the city ever since, moving around between flat shares like Hannah. Her current home is a flat shared with two 'difficult women', but she doesn't elaborate and instead goes on to talk passionately about shows she's recently seen.

Throughout the evening people come and go in the kitchen, but Hannah and Mona stay talking to each other. Hannah feels at ease, as though she has known Mona all her life. She admires the way she talks about dancing, how she lights up and her whole body seems to come alive, as though she might start dancing herself any second.

'There's nothing like it,' Mona says, and Hannah thinks immediately of singing – how it feels to close her eyes and surround herself with the music.

'I know it might sound silly,' continues Mona, 'But when I'm dancing I feel as though I'm doing what my body is meant to do. I'm more myself than I am at any other time. I sometimes feel like someone should watch me dance if they want to really get to know me. It's like my body can describe me better than me talking ever can. It's more eloquent, somehow. Does that sound mad?'

Hannah finds herself swallowing hard as Mona's words hit her in the chest. Because they don't sound mad at all – they make perfect sense. Since breaking up with Sam, she hasn't been singing or playing her guitar every day like she used to, and she suddenly realises how much she misses it. It's the thing she has loved since she was a young girl living in a village in Wales and dreaming of the city. It's the thing that is always there, no matter what else is going on in her life. Her upcoming gigs might have been cancelled and she might be starting out on a new, unexpected chapter of her life, one she didn't choose for herself, but no one can take away the ache in her heart and the dream that is still there beneath the sadness and the disappointment. No one can take away the music. She decides suddenly and firmly that she has to start singing again, and that this change in her life could be her opportunity to devote herself to her music – to finally get her big break.

'Not at all,' Hannah says eventually to Mona, 'I know exactly what you mean.' From the start they understand each other completely.

The day after the Halloween party Poppy triumphantly announced that her plan had worked and someone wanted to move into the spare room.

'You met her, Hannah,' Poppy said, 'Her name's Mona.'

When Mona moved into the room opposite hers a week later, Hannah helped her unpack and they got to know each other as they sorted through the boxes and assembled Mona's wardrobe. They talked and talked and Hannah felt the giddy excitement of an instant connection – that feeling when you meet someone and it just clicks. She already associated meeting Mona with inspiring her to get back to her music; the day after the party she had picked up her guitar again despite her hangover. And now it seemed as though this new friend would also help her feel at home in the house that up until then she'd still felt somewhat reluctant to be in.

They very quickly became close friends, staying up late in one or other of their rooms and talking. Mona took Hannah to shows at Sadler's Wells and Hannah showed Mona her favourite music venues. They started cooking together, sharing food shops and a shelf in the communal fridge and leaving each other leftovers in Tupperware boxes when they were working different schedules and couldn't eat together. And when Mona moved from a job she hated as a bartender in a seedy nightclub to a job waitressing at Stella's, the all-night café on Liverpool Street, she told Hannah how flexible the owner was about shifts and taking time off for auditions and about an opening they had for another waitress. Mona put in a good word and

Hannah got the job; suddenly they were working together as well as living together and they grew even closer, bonding over gossip and speculation about customers and shared late-night shifts.

At first Hannah was cautious about letting Poppy see how close she and Mona had become; if they went out somewhere together she would always invite Poppy too, not wanting her to feel left out. Hannah was aware that Mona was Poppy's friend first, even if they hadn't seen each other in a while and even if she knew that sounded petty. She didn't want to offend her new housemate and knew that even though they were in their mid-twenties none of them were immune to the hurtful effects of being left out. But Poppy, a young woman who collected friends like some people collect shoes or toy cars, was usually too busy to commit to plans. Over time Hannah and Mona stopped expecting her to come, and then stopped inviting her. The housemates very quickly forgot that Mona had joined the house as Poppy's friend, not Hannah's.

'Do you have to spend your whole time on that bloody phone?' comes a sudden loud voice. Hannah turns to the booth where the couple in fancy dress are still sat. The woman dressed as Marilyn Monroe is staring at the man dressed as a gorilla, and the man dressed as the gorilla is staring at his phone. But at the sound of her voice he looks up.

'Oh shut the fuck up,' he says. All the laughter that was in his voice earlier has disappeared and his tone is coarse and bitter. He thumps a furry fist down on the table so hard that it rattles and Hannah jumps slightly. The young man on the nearby table looks up at the sound but then looks away again quickly. Hannah stares, wondering if the man in the gorilla suit will start laughing again as though he was just joking, but he doesn't. The woman, who seemed so confident when she first arrived, sinks a little into her seat and says nothing. They stare at each other for a moment and Hannah prepares herself to head over or shout for Pablo if a more violent argument kicks off. It wouldn't be the first time that has happened in the café. But the man dressed as the gorilla goes back to looking at his phone and the woman sits opposite him in silence. After a while she stands up and pays at the counter, avoiding Hannah's eyes. She returns to the table and without a word the man in the gorilla suit picks up his mask and stands up.

'Let's go,' he says, reaching for the woman's hand. Hand in hand, the gorilla and Marilyn Monroe step outside into the street. Hannah watches them as they walk towards the bus stop. She wonders where they have been and where they are heading. Whether the shouting was a tired one-off or a sign of something more serious. But of course, she will never know. A bus pulls up and they step on, the doors closing behind them.

'Are you OK?' says Pablo, suddenly in the doorway between the café and the kitchen, a tea towel flecked with chocolate flung over his shoulder, 'I heard someone shouting but was at a very important moment with my cake.'

His face is pink and glistening with the warmth from the kitchen and chocolatey handprints stain his chef's whites where he must have rubbed his hands while baking.

'I'm fine, thanks,' replies Hannah, glad of Pablo's presence even though she has seen far worse fights here over the years, 'Just an angry customer, but he's gone now.'

Pablo nods and then hesitates, pausing in the doorway. Hannah suddenly thinks how lonely it must be working in the kitchen with only the radio for company and without these customers to observe and wonder about.

'Do you remember when Mona and I first started working here?' she asks him. He smiles.

'Of course,' he says, nodding, 'You made me coffees to practise using the machine and they were terrible. They are better now though.'

'I should hope so, I've been making them for five years,' she replies. As she says it her mind rests on the number – *has it really been that long?*

'It's seven years for me,' Pablo says. Hannah thinks again about his life before the café, and how little we often understand about the people we think we know so well.

The café door opens and a woman walks inside.

'I better get back to the cake,' says Pablo, 'It won't ice itself, the bastard.' He disappears into the kitchen.

4.00 A.M.

HANNAH

The new customer is petite, perhaps only just five foot, Hannah guesses, and wearing tracksuit bottoms, trainers, a trench coat and a large grey cable-knit jumper that looks much too big for her and has a small pale stain on the chest. One of the legs of her tracksuit bottoms is tucked into her sock: pale blue with puffins printed on it, reminding Hannah of a pair she owned as a child. With wide, dark eyes the woman looks around her as though she has landed there by some magic, instead of having just stepped off the night bus. Her hair, blonde at the tips but dark from the roots, is tied back in a messy ponytail. As her eyes meet Ernest's she shudders a little and moves to a table facing the opposite direction without looking at Hannah. Once she is seated she sits very still, staring ahead out the café window.

The boy in the green hooded jumper is still sat at his table surrounded by books and glances across at the new customer. He looks at her for a long time, something like but not quite a frown on his face. Then he shakes his head slightly and returns to his books, his head resting in his hands as he reads them. Every now and then his eyes dart back to the woman in the tracksuit, and then back to his book.

'Can I take your order?' asks Hannah, standing over the woman's table. As she speaks, a buzzing sound comes from the woman's coat pocket.

'A cappuccino,' says the woman, the buzzing continuing.

Hannah nods and turns to leave, but then turns back.

'Your phone?' she says, indicating the woman's pocket which is vibrating from the buzzing of the phone.

'Oh, yes,' says the woman distractedly, taking the phone out of her pocket. She presses the 'decline call' button and places it on the table in front of her. Then she turns back to the window. Hannah looks at her for a moment, the woman clearly oblivious that she is still there. Her shoulders sink slightly as she settles into the chair. Everything about this woman makes Hannah want to reach out and place a hand on her shoulder, but instead she turns back towards the coffee machine.

'Your coffee will be with you in a sec,' she says. The woman says nothing in reply.

DAN

He is used to bumping into his mum in the street or staring at her in a TV programme. He always realises very quickly that the person is not actually his mum, just someone who bears a faint resemblance to her, but it stills sends a jolt through him every time.

The woman who just walked into the café has the same shade of hair as she had and is around the same height. He stares at her for a moment as she looks out the window. Her phone buzzes repeatedly on the table but she ignores it. As he looks closer he realises this woman is much younger – she looks almost like he remembers his mum did when he was little.

She had him when she was still quite young – twenty. He didn't realise this was unusual until he met the parents of his school friends and noticed that they seemed older than his mum. He was always proud of that fact – she was young and slim and wore tight jeans and jumpers that he thought made her look nice. He saw the other parents looking at her at the school gates and he felt proud in a way he couldn't describe. He loved the big gold hoop earrings that she always wore – how they shimmered in the light as though they were made from *real* gold.

It was through meeting his friends' parents that he also realised lots of families had both a dad and a mum. Not all of them – some of his friends lived just with their mum like he did (none of them lived just with a dad) – but a lot of them did. He liked visiting his friends who had both – like Aaron and Sadir at primary school. He enjoyed observing the fathers in each of his friends' homes. He watched them closely, noticing how they were with their wives, how they were with their children, how they were with him. Sadir's dad always kissed Sadir's mum on the mouth when he arrived home – it made Sadir squirm and shout at them to '*Cut it out!*' but Dan secretly liked it. It made him feel slightly uncomfortable too, but it also made him smile. Aaron had two sisters but his dad didn't treat them particularly differently to how he treated Aaron. He worked from home and would greet them at the door when they arrived (Aaron always walked his younger sisters to and from school) and hug each of them in turn and plant a kiss on their cheek. When Dan visited after school Aaron's dad would do the same to him, except missing out the kiss. He would never have admitted it, but as he sank into Aaron's father's hug (he smelt like peppermint tea), he wished for a kiss on his cheek too just like the rest of them.

But despite Dan's interest in fathers, he liked the fact that it was just him and his mum. He liked that they could share a two-person pizza on a Friday evening when she finished her shift early, and that she let him have half of the bookshelves in the sitting room for his own books. She never brought a man back to the house, not once, and he didn't know how he would have felt if she did. The thought makes him sad now – sad that she didn't have anyone other than him to look after her when she was sick. And, although he dismisses the thought as selfish, he regrets that he has to carry the weight of his grief alone – that there is no one who feels it as keenly as he does or who he can call to say, 'I saw someone who looked just like her today'.

He looks at the woman again. Her body is hunched over slightly and she tightens the belt of her trench coat around her waist. As he looks closer, he realises her hair is actually much darker at the roots than his mum's was, and she is much shorter too. In fact, he realises that she looks nothing like her at all.

HANNAH

When Hannah's phone buzzes she thinks it is the customer's again – it has been going off since she arrived in the café but she hasn't once picked up. So she continues to stare outside to where two drunks are shouting at each other in the middle of the street. Luckily the road is empty. One throws a can towards the café and it lands on the pavement, rolling down into the gutter. Hannah watches and wonders if she should step outside and warn them that they're in the road. But as quickly as the fight started it stops and the men turn and go separate ways, one towards the station, one towards Spitalfields.

But then she hears a buzz again and this time reaches into her apron pocket. She pulls out her phone and sees she has a message from her old housemate Lily, including an invitation to her daughter's christening. If it was any other friend, Hannah would be surprised to receive a message at this hour. But Lily's daughter Mabel is teething and over the past few months she and Hannah have had several late-night WhatsApp conversations, while Lily tries to soothe her daughter and Hannah works a late shift in the café.

'How is she this morning?' Hannah types.

'A little devil,' replies Lily, then, 'You will come to the christening though, won't you?'

'Of course,' replies Hannah, 'I'll look up trains later.'

Lily no longer lives in London – when she left the Bounds Green house she moved back to her home town in Yorkshire. At first she stayed with her parents then eventually moved into a flat of her own. Writing to Lily, Hannah thinks with a pang back to when she still lived in Bounds Green, back when Lily was still there.

Although they were not as close with the other housemates as they were with each other, over time both Hannah and Mona came to know the other women well. They overheard the fierce arguments between Bemi and Sophie – Sophie accusing Bemi of having her girlfriend Anya round to visit far too often and saying she should contribute towards the bills and Bemi complaining at Sophie for her late-night practising sessions on her double bass. Despite the arguments they could also be thoughtful too, Bemi and Anya often cooking for the whole house (Anya was a wonderful cook) and Sophie always remembering birthdays, without fail. But to Hannah, Lily was always something of a mystery. She lived on the top floor of the house and Hannah was on the bottom, and even though the distance was only the length of two flights of stairs, it was enough to make a difference.

All she really knew about Lily while they lived together was that she was an artist and worked part-time in an art supply shop, and that she dressed in many baggy layers but always seemed to have bare feet, a silver anklet with a crescent moon charm dangling from her petite ankle. She had a nervous energy to her back then. One week, not long after Mona moved in, Lily set up a makeshift art corner in the living room, arguing that there was more space there and she needed the light. For several days she didn't seem to leave the living room, painting frantically all day. One night, Hannah came through the living room to the downstairs bathroom at two in the morning and Lily was still there, staring at a canvas that was smeared in shades of red and orange that Hannah found alarming. Hannah knew some of the other housemates were getting frustrated by Lily's takeover of the living room – she'd caught whispered snippets of conversations seeping out from not-quite-closed doors – but by the end of the week all Lily's things had been packed away, the room returned to normal. The following week Lily barely left her room. Hannah soon found that these bursts of energy followed by extreme lethargy were normal. 'She's having a quiet night,' Poppy would say when the housemates, hanging around in the kitchen making separate meals but chatting while they cooked, asked where Lily was. 'Best to leave her to it,' she would say, and most of the time they did.

As well as the arguments between Bemi and Sophie, other annoyances and fights became more common in the house: Sophie shouting at Hannah for spending too long in the shower, Bemi getting annoyed at the sounds of Mona's strict morning workout. And being on the ground floor, Hannah and Mona were both woken up when someone started opening and closing the front door in the middle of the night. It happened at first just once, but then became a regular occurrence, interrupting their sleep. They assumed it was one of their housemates heading out on a late night 'date'. Mona wanted Hannah to help her confront the others about it, but Hannah refused. So Mona brought it up one evening herself. Sophie took particular offence. 'Are you calling me a whore?' she had shouted at Mona, who had shouted back in a dramatic voice, 'Don't be so theatrical.'

Then food started to go missing from the fridge and freezer, causing endless passive-aggressive Post-it notes and accusatory conversations. There was one particularly heated argument about a missing frozen lasagne that belonged to Bemi.

'It's just a lasagne,' Hannah had said, trying to play peace-keeper.

'But it belonged to me, Anya cooked it,' shouted Bemi, 'I was saving it. I've had a long shift, I was looking forward to it.'

'Maybe it was a mistake,' suggested Hannah.

'A mistake? Oh whoops, I've just eaten an entire lasagne that doesn't belong to me. My mistake!'

No one admitted to the theft and Bemi stormed to her room, shutting the door so firmly that the thin walls rattled.

Looking back, Hannah realises the tension that had grown in the house for months could only go on for so long. Something had to give. In the end, someone had to leave.

Lily was the first to go. Really, it had been a long time coming. Once it all came out and Lily decided to pack her things it seemed so obvious. But in a house of six women, secrets were easy to hide.

Hannah has learnt to give Lily space – they all have. When she is painting she prefers to be left alone and Hannah and the other housemates respect this. That's Lily – she is quiet and happy in her own company. It's just who she is.

So, when late one night Hannah is woken by the front door again and gets up quickly, careful not to wake Mona, she is shocked by what she sees in the living room. Lily is standing by the door to the kitchen. The light in there is on but the living room is dark. Lily stands in a frame of bright white light between the two rooms. One hand grips on to the frame of the door, the other holds a pair of trainers, her socked feet planted on the kitchen tiles. Her face is damp with sweat. She is dressed in running leggings and a tight Lycra top, and as Hannah looks at her, she realises she has never seen Lily in anything other than the loose, draping styles she favours. She suddenly understands why. What Hannah thought was just Lily's style has been a way to hide the truth. Silhouetted by the bright white kitchen lamp she looks like a flickering shadow, close to disappearing, a person faded and rubbed out at the edges. She pauses between the two rooms and Hannah sees a woman on the threshold: life and brightness behind her but only darkness ahead. As Lily spots Hannah her eyes widen and she reaches for the hooded jumper tied around her waist, quickly covering her body again. But as she reaches to pull it over her head Hannah sees the veins in her thin arms and the protruding collar bones that slice across her chest like knives. She sees the way her arms shake with the effort of lifting them above her head, and her hip bones that are visible above the line of her leggings as her top rises. In the baggy jumper she looks almost like Lily again, except she is shaking. Her face is twisted in a look of pain and terror that Hannah has never seen before.

'What's going on?' says Hannah quietly, aware of Mona sleeping just down the corridor, and the others in their rooms upstairs. Part of her wants to shout, to wake them all, or Mona at the very least. She doesn't know what to do and wants someone else to bear witness to what is happening. She wants a grown-up, knowing how ridiculous that seems, aged twenty-five. But Lily looks so afraid that she remains quiet.

'It's three in the morning,' says Hannah, her eyes flicking to the clock on the kitchen wall behind Lily's head, 'What are you doing?'

'I ... I,' Lily falters, staring at the shoes in her hand and then back at Hannah, but without meeting her eyes, 'I just went on a little run. I couldn't sleep.'

'How often does this happen?' asks Hannah, already knowing the answer. It was months ago that she was first woken by the door in the middle of the night.

'It's only been a few times,' says Lily, still looking down.

As Hannah watches her she realises how sunken her eyes have become, something she is ashamed to admit she hadn't noticed until now.

'How far do you go?' Hannah asks, trying to remain calm.

'Oh, not very far,' replies Lily. But as she reaches for the doorframe again and grips it tightly, Hannah realises she is struggling to stand.

'You should sit down,' says Hannah, 'I'll get you something to eat and a sugary drink.'

But as Hannah moves as though to head into the kitchen Lily reaches her other hand for the frame so that she is blocking the door.

'I'm fine,' she says, her voice hardening, 'It's nothing.'

'It's not nothing,' says Hannah.

'Honestly, I'm fine,' snaps Lily again, 'And anyway, I just want to go to bed. I'm sure I will sleep better now. As I said, it's just to help me sleep.'

Hannah stares at her a little longer. She wants to question her more, to get to the bottom of what has been going on, but Lily is probably right – she certainly does look like she needs the sleep. And Hannah is tired too, too tired and caught off guard to think clearly about what to do. She'll talk to Lily again in the morning, and if she doesn't get anywhere, she'll tell Mona and Poppy.

'Please,' says Lily, quietly now, 'Can I just go to bed?'

'Fine,' replies Hannah. She steps aside and Lily walks slowly through the living room. Hannah can tell she is trying to walk normally but she is unsteady on her feet. As Lily climbs the stairs to her top floor room her footsteps make no sound at all.

The next morning when Hannah wakes she knocks on Lily's door, but Poppy, who is just heading out of her room opposite, tells her Lily has already left for work. Hannah has to get to work too, and while she is there her mind is distracted by coffee orders, difficult customers and the news from Pablo that his daughter is getting married.

But later that evening it all comes crashing back to her. She is just back from her shift and is sat in the living room with Bemi and Sophie. They'd been deciding on a film to watch but so *far haven't been able to choose one they all wanted. Instead the three of them are sat on the sofas and chairs scrolling through their phones.*

'Whose soup is this?' shouts Poppy from the kitchen, stepping into the living room holding a pot of leek and potato soup in her outstretched arm. Bemi and Sophie look up from their phones but back down again.

'It's mine,' says Hannah, jumping up from the sofa.

'Can you move it off my shelf and onto your own? I've just done a big food shop and need the space.'

'I put it on Lily's shelf – Mona and I ran out of space on ours so I asked her and she said it was fine.'

'It's not on Lily's shelf, it's on mine,' says Poppy.

Hannah feels her stomach twisting at the sound of Lily's name. She follows Poppy into the kitchen, the others watching as she leaves. Poppy opens the fridge door and points at the top shelf.

'Everything on here is mine,' she says.

Hannah peers inside the fridge, looking at the contents of the top shelf: a bag of spinach, a packet of stir-fry veg, a pot of yoghurt, a packet of chicken – all things she has seen Poppy eating, now she thinks of it.

'Where's Lily's shelf then?' Hannah asks.

Poppy points at the one below it.

'That one.'

Hannah shakes her head, 'No, that's the one that Mona and I share.'

Poppy's face drops for second.

'Maybe the one below that?'

79

Hannah shakes her head again, 'No, that's Bemi's – I remember borrowing something from there the other week.'

Poppy holds open the fridge door, the light inside shining on the pale inside of her arm. She looks up and her eyes meet Hannah's.

'Can you come in here a sec, guys?' Poppy calls into the living room. Bemi and Sophie shuffle into the small kitchen and Poppy gets them to point out their shelves in the fridge. They seem irritated, but they each claim their shelf until there is no space left in the fridge.

'What's going on?' Bemi says, her face shifting from irritation to confusion.

Poppy and Hannah look at each other again and Hannah's heart starts to race as she realises what it means. Nothing in the fridge belongs to Lily. In horrifyingly high speed, this and the events of last night fit together until Hannah is confronted with the picture that has been right there for months, unnoticed. Poppy must be coming to the same conclusion because she seems frantic, nothing like her usual cheerful self.

'Open the cupboards,' she says, almost shouting now. The housemates glance at each other but follow Poppy's orders. Poppy stands by and watches in dazed horror as Hannah, Sophie and Bemi open their cupboards one by one. Boxes of cereal, packets of biscuits, half-open bags of rice that spill grains as the cupboards are opened, tubs of Nutella and chocolate spread … The contents of all the cupboards are carefully inspected and claimed. Poppy's wholegrain pasta and brown rice, Bemi's pot noodles and cans of tuna, Sophie's porridge oats and packets of Mini Cheddars. Hannah speaks for herself and for Mona, who is at work; they shop together so she knows everything that belongs to her. Eventually, they run out of cupboards. Every shelf and every piece of food is claimed by someone in the room.

Bemi and Sophie look back and forth between each other as Poppy stands in the middle of the kitchen for a moment, silent but starting to tremble slightly.

'So, nothing in this entire kitchen belongs to Lily?' she says.

The housemates look at each other, and back at Poppy.

'Not one single thing?' she says, her voice suddenly very quiet.

Everyone is silent.

'We're probably overreacting,' says Sophie, 'I'm sure Lily can explain.'

'It's probably nothing,' says Bemi, but her voice is full of hesitation. That's when Hannah decides to speak.

'There's something I've been wanting to tell you,' she says, talking quickly as though letting out a guilty secret, 'Something that happened last night. I thought it was nothing, but it now seems to make sense.'

So she tells them about catching Lily back from a night-time run, about how unwell she looked in her exercise clothes, about how, guessing from how long Hannah has been disturbed by the sound of the door, these runs must have been going on for a long time. As she speaks she watches the faces of her housemates, as, like her, they begin to understand. It begins to make sense. The lethargy, the baggy clothes and Lily's general absence from the house, from life in general.

Poppy shakes her head, her face drained of all colour. It's the first time Hannah has ever seen her like this: not sunny,

81

or distracted, but afraid. She looks younger: a child seeing the ugliness of the adult world for the first time.

'She's my friend,' she says in a small voice.

The others watch her, no one seeming to know what to say.

'She's my friend,' Poppy repeats, 'And I had no idea. What kind of a person am I? I should have known.'

That's when Hannah steps forward, wrapping her arms around Poppy's shaking body.

'It's OK,' she says as the other housemates look on, 'It's not your fault.'

But despite her words and the strength with which she hugs Poppy, inside she wonders. Why didn't Poppy know? Why didn't any of them know? As she hugs Poppy and Bemi and Sophie say softly that it will be all right, Hannah realises that it isn't all right. And that, although she would never say it out loud, perhaps Poppy has a point. They should have known. She thinks of Lily, imagining her shut away alone in her room, picturing her in the living room last night, her body exhausted and her eyes wild as she told Hannah it wasn't what it looked like. She thinks of Lily's gentle smile and the frenzied painting in shades of orange and red that stuck with Hannah long after the canvas disappeared from the living room. And although no one else says it, Hannah can hear the words resting in the air in the house where the cupboards are full but their housemate has been starving: oh Lily, we have let you down.

*

At first Lily was defensive. Poppy and Hannah confronted her together and explained what they had learnt, and that they felt she needed help.

'There has obviously been a problem for a long time now,' said Poppy, sitting next to Lily on her bed, the sheets covered in a daisy print similar to one Hannah remembers having as a child, 'I'm so sorry I didn't notice sooner.'

'There's nothing to notice,' said Lily tersely, wrapping her knees up to her chest and almost disappearing within the folds of her oversized top, 'I'm fine.'

When they pressed her she grew angry, shouting at them that they were spying on her, that they didn't know what they were talking about, that they weren't her friends, they didn't care about her.

That first conversation didn't go anywhere: Lily withdrew inside herself and eventually went out, slamming the front door behind her. For the next couple of days Hannah, Poppy and the others tried talking to Lily about it again. At first they were all met with the same response – denial, fiery anger and sharp words that left them stinging. But eventually she gave in. It was Poppy whom she finally confided in, but Poppy told Hannah and Mona what she had said. That it had been happening for a long time now – the starving and the secrets. How she was too afraid to have food in the house, so stopped going food shopping, but would occasionally be so painfully hungry that she would take something from the fridge or freezer, anything, feeling wracked with guilt as soon as she finished eating. She went on her first run after stealing a handful of cereal from Hannah and Mona's cupboard. She went late at night so that no one would see her. At first the runs were relatively short, but they became longer and more frequent. 5K, 6K, 10K. On the night that Hannah found her in the kitchen, she told Poppy, she had just run 20K. Lily told Poppy that she had been taking her running gear to a local launderette, not wanting the housemates to see her exercise clothes drying in the house and know how often she had been going.

Poppy suggested that Lily go back home to her parents for a while. She said she could call her mother and help her pack her things. By that point, Lily was too exhausted to refuse. After her mother had arrived a few days later with her car and the housemates had helped Lily pack her things inside and waved a strange, sad goodbye, Hannah and Mona retreated to Hannah's room.

Hannah remembers sitting next to Mona on her bed. They both stared ahead in silence.

'Promise we'll always look after each other, OK?' Hannah said eventually. Despite her guilt around Lily, her sense of shame at having let one of them drop off the edge unnoticed, there was one thought that Hannah held on to throughout it all. She knew what food in the fridge was Mona's. She knew from her complexion and from her body that she was healthy. And they were fierce, close friends; if Mona ever had anything on her mind, Hannah knew she would tell her. There would never be secrets between them.

Mona didn't say anything but nodded and reached an arm around Hannah's shoulder.

Lily never came back to the house in Bounds Green, but the housemates made a trip to Yorkshire to visit her. It was there that Hannah felt she finally got to know her former housemate, wrapped in a blanket on the sofa of her parents' house, looking out across the rainy moors and talking honestly for the first time. They stayed for a weekend but after they left, Hannah started writing messages to Lily. They kept in touch that way – words reaching each other across the distance between them. Hannah's messages to Lily might have started because of guilt and concern for the fragile woman she once shared a house with, but over time it became a real friendship, even if they saw each other rarely. Their messages were often infrequent too, but the flow of them never stopped. A year after moving back to Yorkshire, Lily told Hannah she had reconnected with her first boyfriend, whom she broke up with when she moved to London. Nine months later, they were engaged. Lily said it was partly Tim who finally helped her to get better – they wanted children and her doctor told her she wouldn't be able to have them until she put on more weight. Although Lily didn't go into details, Hannah gets the sense it was a struggle; but eventually she reached a healthy weight, and six months ago Mabel was born.

Hannah feels her eyes growing damp as Lily types another message.

'See you soon,' she says, and attached to the message is a photo of Mabel, asleep in Lily's arms.

'See you there,' Hannah replies.

For a while she stays very still, staring at the photograph of baby Mabel. Hannah is delighted that Lily has found happiness in the shape of this tiny bundle of pink cheeks and scrunched fists. She deserves it, after the difficult few years she has been through. But Mabel's approaching christening is another reminder of how different Hannah's life is to that of so many of her friends. She pictures the flat that is waiting for her at home. She loves living with Mona, but their place is small and not truly theirs, even though they have lived there for four years. There is no living room, no garden and no dishwasher, all things that it was normal not to have at twenty-one, twenty-three, twenty-six. Back then most of her friends were living similar lives to hers, chasing dreams and holding down low-paid jobs, living in tatty apartments where damp and mould were common decorations. But as the years have drawn on, things have changed.

Each year that passes, Hannah wonders if it is time to give up on her dream and to accept that the things she hoped for are never going to come true. And each year something always keeps her holding on a little longer. But as she stares at her phone, her feet already aching and the smell of grease and coffee surrounding her, she wonders what that thing is and whether it's enough to keep her doing this for much longer.

5.00 A.M.

HANNAH

'FUCKING BITCH!'

Hannah barely has time to register the café door opening before the woman is there, shouting so loudly it makes her jump and the other customers turn around quickly in their seats.

'BITCH! FUCKING BITCH!'

Hannah shoves her phone in her apron pocket as the woman staggers into the middle of the café, jeans half open, a plastic bag in one hand and an empty dog lead in the other, trailing on the floor. Her long hair is matted at the ends and her eyes are open very wide. She is missing a front tooth. Hannah recognises her immediately.

As Hannah backs away slightly behind the counter and the young boy in the hoody stands up, the woman stops swearing and instead opens her mouth and starts suddenly and very

87

loudly to scream. The sound fills the café and the woman at the table by the window puts her hands over her ears. *She's back again*, thinks Hannah. Hannah, Mona and the other café staff know this woman well. They refer to her as The Screamer.

In an instant Pablo is out of the kitchen and at Hannah's side. He places a hand on her shoulder. Hannah looks back and forth between the young man and the female customer, trying to reassure them with just a glance that everything will be OK. But she is startled herself, the screaming bothering her so much more this time than it has in the past. It pierces her ears and makes her heart rate rise rapidly and she realises suddenly that she has no idea what to do. She notices that the young man is still standing, and after taking a deep breath he turns towards the screaming woman.

'Hey,' he says in a gentle voice, 'Where's your dog? I love dogs.'

Abruptly, the woman stops screaming. Her head spins quickly to face the young man. She fixes him with a glare.

'Dog? What dog?'

She takes a step closer to the young man and Hannah flinches, as though the woman is lunging at her. The young man moves backwards too, knocking into the table behind him. He looks at the lead in the woman's hand and then at Hannah, but he doesn't say anything further.

It's Pablo who eventually steps forward towards the woman. Hannah's mind was elsewhere and it disturbs her to find that she feels unable to cope, that she needs Pablo and his soft voice as he tries to comfort the woman. She stands behind the counter, feeling suddenly helpless.

The first time Hannah encountered The Screamer she was so frightened she nearly screamed too. It was at a similar time of night and that time the woman simply came and stood in the middle of the café and screamed non-stop for about five minutes, before turning around and leaving again. When it happened then the few customers were so startled that Hannah gave them all free coffees. Over time, though, Hannah and Mona have both grown used to her.

There are all sorts of strange customers that come into the café, particularly late at night. Hannah knows they all have their own stories; she has often wondered how The Screamer got to this point in her life. But it doesn't make it any less distressing, especially if she is the only waitress in the café. Most are completely harmless, like the very old man who comes in some nights and asks again and again to speak to Margaret. Hannah always tries to kindly explain there is no Margaret here, and eventually, he always leaves, but not before asking every customer in the café if they are Margaret. Then there's the woman who tries to hand out home-made religious flyers to all the customers, and leaves them taped to the bathroom mirror too. Sometimes she recites a passage from the Bible in a loud voice before leaving.

By now, Hannah knows the soothing voice she has to adopt with The Screamer and not to attempt to get too close, as it only panics the woman. She knows all of this, and yet she watches in silence as in patient but firm tones Pablo is able to calm the woman and steer her in the direction of the door. Hannah feels her shoulders sinking in relief as the woman lets herself be guided out. But at the last minute she stops abruptly. In a swift movement she kicks a chair so hard that it skids across the linoleum and crashes into a table, knocking the cutlery, napkins and sauces onto the floor. Without another word, the woman hugs her plastic bag tightly to her chest and steps out into the street.

Once she is gone, both the young man and the female customer head to the table and begin to pick up the things from the floor. They crouch down, collecting cutlery and packets of sauces.

Hannah finally gathers herself and pounces into action.

'Thank you,' she says, reaching down to the ground and helping collect the disturbed cutlery. As she leans down she catches Pablo's eye. He gives her a thumbs up and a questioning look. She returns the thumbs up and he nods and heads back into the kitchen.

Hannah focuses on trying to reassure the customers and right the table.

'I'm sorry about that,' she continues, 'She comes here every now and then. She's harmless really but can get a little ... aggravated.'

'I'll say,' says the woman in the tracksuit and trench coat, passing Hannah a pile of napkins. The young man collects a handful of cutlery and hands it to Hannah with a shy smile.

'Thanks,' Hannah says, and the three of them stand up, placing the fallen debris back on the table. She is about to ask them their names and to offer them a coffee on the house when the woman's phone rings again. This time she pulls it from her pocket and answers it, turning back to her table. The young man returns to his too, opening a new textbook and staring intently at the pages.

'I'm just at the corner shop,' says the woman into her phone. Hannah listens to one side of the conversation as she continues to straighten the disturbed table and chairs.

'I popped out for some air,' continues the woman, twisting the belt of her trench coat in her hands and looking at her nails. 'Yes, I know how late it is. I just needed five minutes, OK?'

Hannah quietly tucks the chairs back under the table. The woman on the phone is now staring out the window to where a man is urinating against the front of the station on the other side of the road and a group in high visibility jackets are making their way down the street. In a couple of hours this road will be heaving and will stay that way for the rest of the day. But for now it is still quiet, the bin bags still waiting on the pavement and the few people who are here still cause for intrigue.

'I've only been gone five minutes. I'm walking back now. Yes, I can hear she's crying. Just comfort her until I'm home. Yes, I know you don't have breasts, darling, I'm not insane. Wow, thanks. Yes, I said, I'm walking home now. I'll be home soon.'

The woman hangs up her phone and slips it back into her pocket. Hannah straightens the table and tries to look as though she wasn't listening. Her breathing has returned to normal and her mind is now drawn to the woman in the track-suit and her story, wondering at the baby waiting for her at home. She knows she has no right to judge her for clearly lying to her husband, but she still feels a question flash through her mind – *why is she here?*

The woman doesn't seem to have noticed the fact Hannah was listening, or the expression on Hannah's face, which Hannah is sure is concerned without her meaning it to be. Instead she leaves a pile of coins on the table, tightens her coat around her and leaves without glancing back. Hannah watches as the woman steps out onto the street. She stands on the pavement, her shoulders heaving as though she is taking long, deep breaths. She stays that way for a while and then she thrusts her hands in her pockets, tilts her head down and walks quickly away.

Hannah feels a calm descend on the café now that The Screamer has left and the tables are all empty, apart from the young man in the green hoody who has been here so long that he feels like part of the furniture. She lets herself rest on a chair by the counter. In the quiet, her thoughts return to Lily and her other former housemates.

Shortly after Lily left, Bemi told the housemates she was leaving too. She was moving in with Anya, into a small flat above a fish and chip shop in Tottenham, the only place they could afford but somewhere that would be theirs. She seemed nervous telling the others, but they were all supportive and Bemi was relieved. All of them apart from Sophie, who surprisingly didn't take the news well. She stormed out of the room after Bemi had finished telling them and on the day Bemi left, carrying Maud's tank out to the removal van, Sophie burst into tears.

It was when Poppy left that Hannah and Mona both decided it was time to move on as well. Poppy called a house meeting one evening. She had bought doughnuts for everyone, a huge box of Krispy Cremes that sat on the coffee table in the middle of the room, sweating sugar in the waxed box.

'I'm moving to Paris,' she told them all, 'I'm moving in with Antoine.'

Hannah remembers turning to Mona, meeting her eye and seeing her own shock reflected on her friend's face. Poppy had mentioned Antoine before, but she mentioned so many people and was out so often that Hannah had no idea Antoine was her boyfriend. It turned out they had met through a friend at a house party when he was visiting from Paris for the weekend. Since then they'd been seeing each other regularly, Poppy said, Poppy staying with him in the apartment his company rented for him when he was over for business. Hannah remembered several trips Poppy had made to Paris since she had been living in the house – Poppy had said it was to visit her cousins who lived there, but it must have been to see Antoine. For such a sociable person, Poppy's strong sense of privacy came as a surprise. It seemed that although she surrounded herself with people, when it came to those who were truly close she held them to her tightly like winning cards.

'Why didn't you tell us?' asked Sophie.

Poppy shrugged in that light way she had.

'I didn't know if it was going to become anything serious,' she said, 'I didn't want to jinx it. But when he asked me to move it just suddenly seemed to make sense. Why not? I've always wanted to live in Paris, and there are loads of cabaret shows there that I'm going to audition for once I've moved. Sometimes you have to make a leap of faith.'

Hannah, Mona and Sophie congratulated Poppy and

together they shared Krispy Cremes and whatever they could find in the kitchen to drink (a quarter of a bottle of gin and a few cans of beer). But there was an unspoken sense that with Poppy leaving, things had changed too much. Hannah couldn't imagine living there without Poppy to bind them together – the ringmaster who assembled the house of misfits. And with Lily's room still empty, they would need to find not one but two new housemates. The dynamic of the house would change completely. Once the doughnuts were eaten and the drinks were just sticky dregs at the bottom of glasses, Poppy mentioned that the lease was due for renewal in a month's time. Did the others want to take it on and renew it for another year?

Hannah, Mona and Sophie looked at each other. Without needing to say anything else, it was decided. Sophie said she had friends who had a spare room going, so she would get in touch with them. Hannah and Mona started looking for flats that evening. They moved three weeks later.

The new flat with just Mona felt so much more like home that she didn't miss the Bounds Green house, but she did find herself missing Poppy in particular. Taking her phone from her pocket again, Hannah clicks on Poppy's Instagram page and scrolls through the images. She pauses on a photo of Poppy and Antoine in a bar in Paris. They are both holding wine glasses and Antoine is smiling at the camera but Poppy is smiling at Antoine. Hannah wonders who took the photograph and where the bar is. Perhaps it is their local favourite. Hannah looks again at Poppy, thinking how happy she seems. Her hair is shorter but other than that she looks the same.

Four years have passed, and despite the warmth that Hannah feels whenever she thinks of Poppy, they have drifted apart. They have seen each other a few times when Poppy has been in London visiting friends and family, but Hannah has never been to see her in Paris, or to watch the cabaret show she has been dancing in for the past three years. Each year she says she will, but somehow it has never happened.

Hannah and Mona planned a trip together once. It was January and they were both between theatre jobs – Mona had finished a Christmas job tap dancing in nursing homes around London and Hannah had come to the end of a small singing role in a musical at a community theatre in Tooting. She was exhausted: she had continued working at the café during the day throughout the three-week run, and the theatre was more than an hour away from their flat. But the thought of Paris had kept her going. She pictured drinking espressos outside busy bistros with Mona and Poppy, people-watching. And she just desperately wanted a few days away from it all: away from the café but more importantly away from the auditions and the yearning to make something of her music, and the growing fear that she wasn't a star but rather a dull lump of rock. But in the end Mona caught a stomach bug the week before their trip. They never made it to Paris.

*

'Go without me,' says Mona from the nest of duvets and blankets on her bed, her face clammy and pale, 'I'm sure someone else will want to go with you – or just go on your own.'

It is the day before their planned departure date and their full suitcases stand in the hallway. Hannah packed for them both just in case Mona felt better and wanted to go. Her rucksack holds a guide to Paris she bought for the trip, pages folded down to mark the places she particularly wanted to visit or thought Mona might like. The Musée Rodin, the Musée Picasso, the Shakespeare and Company bookshop and a café she read about that apparently serves the world's best lemon meringue pie – Mona's favourite.

'I'm staying here with you,' Hannah replies, placing a mug of hot water and crushed ginger on Mona's bedside table. She places a hand on Mona's forehead – it is hot, and Hannah gently eases back the duvet. At that moment, Mona starts to tremble. Her face turns a shade of grey and she leans forward – as she does so, Hannah reaches for the washing-up bowl on the floor and lifts it towards Mona just in time.

'It's OK,' says Hannah, holding the bowl with one hand and pulling strands of Mona's hair away from her face with the other. Mona starts to cry and Hannah reaches for the tissues and a damp flannel that she has left beside the bed.

'It's OK, you're going to be OK,' says Hannah gently.

Once Mona is sleeping again, Hannah cleans up and opens a window, moving the jug of gerbera she bought earlier that day from her bedroom to Mona's bedside table. Later, she runs a bath and helps Mona from the bed to the bathroom.

'Just put your arm around me,' she says, letting Mona lean in to her, 'It's OK.'

It is strange to see her friend, usually so strong and collected, like this. Being able to look after her gives Hannah a strange rush of confidence and pride. Last week she received another rejection from a music venue and attended another failed audition. But here is somewhere that she can be of use. She throws herself into the task with the enthusiasm she knows she should have given to last week's audition but that she found suddenly so hard to muster, a fear of failure making her hold back. She had been ten minutes late for the audition and knew immediately that she wouldn't get the part. But lateness seemed a more palatable reason for her failure than what she increasingly fears is the truth – that she just isn't good enough.

But this, being there for her friend, she feels good at this. She helps Mona undress out of her pyjamas (Hogwarts leggings and an over-sized, faded T-shirt with a hem dotted with moth holes), turning away discreetly and throwing them in a pile for the laundry basket and giving Mona an arm to lean on as she climbs into the bath.

'OK, now lift your right leg, there we go, you're in,' says Hannah, keeping her voice gentle but firm. Mona silently follows her instructions.

Once Mona is in the bath, Hannah carefully rolls a towel and places it at the head of the tub, encouraging Mona to lean back against it. Her slim body sinks into the clouds of foaming lavender bubble bath that Hannah swirled into the water.

After a while, Hannah encourages Mona to sit up. She holds out an arm for her to lean against while she reaches for the shower head with the other. Carefully, she starts to wash her friend's hair. As she sprays the warm water she sings quietly, practising a folk song she needs to learn for a gig. She hasn't been practising as much as she knows she should, but here it *doesn't feel like practice. Here, in the warmth of the bathroom with Mona leaning weakly against her arm, it feels like how singing felt before she put the pressure on herself to make it her career. When singing was just singing.*

'Is the water warm enough?' says Hannah, remembering the words the hairdresser used at the salon last time she visited. Mona nods.

Hannah squeezes shampoo into her palm and rubs it gently into Mona's scalp, picking up her song again. Her voice echoes around the small room, rising above the sound of the bathroom fan and the broken tap that they have never been able to stop dripping. As she rinses out the shampoo she places a hand at the top of Mona's forehead and instructs her to lean her head back, careful not to let any shampoo suds into her eyes. Mona closes her eyes as the water falls and shampoo trickles down the length of her hair, so dark it is almost black when it is wet.

Once her hair is washed, the room smelling of the bottle of aloe vera shampoo they both share, Mona leans back against the towel and looks up at Hannah.

'I think this probably makes us best friends now,' she says quietly. Hannah even spots the start of a smile. She laughs quietly.

'I'd say so,' she says.

After two more days of illness, Mona is feeling better. On the fourth day, she takes Hannah out for dinner at a French restaurant in Islington. To look at her you wouldn't think she had just recovered from being unwell: she is dressed in a chic pair of high-waisted trousers and a polo neck, her dark hair worn loose tonight. She orders wine for them both and tells Hannah about an audition she has lined up for the next week as they share the lukewarm carafe of red, the sound of Serge Gainsbourg coming quietly from the restaurant's speakers and a couple with strong South African accents talking animatedly at the table next to them.

Mona suddenly puts down her cutlery and looks seriously at Hannah.

'I know this isn't the same as Paris,' she says, 'I'm so sorry we didn't make it. And thank you so much for looking after me – you were amazing.'

'Don't worry about it,' Hannah replies. Mona reaches for her hand and Hannah squeezes her friend's hand back as the waiter clears their plates and asks them if they want dessert.

'Remember, this is my treat,' says Mona.

Hannah smiles.

'Why not then?' she says. They order two different puddings so that they can share.

*

At the coffee counter, Hannah starts typing a message to Poppy and then remembers what time it is. She finishes the message but closes WhatsApp before pressing 'send', making a mental note to send it at a more reasonable hour. Perhaps she could plan another trip to Paris, she thinks to herself. It would be good to see Poppy again and might be the perfect distraction from her worries about her career and the pain of her recent split with Jaheim. Maybe Stella would let Mona have the time off so she could come too, Mona, Hannah and

Poppy reconnecting over red wine. It could be a break, and as she leans on the coffee counter looking out over the nearly empty café, Hannah realises that's what she needs more than anything. She just needs a break.

6.00 A.M.

DAN

As the morning edges closer to day, he feels exhaustion pressing down on him, melting his thoughts until they swirl into one another like marbled paints. Brief snippets of things he has read in his textbooks merge with snatches of overheard conversation in the café around him, as well as remembered words that seem just as real to him as he sits alone at the table.

'Not long until breakfast,' says the dark-haired man in chef's whites as he steps through a door at the back of the café and is handed a coffee by the red-haired waitress.

'Just one more chapter,' says his mum as he struggles to read another page in another textbook, *'Just one more chapter.'*

The thought distracts him, and he is no longer in the café but instead lying in his bed in the old flat, his mum sat on the edge with her legs tucked under his duvet. A copy of his library book, *The Hobbit*, rests in her lap. They have read it together twice already, but it is his favourite, and when she took him to the library on Saturday morning it was the one he chose. He sat in one of the colourful chairs reading the beginning that he knew so well while his mum walked slowly up and down the aisles in the adult section. He was proud that a love of reading was something he got from her, just like the bump in his nose that she told him gave his face character, his green eyes and his light blond hair. They are all he has left of her now.

A new customer pushes open the door: a small woman Dan guesses is in her fifties or sixties, with grey hair worn short and a frown on her face but bright, smiling eyes, who nods at the red-haired waitress as she takes a seat at one of the bar stools. She carries a large bucket filled with colourful bottles. Dan remembers the cupboard under the sink in the old flat that was full of similar bottles, and how every other Sunday his mum would get them out and they would spend the morning cleaning the flat. Even when he was very little she gave him a task to do, starting off with dusting or changing the sheets and moving up to hoovering and cleaning the bathroom.

'It's just the two of us,' he remembers his mum saying when he must have been six or seven, 'We've got to help each other out, OK?' He nodded and climbed onto a chair to dust the bookshelves and the top of the TV.

When he was much older and she got sick, he took on more and more of the Sunday jobs until he knew how to clean the entire apartment and did it while his mum sat on the sofa.

'You're an angel,' she said quietly to him as he worked around her in the living room, refilling her mug of tea as well.

His cleaning skills had come in handy when he stayed with Rob. The flat had been a mess when he first arrived, but he cleaned the kitchen thoroughly before cooking for them all on his first night there.

'Wow, this is great,' he remembers Rob's flatmates saying as he served them steaming bowls of spaghetti and meatballs, and he had felt the warmth from the steam and his own pride flushing his face.

Dan is modest but knows he would make a great housemate or tenant. His mum brought him up well, he can see that now.

The new customer looks up and catches his eye. He smiles and she smiles back, and although she is years older and at least a foot shorter, there is his mum again in the warmth of this stranger's smile.

HANNAH

On the street, a dustbin lorry is parked with flashing hazard lights. Four men in dark green trousers and fluorescent jackets jog up and down this stretch of road, grabbing full bags from the pavement and slinging them into the mouth of the dust-cart. There is something graceful about their actions: the light-footed running to keep up with the lorry as it slowly moves down the road and the ease with which they seem to swing the bags.

Seeing the lorry, Hannah suddenly remembers the bins in the kitchen and beneath the counter. As she reaches for them, holding her breath to avoid the wafting smell of bin juice as she puts in the new liner, a favourite phrase of Mona's comes into her head.

'I feel like this is going to be our year.'

It's a phrase that Mona says every year and that Hannah usually nods along to. But as she ties a knot in the full bin bag she wonders again whether her year is still to come, or whether time has simply marched away with her dreams, leaving her behind. After fetching the kitchen bins too, she dashes out into the street, asking Pablo to watch the café while she does.

She catches the lorry just in time.

'Sorry!' she says to one of the refuse collectors as he takes the bags from her and slings them into the back of the truck. She normally puts them out in plenty of time, but this morning she has been distracted and on edge. It started with news of Mona's call-back and has become worse throughout the night, a sort of agitated nervousness that she feels now rushing through her body like electricity.

For a moment she stands on the street, watching the sky growing brighter as the sun rises above the city. Sunrise is usually her favourite part of her shift – she loves watching the sky change colour and the buildings bathed in light. She never actually sees the bright orb until much later when it is no longer hidden behind the buildings and her shift is over. But throughout the day she charts its effects, the colours it spreads and the shifting quality of the light. She knows it is there and that if she were to be standing at the top of the Gherkin or the Heron Building or one of the others that scrape the London sky, she would see it rising out of the grey streets like a phoenix spreading its wings. In the past it has been a comfort just to know that, even if she can't see the sunshine for herself.

Today though, the morning light seems to have lost its charm. Instead of noticing the colours in the sunrise she sees the homeless man crouching by the station and the litter scattered at his feet. Her eyes fall on the newsstand plastered with adverts: a local fish and chip shop and an unappealing brown and orange ad for a tanning salon. The air is heavy with the smell of the dust on the street and the tang of the bin lorry. This street that she knows so well seems all at once like any other street in any other city – a pulse of anonymous faces beating past and the same hum of traffic and layer of dirt and grime that coats the street and pavements.

Suddenly she wonders what would happen if she didn't return to the café. It would be so easy to just walk away down the street and not look back. With the air on her face it feels like an easy decision and a voice shouts loudly at her to run. For a moment she pauses, her feet ready to take her towards the bus stop and then home. But then the sensible side of her brain switches back on, as though she is waking up out of a dream. She thinks of Pablo and of Stella, who might be coming in to the café later and whom in any case Hannah feels indebted to for always being flexible and letting her have time off for gigs and auditions. Eleanor, one of the café's other waitresses, will be arriving soon for the morning shift. She is fairly new and Hannah knows she can't leave her on her own, it wouldn't be fair. She takes one last look down the street and then turns back towards the glowing red sign of the café, following it inside.

'Sorry,' Hannah says to Pablo, who is standing behind the

counter watching the café for her, 'I had to chase the lorry down the street a bit.'

'No problem,' replies Pablo, stepping out from behind the counter to let Hannah retake her position.

'Pancakes soon,' he adds, winking. Around 7 a.m. every morning when they are on a shift together, she and Pablo sit down to a quick breakfast of fresh pancakes. Her stomach rumbles and she realises how hungry she is.

Once Pablo has returned to the kitchen, Hannah washes her hands, then scans the café. By now the student with the rucksack has abandoned his textbooks and instead stands in front of the lending library telephone box, his head tilted as he reads the titles. He reaches for one particular book and pulls it out, smiling with recognition as he sees the cover. He brings it back to his table and settles himself to read.

As well as the student, there is a man in a Transport for London uniform reading a magazine (*Hello!*, Hannah notices with a smile) and Flavia, the local cleaner who often comes in at this time of day and sits at the same table not far from the counter. She is a small woman in her fifties with a stern expression that clashes with the bright blue of her uniform and the lilac eyeshadow she always wears. She sips her Americano (no milk), occasionally smiling up at Ernest the bear as though gloating over the fact that he is dead while she is alive.

Hannah checks on the customers and brings the man in the TFL uniform a cappuccino and puts in his order to Pablo for a bacon butty. She glances at the clock: it is halfway through her shift. She knows it should bring her some relief to know she has already made it through to that point, but the remaining six hours loom ahead of her. As she is looking at the clock the door opens. It is Eleanor, arriving for her shift and Hannah breathes a sigh of relief.

'Morning,' she says quickly to the petite woman in her early twenties who is making her way through the café. Eleanor is currently completing a masters and works part-time in the café to support herself. She is Spanish and speaks in Spanish to Mona, Pablo and Sofia, another waitress who works part-time at the café. Mona and Pablo always reply in English, but when Sofia and Eleanor are in the café together they only speak English to take orders from the customers. It has made it difficult for Hannah to connect with them and she usually finds herself bristling slightly when either of them arrives on a shift, but today she is relieved to see her.

'Now you're here, I'm going to take a quick break,' says Hannah, as Eleanor reaches for an apron and ties it round her waist. Before Eleanor can say anything, Hannah is heading for the small storeroom at the back of the café. As soon as the door is closed behind her she feels herself breathing more deeply, happy to be away from the café for a moment even if the storeroom is a mess. It is piled high with boxes filled with bottles of drink, napkins, receipt rolls. This is where the cleaning products are kept, too, a mop, bucket and hoover tucked in one corner, as well as spare crockery and glasses. There are a couple of chairs wedged between all the boxes and Hannah sits down heavily on one, stretching out her legs and resting her feet on the other. It is cooler and more dimly lit in the storeroom than in the café and the chill feels pleasant on Hannah's hot, tired body.

With nothing much to look at in the storeroom apart from the boxes, she reaches for her phone and sees a missed call from her mother. To anyone else, a call from a parent at 5 a.m. might be cause for alarm, but Hannah is used to it. Her mother is an insomniac, and if she knows that Hannah is working a late shift she often calls her, hoping to catch her on a break. It has been over a week since Hannah last spoke to her mother so she settles into the chair and dials her number.

'Hello, darling,' answers her mother, so quietly that Hannah can hardly hear her, 'I'm just going to go downstairs so I don't wake your father; wait one second, honey.'

Hannah can hear the low rumble of her father's snoring in the background. She covers her mouth to stop herself from laughing. A few moments later her mother resumes talking at a normal volume.

'Sorry about that,' she says, 'After I couldn't get through to you I went back to bed for a bit but of course couldn't drop off.'

At thirty, Hannah supposes she shouldn't derive quite so much comfort simply from the sound of her mother's voice, but as she sits, tired and anxious in the café storeroom, the chat reaching her down the phone soothes her.

Hannah wishes suddenly and fiercely that she was in her bed at her parents' house in Wales, the room truly dark, unlike any she's had in London. The room is not really *her* room any more – her parents redecorated it several years ago and turned it into a generic guest bedroom. But the bed is still more comfortable than the one she has in London and the cool blue shade her mother chose for the walls is peaceful and calming.

She pictures waking up and joining her parents for breakfast, her father reading the paper and her mother chatting and pouring the three of them coffee. In her mind she can see the kitchen that looks out over the garden and the hills beyond and she realises how much she misses the colour green.

'So how are you? How's work?' her mother asks.

Hannah knows that her mother doesn't understand why she still works at the café. Over the years, both her parents have been incredibly supportive of her dream to be a singer, attending gigs and loaning her money for new guitars and other equipment. But as more and more of Hannah's friends have bought flats and settled down, she can tell that her parents' understanding of her choices has faltered.

'I just want you to be happy,' her mother had said to her a few months ago. 'Is your life really making you happy?'

'Yes,' Hannah had snapped at the time, despite the fact that she was just back from a shift, felt exhausted and didn't dare check her bank balance because it was nearing the end of the month and she didn't want to see how little she had left in her account.

Since then her mother has been more cautious, asking questions but avoiding saying anything confrontational. Hannah supposes that's where her fear of conflict comes from and can't decide whether that's a good or a bad thing.

'It's OK,' Hannah replies, reaching down with her free hand to rub her shins, which are aching from standing all morning, 'Sorry I missed your call – Eleanor's just arrived so I'm taking my break now. Pablo's granddaughter has started walking.'

Hannah keeps her mother updated with news of the café

staff – it seems a good neutral topic, and she knows how much her mother loves babies.

'Oh, that's such a gorgeous age,' she says, her voice soft. Hannah knows her mother would never dream of expressing it, but she wonders if she is sad not to be a grandmother. As her parents' only child, she is their only chance of becoming grandparents. She has never felt an urgent broodiness like some of her friends have described, but Hannah realises she always assumed that she would have children someday. Except as she has got older, the prospect of 'someday' has become less of a faraway thing and more of a cause for panic. Now that she is single again, she wonders whether 'someday' is ever likely to arrive for her. It's something she has been grappling with since her break-up with Jaheim, and the photo of baby Mabel this morning stirred those feelings once more. But she realises she hadn't properly thought about it from her mother's perspective. She knows that's not a *reason* to have children, but she also hears for the first time the longing in her mother's voice and feels not anger at her hopes and expectations for her, but some sort of understanding. So many of her mother's friends are grandmothers and she often talks about spending time with them and their grandchildren. Hannah thinks her mother would make a wonderful grandmother.

'How's Dad?' Hannah asks, changing the subject and trying to push away the thoughts that she isn't ready to confront because she has no answers to them.

'He's doing OK,' replies her mother. Her father's mother, Hannah's grandmother, passed away at the start of the year and since then Hannah has felt a need to check up on him. It has been a strange shift, feeling like she needs to look after her parents rather than the other way around.

'We went down to the coast last week,' her mother continues, 'Just packed some lunch in the morning and headed off. The weather wasn't great but we didn't mind.'

Hannah's parents have both recently retired and are enjoying the new freedom. She pictures them eating their sandwiches on a windswept beach and finds herself smiling.

'And how's Jaheim?' her mother asks.

The question catches Hannah off guard. She takes her feet off the chair and places them on the ground, leaning forward in an attempt to calm the sudden spinning in her head. Her throat feels dry and the storeroom seems suddenly not pleasantly cool, but painfully cold. She takes a long breath, wondering what to say.

'He's fine,' she replies eventually.

When Hannah and Jaheim broke up three weeks ago she was too upset to talk about it. She felt plunged into a darkness that she couldn't find a way out of, and she stayed there for a week. In the second week she emerged, bleary-eyed and dazed, but trying to get back to her life. She considered calling her parents then, but she couldn't find the words to tell them how Jaheim had betrayed her and that the relationship that she'd put so much hope and energy into was over.

'That's good,' says her mother, not seeming to have noticed the hesitance in Hannah's reply, 'He's a good egg – your father and I like him very much. We're so glad you're happy, darling, especially after what happened with Sam.'

Hannah holds a hand over her mouth, holding back a gasp

111

of pain. She knows she should confide in her mother and that the longer she doesn't tell her the truth, the worse it will be when it eventually comes out. She doesn't want to hurt her mother by keeping secrets from her. And yet she still can't find the words. She can't bring herself to tell her mother that in the end, Jaheim had been just the same as Sam, even if his cheating wasn't with another woman. She can't admit how deeply she was tricked by both men, that she clearly learnt nothing from her first relationship because she let herself trust again so easily, so openly. And she doesn't want to break it to her mother that now she is alone again and is worried that this time it is for good, that those children she thought she would have 'someday' are just a fantasy, like so much about her life.

Swallowing hard and closing her eyes, Hannah speaks as calmly as she can into the phone.

'Thanks, Mum. I'm sorry, Eleanor's calling me from the café, I'd better go. Send my love to Dad.'

Her mother says goodbye, and as soon as Hannah has hung up and double-checked the call has ended, she lets herself cry. Tears flow down her face and she wraps her arms tightly around herself, trying to stave off the fierce sobs that threaten to shake her apart.

Without really realising what she is doing, she reaches for her phone in her apron pocket again. She is opening her photos before she can stop herself, scrolling through the pictures of her and Jaheim that she hasn't yet deleted, tears still rolling down her cheeks. The photos have a folder to themselves and there are hundreds of them. Hannah and Jaheim in restaurants, cafés, parks and in Hannah's parents' garden last summer. There are several of Jaheim sleeping, photos she never showed him but which she couldn't stop herself from taking. She meant to delete them all weeks ago, but she didn't.

She knows she shouldn't look at them – it's like picking at a scar that hasn't quite healed. She can't help herself though, and there is some kind of twisted relief in finally letting the pain wash over her after spending the last two weeks trying desperately to ignore it. In the silence of the storeroom she digs a little deeper, this time running her nail under the memory of the first time she met Jaheim, back when he was just another face in a crowded pub in this city full of strangers.

*

She doesn't notice him at first. The gig is in Camden and Hannah is performing before the main act. She knows the gig was really a favour from one of Mona's friends who is the manager here. When Hannah got the call saying they wanted to book her she pretended not to be aware of the connection, but as the evening drew closer the fact repeatedly tapped her on the shoulder, making her doubt herself. 'They don't really want you,' she said to herself as she put her make-up on in the bathroom mirror, carefully painting her face in an attempt to hide her nerves, covering her worries with blusher and lipstick. It had taken nearly an hour to decide what to wear; she eventually opted for a red dress that clashes with her hair but in a way she hopes works.

But as she sits on the bar stool preparing to play she suddenly worries she misjudged the colour of the dress and the style, which suddenly feels too formal. Looking around she notices most of the customers are wearing jeans. She spots leather jackets, battered Converse and Doc Martens. Mona is at the bar chatting with the manager. She came straight from a shift in the café but still manages to look effortless. She fits in here, and as she leans against the bar and laughs and the manager laughs back, Hannah sits alone with her guitar and envies her friend nearly as much as she loves her.

While she waits to begin playing, no one seems to notice she is there. Conversations continue around her: the buzz of a Thursday night just after pay day. A man with a shaved head and a neat beard loudly orders five packets of crisps and carries them in his arms back to a table in the corner where his friends thank him and reach for the packets, ripping them open to share. A young woman waiting at the bar is nudged to the side by a broad-shouldered man who tries to get the attention of a pink-haired waitress wearing dungarees and a striped shirt. She ignores the man and instead asks the woman what she wants. The young woman smiles with relief and soon turns back to her friends clutching a bottle of rosé and four glasses. They smile at her and immediately start talking, looping her into the conversation they'd been having while she was at the bar. Hannah picks out Mona's laughter again and wishes, despite her dreams of making it as a singer, that she was leaning against a bar instead of teetering on a stool clutching a guitar.

Her eyes wander to a group near the door: men and women a similar age to Hannah huddle around a table filled with pint glasses, some full, some empty. They look like they've come straight from an office – they are smart but not too smartly dressed and sit a little apart from each other but talk quickly and animatedly. A slightly older woman still wearing an office lanyard places three full pints on the table that overspill slightly. No one seems to care as they lean forwards to grab their drinks. At first Hannah doesn't know why her eyes are drawn to the man with the large brown eyes and hair so short that it emphasises the size of his ears, which are not small. He isn't the most attractive one there – even sitting down, she guesses he is shorter than she normally likes. Yet he's the one she focuses on and she quickly realises why: while the others in the group drink and talk, he is watching the woman in the red dress with the guitar balanced on her lap. Hannah looks away, adjusting her guitar strap and shifting slightly on the stool. When she looks up again he is still watching her. He smiles, and suddenly he becomes the most attractive in the group. His smile takes up most of his face and is the type of smile that can only belong to someone who knows how to laugh and is kind to their mum. You can just tell, or at least Hannah thinks she can. There's something about his smile that makes her feel more at ease. Hannah smiles back, watching him for a moment and waiting for him to break eye contact with her or to stop smiling. But he doesn't.

Hannah is the first to look away. She glances over to the bar manager, nods at him, and he nods back. She places her hands on her guitar, the feeling of the strings so familiar against the pads of her fingers. Then she starts to play. As soon as she begins to sing the conversation and laughter in the bar quietens down and eventually stops altogether. She knows that when she's at her best she is able to do that – to quieten a room. It feels almost arrogant to admit it, but she has sung in enough rooms to know that it is something like her superpower. The problem for

Hannah has never been the singing. It's been getting into those rooms in the first place.

Normally when she performs she looks for Mona's face in the crowd. If she can, Mona will always be there for Hannah's gigs, just like Hannah is there for all of Mona's performances. Hannah knows that her friend will always give her the smile and the nod she needs to tell her it's going well and that she believes in her. But tonight Hannah doesn't look at Mona. Instead her eyes fall on the face of the man with the most wonderful smile she has ever seen. The man who saw her when no one else did, before she revealed her superpower. When she was just Hannah. He looks back and everything else in the bar is just background noise.

As they lock eyes she knows very clearly what will happen when she finishes her set. For someone so often filled with self-doubt, there is suddenly no question about it. She knows that when she stops singing she will cross the bar and find the face of the man with the big smile, the slightly too-large ears and the brown eyes, and she will kiss him. He will kiss her back and after talking and drinking, they will go home together. There is no question about it. And being certain for once of how things are going to go makes Hannah happier than she has felt in months. In the warm bar in Camden that smells of beer and cigarette smoke that clings to the jackets of the customers, Hannah sings and he smiles. Everything else is just background noise.

*

116

In the storeroom, Hannah stares at the photos on her phone, her hands still trembling. She fell for Jaheim quickly and fiercely. Looking back, she wonders why she wasn't more guarded and cautious, given what happened with Sam. But when love struck her she found she suddenly forgot everything else, entirely consumed by the sweetness of it. She cringes at the stupidity of it, wishing now that she had been more careful.

They might have met at one of her shows where for a short while all eyes were on her and she held the room with her voice. But very soon Jaheim became the centre of her world. Because he saw her when no one else did and that meant everything. Because he was something to count on when everything else was uncertain. Because their relationship was something to pour her attention into, something to focus on.

That's why she can't tell her mother that it's over. Because she was so wrong, and she feels so ashamed.

Hannah returns her phone to her pocket. She looks around the storeroom, trying to calm herself by taking in all the small details and the fact that she has six more hours of her shift to get through. She can't fall apart right now, she has to work. After a few more moments she wipes her face, wondering at the state of her make-up. Before heading back to her shift, she sneaks to the bathroom to reapply her eyeliner and mascara, staring at herself in the mirror and trying to set her face into a confident, calm expression. Once she is happy with her mask, she takes one final deep breath and returns to the café. She has been a performer for long enough to know that the show, and the shift, must go on.

'There you are,' says Eleanor, 'I was about to come and find you. I know you showed me last week but I can't remember where the coffee beans are, the machine is low.'

Hannah focuses on helping Eleanor drag a fresh bag from the storeroom and fill the machine. It feels good to have a task to throw herself into, but as they work a thought flashes into her mind. She wonders how long Eleanor will be working here for. Once her masters has finished, will she stay, or will she find a full-time job that excites and inspires her? Will she stay for five years, like Hannah has, or will this café just be a fleeting chapter in her life, a chapter to flick through quickly before getting on to the main story?

'There we go,' she says, once the machine is full, 'If you have any other questions today, just shout.'

Eleanor nods and heads over to serve a man who has just arrived at a table in the corner.

'I'm off now,' comes a voice, and Hannah turns to see Flavia, the cleaner, picking up her bucket of cleaning products and heading to the counter to pay.

'Good to see you,' Hannah says as she deals with the payments, 'See you again soon.'

Hannah watches as the woman crosses the road towards the office blocks on the other side, where she will spend the morning wiping desks and stacking abandoned mugs into a dishwasher. Hannah wonders if the office workers will even notice that yesterday's crusty cereal bowls have been removed from their desks, or the faint smell of antibacterial spray. The bright flash of the cleaning bottles is visible against the grey of the street and then Flavia walks away and Hannah can no longer see her. Because that's how it goes. People come and go and Hannah stays. She blinks quickly.

On the street outside newspaper sellers in branded uniforms push wheeled trolleys stacked high with copies of the *Metro* and *City AM*, each pile covered in a coloured piece of paper and wrapped tightly with a cable tie. Soon they will be snipped open and the newspapers handed out to commuters as they stream out of the station, copies slipped under arms or stuffed into bags.

It is still quiet at this time in the café. She has a little longer until the office workers start to come in and a queue starts to form by the counter. Although her feet ache, Hannah suddenly welcomes the thought of the approaching rush – anything to occupy her and make the rest of her shift pass quickly. She feels like she is fraying around the edges; but perhaps work, mindless work, can keep her together for a few more hours. She wipes vigorously at tables that are already spotless and waits for the rush of customers to arrive.

7.00 A.M.

DAN

He only manages a few chapters of *The Hobbit* before he falls asleep again. His head nods and his eyes burn as he tries desperately to keep them open. He focuses on the clock above the counter, its hands bringing him gradually closer to his first lecture but seeming to him to be frozen in the same spot. Fatigue circles him but he pushes back against it, pressing his fingernails into his palm until it is covered with indented crescent moons.

Sleep eventually comes to him like a dark, cold wave pulling him under. He is too exhausted to fight back and resist as he slips beneath it and down into the deep. It is not a restful sleep. It is not the kind of sweet dreams and calm, heavy breathing that you wake from feeling refreshed. Sleep for Dan is sinister – it claws at him and drags him down, down into a place that he feels he can't escape from.

Sounds from the café enter his mind like wind through a gap in a windowpane. He hears the hissing of the coffee machine, but in sleep it becomes the sound of the Orient Express, sighing great clouds of steam as it stands at a station platform. It looks like Paddington; he remembers it from trips to visit his grandparents when he was very young, before they both passed away. He is at the station with his mum, old-fashioned suitcases piled beside them. She is wearing one of the smart trouser suits he remembers the women wearing in the murder mysteries that she liked. She is smiling. It makes him smile too. But as the steam parts he realises that something is wrong. The train is nothing like he imagined. It doesn't look like the shining, glamorous vehicle that hung in a frame, the page cut from a magazine, in their kitchen. The paint is rusting and peeling, the windows are smashed and as he looks through them he sees that the carriages are completely empty – there are no seats or tables or the bar he remembers his mum talking about. He turns to her and she must not have noticed yet because she is still smiling.

'Shall we get on?' she says, reaching down for one of the suitcases. He feels panic rising inside him. He can't let her see this – he can't let her know how their plan has come to nothing, that what they hoped for and dreamt of is nothing more than a broken-down old train with shards of smashed glass scattered among discarded rubbish on the tracks.

She starts walking and the train hisses again and obscures her with a cloud of steam.

'Mum?' he shouts, following her through the fog. For a moment he spots the bright cream of her trouser suit, but then she is gone. He has reached a door to a carriage and tries the handle but it is locked. He rattles the handle a few times, but it won't shift.

'Mum?' he shouts again, starting to run along the platform. He tries each door and peers in each window, but each carriage is empty.

'Mum?'

His voice rises above the sound of the engine but he is alone at the station, peering through fog at an old, abandoned train. He feels the same childish fear he felt when he lost his mum at the library when he was seven (she wasn't lost, just sat at a chair propped against the end of an aisle, absorbed in a book). Except this time there is no librarian to run to, sobbing, who can walk with him around the place until his mum is found. He is completely on his own.

When he wakes it takes him a moment to realise where he is. His eyes adjust to the bright lights and focus on the linoleum floor, the flash of red napkins in the middle of the table, the clock and the outstretched paws of the bear on the wall.

'Mum.'

He says the word so quietly that it is less than a whisper.

HANNAH

The boy with the rucksack and sleeping bag is still sat quietly at the same table he has occupied nearly since the very start of Hannah's shift. To begin with, Hannah headed over every now and then to ask if he wanted anything else, but the way he shifted in his chair and looked from his books and back to her again told her to leave him alone. It's not as though they have been short on tables this morning. He is awake now, head tilted down as he reads the battered copy of *The Hobbit*. Hannah noticed him sleeping earlier, although she pretended not to. She knows that Stella wouldn't approve of a customer sleeping here – as an all-night café it happens quite often and when Stella is working she asks them to wake up or leave. But Hannah doesn't mind the sleepers. They're no trouble – it's the night-time and early-morning drunks that she fears. The ones who look at her with wild eyes and ask her for things she isn't prepared to give.

The door opens and a construction worker with a weathered face and tattoos circling his neck orders a filter coffee to go. He carries his hard hat in his hands and has dust under his fingernails. As he pays, Hannah spots a photograph in his wallet of a young girl dressed in a ballet outfit. He catches her looking as he returns his credit card. He places a large thumb over the photo.

'My daughter,' he says and his face softens into a smile and his eyes shine. Hannah nods and smiles back, passing him the coffee. The man returns his wallet to his pocket and his hard hat to his head as he leaves.

Outside, the street is starting to grow busier. The keenest office workers head out of the station and towards the offices along the streets, some grabbing newspapers from the out-stretched hands of vendors, others keeping their heads down as though staring at their feet could trick them into being somewhere other than this – another street somewhere sunnier, perhaps.

123

In less than an hour's time the café will become too busy for Hannah to think. But until then, her mind floats, unrestrained and untethered. She still feels shaken by her conversation with her mother, and guilty about not speaking the truth. And however hard she tries not to go there, she finds her thoughts returning to Jaheim.

*

Mona is working tonight, dancing in a new production being performed at the Bush Theatre. Hannah has already been to see it twice, but tonight she stays home. Some of their friends are attending the show; she knows that Mona will stay with them afterwards for drinks and won't be back until late.

'That will be fun,' said Hannah cheerily in the morning, 'I'm sure it will be nice to catch up with everyone and let your hair down, you deserve it. I'm just sorry I can't make it too.'

She had told Mona that she was working and that's why she couldn't join her for drinks. It was nearly true – that afternoon she had been offered a last-minute slot in an open mic night in a bar she'd played at before. But without really thinking she had turned it down, saying that unfortunately she was unwell and couldn't sing, but that she'd love to do it another time. They were understanding and she hung up feeling pleased, like she'd done the right thing. It was important to let herself have some time off, she told herself, and besides, it was just the one gig. She didn't mean to lie to Mona about what she was doing this evening, but she didn't know how to explain how important to-night was – that she and Jaheim hadn't had either her flat or his

124

to themselves in over two weeks. That she felt like she was going crazy because of it. She knew that Mona wouldn't understand and she didn't want to offend her either. Lying felt kinder.

For the first time since living with Mona, Hannah has started to feel bursts of relief when Mona is not home. Usually when she arrives back from a shift she looks up to their flat as she approaches the building, picking out their front door and checking to see if a light is on. In the past she searched for that light like a beacon. But recently she has found herself turning the corner into the housing estate and looking up somewhat nervously. No light means an evening alone with Jaheim. Although they have only been together for two months, they have spent most evenings together since they met. But he has three housemates and she, of course, has Mona. Nights alone with Jaheim have very quickly come to be Hannah's greatest source of happiness. She feels greedy for them and even though a quiet voice tells her that perhaps things are moving too fast, or perhaps some time apart might be good for them both, the voice is so quiet that it is very easy to ignore.

Hannah, not usually bothered by the state of her bedroom, does a quick tidy up while she waits for Jaheim to arrive. She pushes her shoes under her bed and removes a pile of clothes from the floor. She applies her make-up carefully, her hands shaking slightly with anticipation. As she clears up she spots a book that Mona must have left for her, balanced on top of a pile of clothes on the end of Hannah's bed. Hannah picks it up and glances at the cover – it seems to be some sort of motivational non-fiction book of the kind that Mona devours – and notices a card slipped inside. On the front is a picture of two toddlers dressed in superhero outfits. They are holding hands and laughing. Hannah opens the card.

'Darling Hannah,' it reads:

I know things have been tough for you recently with auditions and gigs and everything that comes with trying to get the world to see how fabulous you are. I'm sorry they don't always see it straight away, because to me it is just obvious. I'm so proud of you for sticking at it, even when it's hard. I hope you might like this book, and that it might encourage you. Good things are just around the corner, I'm sure of it. And I will always be here, cheering you on and believing that you are in fact a superhero. Mona xx

Hannah blinks back tears as she reads the card and imagines Mona choosing it. She suddenly feels guilty for wishing her best friend away. But then the doorbell buzzes. As soon as she hears the sound she feels her heart rate rising so rapidly it feels like her heart is going to break out of her chest and run away from her. Everything else falls suddenly away. Quickly, she stuffs the card and the book under the bed, along with the pile of clothes and turns to the door buzzer.

'It's me,' says Jaheim, and just those two words are enough to drive Hannah crazy.

He arrives carrying tulips and smiling that smile. Since Hannah has met him they have spent hours talking, staying up late and asking each other questions that feel like questions no one has ever asked them before – details no one has ever truly cared about before this, before each other. Even with Sam it had *felt different, or perhaps she has just forgotten how exactly the same it was. Love has made her forgetful.*

Jaheim works for a young TV production company as an assistant for a demanding but fair boss who is going through a divorce and whom Jaheim told Hannah he saw crying over the photocopier one day. 'I pretended not to see and she pretended too,' he told her, and Hannah had nodded, loving him for that. He has two older sisters and one younger brother and admitted to Hannah late one night that although he loves them all equally, he looks up to his older sister the most. She was the one who helped him with problems with friends and girls when he was young. She is also the person in his family he most strives to impress, but whose attention is hardest to win (she has twin toddlers and a new baby). Jaheim is a vegetarian and tells his friends it's because of environmental reasons but admits to Hannah it's because of a school trip to a farm when he was young, where he fed a lamb and has always remembered the feeling of its warmth in his arms as it sucked hungrily on the bottle. He blushed when he told her that but she didn't care – there was nothing he could tell her that didn't somehow contribute to the miraculous picture that was him. No detail is uninteresting to her: his favourite toast topping is peanut butter and sliced bananas, he has size ten feet, he prefers Star Trek *to* Star Wars, *he wants to own a German shepherd one day and to write his own TV show and to drive a forest-green Jaguar. He prefers autumn to spring; he is, as she guessed, kind to his mother but is frightened of his father; he talks in his sleep, he has a big group of friends but only a few he can really count on,*

127

he is competitive, he has never been to Scotland, he never wears matching socks, he is scared of snakes.

She feels she knows him, even though they haven't been together for a long time. There are so many things that she loves about him already. But her favourite thing is still that smile.

As soon as he steps inside the flat their hands are on each other. He wraps one arm around her and kisses her. She takes the flowers from him and places them on the table in the hall so that both their hands are free to hold each other. He kicks the front door shut and pushes her gently against the wall, his arms tight around her waist, his lips warm against hers. Their hips press against each other. She wonders if there is any greater satisfaction than this.

Last week they said 'I love you' for the first time.

'Tell me,' she whispers into his ear as she starts walking backwards towards her room, his arms still tight around her.

'I love you,' he says, kissing her earlobe and working down her neck to her collarbone.

'Tell me again,' she says as they stumble inside her room.

'I love you,' he says again, gently tilting her face towards his so he can kiss her hard on the mouth.

'I love you,' he repeats when their lips are parted, 'I love you and I want you.'

They are her magic words and as he says them they fall together onto her bed, the door still open, her moans filling the flat unrestrained. Because nothing feels better than this – to be this wanted, this needed. When they are together Hannah forgets everything else. But letting go is addictive; the longer she spends with Jaheim, the less she wants to go back to real life.

A different type of hunger finally sends them out of bed and into the kitchen, Hannah dressed in Jaheim's shirt and Jaheim wearing her dressing gown. She puts the tulips in a vase and pulls ingredients out of the fridge for the dinner she planned for the evening.

'You chop and I'll start frying?' she says, handing him a knife and a board.

'Yes, chef!' he says with a salute. She can't help but laugh at the vision of him saluting in her floral dressing gown. She puts on some music – Ella Fitzgerald – and pours them both a glass of red wine as they cook together, sharing the small space comfortably. The kitchen soon warms and fills with the smells of a rich tomato sauce, heavy on the red wine. She normally hates cooking but this feels different. She feels relaxed and she likes watching him move around the room, likes seeing him in this space she knows so well.

She thinks briefly of Sam, remembering not the affair, but the flat they shared together in Stoke Newington. She knows it is still early days but she wonders how long it will be until she and Jaheim want to find a place of their own. The thought makes her smile. This time it will be different, she thinks to herself, this time it will be for good. She just has a good feeling about Jaheim, and about this new relationship.

'I could do this forever,' she finds herself saying, stirring the sauce and looking up at Jaheim, who is leaning against the counter, a glass of wine in his hand and his bare foot tapping along to the music. And she means it. She always thought she wanted so much more: to see her name on a programme she felt truly proud of, to travel and live abroad, to sing at Ronnie

Scott's and listen to her own music on Spotify. But in this moment, all she wants is for this to continue forever: the sound of Ella Fitzgerald and the bubbling of the pan, the steamy warmth of the tiny kitchen and Jaheim's smile. She doesn't want it to end, and right now she doesn't need anything or anyone else.

'Me too,' he says, as he leans in to kiss her.

*

As she remembers the intensity of the start of their relationship, Hannah feels a wave of guilt at those nights when she wished Mona away so she could be alone with Jaheim in the flat. Since breaking up with him, she has started to look for a light on when she arrives with a sense of hope again. She doesn't know what she would do without her friend. Now the fog of her relationship has lifted she sees her clearly again. Mona is someone she knows she can rely on and Hannah feels a surge of gratitude for that – a glimmer of brightness to keep going for.

Hannah is relieved that things seem to have gone back to normal with Mona – they haven't spoken too much about Jaheim, or about how Hannah's love for him turned into what she can now see as a sort of obsession. But they have started to slip back into their old routines together and that has been a huge relief for Hannah.

Glancing at the clock, she wonders if Mona managed to sleep. She knows her well enough to know she probably stayed up practising instead, perfecting her routine as a way of calming herself. Forcing herself to go over and over the same thing, even when she is exhausted. Because that's just who she is.

As though anticipating the morning rush, the young man in the green hoody stands now and starts piling his textbooks into his bag. Hannah attempts to read the titles of the books as he tidies them away, and works out they are to do with engineering. She spots a Kings College London key ring on his rucksack, just below where the sleeping bag is wedged in the top. His hair falls in front of his face – it's a nice blond shade, perhaps a little too long, but she thinks it suits him.

'Thanks then, bye,' he says quietly as he heads to the door.

'See you,' she replies, watching as he heads out into the early morning.

Once he is gone, she heads over to clear the table, pushes the chair in and wipes down the surface. That's when she spots the crossword book. She looks towards the café door – it has already swung shut and she can no longer see the young customer. She picks up the book, and as she does, a white envelope flutters out from inside the pages and falls on the floor. She stoops to catch it. It is not sealed.

Quickly, before she can change her mind, she opens the envelope and pulls out two crisp fifty-pound notes. She stares at the fifties. They are dry and stiff beneath her fingers and a shade of pinkish red that seems to her incredibly pretty. She can't remember the last time she held a fifty. She looks around her in the café. Pablo is in the kitchen and Eleanor has her back to her, serving a customer on the other side of the café. No one is watching her, and in a swift movement she slips the money, as well as the crossword book, inside the pocket of her apron.

'Good morning,' she says, trying to keep her voice bright as a customer approaches the counter, a pale blue handbag tucked under her arm.

'What can I get you?'

'Something strong,' replies the woman. Hannah spots an NHS lanyard hanging around her neck.

'A double espresso?' offers Hannah, reaching for a cup.

The woman nods and sits heavily in a chair at a small table facing into the café, the same table where the boy with the rucksack spent most of the early hours of the morning. Hannah notices the choice and feels her cheeks growing warm as the weight of the crossword book, and the money, nudges against her stomach. She tries to ignore it though – she will think about it later.

'Coming right up,' she says as she turns to the coffee machine.

'Bloody hell!' says the woman suddenly, the noise rising above the sound of the machine. It makes Hannah jump and she spills hot milk onto the floor.

'Sorry,' says the woman as Hannah leans to wipe up the spill, 'I just noticed the bear.'

When Hannah brings the woman her coffee, she notices she is reading the book that the young man left on the table from the lending library, *The Hobbit*. The woman smiles up at Hannah as she reaches for the coffee.

'This was my favourite when I was a girl,' she says, 'My friends preferred books about ponies and all-girls boarding schools, but for me, it was *The Hobbit*. I haven't looked at a copy in years, though.'

'Enjoy,' says Hannah with a nod. The woman returns to the book and smiles, her eyes growing misty.

Hannah sits down at an empty table, keeping an eye on the door in case of new customers. It feels good to rest her feet. She tries not to think about what is in her apron pocket, or about Jaheim, or anything other than the prospect of breakfast. A few minutes later Eleanor joins her at the table, followed by Pablo who carries three plates of pancakes drizzled with maple syrup and scattered with berries.

'Breakfast is served,' he says.

They only have time to chat for a short while: soon the morning crowds are flowing from the station into the street and a queue of caffeine-hungry customers gathers in front of the counter. Hannah rises to her feet, her breakfast only half-finished on her plate.

'You finish yours,' she says to Eleanor, as she goes to rise too, 'I'll be fine on my own for a bit.'

'Thanks,' replies Eleanor, but she eats quickly, finishing up just a few moments later. Pablo takes the plates and returns to the kitchen.

As the morning crowd starts to fill the café, Hannah focuses on making their coffees, trying to ignore the book inside her apron pocket and the choice she is already making that she knows is not right but seems somehow inevitable.

8.00 A.M.

HANNAH

A nervous-looking young woman in a grey trouser suit pulls a scrap of paper from her pocket as she reaches the front of the queue.

'One soya latte, one decaf cappuccino, one regular cappuccino, two Americanos and a macchiato. Please. To go. And can I get a receipt please?'

Hannah nods and turns to make the orders. She can hear impatient tuts coming from behind the young woman – a need for coffee makes some people merely grouchy, Hannah has found; for other people it makes them lose their minds.

'Can't I go first?' comes a loud man's voice, 'I've only got one order and I'm late for a meeting.'

Hannah doesn't turn around.

'As you can see, I am already serving this customer. I'll be with you next.'

Eleanor is busy serving customers at their tables. She hasn't been here long but she already looks frazzled – morning shifts do that to you, Hannah has found over the years.

She is tempted to go even slower with the order just to annoy the rude man, but she feels for the nervous young woman who she imagines is collecting an order for a whole team in her office. She looks around nineteen: Hannah guesses she is on work experience and wonders where she is working and whether her colleagues are friendly to her. The way she carefully consults her list for a second time as Hannah turns around with the drinks makes her think perhaps not. The young woman shuffles uncomfortably on her feet, clearly mortified to have made a scene and held up the queue.

'I've written the orders on the side of the cups,' says Hannah, slotting the drinks into a cardboard carrier, 'And I'm putting the decaf and the regular cappuccino far away from each other so they don't get confused, OK?'

The young woman smiles, folds the order and places it back in her pocket, and reaches for the coffees.

'Thank you,' she says, her shoulders sinking slightly and a shy smile reddening her face. She turns to leave but Hannah calls after her, 'Don't forget your receipt!'

She leans across the counter to hand it to the young woman. Their hands meet briefly and then the young woman nods and carefully weaves her way through the line of customers to the door, where a woman with a baby held in a carrier on her chest opens the door for her.

'Right, who's next?' says Hannah, trying to sound cheerful.

'An espresso to go,' says a man at the front who doesn't

look up from his phone as he speaks. Hannah recognises the voice as belonging to the queue-jumper. She had wondered if he might leave in frustration, heading to his meeting instead, but once a customer is in the queue they very rarely do leave, regardless of how late they are running. This is a part of their day they can't seem to skip and Hannah usually takes some satisfaction in filling that role for them, as though she is a pharmacist handing out over-the-counter drugs to the morning's coughers and sneezers. With this man, though, she finds herself feeling only anger at his sense of entitlement and the way he doesn't look at her as she takes his payment. For a brief moment she considers spitting in his coffee. But of course that would be terrible. And besides, the café is far too busy – someone would certainly notice.

Next comes a steady stream of customers dressed in office-wear in varying levels of formality. One young man is still in his cycling clothes, a helmet and a rucksack held under his arm and one earbud in his ear. Two women chat while they order.

'So you find out about the promotion today?' says one. The other nods.

'If I don't get it I'm looking for a new job. I'm sick of seeing all the men in my team promoted ahead of me.'

There are a few customers sat at tables too and Hannah glances over to them, checking that Eleanor is doing all right serving them. In the far corner a woman in a Tesco uniform does her make-up, brushes, lipsticks and an eyelash curler laid out on the table as she peers into a small portable mirror that is propped up against her coffee cup. A few seats away from her, a man in hospital scrubs and a navy-blue coat pushes scrambled eggs on a plate, barely taking any mouthfuls. The mother who just arrived with her baby orders a hot chocolate from Eleanor and chooses a seat by the window, taking her baby out of its carrier and sitting it on the table so it can look outside. Hannah watches as the baby leans forwards, pressing both hands on the glass. She follows the baby's gaze outside and spots John, the *Big Issue* seller who has worked outside the café for the past few years. With one hand he holds a stack of magazines, with the other he waves at the baby.

Hannah smiles and turns back to the queue that doesn't seem to go down.

'What can I get you?' she says, trying to keep her voice light and ignoring the thoughts that threaten to distract her.

JOHN

He laughs and pulls a face and the baby inside the café laughs back.

What a dote, he thinks, the laughter leaving the imprint of a smile on his face. Reluctantly, he turns away from the window and back to the street, back to work.

'BIG Issue, Big Issue, Big Issue!' he says in a sing-song voice. No one looks up. The flow of pedestrians continues around him like a river around an islet.

So many of them are on their phones. Either walking with them held to their ears, having loud conversations that he catches snippets of as they walk past, or staring at them in their hands, only looking up to cross roads or when they nearly walk into other people or the occasional lamp post.

'Let me finish!' says a short man with a loud voice and a flushed face as he walks past John, 'Let me finish! I said, let me finish!' He is nearly shouting now and a few of the people around him turn to watch. He seems oblivious to anyone aside from the person speaking to him on the other end of the phone.

'Mum! Will you just shut up?' he says, and then he turns down a passageway at the end of the road and disappears.

The lights change and a stream of pedestrians cross the road. An old woman with a rucksack on her front and a map in her hand walks slightly ahead of an old man with a hooked nose and a creased, pink face who walks slowly, looking all around him. Straining against a lead is a dog wearing a high visibility jacket with 'NERVOUS' written in large letters. It jumps and jolts away from the feet of pedestrians and John can hear its owner, a young woman in a bright orange beanie hat, talking to it in a soothing voice. He feels for the dog; although John hides his anxieties well, there are days when he'd like to wear a jacket like that himself. *Wouldn't we all?* he thinks to himself.

Pedestrians weave in and out around John as he stands on the pavement, some continuing along the street, a few veering off into the café.

John takes a deep breath and tries again.

'Good morning sir, can I interest you in a *Big Issue*? Well, have a great day. Madam, *Big Issue*? Have a lovely day. Who's going to make me a happy man on this grey day then?'

Most people ignore him but some look up at the sound, make brief, awkward eye contact and then look hurriedly down again. He is not surprised. Resilience is a key requirement of this line of work.

'Get a fucking job!' shouts one voice. It belongs to a man in his sixties, wearing a tweed jacket and yellow trousers.

'This is my job!' John shouts back, but the man has already walked away.

That always pisses him off. He doesn't come to other people's workplaces and disparage them, does he? He is always polite, even when people refuse a copy (which is most of the time). Sometimes it's hard – when it's raining and he has a few copies left and is determined to sell them before leaving. But he doesn't pester people – it's not professional.

He's been doing the job for three years, working on the same pitch opposite Liverpool Street station and outside Stella's. It's more than a job, though – he likes to think of himself as an entrepreneur. He buys the stack of magazines from head office, just like any other business owner purchasing their stock, and then keeps the profits on what he sells. It's up to him what time he arrives and leaves work – whether he works late on a busy day and packs up early on a slow, rainy one. He likes the flexibility and feeling, finally, as though he is taking back control of his own life.

'John!'

He looks up and sees Paul, one of his regular customers, heading towards the door of Stella's, his hand raising briefly in a wave. He is a tall, middle-aged man with a broken nose and dark eyes. He carries a briefcase and a weight on his shoulders that slumps them forwards. John waves back at him.

'Good to see you Paul,' he says, as Paul fishes in his pocket for coins. They make the exchange swiftly and quietly and once Paul is holding a copy of the *Big Issue*, which he rolls and puts into his pocket, they move onto the important part.

John thinks of his job as part entrepreneur, part therapist. He has plenty of regular customers who stop by for a chat, but often someone new pauses by him after buying a copy and starts telling him something about their life. When he first started the job it had surprised him, these conversations. But now he thinks of it as completely natural – he has learnt that everyone just wants someone to talk to. And he is here every day, rain or shine. They know where to find him, and his conversation can be bought for as little as £2.50 (much cheaper than a therapist). He'll talk for free, of course, but the serious customers understand the etiquette. Buy a magazine, and then let's chat. Let's chat for as long as you like.

'How are things?' says Paul. He is still wearing his suit, poor man, and a purple tie. He lost his job several weeks ago but still comes in every day, dressed as though he's going to the office. John gets it – when things started going wrong for him it took him a while to admit to himself how bad it was getting. When he finally did so, it was too late. The thing that he has learnt is that it can happen to anyone.

'Not too bad thanks, mate,' he replies, 'And how about you? Any luck with finding a new job?'

Paul sighs.

'Not yet, no,' he says slowly, 'But I've got a few leads. I'm hoping at least for some interviews in the next few weeks. I hope by the end of the month I'll have good news for Sandra.'

'I know it's not my place, mate,' says John, 'But do you

think perhaps you should tell her? She's your wife, I bet she'd understand.'

'I expect she would,' says Paul, 'But with that would also come her pity. And I just can't bear it. Not yet, anyway. I just need a bit more time.'

And John understands that too.

'Righto, boss. She's your missus after all – you know what's best. I'm keeping my fingers crossed for you. And my toes!'

He makes a show of wobbling on the spot and Paul laughs. It feels good to make someone laugh. They say goodbye and John waves his magazines as Paul opens the café door and steps inside.

As he thinks about Paul, he can't help but think about his own story. It started with a lost job too. He was working in construction but when the crisis hit he was let go. He tried looking for other work but it was made hard by the drinking. Without a job to get up for each morning he was drinking more and more. He didn't think of it as a problem – it was just his way of coping. Everyone had their own thing, didn't they? His was drink. It softened everything: his aches and pains after years of working on building sites and his fear of what to do next. But it also softened his brain, made him sluggish and unmotivated. What started as a coping mechanism became the thing that prevented him from moving forwards at all.

He lived in a nice flat, a little one-bed that he'd been proud to be able to afford when many of his colleagues lived in shared accommodation. But the longer he remained unemployed and the more he drank the harder it became to meet the rent. At first the landlord, who lived in the flat above his, was understanding. John had been there for several years and they'd become, not exactly friends, but friendly. They'd even been to the pub on the corner of the street for a beer a few times. But John found that kindness only went so far when it came to money. He was evicted a few months later.

John knows that most people would disagree, that they'd think themselves above it somehow, but he has come to believe that addiction can happen to anyone. Give them the right situation (or the *wrong* one, more accurately) and they too would find some way of numbing the pain and would soon see how hard it is to stop once you've found that rush, that pleasure in a grey world. He has always been somewhat proud that at least his substance of choice is legal. Because it would be easy to fall the other way too.

After the eviction he moved in and out of temporary accommodation – sometimes with friends, sometimes in hostels. But it never worked out. His vice always made it difficult: by then it had taken up so much of his existence that living a normal life seemed impossible.

Thinking back to that time, two years sober, John shudders. Some of his old friends he has been able to apologise to. They are still wary, but he hopes he is proving to them day by day that he has changed. But there are also those whom he knows he can never talk to again. He pushed them too far, did things that wake him up in the middle of the night, terror and shame caught in his throat. He mourns the loss of those friends with a pain stronger than that of his failed romantic relationships (because there have been many of those too), feeling as though a part of him has broken away – that he is somehow less whole now. Then there are the friends whom he simply can no longer see because they don't understand that for him, being sober means he will never be able to set foot inside a pub again. The place that felt for a while like some sort of shelter, a kind of home even at his worst, is now dangerous, off-limits.

Over the past few years things have steadily improved. He is proud of the room he now rents – just a small place with a sink in his bedroom and a shared bathroom and kitchen down the corridor – and of his job selling the magazines. But he still has a way to go. He would like to have a little balcony one day and to grow his own chili plants and maybe some tomatoes. And most of all, he would like a dog. He will get one, he promises himself, once he is confident he can look after himself. When he feels back on his feet. He already knows what he will call his dog: Lucky. Because although it sometimes doesn't feel that way when the hot water in his flat stops working or customers are particularly rude to him, he knows he is lucky. He is lucky to be alive.

As he waits for more customers he watches the sky. The clouds are the same colour as the backs of the pigeons that huddle together on the roof of the station. For a moment he forgets about his work and watches them, picking out the stripes of blue and black in their grey feathers. Most people who look at pigeons see pests, he thinks as he watches them. Rats with wings that are as bleak to look at as the city on a winter's day. But if you look a little closer you notice an iridescence to them. You see how soft their feathers look and how bright and inquisitive their eyes appear. They are not what

143

they seem from a first glance. They are more than what people make of them.

HANNAH

After a while, Hannah and Eleanor swap stations, Eleanor taking over at the counter and Hannah waiting on the tables. After taking the order of the woman with the baby, she approaches a man in a suit and purple tie who she guesses is in his late forties. His posture sags, as though a child who is slightly too old to be carried sits on his shoulders. A laptop is open in front of him but he looks fixedly out the window, at John and the office workers who clutch coffee cups and sidestep one another on their paths towards their buildings as though performing a perfectly choreographed dance. Hannah has to bend down to catch the customer's eye and ask him what he wants to order.

'An orange juice and a full English please,' he says, barely moving his eyes. Hannah nods and turns away just as a broad-shouldered man in a navy suit worn with a pale pink shirt opens the door and heads towards the queue. But before he reaches the end he stops, looking at the man by the window. He holds a phone tightly in one hand.

'Paul!' he says loudly, raising the phone in a wave. Hannah looks up and watches the interaction as she pours the orange juice and prepares the other orders. The man sat at the table, who by his acknowledgement Hannah assumes is named Paul, is turning to follow the noise and seems to shudder slightly at its sound. He nods, and the pink-shirted man walks over. He stands next to Paul's table, his legs apart and planted firmly on the ground. Hannah notices the flash of silver cufflinks poking out from beneath his jacket sleeves. His hair is a somewhat unbelievably rich brown and worn in the style she sees so many male office workers favouring: short at the sides and long and gelled into a sort of mound at the top.

'Good to see you,' he says, reaching out his right hand, his left still gripping his mobile like a baton he is not about to pass over any time soon. Paul stands up, and after the handshake remains standing somewhat awkwardly, one hand resting on the table and the other in his trouser pocket. The table is too low down though for him to lean on it comfortably, so he tilts to one side slightly. Watching him, Hannah realises his face is familiar. She must have seen him in here before and suddenly wonders why she took so long to recognise him. But unless they are steadfast regulars she loses track of customers easily. There are just too many to hold inside her head.

'Same to you,' Paul replies quietly.

'I can't deny it's a surprise,' says the other man. He has a deep voice that rises above the noises in the café. It is a voice that seems used to filling a room.

Paul says nothing in reply. The other man continues.

'But still. Anyway, I'm sorry about what happened. Just one of those things, you know? But I take it you've found something new?'

Paul nods, 'Yes, just around the corner.'

'Excellent! Excellent. Late start then?'

'Flexitime.'

'The dream!' says the other man, 'Well, good for you, good

for you. Right, I'd better get my caffeine fix and get back to the old ball-breaker. If you're working around here now, then maybe see you in the usual one evening?'

'Yes, that would be great,' says Paul.

'Bye for now!'

Paul stays standing until the other man has ordered his coffee and left, his cup held aloft in a salute. He raises his hand in a wave too and then sits down heavily in his chair.

Hannah slips out from behind the counter again, taking the orange juice to Paul's table.

'Your breakfast will be with you soon,' she says, 'Can I get you anything else?'

'Gin?' he says, looking at her almost seriously and then breaking into a weak laugh.

'Too early for gin, I suppose?'

'I'm afraid so.'

'This will do then, thanks.'

And he turns back to the window, his hands resting on his laptop keys but his eyes focused outside. Hannah returns to the queue, concentrating on the orders and trying to ignore the feeling of the crossword book in her apron pocket, her thoughts of Jaheim, and her anxieties about her career and whether she has the energy to keep fighting for it.

9.00 A.M.

HANNAH

The takeaway orders continue into the morning. The mother and baby who sat by the window leave and Hannah misses the sound of the child's laughter. They had played together while they sat there, the mother pointing out dogs on the street and the baby giggling. The mother laughed too as though she genuinely enjoyed nothing more than playing with the little ball of flesh who couldn't even speak yet.

As she makes the orders, sharing customers efficiently and quietly with Eleanor, she is aware of the middle-aged male customer in the suit and the purple tie who arrived earlier and ordered a full English breakfast and an orange juice. Since they last spoke he has been sat in the corner tapping away at his laptop. Every now and then he stares out the window, before returning to typing so fiercely that the keys sound like a crowd of marching footsteps on a stone floor.

She lets herself pause and glance outside for a moment. Discarded copies of that morning's newspaper lie like autumn leaves around the station. In the city, today's news is already old news. As she looks out, the street abruptly darkens and the rain that has been threatening all morning beats suddenly on the pavements, on the cars and buses on the road and on the windows of the café. At first Hannah is relieved; the café windows rarely get washed and are constantly covered in a thin layer of dust and grime from the street and its endless pulse of traffic. But then she spots John the *Big Issue* seller hurriedly reaching for a plastic cover in his pocket and slipping his magazines inside. Around him people huddle under the awnings of shops and open umbrellas or lift their jackets over their heads as they dash across the road. A bottleneck has already formed at the station as people rush to get inside while struggling to close umbrellas.

'Are you OK for one sec?' Hannah asks Eleanor, who nods. Hannah quickly rummages in a box under the counter and steps outside, her coat held aloft over her head.

'Morning, John,' she says over the sound of the rain and the traffic.

'Morning!' he says cheerfully, a large raindrop dripping off the tip of his nose.

'I thought you might like this,' she says, 'It was in our lost property. I'm sorry about the colour.'

She hands him a bright pink umbrella. The handle is in the shape of a flamingo's head. They both look at it for a moment. He pushes it open and is sheltered in a glow of pink.

'I'm afraid that's all we had,' Hannah says.

'I think it suits me, don't you?' John says after a moment. He laughs, a bright peal of sound that seems at odds with the gloomy surroundings. Hannah smiles, relief spreading across her face.

'Can I get you a coffee?' she asks, then spots a paper cup in his hand. If she or Mona are too busy to step outside and chat to him and offer him a coffee, a customer usually gets there first.

'I'm all set, thank you,' he replies, 'Now you get back in the dry. I'll be right as rain here.'

He chuckles at his own joke. She smiles too and glances at him briefly, sheltered by the pink flamingo umbrella, before waving and dashing back into the café. As she steps through the door she catches sight of the clock. *Not long until Mona's audition,* she thinks to herself. She imagines Mona waiting nervously for her second audition before being called in and walking with an artificial confidence into the room. She wonders what the casting team will think when they see her – perhaps some for the second time and others for the first (the panel is usually larger for call-backs). They will notice her slender build and the graceful way she carries herself – instilled by years and years of dancing – and her height and the way she tilts her head just a little too high when she is nervous. She wonders if they will see what Hannah sees. The determination, the focus and the *shine* that comes off her friend. Because Mona is one of the special ones. She sparkles.

Hannah glances around the café, checking if there are any customers who need her attention. And that's when she notices that the middle-aged man with the purple tie, Paul, she remembers his name was, is shaking. Hannah stares at him in alarm. It's only after a few moments that she realises he is crying. Tears drip from his face onto his laptop keyboard and he makes no move to wipe them away.

Watching him, Hannah thinks first of her tears in the storeroom earlier, feeling her cheeks flush at the memory. Next, she thinks of her father.

As a child, she never saw her father cry. Her mother was always the emotional one, breaking into tears watching anything from RSPCA adverts to emotional stories in the London marathon or the Olympics. At every school performance, Hannah's mother would stuff tissues into the sleeves of her cardigan and sometimes audibly sob when Hannah took to the stage. It embarrassed Hannah, particularly when she was a teenager, but she didn't want her to stop, either. It was part of who her mother was, and showed a softness that meant Hannah felt she could come to her with any worry, however small. With her father, she always felt warier. She knew he loved her; but they rarely spent time together without her mother being there too and when, later, she had left home and called her parents, if her father answered he would always say, 'I'll get your mother' as soon as he heard Hannah's voice on the other end.

Now, Hannah remembers the first time she saw him cry, at her grandmother's funeral earlier that year, and wishes that she had taken her break later so she could have spoken to her father too when she phoned her mother this morning. The customer's tears make her ache suddenly for her father, remembering in painful detail his breakdown at the funeral. Despite her discomfort at holding back the news of her break-up from her parents, Hannah suddenly longs to be with her father with a simplicity and an intensity that overpowers everything.

*

Her grandmother dies on New Year's Day.

Hannah and Mona held a party at theirs the night before and when Hannah wakes her room is bright with winter sun. Her head is foggy and she is aware of the empty bottles discarded around her room – the room they used as the main space for the party. There are a few half-empty bin bags scattered around too from when Hannah and Mona had, still drunk, attempted to start tidying in the early hours, before giving up and crashing asleep, both in Hannah's bed. Jaheim was there for the start of the party but left early as New Year's Eve is also the birthday of one of his best friends. Hannah had tried to leave with him, but by that point she was already drunk and he persuaded her, reluctantly, to stay behind.

As she shifts she feels the warmth of Mona's body next to her and hears the quiet snuffle of her snores. When they first lived together they sometimes fell asleep like this after staying up late watching a film, but it's been a long time since it last happened.

When she opens her eyes, Hannah reaches immediately for her phone. She notes the time – it is midday – and sees that there are no messages from Jaheim. Instead, there are four from her mother. There is a voicemail too and she slips out of bed, wrapping a blanket around her, to listen to it without disturbing Mona.

Her mother's voice has a shake to it, but Hannah can tell she is trying to stay calm.

'Will you give me a call back when you get this, sweetheart?' she says, 'It's your gran.'

Hannah phones home immediately, glad that it is her mother who picks up, not her father, when she hears the news. She doesn't know what she will say to her dad when she sees him. They talk briefly and stick mainly to logistics. Her mother has already looked up the train times for the next day. Hannah says goodbye and tells her mum to give her dad a hug from her.

When she hangs up the phone she notices Mona in the doorway. She is wearing her dressing gown and has last night's make-up smudged around her eyes.

'Are you OK?' she asks.

Hannah shakes her head and feels herself starting to cry.

'No,' she says, as Mona crosses the room and takes her into a hug, 'Gran died.'

Mona cooks them both breakfast, which they take back to Hannah's bed, eating wrapped up beneath the duvet. Hannah tries calling Jaheim but he must still be asleep, or too hungover to answer. Mona listens as Hannah tells her about her grandmother – the sweets she always kept buried somewhere in her pockets and that were sneaked into Hannah's outstretched hands as a child, her famous apple pie that to Hannah was the sweetest thing in the world, and the way she always smelt of mothballs, cigarettes and Astral face cream.

They watch Disney films in bed (Mona's idea) and Hannah finds it hard to work out where her hangover ends and her grief begins.

At five o'clock in the afternoon her phone rings. It's Jaheim and she jumps out of bed to talk to him, walking out onto the balcony despite the cold.

'I'm so sorry I didn't answer your call earlier,' he says when she tells him the news, 'You poor thing, I hate the thought of you being on your own at a time like this.'

Hannah leans against the balcony railing and turns to look inside. Mona had left the room for a moment but is back now, sitting on the bed and looking worriedly out the window at Hannah. She nods at her.

'I wasn't on my own,' she says, her voice slightly cold.

'I still wish I'd been there, my love,' he says, and she softens. Because this is Jaheim, and because she loves him.

'I do too,' she admits, 'But I'll come over later?'

'As long as you're sure,' he says, 'I can easily come there?'

'No it's fine, it'd be nice to have a change of scenery.'

They chat for a little longer. The sound of his voice makes her smile, despite it all. They talk a bit about her grandmother and he tells her about last night's party for his friend – it distracts her and she enjoys listening to him (she could listen to him talk about anything). By the time they hang up and she steps inside, she is feeling calmer.

As soon as she closes the door behind her, glad to be back inside the warmth of the flat, Mona, who has placed two mugs of tea on the table, starts talking.

'I just spoke to Stella,' she says, 'And she's given you all of next week off work – she says there's no rush to come back in, Eleanor and Sofia can cover your shifts. So that's one less thing

to worry about. And as soon as you know the date of the funeral she says I can have that day off too.'

Hannah walks across the room and gives her friend a hug.

'Thank you so much,' she says, squeezing her before stepping away, 'But don't worry, you've already done plenty. Jaheim's going to come with me to the funeral.'

Mona looks down at her tea.

'Oh, right,' she says.

'It's just I knew you said you wanted some extra shifts this month to catch up after the show at Christmas,' says Hannah quickly, 'And it's a long way to travel. I don't want you to have to do that.'

Mona nods.

'Yes, you're right,' she says, 'I could certainly do with the money if you don't need me there.'

Hannah smiles, pleased to have made the right decision. She knows how stressed Mona gets about money and the train tickets to Wales can be expensive.

Hannah catches the train home the next morning, her mother greeting her at the station. Normally she pulls up in the drop-off area and beeps as she sees Hannah walking outside. Today she parks in the car park and is waiting for Hannah on the platform. They hug, then walk slowly back to the car, their steps syncing up without meaning to.

'How's Dad?' Hannah asks, immediately regretting the obviousness of the question. It feels pointless, and she wishes she could find words with more meaning.

'He's just about coping,' her mother replies, turning to her and squeezing her arm, 'He'll be very happy to see you.'

Hannah isn't sure she'd describe her father's reaction to her arriving home as happiness, but happiness probably isn't something he is capable of right now. He is sat in one of the three armchairs in the sitting area just off from the kitchen. He is staring intently out the window to where a sparrow hops along the top of the garden wall. Hannah watches the sparrow fly away but her father's gaze does not move. Hannah's mother kisses his forehead and busies herself filling the kettle while Hannah sits in the chair next to him and reaches to place a hand on top of his.

'Hi Dad,' she says.

He flinches slightly then turns to her.

'Hannah,' he says softly, 'You're home.'

'I am,' she replies, 'Mum just got me from the station.'

She pauses for a moment.

'Dad, I'm so sorry,' she says.

He turns his hand over so that his palm is facing up and she links her fingers through his.

'Me too,' he says.

'I'm so glad I got to know her,' Hannah continues, 'She was a great woman. I'm going to really miss her.'

'Me too,' her father says again.

Her mother joins them, bringing them coffee with a spoonful of cream, something usually only reserved for Christmas and birthdays.

'We'll let ourselves have a little treat to cheer ourselves up, won't we?' she says as she pours, Hannah watching the cream swirl into the black coffee.

Then the three of them sit in a silence that only families can manage, Hannah not letting go of her father's hand. She feels, not for the first time, the physical absence of a sibling. She wishes for a brother or sister to share this moment with – a solid comfort between the raw grief of her father and the worry and sympathetic heartache of her mother.

It's partly why she feels so relieved when Jaheim arrives on the day of the funeral. It's the first time he's met Hannah's family and the formality of it holds them all together somehow. Her father even talks to him about tennis (a shared passion, they discover).

In the church, she introduces Jaheim to distant relatives, her grandmother's friends and friends and colleagues of her father (there are many of these, and it makes her feel a brief, golden burst of pride amid the darkness). She feels stronger on Jaheim's arm, somehow.

It is Jaheim who suggests he sit at the back of the church, instead of next to her at the front. She says he's welcome with her and her family but he shakes his head and insists.

'I'll see you afterwards, OK?' he says, 'You look after your dad.'

So she takes her place in the pew between her parents, the first time that they have sat at the front of a church together. She remembers all the Christmas carol concerts they took her to when she was young – not because they were religious, but because she loved the singing. They used to hide at the back, eating chocolate buttons and then joining in with the carols. This time, she tries her best to sing along with the hymns – she doesn't know their tunes but tries to pick them up from the older members of the congregation. She wonders if Jaheim can hear her at the back, and whether he is singing too. Her mother and father are mute during the singing, so she sings a little louder as she finds the melody, realising that this – her voice joining the others that rise above the heads of the congregation – is all that she has left to offer her grandmother.

Eventually it is time for her father's eulogy. He stands up from the pew and stumbles forward, drawing from his pocket a crumpled sheet of paper that he clutches tightly between two hands. Hannah's mother rises slightly in her chair as though about to reach out for him, but then she sits back down again, folds her hands in her lap and locks her eyes on him instead. Hannah watches too, her heart beating fast as he stands alone at the front of the church. There is silence, then the shuffling of people in their seats as they wriggle with the awkwardness of it all. Someone coughs.

And then Hannah's father begins to speak. His eyes are fixed and unmoving from the sheet of paper. He talks in a flat and steady voice free from emotion. He sounds as though he is reading from a teleprompter and reminds her of the stilted speeches of un-charming politicians.

But halfway through he stops. His voice cracks and he takes a breath as though to continue speaking, but the only sound that comes out is a soft moan close to a howl, and then his face crumples and the tears start to fall. His shoulders shake as he cries, watched by the black-clad congregation. He looks completely lost, this large, weeping man who is her father.

For a brief moment, Hannah feels a flood of embarrassment. She thinks of Jaheim sitting at the back of the church and wishes suddenly that he had met her father sooner, on a better day. She turns to her mother, who looks too surprised to move. And then in the next moment Hannah is on her feet. What was she thinking? She pushes away her initial embarrassment as she walks forward to stand by her father's side. Gently, she eases the piece of paper out of his trembling hands and links her arm through his. She squeezes his arm. And then she looks down at the sheet of paper and reads the end of his speech for him as he stands and cries, mostly silently but with the occasional sob shuddering through his body and echoing in the cold church. She feels his arm squeeze hers back and it requires all her strength to keep her voice clear and loud. As she speaks she thinks of her grandmother, but mostly she does it for her father.

*

Hannah breathes deeply as she thinks of her father and remembers her grandmother's funeral. She approaches Paul's table slowly. Tears drip onto his keyboard and his face – previously serious-looking and lined with middle-age – twists into an expression of pain that makes him look ageless.

'Can I sit here for a minute?' Hannah asks gently, although she is already sitting down. She spots Eleanor throwing her a glance from the counter, where there is still a queue of customers, but she ignores her. The customers will just have to wait.

Paul looks up and wipes at his face suddenly, as though actually looking at another person has snapped something inside him and made him remember who he is: a middle-aged husband and father who doesn't cry.

'I'm sorry,' he says, using one of the red paper napkins on the table to wipe his face, 'I don't know what's come over me, I never cry.'

The paper shreds slightly in his hands and there is something about it that makes Hannah very sad.

'Neither does my father,' she says gently, 'Apart from at really sad films, funerals, children's charity adverts and when his football team loses.'

She smiles, and Paul sniffs and smiles too.

'Does it embarrass you when your dad cries?' he asks, scrunching up the soggy paper napkin and stuffing it in the bottom of his empty juice glass.

Hannah winces as she thinks about that initial flash of embarrassment at the funeral. She hates herself for it. Perhaps it had partly been because his tears came as such a shock. They unsettled her, as though some fundamental fact in her life had suddenly been disproven. Father Christmas does not exist, and men do cry. But afterwards something had shifted in their relationship. Recently when she has phoned, he has chatted for a little longer if it is him who picks up the phone. It seems to Hannah as though the crying and the new, more approachable man wearing her father's shoes have something to do with each other. She misses him and thinks again of her parents' house and the bedroom where the bed is always made, just in case she were to come and visit. She wonders if they are ever lonely, just the two of them, and realises that although she has seen them in London several times since, the last time she visited them in Wales was for the funeral.

'Not at all,' she says to Paul, 'I sort of like it. It makes me feel better when I get sad. We all do it, whether it's behind a bedroom door or in a café.'

Her thoughts return to her earlier outburst in the storeroom.

She thinks she did a good job at redoing her make-up and hiding any sign of her tears – surely no one could tell that earlier she was weeping in a small room surrounded by boxes. Part of her wants to tell this customer about her earlier tears so he knows he is not alone. But she knows she won't.

'I never thought that would be me,' the man says eventually, 'My father would turn in his grave if he could see me right now. I look like a fool.'

Hannah shakes her head.

'Not at all. I'm sure no one noticed. Besides, even if they did you'll probably never see them again.'

He winces.

'I used to work with a lot of them,' he says, gesturing towards the queue, 'This is their local café. It used to be mine, too. God, I bet word will get back to the office that I'm sat here at nine-thirty on a Thursday, crying like a lunatic. They'll feel even more sorry for me than they already do.'

Hannah doesn't know what to say to that so she says nothing, she just smiles, hoping it is enough.

By now the man's breathing has returned to normal, and his face, while still slightly blotchy, is returning to its former composed state.

'Thank you,' he says quickly, then, 'Can I get the bill please?'

And with those words he goes back to being a customer and she goes back to being a waitress.

'Of course,' she says. She returns with the bill and the card machine. He pays without saying anything else, piles a large tip in coins on the table and leaves.

10.00 A.M.

HANNAH

The café is quieter again now – there is no longer a queue. The rain has subsided and Hannah watches John out the window as he closes the flamingo umbrella, shakes it and props it next to him on the pavement. He takes his magazines out of their protective cover and tries to talk to a woman who walks close past him, a phone held up to her face. She shakes her head vigorously and walks off. John shrugs his shoulders.

The door swings and two men step inside, one holding the door while the other drags a huge red suitcase into the café. They both look tired or sad, Hannah can't tell which.

Before she has time to head to the table to ask them what they want, one of the men is standing at the bar ordering two lattes. Tired *and* sad, she thinks as she takes his order – his hands rubbing the back of his neck and his face drained. His eyes look slightly above Hannah, not at the bear – as is normal with customers – but somewhere else entirely. Somewhere, she guesses, that is not inside this 24-hour café opposite Liverpool Street station. She watches him as he returns to where the other man waits for him, staring down at the table. A few moments later she carries the drinks over to the pair, setting them down between them.

'Here we go,' she says.

They don't say anything; instead they simply nod, their eyes turning down again.

The mood of the café has changed from morning rush to subdued lull. Eleanor has taken a break and the only sign of Pablo is the sound of the radio coming from the kitchen. In the middle of the café, looking out on the street that heaves with people, traffic and fumes, Hannah suddenly feels very alone.

Nearby, the couple with the red suitcase sit in silence.

JOE AND HAZIQ

'How long have we got?' says Joe after a while, reaching for his coffee and taking a long sip. They sit at a table with three chairs. On the third chair sits the large red suitcase.

Haziq looks at his watch.

'We've got about an hour until the coach arrives.'

Joe sighs and reaches for his coffee again. The café is quiet apart from the background music and the soft buzz of conversation. Joe shuffles uncomfortably on his seat, feeling exposed.

He nods and looks down at his coffee cup again. The café door opens and a group of men in high visibility jackets and overalls jostle inside, carrying hard hats under their arms. Joe doesn't think he's ever been relieved to see a group of builders before, but as the room suddenly fills with noise – overlapping conversations and the shuffle of work boots on the checked linoleum – he feels himself relaxing slightly. It makes the silence between him and Haziq less deafening.

The men order bacon and egg rolls from the counter and head to one corner of the café, where they pull tables and chairs together in a messy group. Some of them laugh, others sit quietly, resting their feet on spare chairs. Joe wonders if they are taking a late morning break, or whether they have been working since the early hours, making this their lunch time. Either way they seem relieved as they sit down, clicking knuckles and rolling shoulders.

Under the table their legs are close together. They can feel the warmth from each other's bodies but they don't quite let themselves touch. Too much physical contact right now would be too much to bear.

Haziq shifts in his seat. He can feel the bulk of his passport in his pocket. It seems heavy, as though it is weighing down that side of his body. He looks out the window: a bus stops outside the café and a ramp extends, those who want to get on the bus standing aside to let a wheelchair user off. A man and a woman in running gear jog along the pavement, talking to each other as they run. Above, glass and metal buildings tower into the grey sky where a soft blue is starting to break slowly through the clouds like a pale ink stain.

'We should have got married,' says Joe suddenly, looking up and meeting Haziq's eyes.

Haziq flinches at Joe's words. They are the words that they both know they have been skirting around for weeks but hearing them finally said out loud still sends a shock of pain to his heart.

'But we haven't even lived together yet,' Haziq replies, turning away from the window. His voice is gentle but tired.

'But we were about to.'

'I know,' says Haziq, glancing quickly and instinctively to the group on the other side of the café before reaching for Joe's hand. Once he is holding it he has to use all his strength not to pull away, however calming it is to feel the warmth of Joe's skin against his. The fear doesn't go away easily, however hard he wishes it would.

They had even booked the removal company to move Haziq's things into Joe's flat. They had chosen new bedding: simple grey pinstripes to replace the old sheets they'd both had since before they met each other. They both agreed that it was important to have new bedding for their new life together. Neither of them had ever lived with a partner before and they were excited. Joe had bought some interiors magazines and had taken to turning down the pages to mark things he liked: whisky tumblers, a cactus plant, a mustard yellow beanbag. They were both ready for the next stage in their lives. And then Haziq got the letter.

'Nearly living together is not quite the same thing,' continues Haziq, 'What if you couldn't stand me once you'd had hundreds of mornings of me being grumpy and leaving my cereal bowl in the sink? Maybe you'd be not so happy to be married to me then.'

He laughs softly, trying to keep his tone light but knowing it seems forced. Joe looks down at the table and up again.

'I really would have married you, you know,' Joe says.

Haziq's smile slips away and he sighs. He looks at Joe, the dark hair he is used to running his hands through falling slightly over his face, his eyes wide and dark.

'I know,' Haziq says, 'And I would marry you too – one day. But I just hate being forced into it like this. I don't want to do it like that – out of necessity, I want it to be when we're both ready, not because of immigration laws.'

The letter came out of the blue. After finishing his studies Haziq found a dream job in a publishing house and they had sponsored him to stay in the country. He was doing well in his job – he'd just had a promotion. But then the rules changed about how much he had to earn to be here, and even with his promotion it wasn't enough. The company was apologetic – they wanted to keep him but just couldn't justify that leap up in salary. They told him he would have got there eventually, in the next few years, but as a recent graduate they just couldn't stretch to it. It wouldn't be fair to the other employees.

Haziq understood – it wasn't their fault. But it meant his fate was sealed. He had to leave voluntarily or face deportation. He booked the flights himself but it didn't make a difference – right now it feels just the same to him as if he was being led to the airport in handcuffs.

'But I love you,' says Joe, his eyes damp, droplets resting on his long lashes.

'And I love you too. God, do I love you.'

Haziq turns away so he doesn't have to look at Joe's face. Those big brown eyes are breaking his fucking heart.

He pictures what is waiting for him back in Indonesia. He will be happy to see his parents at first – it's been a long time since he's been able to go home. They are both getting older and at times over the past few years he has woken suddenly in the night, having dreamt that they had both died. If he was at Joe's when it happened Joe would reach across on hearing him wake up and pull him over to his side of the bed, his arms held tightly around Haziq's shaking body. He held him until he settled again and fell back to sleep. When they woke in the morning they would usually still be curled up like that.

But beyond seeing his parents, Haziq doesn't know what else to be hopeful about. None of his extended family knows he is gay. At high school he had dated a sweet, bookish girl called Dhia. He always thought she knew, but she said nothing, holding his hand at lunchtime break but never asking for anything more. He lost touch with her after high school and wonders what she is doing now and wishes he had expressed his thanks to her. At the time he felt too bitter to acknowledge her with much more than the most basic conversation – just enough to convince people and not arouse suspicion.

For the past four years in London he has lived the life he had always dreamt of but never quite believed would be possible. As a student at LSE he had taken a while to come out of his shell – it was hard to let go of the fear that followed him. But once he realised that not everyone was judging him – that actually in huge, anonymous London most people weren't even interested – he let himself loosen up and be himself. He made a tight group of friends and went to G-A-Y in Soho most Saturdays and went on Pride marches and cried each and every time. He loved his job at the publishing house and shortly after starting there he met Joe at a book launch. Joe was a friend of the author's but revealed that he was a writer too. They talked about books, and London, and their childhoods, and left together without even having to ask the other where they were going next. It felt the most natural thing in the world to go home together. For the past nine months their lives have grown more and more entwined.

As he sits in the café Haziq pictures a Saturday from several months ago, before it was all taken away from them. It was a normal Saturday, typical of their life together, and he doesn't know why it enters his mind now – perhaps because its ease, its casual warmth is what he will miss the most. They stayed in bed late, nestled in the sheets and each other's smells and body heat. After waking slowly, showering together and dressing they went for brunch, meeting friends at their favourite local restaurant. It turned into a boozy brunch and they laughed loudly and he and Joe returned later to Joe's flat, a bit pissed, and rolled back into bed for the afternoon. In the evening they got up again and went out to an art exhibition one of their friends was holding in Dalston. They didn't stay next to each other all night – instead they milled around speaking to friends. But at some point in the night they caught each other's eye across the room and Haziq's heart pounded as he thought, *I'm going home with him.*

In the café he looks again at Joe. Despite his height he

looks small, hunched over in the old-fashioned school chair. The construction workers are laughing and he throws them a nervous glance, but they haven't even noticed Haziq and Joe – they are completely oblivious to them and their pain.

'It will be OK,' Haziq says, 'We'll work something out.'

Haziq is going to apply again for a visa when he gets back home, and they have both agreed to book a holiday somewhere part-way between the two of them. Haziq pictures a sunny villa somewhere and the two of them sitting on the terrace drinking wine. He imagines lying side by side by a pool, each of them reading but holding hands, binding them to one another even though in their heads they are in different times, different places, different worlds. Because that's how Joe makes him feel.

But it is time to leave, time to let go.

'I should probably go and wait outside now, the coach will be here soon.' Haziq goes to stand up but Joe reaches for his hand.

'Just a few more minutes,' Joe says, his voice rising with panic, 'Please, please.'

The look on Joe's face makes Haziq sit back down. They hold hands across the table, squeezing tightly. Their fingers entwine and warmth flows between them back and forth like a conversation, saying everything they can't put into words. Haziq dares himself to look, to properly look, across into Joe's eyes. And that's when he feels himself breaking. He had tried to stay calm and strong, for Joe but for himself too. But inside he splinters. In Joe's eyes he sees his best friend. He sees all the goodness and all the love he has ever wanted. He sees a life that he was only just starting to believe was really possible when it was taken away from him.

The construction workers finish their breakfast and head out into the street. As they open the door the sound of traffic mingles with the quiet music in the café. The rain clouds are melting away and the sky is brightening, sunshine reflecting on the wet pavements and the puddles that have formed near the gutters. The sun rises over London, but at the small table in Stella's it sets on Joe and Haziq.

HANNAH

When the group of builders have left, and with Eleanor on her break, Hannah feels inside her apron pocket, checking that the crossword book and the money are still there. Without pulling the book out she feels inside its pages, her fingers meeting the crisp, waxy feel of the fifty-pound notes. She is almost surprised to find it there, still waiting for her to decide what to do with it.

Perhaps she should have run after the boy when he left earlier, she thinks to herself, but it was a few moments after he had gone that she found the book and he would have disappeared by then. There was nothing she could have done. At least that's what she tells herself.

When both Hannah and Mona are low on tips or have taken time off from waitressing to focus on creative projects that sometimes pay a little, but often pay nothing, their evening meals become an amalgamation of things in their cupboards or freezer. Tinned mackerel on toast, tuna and kidney beans stirred into pasta, frozen vegetables and fishcakes. When she was younger these mismatched meals were somehow exciting, but they long ago lost any sort of charm. She hates that she still lives like a student, that she has no savings to speak of and is constantly worried about money.

So when she found the money left on the table she acted on impulse, the side of her that is exhausted and stressed taking over. No one had been looking, it was so easy just to slip it into her apron pocket. That money would mean several weeks' food shopping, or a trip home to Wales to visit her parents. That's how she tried to justify it to herself, even though she knew it was wrong. And part of her did it just because she could, because there was a thrill to it, however tinged with guilt, because it was there.

As she slips the money back inside the notebook she wonders if this is how it happened with Jaheim. Is that what led him, the man she loved, to deceive her? Sometimes it starts with just one bad decision.

*

They have been together for nearly a year. During that year she has spent less and less time with other people and more and more time with him. When she broke up with Sam she told herself she would never distance herself like that again, but now that she is in love again she has completely forgotten her earlier promises to herself. Very occasionally it crosses her mind that perhaps she has cut down on her social life like she did before. But she always talks herself out of it. This time it's different. Jaheim is different. It's still a relatively new relationship and for it to work out she has to dedicate time to it, to them. Love is a drug and she is a junkie.

It's not just her social life that has become secondary to the all-consuming force that is her relationship. She hasn't performed in public in months; instead she prefers singing to Jaheim. He says he likes nothing more than to listen to her and sometimes after sex she reaches for her guitar and plays naked while he lies in her bed and watches. She has never felt more relaxed than in these moments. With him she is safe and adored. She can never even hope for that from a gig, let alone depend upon it.

As a result of this lack of motivation for performing, she is short on money. She still works regular shifts at the café but working enough to be more comfortable in her finances would mean no time to see Jaheim. It seems that every time she goes to her wallet or to check her bank balance there is less there than she had been expecting.

One Friday evening they order pizza to eat in Hannah's room: as much as they enjoy going out, love often makes them too lazy for it. The door buzzer rings and Hannah leaps out of bed where they had been lounging together, a film playing on her laptop. She reaches for her wallet on the top of her chest of drawers and leafs through it.

'That's weird,' she says, a frown creasing her forehead, 'I could have sworn I had a twenty in here – I got it out specially.'

Jaheim props himself up in the bed. He yawns.

'Have you checked all the pockets?'

She unzips the coin purse but there is nothing except a lone twenty pence.

'Nothing,' she says.

'Maybe you dropped it at the ATM,' he says, 'There's some money in my jeans pocket. Take that.'

He points to the floor where his jeans lie in a heap.

'I'm sorry,' she says bending down and rummaging until she finds a crisp twenty, 'I wanted this to be my treat.'

He waves his hand as she heads to the door with the money. 'Don't worry about it, babe.'

They eat the pizza in bed and she forgets about the money.

But a few days later the same thing happens. She goes to her purse, expecting to find ten pounds, and instead it's empty. This time she mentions it in passing to Mona, asking if she's borrowed any without telling her. But Mona says she hasn't, and Hannah immediately believes her, regretting bringing it up. Of course Mona wouldn't take any money from her without asking.

'I think I'm going mad,' she says to Jaheim one evening, 'I keep losing stuff. That or I'm way more broke than I thought I was.'

He kisses her on the tip of her nose.

'We'll just have to have more cosy dinners in,' he says, 'I can think of worse things, can't you?' She settles under the nook of his arm and breathes in his smell that she knows so well. It calms her, and she asks Jaheim about his day at work, happy to move the conversation away from money.

But it is a pattern and a conversation that will repeat itself regularly over the coming weeks. One day when she logs into her online banking she decides to take the time to read through her statement. She spots a few transactions she doesn't recognise but decides not to worry about them – they are only small amounts and she knows she is disorganised and prone to forgetfulness.

She is never going to remember every single cup of coffee or supermarket shop or takeaway ordered.

She starts trying to be extra friendly and smiley at the café. She checks up on all her customers and brings them a jug of tap water before they have to ask. Gradually her tips do improve; she keeps them stored in a glass jar on top of her chest of drawers. Usually it's just coins, but one day a customer leaves her the biggest tip she has ever received from a single person: a crumpled ten-pound note that has a rip through the middle and an ink stain on the corner but is still definitely usable. She arrives home that evening in a good mood, placing the ten-pound note in the tip jar and changing out of her work clothes into a figure-hugging dress. When Jaheim arrives at the flat after work she suggests that they go to the pub for a drink.

'Good idea,' he says with a smile.

'I'm just going to redo my make-up,' she says, disappearing into the bathroom, leaving him sat on her bed. When she is ready they head out, shouting a goodbye to Mona, who has just got back from a dance class.

It's one of Hannah's favourite local pubs and they order two pints.

'I'll get this round, you get the next?' says Jaheim, leaning on the bar. Hannah smiles and rests her head on his shoulder. As she does, she sees as he reaches into his pocket and pulls out a crumpled ten-pound note. There is a rip through the middle and an ink stain in the corner, but it is still usable.

The bartender hands Jaheim his change and he stuffs it into his back pocket. Jaheim hands Hannah the drink and she focuses hard on keeping her hand from shaking. The bar is noisy, filled *with the sound of conversation and music. But Hannah's ears suddenly fill with the silence and emptiness of realisation.*

'Hannah?' he says, 'Did you hear me?'

She turns back to him. That smile that she loves so much looks different now.

'I said, shall we sit over there?' he asks, his smile faltering as he looks at her questioningly.

For a second she wavers, suspended part-way between two potential decisions, two potential endings to this evening. As though returning to her body, she becomes aware of the noises around her again – the bartender talking to a customer, a group of friends at the back of the room clinking glasses and shouting 'cheers'. Her stomach tightens and her legs feel weak. But she smiles.

'Sure,' she says, letting herself be led to the table by the man she loves, and the man who has been stealing from her.

*

It took her a while to confront him. At first, she was too shocked to accept the truth. Although she had seen the proof very clearly, she still couldn't quite believe it. Her feelings turned quickly to embarrassment. How could she have let herself be so misled, especially after what happened with Sam? She'd had no idea about his affair, and now she'd had no idea Jaheim could be so deceptive. She thought of Mona too, flinching at the memory of asking her if she'd stolen from her, and of all those nights when she'd shut herself away in her room with Jaheim rather than spending time with her friend.

Among it all was the fear of the end. She loved him and she knew when she admitted to herself, and to him, what she knew, it would all be over. He would go, and she would be alone. The time spent with him would have been for nothing, and she would be single again, having just turned thirty. So she put it off, delaying the inevitable, holding on to the idea of their relationship for just a little bit longer.

When she finally did tell him what she knew, she expected him to be defensive, but in the end he was surprisingly honest.

He told her it started as twenty pounds borrowed for the food shop one night. Her purse had been right there on the side, he said. She was in the shower and he'd promised to nip out to buy something for them both to eat. It was so easy, he told her when it all emerged and when their relationship came tumbling down like an earthquake had rocked the house she had spent so long building – that they had built together. At first it didn't even feel like he was doing anything wrong, he told her. He had meant to tell her and replace the money that first time, but he forgot, and she didn't seem to notice, or at least she never mentioned anything about it. And so it continued. It was around this time that he started online gambling, a revelation that filled her with just as much shock as the stealing. She had no idea. At first it had started as a distraction and a release while he commuted to and from work, he said, but he started winning and got a buzz from it. So he kept playing. But then his winning streak changed, which meant his commitment to playing only increased. He had to win back what he had lost. He would stop as soon as that happened.

The money he stole from Hannah was always to pay for food

shopping or dinners out, or even gifts for her, he told her. To be able to afford them while his bank balance slowly dripped away down the gambling sink. He always used his bank card for the gambling – he found it important to make this distinction, as though it made it somehow better. For Hannah, it made it much, much worse.

When Hannah saw her ten-pound note in his hand in that bar, she thought it was something that had only happened a few times. But it turned out it had been going on for most of their relationship: she just didn't notice it until she was suddenly really struggling for money and very aware of every ten pounds, every twenty pounds. He had used her bank card for so many online transactions (he kept them small so she wouldn't notice) that he admitted he knew the numbers by heart.

By the time their relationship ended Jaheim shamefacedly guessed he had stolen several hundred pounds from her.

In the café, Hannah winces as she thinks about the stolen money and Jaheim's deception. He has promised to pay her back in instalments. He seems genuine about it, so she hopes that in a few months she will have regained the money. But that fact gives her next to no comfort.

Over the past few weeks since they broke up, she has spent a lot of time wondering how she let it get to that point, how she was so blind to what was happening. But she knows the answer. She loved him. And for her, it became more than just a relationship. She had been feeling so lost when she met him, so unsure of herself and her future, that he became her whole life.

Hannah feels suddenly filled with an overwhelming desire to apologise to Mona for the way she behaved while she and Jaheim were dating. She hadn't thought about it at the time, but looking back she can see that her obsession made her at times forget her friend and the impact that her new relationship might be having on her. The pain of the break-up might still be fresh, but enough time has passed for Hannah to now be able to see that she should have behaved better and to want to make it right with Mona. She thinks about the dinner she plans to invite Mona to, the one that was originally supposed to be her anniversary celebration with Jaheim. Perhaps they can have a proper heart-to-heart then. She will apologise and tell Mona how foolish she feels. And that's when she will suggest the trip to Paris, Hannah suddenly decides. She'll tell Mona that she wants to spend some proper time with her, that she loves her and values her as a friend and wants to make things right.

And as Hannah thinks it, she feels a rush of guilt for the crossword book and money in her apron pocket. *What was she thinking?* She is not Jaheim. She took the money in a moment of weakness, taking advantage of a brief opportunity and thinking about how much that money would mean to her. But it's not hers, and she doesn't want to steal or lie. Because it's the deception that hurt her most about the endings with Sam and Jaheim. They kept things from her and lied to her and she never wants to be like them.

Hastily she withdraws the stolen crossword book from her apron pocket. Searching beneath the counter, she finds a large envelope and slips the book inside. Before sealing it, she suddenly reaches for her own bag, stashed beneath the counter beside sacks of coffee beans. She glances briefly towards Eleanor, who is back from her break, but she is busy serving a customer at a table in the corner. Crouching, Hannah rifles through her purse, finds a couple of notes from last week's wages and slips these carefully alongside the others that were there inside the crossword book. Then she seals the envelope and places it in the lost property box, alongside a single glove, a pair of keys with a pom-pom key ring that have been there for months, a baby's dummy and a silver card holder stuffed with business cards that was dropped by one of the morning's customers.

Standing again, she writes a note addressed to Mona and secures it to the front of the till so she won't miss it when she starts her shift. She will tell her about it too and describe the young man to her so she knows who to look out for, but just in case they are caught in a rush and don't have time to talk, this note will be here for her.

Now, every time the café door opens Hannah looks up quickly, hoping it will be the young man in the green hoody so she can hand over his lost book and the money. She scans the faces beyond the window too, hoping to see a flash of green outside so she can rush up to him and right the wrong she committed easily, but which now gnaws at her like the residue of a bad dream that won't disappear with the brightening day. But he never comes. Instead, the café starts to fill with workers taking their morning coffee break, heading here for their dose of caffeine administered in a paper cup, before disappearing into the many buildings that spread out around Stella's and on into the sprawling streets of the city.

And in the middle of the café the two young men with the red suitcase hold hands across the table. They have been like that for a long time now, gripping tightly but saying nothing, as though they are each other's lifebelts and if they simply hold on, eventually the choppy seas will calm or someone will come and rescue them.

11.00 A.M.

JOE AND HAZIQ

'Fuck it,' says Haziq.

Joe looks up in shock. It is the first thing either of them has said in over an hour, since they watched Haziq's coach pull up opposite the café and then roll away again, and since they looked up at the clock and realised that check-in for his flight would now be closed.

'What?' says Joe.

Haziq is standing up and in a moment of panic Joe wonders if he is leaving now after all, if he has decided to catch the next coach to the airport and to try to buy a new ticket. He thought he would be able to say goodbye, but after hours of sitting together in silence, watching time passing, he realises he is incapable. He cannot let him go, he cannot say goodbye.

But Haziq isn't leaving, instead he bends down. Joe wonders

if he dropped something and looks down on the floor, but when he looks up again Haziq is kneeling, his eyes meeting Joe's.

'Joe,' Haziq says, reaching out and taking Joe's hands, wrapping them in both of his, 'I want you to marry me.'

Joe's mouth grows dry, his head is spinning. He notices that the two waitresses and a line of customers by the till have turned to watch them. He doesn't care.

'I want you to marry me,' Haziq repeats, without looking at the others in the café, oblivious to the fact they are all staring at him. He looks only at Joe. Haziq's eyes are damp and he quickly wipes at them before returning his hands to Joe's lap. 'I want you to marry me, and not because of immigration laws or the fact I am being forced to leave. I want you to marry me because I have never met a kinder man than you, because there is no greater happiness in my life than waking up next to you, and because I don't believe I could ever meet a better friend, a better partner, than you.'

Joe feels his eyes filling too and he lets the tears fall. Haziq holds his hands tightly and continues, his voice shaking.

'I want you to marry me because the thought of a life without you in it doesn't seem like a life at all. And I know what you'll be thinking, because I know what I said earlier, but I was stupid. I was just scared, but after sitting here with you I've realised that nothing is scarier than the thought of leaving you.'

Joe finds himself sobbing with the strength of someone who has just been broken and put back together again.

'What do you say?' says Haziq, wiping his eyes again.

Joe takes a deep breath.

'Of course,' he says, 'Of course I will.'

As he leans forwards to kiss Haziq his ears buzz with the sound of cheering.

HANNAH

She watches the proposal from the coffee bar, speechless and smiling. Throughout her five years working in the all-night café she has seen many things, some that have made her laugh and smile, others that she wishes she could forget. But she has never seen a proposal. She notices that Eleanor is staring at the couple too and when their eyes meet they find themselves suddenly sharing a hug. Hannah has never hugged her young colleague before, but it feels necessary somehow – she wants to share this happy moment with someone. They step away from each other, both looking slightly surprised at the sudden physical contact, but happy too.

Several customers in the café are clapping and a cheer erupts from a table near the bar. The couple blush and smile, both looking a little stunned, their eyes swollen from crying but their faces happy.

Hannah wishes that she had thought to whip out her phone to take a photograph of the proposal – she thinks it's a moment the couple would be pleased to have captured on camera. But it was so unexpected that she didn't think of it at the time. She noticed one of the men bending to the floor but assumed he was reaching for something or leaning to stuff a paper napkin under their table to correct a wobble. When he dropped to one knee she could hardly believe it.

Hannah brings the couple two milkshakes on the house, grinning at them as she sets them down on the table. She wishes she could speak to them and ask them dozens of questions about themselves and their lives and their engagement. But she gets the sense that they want to be left alone, so with great restraint she nods at them and returns to the bar.

She is still beaming when she feels her phone buzz in her pocket. She glances across to the coffee counter; Eleanor is serving a woman who wears a shiny red raincoat, despite the fact it long ago stopped raining. She seems to have things under control, and there is no one else waiting, so Hannah discreetly pulls her phone from her pocket. She has received a new email, and she clicks on the icon to open it.

As she does, she feels her head start to spin.

'We are really sorry but ...'

At 'sorry' she feels the tears pricking her eyes and a lump forming in her throat. But she fights hard not to let the tears fall. Not here, not on the café floor. With what tiny scrap of energy she has left, she focuses on holding herself together.

The email is from the manager at the hotel who booked her for the upcoming gigs next month. He is writing to tell her that they are going in a new, more modern direction in the bar and as such have decided to go for a different option for their music. They want to attract a younger business crowd and think her jazz style might be too old fashioned. They are sorry, but they will let her know if anything comes up in the future. But Hannah feels suddenly sure that it won't. They have made up her mind. They don't want her – she is old fashioned and irrelevant. Although it is just the one hotel and just one gig, it feels suddenly more significant than that. With a clarity and certainty that she has never quite felt before, she feels suddenly certain that if she keeps going, this is the way the rest of her life is going to go. Endless 'no's, endless disappointments. And finally, after years and years of trying, she realises she can't do it any more.

She is still holding her phone, and as she looks down she notices she has received another message, this time a text. Not quite ready to face getting back to work, Hannah opens the message.

'I GOT THE JOB.'

She stares at her phone and at Mona's message. Around her, life in the café continues. She can half hear Eleanor speaking to a customer and the quiet chatter of the happily engaged couple with the suitcases. Pablo's radio in the kitchen competes with the music playing from the café speakers. But Hannah is frozen to the spot, gripping her phone tightly and staring at the screen.

It takes all her strength to type a reply.

'That's amazing,' she writes. **'We'll celebrate later. I'm so proud of you. H xx'**

And she is proud of her friend. She knows how hard Mona works – ever since Hannah has known her Mona has been driven to the point of obsessiveness, practising far longer than Hannah thinks she really needs to and spending spare hours and money on dance classes. But she also aches.

'Excuse me,' comes a sharp voice, 'Can you put your phone away and take my order?'

A woman in a pale grey trouser suit is staring at Hannah, a hand on one hip and the other tightly clutching the bag slung over her arm.

'I'm sorry,' says Hannah, quickly putting the phone in her pocket and returning to the counter.

'What can I get you?'

'A black Americano,' says the woman in a clipped voice.

As Hannah makes the coffee, her mind circles around and around the same collection of thoughts. Jaheim, and how he lied and Hannah was fooled by him. The message from the hotel, her mind sticking on the phrases, 'we're sorry', and 'old fashioned'. Baby Mabel, and Hannah's mother who might never become a grandmother. Mona, and how her career has suddenly leapt forwards at the same time that Hannah's has come to an end.

As she hands the coffee over, the woman in the trouser suit looks down at it and frowns.

'This has milk in it,' she says, thrusting the cup back at Hannah, 'I asked for a black Americano.'

Eleanor flashes Hannah a glance, but when Hannah says nothing she returns to the customer she had just been serving, an elderly man with a dachshund poking its head out of a bag on his shoulder. Hannah makes the woman's coffee again, thinking about the thousands of coffees she must have made here over the years, and wondering what it has all been for.

12.00 P.M.

HANNAH

Hannah can hear Pablo clattering in the kitchen, chopping and slicing, bacon hissing on the pan. It is the start of the lunch rush, two hours of madness in which the café heaves with local office workers. Many queue for takeaway sandwiches; others sit in groups or alone, heads leant over books or phones on the table.

In one corner a pair of older men conduct what looks like an interview with a younger man. A sandwich lies abandoned in front of him as he talks quickly, moving his hands in front of him as he does. Every now and then he moves as if to reach for the sandwich, but one of the other men will always ask him another question making him straighten back up again. Sweat is starting to darken his shirt beneath his arms.

At steady intervals Pablo brings a plate of food through

from the kitchen and rests it on the counter, saying the name of the dish loudly as he does so.

'Fish and chips!'

'Fried eggs on toast with a side of bacon!'

'Pastrami sandwich no pickles.'

Eleanor and Hannah work quickly, trying to keep up with the queue and the orders. Hannah can feel her hands shaking and her feet burning with the pain of twelve hours of standing, but she knows she can't stop. Her shift may be over, but she can't leave until Mona arrives, and even then, in a rush like this she is unlikely to go until the queue has died down. She works as if in a trance. One or two people complain – she burns the milk on one order and adds normal milk instead of soya milk to another. She never usually makes mistakes like this and is aware of Eleanor looking concernedly in her direction. But she doesn't care.

When Mona arrives, Hannah is so busy that all she can do is look up and flash her a quick smile before returning to the coffees she had been making. She is working the counter now, with Eleanor doing table service, and it's hard to keep up with the orders on her own. After a moment Mona is at her side, apron tied around her waist. She places a hand briefly on Hannah's back and then turns to the queue.

'Who's next, please?' Mona says brightly. The queue shuffles forward slightly, and for a while the two of them work silently alongside each other, taking lunch orders and making coffees. It feels strange to have Mona suddenly here. It may only have been twelve hours since Hannah last saw her, but it seems as though so much has changed. She is not the same person who danced with Mona at midnight. Her eyes glance at the clock: it is now midday so her shift has technically ended, but she knows she can't leave Eleanor and Mona during this rush and besides, she needs to speak to Mona and ask her about the job, and perhaps tell her about her own cancelled gigs (she hasn't decided yet how much she wants to say).

Finally, the queue subsides slightly and Hannah makes the most of the pause to do what she knows she should do – hug Mona tightly. Mona feels a little stiff beneath her arms, but after a second she relaxes and squeezes Hannah back.

'I'm so happy for you,' Hannah says once she has released Mona, 'It's so exciting.'

She forces herself to say the words she knows she should, rather than exactly what she feels. She wants to be there for her friend, but it is hard.

'Thank you, I'm excited too,' replies Mona, but her voice is somewhat flat. Hannah wonders why she isn't being more expressive, but presses on, trying her best to be supportive.

'I want to hear all about it,' she says.

Mona pauses. She looks down at her apron, thrusts her hands in her pockets and then removes them again, fiddling with her watch strap. Hannah notices that her cheeks are flushed.

'There's something I need to tell you,' Mona says slowly.

A very short man with very blue eyes and a piercing in his eyebrow approaches the counter.

'Can I get an all-day breakfast wrap to go,' he says. Despite his stature, his voice is incredibly loud and makes Hannah jump slightly. She gives a quick look at Mona, trying to work out her expression, but Mona is looking down at her apron.

'Of course,' Hannah says to the man with the eyebrow piercing, passing the order through to Pablo.

Peering over the head of the short man is a tall teenage girl who wears her height apologetically. A long fringe hangs in front of one eye. Hannah notices a blue badge on her coat that says 'Please offer me a seat' and recognises it as one of the badges available from Transport for London. Without meaning to, Hannah finds herself wondering at the young woman's story and what unseen battle she must be fighting with her body. She hopes that, despite the badge, she is winning.

'What can I get you?' Hannah says. The young woman orders a latte and a ham and cheese toastie and takes a seat at one of the bar stools. As Hannah deals with the order she is very aware of Mona standing next to her, fiddling with her watch and tucking strands of her hair behind an ear, untucking it and then tucking it behind again. Hannah knows her well enough to know that she looks nervous and it confuses her. She should be happy, shouldn't she? Hannah feels a stab of annoyance that she can't control – why isn't Mona happy? Hannah would give anything for a break like that, but Mona seems somehow distracted, as though she doesn't care.

When the sudden rush has died down Hannah turns to Mona again.

'So, what is it?' she asks, less softly than before.

Mona looks up and meets Hannah's eyes with hers.

'The job,' she says, 'It's in Paris.'

Hannah's stomach drops and she stops still. Mona is staring at her, waiting for her to say something. But she doesn't know what to say, because there is nothing to say. She is so shocked and overwhelmed that all she can do is repeat 'Paris' over and over in her head.

'What?' Hannah says eventually. It's all she can muster. She feels as though she is spinning and reaches for the counter without thinking. She can hear her heart beating loudly in her ears.

'The job is in Paris,' says Mona.

In an instant the reality of what is happening hits Hannah. Mona is leaving. And Hannah will be truly on her own again. She suddenly feels overwhelmed by the smell of scrambled eggs coming from the kitchen. It is all she can smell and she feels sick. Her feet give a sudden sharp burst of pain.

'Paris?' Hannah says, unable to think of anything else to say.

'Paris,' Mona repeats.

Hannah wants to say more but a woman with a pinched-looking face is standing at the counter and audibly tapping her foot on the linoleum.

'I'll get this,' Mona says quietly to Hannah before turning to the woman and smiling her best waitress smile.

'What can I get you?'

As Mona serves the woman, who answers her phone part-way through ordering and speaks to both Mona and the person on the phone seemingly at the same time, Hannah stares around the café. As she does so, she suddenly sees it with fresh eyes. Instead of looking cosy and amusingly ironic, the fake leather booths and retro decorations appear tacky and old fashioned, not in a cool authentic way, but in a tedious, predictable one. The smell of the scrambled eggs seems even stronger although she can't even remember anyone actually ordering them. She notices the grease stains on her apron and a line of dirt under her fingernails that she hadn't seen before; she isn't sure where it came from. Outside a dog shits on the pavement and its owner walks quickly away, ignoring the shouts of John the *Big Issue* seller that Hannah can hear even through the café window and above the drone of the traffic.

She stares back inside the café full of strangers. For years she has told herself this is just a passing phase, a part-time job to support her other work, her *real* work. Hannah suddenly sees herself and the life she leads as ridiculous.

'So, what, you're moving out then?' she says when Mona has finished with the customer. She tries to keep the tremble out of her voice but it is hard, she feels as though the ground is shaking beneath her feet.

Hannah already knows the answer but it still rocks her to see Mona nodding slowly. Her face looks pained but Hannah pretends not to see this. It allows her anger more room to grow if she doesn't. She realises that for years she has fought against anger, choosing sadness instead. When she found out that Sam and Jaheim had been lying to her, she felt awful, but not angry at first. And after every failed audition or cancelled gig she has taken it as a reflection on her and her abilities, each disappointment knocking away at her self-confidence. But suddenly she feels a fiery explosion of anger, finally erupting after all these years.

'I start the job in two weeks,' Mona says, 'I'll pay my rent until the end of the month though.'

A jolt of panic flashes through Hannah's body. She pictures the flat they have shared together for four years, the place that might not be perfect but that feels like home. Now she imagines herself peeling their pictures down from the walls and packing her things into boxes, to go where? Where will she go? She can't stay in the flat alone – she couldn't afford it and can't imagine someone else moving in. It would be too strange, too sad. Mona's room is Mona's room. No one else could possibly live there. And she suddenly can't bear it all any more – the café, the rejections, the city itself. She realises she has absolutely no idea what she is going to do next.

'Well, thanks for all the fucking notice,' she says, surprising herself with the sharpness of her voice. This is not her, she hates arguments and she loves her friend. And yet it is her, all her pain and disappointment materialising itself in a sudden rage.

She spots a shift in Mona's face, a hardening as sadness turns to irritation. She knows Mona's expressions better than her own, having witnessed the whole spectrum of them throughout their friendship. She is angry too.

'I thought you'd be happy for me,' Mona says tersely.

Part of Hannah wants to tell Mona about the cancelled hotel gigs and her own realisation that her career is over. Maybe it would help Mona to understand why her news has hit her so hard, that it isn't that she isn't happy for her, but that she is falling apart.

'Why didn't you tell me?' she says instead, feeling her voice growing louder.

Mona shudders a little as though shaking off something uncomfortable that previously sat on her shoulders. One of the customers looks up at the two waitresses but then looks back at his phone.

'We don't talk about our auditions, you know that. We never do.'

'Yes, but when you audition for a job in fucking Paris, that's something you tell me. When you're thinking about leaving the country and moving out of our flat, that's something you tell me.'

Hannah feels herself getting more and more agitated. She hears her voice and how irrational it sounds but finds she can't control it. How can she tell Mona that their friendship, and their home together, felt like the only good thing in her life? The words are there, beneath the surface, but she can't reach them. They seem absurd, embarrassing, pointless. Mona has made her decision – she is leaving.

Hannah senses more of the customers looking at the two of them. She tries to smile reassuringly at the room as though it is an audience, but her face won't quite twist the way she wants it to. Mona has her head down and is wiping the counter. When she speaks again it is in a quieter voice and without looking up from the coffee bar.

'It's a permanent role with a contemporary dance company I've admired for years,' says Mona, 'These jobs just don't come around, and certainly not at this stage in my career. I'm not twenty-one any more. So to find something like this, something with security, where I'll be able to do what I love every day instead of serving coffee to strangers ...'

Hannah flinches at her words, realising that for the past four years she has been deluding herself. She is not a singer/waitress. She is a waitress. She makes coffee for people whose stories she will never know.

'You don't understand what it's like as a dancer,' Mona continues, 'Every year that passes it becomes less and less likely that I'm going to make it. I stand next to these women in auditions – these *girls* really – and I realise I'm old. I'm only thirty but to them I am ancient. Every time I go to another audition I tell myself that perhaps it should be the last one, that perhaps it's time to give up on the dream. It's just too painful to keep trying and failing. Most people do jobs they are indifferent to at best, often that they hate. Why should I be different? But despite it all it doesn't go away, that aching to live another kind of life, to spend my day doing the only thing I've ever felt actually good at, the only thing that makes sense, the thing that feels as normal to me as breathing. I want it so much it feels like a physical pain sometimes. I know that some people don't understand that, but it's how it feels. And this could be my last shot. After this it might be too late for me. So I don't care that the job's in Paris. If it was in Australia I'd still go.'

Mona lets out a deep breath once she has finished talking and places her hands on her hips. Hannah is acutely aware of the physical space between her and Mona – about half a metre – not something she has ever found herself noticing before. Silence swirls between them like a storm.

'And besides,' adds Mona suddenly, 'I applied months ago. I didn't think you'd care if I left.'

A chill runs through Hannah's body as she remembers the months she spent with Jaheim, so in love that everything else started to fall away in her mind. But she never stopped caring about Mona, not for one second. She wishes she hadn't been so careless with her friendship, which she now feels crashing down around her. *I'm sorry. I'm proud of you. I love you* she thinks. But none of these are the words that come to her, instead her uncontrollable rage overtakes her.

'You think I don't understand?' Hannah says, not even really realising what she is saying, 'You think I don't know what it feels like to want to finally, finally get a break? Had you even noticed that I've had hardly any gigs this year? Because no one is interested in me any more.'

Saying the words aloud brings fresh tears to Hannah's eyes. But she is too angry to cry.

'But whose fault is it that you haven't got any gigs lined up?' says Mona, 'You think I don't know that you lied to me about that audition you said you were going to? If you'd told me the truth I could have been supportive, but you didn't let me help you. And what about those months with Jaheim where you barely left your room? It's fine if you've given up on your dream, but why don't you just admit it instead of taking it out on me?'

Hannah steps back slightly, wounded. She didn't realise that Mona knew about the skipped audition and hearing her say Jaheim's name adds an extra sting. She blinks back her tears – she is desperate not to cry. The most painful thing is knowing that Mona is right. Of course she is right, but sometimes you don't want your friends to be right. You just want them to be on your side.

'So you've found somewhere to live already, then?' she asks, deciding not even to acknowledge the other comments because it's too hard to even begin to know what to say.

Mona shifts uncomfortably, any remaining anger in her eyes disappearing quickly.

'I'm moving in with Poppy,' she says.

Hannah blinks quickly at Poppy's name, surprised that she is surprised to hear it. Of course it would make sense for Mona to get in touch with Poppy if she was moving to Paris, but it all seems so sudden, so out of the blue. Her head spins with it all. Mona is watching her carefully now.

'Wait a minute,' Hannah says after a moment, 'How did you possibly manage to arrange all of this?'

Mona shifts her weight again from one foot to the other.

'I went there,' she says eventually.

'You went to Paris? When?'

'Last month,' says Mona, 'Just after you and Jaheim broke up.'

Hannah thinks back to the week following the break-up. She called in sick for the first time ever and mostly stayed in her room, hidden beneath her duvet, staring at her phone and wondering if Jaheim would call. But she had told him not to, and he hadn't. It didn't stop her checking it though. That week was a blur, as though she was barely registering what was happening around her. But she does remember something now: Mona going to visit an aunt who was in the UK for a weekend.

'Your aunt,' Hannah says, 'You didn't really go and visit your aunt, did you?'

Mona shakes her head.

'No, I went to Paris for the first audition. I stayed with Poppy and Antoine. I asked her not to tell you.'

Mona looks straight at her now, barely blinking. Hannah

196

doesn't know what to say but doesn't need to say anything because Mona keeps talking.

'I told you I was visiting my aunt but instead I went to Paris and stayed with Poppy. We talked about what would happen if I got the job, and she said I could stay with them until I found somewhere of my own. And then this week the company have been on tour in London so I had the second audition here. And they offered me a job and I said yes. And I'm moving in two weeks.'

And that's when Hannah does start to cry. The tears fall noiselessly and she brushes them away, furious at her body for letting her down. Despite the anger, there's a part of her that knows that she should maybe be responding differently. She should be happy. Two of her friends living together in Paris. They will have so much fun. But none of this occupies the front of her mind; instead she feels the searing pain of betrayal. She thinks of Mona and Poppy planning all of this behind her back and realises she has been lied to again. First Sam, then Jaheim and now Mona, her closest friend.

Her mind returns to the trip to Paris she was going to suggest to Mona, but instead of the three of them catching up together, she now pictures Mona and Poppy on their own. Her mind journeys to the café that she marked out, back when she and Mona almost visited the city together. She remembers holding back Mona's hair while she was sick and the packed suitcases standing in the hall, waiting for the trip they never went on. At the time Hannah didn't mind; looking after Mona wasn't even a choice, it's just what she did. But now she thinks back to that abandoned visit to Paris and instead pictures Poppy and Mona in the café Hannah had earmarked, sharing the famous lemon meringue pie and cups of peppermint tea without her.

I should be above this, she thinks, *I'm thirty years old*. Her head aches with it all as she realises she is not above these feelings and they rip through her, anger and jealousy tearing her apart.

As Hannah cries, Mona's face suddenly softens again and she reaches out as though to touch her arm or pull her into a hug. But Hannah is already untying her apron and stepping away from her. She drops the apron on the counter and grabs her things.

'Well *bonne* fucking *chance*,' she says as she moves quickly towards the door, tears streaming down her face.

Eleanor and several customers stare at her as she weaves her way between the tables but Hannah ignores them. As she rushes to get to the door she knocks the edge of a table with her hip and coke sloshes over the rim of a glass.

The customers – a mum and her teenage son – mop at the table and throw her strange looks.

'Aren't you going to apologise?' calls the woman.

But no, she is not going to apologise. Not to them, and not to Mona. Hannah's body feels exhausted, not just because of the twelve-hour shift but because of the sadness that hits her like whiplash. Ignoring the stares of the customers she keeps her gaze straight ahead, fixed out the window at the busy street. At the doorway she pauses for a moment. But then she pushes on the door of Stella's. Stepping onto the street brings an onslaught of sensations. The sunlight glinting off the office blocks, the relentless traffic, the people constantly coming or going, never pausing. It is suddenly too much. She thinks of the cool blue room in Wales where it is dark at night and where her parents will be drinking coffee and reading the papers downstairs. She needs to get out of London. She needs to go home. And suddenly home is not here with Mona.

MONA

Mona stands behind the coffee bar, trying to ignore the concerned expressions from Eleanor, who is busy taking orders, and the customers, who glance at her every now and then. She lifts her chin and adopts what she hopes is a calm expression but which probably comes across as a haughty frown. If she were at home and not in the café, she would reach for her weights or practise some particularly difficult dance steps in order to quiet the ringing in her ears and cool the anger pulsing through her body. She notices that her jaw and her hands are clenched and forces herself to relax her muscles, thinking of her new job. She doesn't need this – she knows well the effects that stress can have on the body and her body is her career, now more than ever. In a smooth motion she lifts her arms above her head and stretches.

The thought of her new job sends a ripple of excitement and fear across her skin. She thinks back to the audition this morning –it was only a few hours ago but it seems much longer. Her life has changed in such a short space of time and she is still reeling from it all, not quite comprehending the reality of what has happened and what is still to come. She thinks back to the audition, remembering standing nervously in front of the dance company panel, chatting for a while and then dancing for them for the second time. She had been so nervous that she'd faltered slightly to begin with, something that never usually happens to her. But then she had found her centre and her rhythm and held it like a lifeline. When she finished, her feet and her heart aching, she could feel herself shaking, ashamed and disappointed at the mistake she had made at the beginning. In the café, Mona winces as she thinks about the rocky start to the audition. It still bothers her, even though they had smiled warmly at her once she had finished and called just over an hour ago to tell her they'd made up their minds and wanted to offer her a place in their company.

Mona had been in the flat when the head of the company called, practising the steps she faltered over in the audition. She had been repeating them since she arrived home, fast and furiously, and she was sweating, her breathing heavy. When the phone rang she nearly didn't hear it, she was so focused on what she was doing. But after a few rings the sound shattered her concentration and she reached quickly for her phone, nearly dropping it in her hurry. When they told her they were offering her the job she was silent for a moment, so shocked and exhausted she couldn't reply. When she found her voice she was brief and calm, trying her best to remain professional. But inside she was an explosion of fireworks.

The first thing she had done was text Hannah. She sent it on instinct because she needed to tell someone the news – she felt like a bottle that had been shaken and if she didn't say the words to someone she might explode. After Hannah,

Mona called her parents. She tried her mother but received no reply – she was probably at work and Mona knew she always kept her phone on silent when she was lecturing. She thought about calling her father too but knew that it would still be early in Argentina and the family would be rushing through their morning routine, trying to get the teenage Matías out of the house on time for school. She would call him later.

Mona thinks back to receiving the news, and how it was Hannah she had wanted to tell before anyone else, even her family. For the past five years since they have known each other Hannah has been the person Mona wants to tell all her news, the person who she felt understood her and her life choices more than anyone. Her stomach twists as she thinks about how much has changed over the past year between them, and about the argument that just sent Hannah charging out of the café.

Hannah's anger caught Mona off guard. As she rode on the bus to the café for her shift she had felt suddenly nervous, wondering how to break the news that she would be moving. As the city rolled past the window outside, Mona went over and over what she would say, trying to choose the words as carefully as she might practise a dance step. She'd expected surprise, tears perhaps, but not anger. Since Mona has known Hannah, Hannah's anger has been a rare occurrence. Mona is on familiar terms with her own anger – she blames the fiery natures of both her parents – but Hannah has always been softer and eager to please. Mona knows Hannah is so fearful of conflict that she does anything to avoid it, which often means simply pretending that problems don't exist, perhaps in the hope that if she doesn't look at them directly, they might go away on their own. So Mona arrived at the café prepared to apologise about keeping the truth from Hannah, and ready to comfort her if she grew upset. She would have told her that Hannah could visit Paris whenever she liked. But when she saw Hannah's anger rearing up like a wild animal her own nature responded, ready to fight and defend herself. And as the fight grew more heated, Mona felt her thoughts of an apology slipping further away. Why should she have to apologise? Why couldn't Hannah just be happy for her, especially after everything that has happened this year?

It had still been hard to admit going behind Hannah's back though. When she told Hannah that final part of the truth, Mona had seen her face fall so completely that for a moment everything else had seemed unimportant and all she wanted to do was hug her friend. Despite everything, Mona doesn't want to hurt Hannah, and when she told her the full truth she saw on her face that she had, deeply. But Hannah had left before she could reach her, pulling away and stumbling out of the café.

At the counter, Mona takes a steady, controlled breath and looks around the café properly for the first time since arriving. A teenage girl in a coat with a blue badge peers up behind a long fringe, a book held aloft in one hand. The book and the girl's arm shake very slightly. As if only just noticing this herself, the girl looks at her hand, puts the book down and folds both hands in her lap. There is a small group of men in shirts and ties at a table in the corner, their jackets slung over the back of their chairs, one revealing a polka-dot lining, another a large tear. A debris of lunch is spread on the table between them: crusts of sandwiches, the salad Pablo and Aleksander use as garnish but that most people ignore in favour of fries. The men have returned to their conversation. Next to them Mona spots a group of regular customers; three older women who sit at the same table by the window every week. Unlike the men, these women are all still looking up at her with concerned expressions. She nods slightly in their direction.

The door opens and a few lunch customers arrive, wanting orders to take away. Mona serves them calmly and quickly, working hard to control her emotions. She prepares coffee orders that she knows so well that she imagines she could make them with her eyes closed. As she does so she replays the argument between her and Hannah over and over in her head, right from the first raised voice to the eventual slam as the door shut behind Hannah and she disappeared.

1.00 P.M.

MONA

'Mona! Mona!'

It is only after hearing her name for a third time that Mona's brain switches back to the room. She has been busy taking orders but realises she was working entirely on autopilot. Her senses return to her and she smells oil frying and hears a customer somewhere in the café talking loudly into a phone. There is a brief lull at the counter as customers take seats, and Mona sees Pablo standing in front of her, wearing his leather jacket.

'I'm off now,' he says. Mona's eyes flick to the clock and she realises Pablo has worked an hour longer than his shift – not wanting to leave Aleksander on his own mid-lunchtime rush, she imagines. His voice is cheery despite the fact he has been working for over twelve hours.

'Where's Aleksander?' asks Mona, looking around her, suddenly realising she doesn't remember the other chef arriving.

'He arrived ages ago,' says Pablo, 'He tried to say hello but you were busy serving customers.'

Mona pictures Aleksander slipping silently into the kitchen and feels bad but not surprised – after all their time working together (he started at the café three years ago) she has never got to know him well. He is desperately quiet and impossible to read. Unlike Pablo, whose eyes Mona suddenly notices are filling with tears.

'I can't believe you're leaving,' he says to her.

Mona feels her cheeks growing warm as she thinks with embarrassment and pain to the fight with Hannah.

'So you overheard that then …' she says, 'I'm really sorry, I didn't mean for things to get so heated. I don't know what happened. And I really shouldn't have said all those things here – I haven't even told Stella yet …'

She trails off, thinking for the first time about how she will tell the café's owner that she is leaving. Since Mona started working here Stella has been as flexible and supportive of Mona's other life as she can possibly be, and Mona feels a surge of guilt at leaving with such short notice. Although she doesn't officially leave for Paris for another two weeks, she could do with some time to pack and organise things, but that would give Stella hardly any time to find a new member of staff. Perhaps she should have mentioned the audition to Stella so this job doesn't come as a total surprise, but she'd been so focused on doing well in it that she hadn't thought of anything else. Her mind races, thinking about Stella's reaction. Perhaps, like Hannah, she will be angry and Mona suddenly realises that Stella would have every right to be. Stella doesn't work set hours at the café, but Mona imagines she will be in later that afternoon – she will tell her then. Better to do it in person, she thinks.

'I won't say anything!' says Pablo, gesturing as though fastening a zip over his mouth, 'Of course I won't. It won't be the same without you, but I'm also happy.'

He is suddenly behind the counter and pulling her into a hug before she really knows what is happening. At first she re-sists, taken off guard, but then she sinks into his firm arms and feels a lump forming in her throat. Mona expects him to say something to her about the fight that he obviously overheard, but he doesn't, and she is grateful for his tact. Pablo has always been so good to her and Hannah, and it has made working here all this time easier somehow. She thinks of her own parents, whom she isn't particularly close to, sees perhaps once a year and hasn't had a chance to speak to yet, and realises that for the past five years it's often been Pablo who has heard her news before her mum and dad, as they chat during shared shifts or early morning breakfasts before the café fills with people. Since leaving for London all those years ago Mona has had to find a new sort of family in the city. At times she has felt envious of Hannah and her relationship with her parents. They get on well and it is easy for her to get on a train and see both her parents, and both at the same time. She sometimes thinks that Hannah takes their closeness, and the fact that her parents still live together, for granted. But she doesn't blame her for it – she would do the same if she were in her position. Over the years

Mona has learnt to need her real family less and less, partly because they are so far away that she has had to, and partly because during that time she has grown up and made her own life, her own network. Her London family has shifted over the years and is a mismatched, unusual sort of group made up of friends and colleagues. For the past five years Pablo has been part of that family.

He pulls apart from her and rests his large, callused hands on her shoulders, his familiar, warm face looking intently at her.

'*Chiquita*, I'm so proud of you,' he says, his bright eyes shining, faint wrinkles creasing.

Mona swallows hard as she thinks about saying goodbye to Pablo and also realises that these are the words she so desperately wanted Hannah to say.

'Thank you,' she says in a serious tone, her energy focused on keeping calm. She hopes he knows her well enough to know that she means to say so much more than this but just can't find the words.

'If we don't work another shift together you'll come in and say goodbye before you leave, won't you?' he says, and as he does so it hits Mona for the first time that she will actually be leaving. In the excitement of the job offer and then the turbulent argument with Hannah she hasn't had time to really think about the reality of leaving the café, the flat and the city that is so familiar to her.

'Of course,' she replies, blinking back tears.

'Can I sit here?' a woman asks, pointing at a table close to the bar. Mona settles her face in a calm expression and waves goodbye to Pablo, who is heading to the door, while answering the customer.

'Please, do,' she says, as the door shuts behind Pablo. The sound makes her flinch slightly.

She turns her attention to the customer, who is dressed in office wear and carries a large scrapbook under her arm with bits of paper and fabric peeking out at the edges. She is wearing a blue coat, and the hand that isn't wrapped around the scrapbook grips a black and white polka-dot umbrella. Mona spots the glint of an engagement ring on the hand that holds the umbrella. She watches for a moment as the woman sits down and places the book on the table, staring intently out the window.

'I'll give you a minute and then come and take your order,' Mona says, but the woman doesn't reply, she simply nods and continues looking ahead, out at the view that Mona knows so well that if she were to close her eyes it would still be there, every detail clear in her mind.

SONJA

The forecast is for rain. Not just gentle showers, but torrential, pouring, flooding rain. She has checked both BBC weather and the Met office once every hour for the past three days. The local weather station has issued high alert flood warnings.

Sonja looks out the window of Stella's and the view backs up the prediction. Perfectly on cue, the grey clouds break and a sudden downpour soaks the street. On the pavement outside the café the man selling the *Big Issue* looks to the sky and opens a pink umbrella above his head. The street becomes suddenly more colourful as around him pedestrians reach into bags and pull out their umbrellas too. Others simply dash.

Sonja's blue coat hangs on the back of her chair, her black and white polka-dot umbrella tucked in the pocket in anticipation of this sudden downpour.

'*Who organises a wedding on a flood plain?*' she says to herself, dropping her phone heavily on the table and taking a long sip of the strawberry milkshake she ordered from the dark-haired waitress. It is candyfloss pink and is nearly solid with ice cream, condensation forming on the glass in tiny droplets. She had been trying to be good ahead of the wedding, being prone to breakouts, but there doesn't seem to be much point any more.

When Timur proposed, she knew immediately where she wanted to get married. They both did. There was never any question that it would be anywhere other than at her parents' house, the marquee set up on the lawn at the bottom of the garden, by the river.

His parents still live in Turkey and they were never very close anyway, but Sonja's mum and dad treat him like he is their own. It's one of the things she has always felt proudest of about them – how openly they had welcomed him into their family. It must have been hard, her being their only daughter. Sonja imagines having a daughter and her bringing home their partner – she thinks she would probably take a while to warm to them.

It had taken a while for her to warm to Timur herself. They met at the media agency where they both worked. She took her job very seriously. He didn't. It used to annoy her that he would leave at five on the dot while she was still in the office, often till gone ten o'clock. Just seeing him the next morning infuriated her because of that. But when her mum called her at work to tell her that they'd had to put down Bertie, the family dog whom Sonja had loved since she was a teenager, Timur was the only one who stopped and comforted her when he spotted her crying on a step on the fire escape. He sat with her and listened patiently, not once making her feel embarrassed about her tears, or suggesting that Bertie was only a dog. Instead, he told her about Sage, the pet cat of his childhood who had died not long after he left Turkey for London. Once she had stopped crying, they talked a little more about themselves – asking for the first time questions that weren't just related to work. She learnt that he was passionate about cooking and had always wanted to be a chef but did this agency job to earn enough money to help look after his younger sister, who moved to the UK a year ago but was struggling to find permanent work. He left at five o'clock each evening and went home to practise new recipes or invent and perfect his own. She immediately felt bad for having thought he didn't take his job seriously. Because his real job, his real calling, she found out was elsewhere and not in the office. She regretted having judged him before, and for never having asked the right questions.

They had become close after that, sharing lunches together and often going for a drink after work. But she said she wouldn't date someone she worked with – that she had a rule against it because it could get too complicated. So he quit. He moved to another agency and they started dating, and when his sister finally found secure work he left the agency and found a job as a junior chef in a kitchen. Over several years he worked his way up in the kitchen, she moved up in the media agency, and the two of them became inseparable.

He is the only person who can make her laugh at herself or break her frown into a smile when she is frustrated or anxious. At work she takes pride in being confident, in control and slightly unreachable; behind the door of their flat she clings to him at night and asks him to brush her hair when she is unwell. He always does it very gently, kissing her forehead when he is finished.

They had been saving for two and a half years for the wedding. When people spot her engagement ring and ask her when she is getting married, at first she felt embarrassed to say how long they had to wait. She wanted it to be sooner, she wanted it to be right now.

The problem was that she could picture it so clearly. It annoyed her that it made her fall into a female cliché, but she knew exactly what she wanted her wedding to be like, and had imagined every single detail years before she even met Timur. The marquee in her parents' garden, the flowers by the local florist, Jen (who was her mum's friend), the food supplied by the local deli and the brunch they would hold in their conservatory the next day with a few of their closest friends. In her head every tiny detail was perfect – meticulously organised and chosen with love and care. She knew that she was lucky that Timur agreed on everything too, but then everything was based around her home and he loved it there nearly as much as she did.

But now the image of her perfect wedding has disappeared. All she can picture is a marquee floating on a flood plain, tables and chairs submerged in muddy water. They will just have to postpone it.

MONA

Mona serves the customer with the scrapbook and deals with another flurry of takeaway lunch orders. Every now and then she catches Eleanor's eye and knows she should talk to her and apologise for the earlier outburst with Hannah, but they are both busy, Eleanor dealing with customers at their tables and Mona struggling to keep up with the coffee and sandwich orders at the bar. She is still shaken from the earlier argument and from saying goodbye to Pablo, but works hard to remain professional and to keep the emotion from her face. She doesn't want Eleanor or the customers to see how much she is spinning inside. She almost laughs at herself as she thinks how typical of her it is – it makes her think of her bedroom back in Haggerston that is immaculate, the tidiness giving her a feeling of order and control that she so desperately craves. It is vital that she stays in control, no matter what is going on behind her calm expression.

'I'll have two black coffees, two orange juices, two poached eggs on toast and two pancakes with berries,' says a woman wearing a yellow poncho in a confident American accent, before returning to a table in the corner where a middle-aged man in a similar poncho sits with two small children who point at Ernest the bear and growl at each other before dissolving into giggles. Mona writes very neatly on her pad and passes the order through to Aleksander, who looks up briefly at her before returning to work. Mona wants to apologise for not acknowledging him when he first arrived but has no time – there are customers waiting for her back at the counter.

A latte and a piece of brownie for a woman with red hair who makes Mona think of Hannah without meaning to, three sandwiches for a man in a pale blue shirt with a neat moustache. She passes two smoothies to a teenage girl wearing a spotty headscarf who holds the hand of another girl with the whitest blonde hair Mona has ever seen and eyelashes that seem almost not there, they are so faint. They nod and move to a table at the back of the café, leaning so close together as they drink that their foreheads almost touch.

Among the sounds of laugher, the hissing of the coffee machine, Aleksander's mutterings in the kitchen and the music that fills the room, Mona picks out a flurry of French conversation. It is coming from two men near the back of the queue and she cannot understand what they are saying, but the sound lifts her up and out of the café, taking her back in an instant to three weeks ago when she headed to France for the first audition for the job that would change her life. Suddenly in Mona's head she is not here in this café on Liverpool Street, she is in Paris on the Rue des Martyrs.

*

The charms of Paris reveal themselves slowly at first. As she steps off the train at the Gare du Nord, Mona can't help but feel disappointed. Ever since she left Singapore for London as a teenager, she has told herself she should make the most of the easy travel to mainland Europe. When she first moved, she pictured herself jetting to European cities for weekends away. But she quickly found that her finances and her schedule – partly dictated by her dance degree and partly due to the self-enforced extra hours of practice – didn't allow her much in the way of holidays. Then after graduating came the endless juggling of shifts with auditions, classes and shows. It's a juggling act that she is still performing nine years later, trying hard not to drop any balls. It has meant that over the years she hasn't had much time for the trips away she dreamed of when she was younger. She has travelled, of course – at twenty-two she spent a year working on a cruise ship in the Mediterranean, and there have been a few brief, cheap holidays over the years. But otherwise any spare money goes on occasional flights to Argentina to stay with her father, stepmother and half-brother Matías and to Germany to visit her mother. She feels embarrassed to admit that at the age of thirty, and with a good friend living there, she has still never been to Paris.

So when she arrives she is full of excitement and yet her feelings are quickly dampened by the busy, somewhat drab reality. The concourse heaves with people rushing in all directions or standing and watching the arrivals and departure boards. Women grip their handbags tightly beneath their shoulders and Mona suddenly realises why – within a few moments she is approached by a man who eyes her bag with overt keenness.

She notices groups lurking around the ticket machines too, perhaps waiting for dropped coins or bags left unattended in a moment of opportunity. Mona drags her suitcase quickly behind her and makes her way through the crowds, emerging onto Place Napoléon-III. It isn't much better here – the streets are thronged with people and she notices similar huddled groups waiting around in a way that she can't help but find suspicious. It is getting dark and Mona suddenly wishes she had accepted Poppy's offer to come and meet her, rather than insisting that she could make her way to the apartment by herself.

Pulling her phone from her bag, she checks quickly to see if there are any messages from Hannah. When she left she felt guilty at first – Hannah and Jaheim only broke up last week and Hannah has been in a daze ever since, calling in sick for work and staying in her room. But alongside the guilt was a flash of something stronger too, a hurt and anger that has built up slowly over the past months. It was that anger that eventually allowed her to shout a final goodbye into Hannah's room and leave the flat with her suitcase, telling Hannah she was going to visit an aunt who was staying in Dorset for a few days.

There are no messages from Hannah so Mona looks up Poppy's address and then zips her phone into an inside pocket of her jacket. As she sets off down the street towards Montmartre she looks up and notices the buildings properly for the first time. The top halves are exactly how she imagined them – pale stone and faded silvery blue roofs, black railings marking balconies here and there. But the bottom halves make her think not of Paris, but of any city in the world. The bright façade of a burger bar, a kebab shop, a chain hotel. Taxis line up outside the station, *sounding their horns at pedestrians or other drivers, Mona can't tell.*

She walks quickly, happy to get away from the station and the rush of noise, people and garish lights flashing outside restaurants and bars. Some streets she walks down are quiet, but then she approaches Anvers metro station and is plunged into the crowds again. Her heart sinks in disappointment when she spots a Pret a Manger on a street lined with tourist shops, tea towels decorated in Eiffel Towers flapping outside their doors. Is this really the place she dreamt of? Is she really willing to leave her home and the life she has built in London for this, however much she likes the sound of the job she will be auditioning for tomorrow? Was this all just a huge, rash mistake?

But then she catches a glimpse of the Sacre Coeur, the white domes perching on the top of the hill and illuminated by lights, making it look like paper cut out against the night's sky. The sight of it makes her stop, staring up through the dark garden and the many steps that lead to its doors. Mona can make out the groups of tourists at the top, but that doesn't make it any less beautiful. And it is undeniably Paris. For the first time since stepping off the train, she feels like she has arrived.

By the time she finds herself at Poppy and Antoine's apartment, reached via quieter streets where Mona notes cafés and shops she would like to return to, she is part-way to being charmed by the city but is still not entirely convinced. The flat goes some way towards hooking her. It is on the fourth floor of a building at the top of Rue des Martyrs, reached by an ancient spiral wooden staircase. As Mona climbs the steps she counts the flats, amazed that so many can fit within the one building.

Most have mats outside their doors, one has an umbrella stand, another a pram, another a pair of running shoes.

As she climbs higher, an unexpected sense of nervousness passes over her. It has been a year since she last saw Poppy, on one of Poppy's visits to London, although they have kept in touch via WhatsApp and Instagram. Poppy was one of the first friends she made at dance college, the warm, funny young woman immediately managing to break down the somewhat cold and stand-offish persona Mona had adopted in order to disguise her fear at leaving her family behind and arriving alone in a new country, in a new city she had never visited. They remained friends throughout their degree, but Poppy had a wide circle and Mona knew she was only ever one of many, many people Poppy cared about. After graduating they saw each other infrequently, often among other people, and then one Halloween Poppy invited Mona to her house for a party and that's when she met Hannah. Mona's connection with Hannah was so instant and so firm, that once she'd moved in, jumping at the chance to leave her nightmare flatmates behind, they quickly became closer than Mona had ever been with Poppy. Perhaps it was partly because they both so needed each other's friendship – Hannah had recently split up with her boyfriend and Mona had spent the years since graduating working so hard that she had unintentionally drifted apart from many of her friends. Hannah and Mona threw everything into their new friendship, whereas Poppy was only ever really able to scatter brief, if warm and vibrant, bursts of attention to hers.

As Mona approaches the door to Poppy's flat, she feels suddenly very aware of the distance that has grown between them over the years. Perhaps she should have stayed in a hotel this weekend, but when she told Poppy she was coming to Paris, she had insisted Mona stay with her and Antoine. Mona accepted, conscious of how much the trip was already costing her. But now she pauses on the threshold to the flat.

When she eventually rings the buzzer, Poppy greets her with two kisses, a cheerful 'Bonjour' and a huge hug. The warmth of the hug relaxes Mona, making her feel immediately more at ease. Mona has seen photos of Antoine before but has never met him, so she looks at him with some curiosity as she and Poppy untangle themselves from their embrace. He stands a little behind Poppy in the hallway and is a tall, extremely attractive but, Mona can tell immediately, surprisingly shy man. He has a perfectly trimmed beard and dark, long-lashed eyes which flick up to meet Mona's before looking down again. His hands are plunged in his pockets and Mona nods and smiles at him instead of offering a hug. He nods back and smiles, a look of relief on his face.

'Let me take your bag,' he says in a quiet French accent, reaching for Mona's suitcase.

The flat is small but beautiful. Two huge windows, the shutters currently open, look out at the street below. Mona immediately gravitates towards them and looks down at the café opposite, which is currently closed, and the bar a few buildings along where a large crowd is gathered on the pavement outside, people smoking and laughing. Her earlier nerves and uncertainty melt away and it feels suddenly wonderful to be up here watching the street below. Beneath each window in the living room is a seat lined with cushions in tasteful shades of grey and navy. There is a table where Antoine is currently pouring wine into three glasses, a full bookshelf and a sofa bed. The small kitchen area is in the hallway at the entrance to the flat, and two other doors lead to what Mona presumes are the bathroom and Poppy and Antoine's bedroom. The living room walls are decorated with old botanical prints in modern frames. Underfoot is a pale grey rug and wooden floorboards that slope towards the windows. Candles are burning on the table and the shelves. It feels cosy and lived in, but not too cluttered. It has character and although Mona has called London home for twelve years, she can immediately imagine what it might be like to live here, right at the top of Paris.

'Watch out if you wake up in the night, the first time you stay here you're likely to get seasick because of the sloping floor,' says Poppy, sitting down on the futon that will be Mona's bed for the weekend and taking a glass of wine that Antoine is handing her. Mona receives hers with a smile, and the three of them clink glasses.

'Bienvenue à Paris,' says Antoine with a small but warm smile.

'Welcome!' says Poppy, beaming at Antoine and then at Mona, 'It's so good to see you.'

That night they stay in, Antoine cooking a simple pasta dish for them. He softens gradually throughout the night but it still intrigues Mona that Poppy, the most sociable person she has ever met, has chosen someone so quiet for her partner. They seem comfortable with each other though, and that makes Mona feel at ease too. She is surprised by how welcome and relaxed she feels, despite having never met Antoine and having *not seen Poppy in so long. And she thinks too about the times she spent with Hannah and Jaheim when they were together in the flat and how different that was. She never felt comfortable then. Mona takes another sip of wine, pushing the thought from her mind.*

Poppy and Mona spend the evening catching up, the conversation warm and easy. Antoine fills their glasses and chips in here and there, but seems content simply listening too. Poppy talks about the show she has been in for the past few years – she has this weekend off which is why she is able to host Mona, although she says she regrets that Mona can't come to watch it.

'Another time,' Mona says, hoping already that there will be another time.

They talk about old course mates and what they are up to, sharing knowledge based on whom they have each kept in touch with. Poppy knows far more than Mona does – despite living in France she clearly hasn't lost her interest in her wide collection of friends. Many of them are no longer dancing and Mona is surprised when Poppy tells her news of some course mates in particular. Like Lara, one of the best dancers in their year group, who is now eight months pregnant and who has told Poppy she doesn't intend to go back to work. Some are now teaching dance, but many are working in completely different industries: human resources, advertising, recruitment. As they share these stories Mona feels the bond between her and Poppy tighten as they both realise something without needing to say it: they are two of the few still dancing. When Mona talks about her job at the café she knows she doesn't have to justify it like she sometimes does when she meets people for the first time. She doesn't have to explain the fact she still rents a one-bedroom flat with her friend, or that, however much she loves and admires them, she feels her life is very far away from those of her friends who have married and settled down. Poppy understands. Mona thinks about the upcoming audition and how this could be one of her last opportunities. In a few years' time she just won't be able to keep up with the latest influx of young performers coming out of dance schools and colleges any more. The thought terrifies her.

'I'm so glad you're here,' says Poppy when they eventually decide it is time to call it a night. Poppy helps Mona with the futon and hands her a neat pile of clean towels. They are both in their pyjamas and seeing Poppy in her checked nightie, Mona feels a sudden rush as she realises how much she has missed her. How much she misses living with her and sharing moments like these – moments that have long since disappeared into the distance between them.

'Tomorrow we'll show you the real Paris,' Poppy says before they wish each other goodnight.

Poppy is true to her word and it's this that makes Mona fall finally deeply, head over heels in love with the city. In the morning they visit Pain Pain, the local bakery where the staff wear pretty navy-blue uniforms and the cakes look almost too beautiful to eat (almost, because they also look delicious). Antoine buys the three of them a parcel of pastries that are handed to them in a paper bag decorated with gold and navy and that smells to Mona like heaven, even though she usually doesn't let herself indulge in food like this. They eat the pastries walking down the street, crumbs dropping at their feet.

'Do you mind if we quickly do a food shop?' says Poppy, her

arm slung through Antoine's and the sun shining on her smiling face, 'We've both been working late this week so haven't had time. And it's a bit of a Saturday morning tradition.'

Mona doesn't mind at all because their food shop doesn't involve a quick stop at the supermarket – instead they spend the morning hopping from small shop to shop. First, they visit the local greengrocers where the staff greet both Poppy and Antoine by name and Mona listens, impressed, as Poppy chats away in French.

'I'm still not fluent,' she says as they leave, Antoine carrying a canvas tote bag full of fruit and veg, 'But I've definitely picked it up since living here. And Antoine's been teaching me, haven't you, darling?'

She turns to Antoine and Mona watches as he returns a smile full of such love that she suddenly understands why Poppy left London four years ago.

Next, they stop at the butchers, then a shop where Poppy and Antoine carefully pick out their favourite brand of olive oil, and finally the florist, where Antoine buys a bunch of delicate pink blooms that he tucks under his arm. After dropping the shopping back at the flat and arranging the flowers in a vase the three of them head out again, spending the rest of the day wandering around the twisting labyrinth of streets that makes up Montmartre. Occasionally they come to a busier street, noisy with crowds and backpacks, but when this happens Poppy and Antoine lead them off the main path, choosing a smaller road instead. And then the sounds quickly die away and it is as though they have stepped through a door into a completely different city. This city, the city of Poppy and Antoine, feels more like a village than a city. It is the tiny coffee shop they stop in for espressos where there is only room for three tables and a well-stocked bookcase, and where the barista immediately gets chatting to them, Antoine translating the entire conversation for Mona's benefit. It is a dog barking on the roof garden of an old building, a small dog on the street looking around in confusion at the noise. It is white shutters and colourful window boxes. It is a grandfather carrying a baguette in one hand and holding the hand of a small child in a bright yellow jacket in the other, perfectly round red glasses making the child's eyes wide like a puppy's.

Poppy and Antoine show Mona the small cemetery where a fluffy cat presides over the graves, sunbathing on one tombstone before sleepily wandering over to another as if giving each its turn at attention. They point out the beehives and the small vineyard that have sat in this part of the city for generations.

Every now and then the tightly packed buildings break apart for a moment, offering a gap and a view down the hill and across Paris. Each time they stumble across one of these Mona finds herself nearly breathless with the view. She can't quite believe she waited thirty years before seeing it. It is a sunny day and a haze rests over the rooftops of the city. She spots domes and spires and an endless web of those silvery grey roofs. When she first catches a glimpse of the Eiffel Tower she feels the same way she did on spotting the Sacre Coeur for the first time. She knows exactly where she is in the world and it feels a long way away from the crowds at Gare du Nord or that spill out of Liverpool Street station back home in London.

They spend the evening in a wine bar not far from the flat,

sharing a large charcuterie board and a bottle of red wine recommended by the bartender. The bar is small and filled with the glow of candlelight and conversation. It is exactly the kind of bar Mona pictured when she thought of Paris but didn't believe would be quite as perfect. Poppy and Antoine spot friends at a nearby table and they try out their English on Mona, making everyone laugh. At one point her thoughts return to Hannah, realising she hasn't thought about her all day. She wonders if she is OK at home in the flat and whether she should call. But she doesn't. Instead she allows herself another glass of wine, relishing being decadent. She didn't even bring her exercise clothes with her – it is the first weekend in a very long time that she has not worked out and she can feel her body sighing, enjoying the break.

When Mona falls in love with Paris, it is not love at first sight. It grows and strengthens over the weekend so that by the time of her audition on Monday, what started as a frivolous idea has become something much more. She applied for the job on a whim and because she thought it would be a good excuse for a long weekend with Poppy and Antoine, and a chance to escape London. Because she had felt a sudden, urgent need to escape from everything that had been happening in the flat. But as she waits in the corridor of the dance studio it hits her very suddenly that she doesn't want to leave. She doesn't want to say goodbye to the pretty streets dotted with bakeries and cafés, or those views that make her stop still and simply stare. When she first moved to London she had those moments, but she knows it so well now that it's as though she doesn't always see everything any more. After twelve years she has stopped noticing quite so much. She misses that feeling of truly taking in every single detail, the way she has this weekend.

As she waits for her audition her mind drifts to Hannah and their flat together in Haggerston. Normally those are thoughts that would make her smile, that would calm her before an audition. But recently, something has changed. She isn't even sure if Hannah has noticed it, but it is there, a shift in things. It isn't the same as it was before. Mona hasn't decided yet whether she even wants to get back to how it was; whether she wants to get back to her friend. That thought frightens her, so she pushes it from her mind and thinks instead about dancing. She is going to dance better than she has ever danced in her life.

*

Mona is usually the last to admit it, but even she could tell that that first audition went well. She could feel that her body had done exactly what she had wanted it to and more – it had added its own extra quality that she couldn't exactly explain.

Despite it all, dancing hadn't come naturally to her at first. She loved to dance as a child, but she was always taller than the other girls and often felt as graceful as a young giraffe in tights. She might have given up if it wasn't for her first dance teacher in Singapore. Ms Lake was in her fifties, with an elegance to every movement even when she wasn't teaching a step, or wasn't even in the dance studio. You could tell just from watching her reach for something on a supermarket shelf (she lived in the same complex as Mona so they often bumped into each other) or turn her key in her car door or brush hair away from her face, that she was a dancer. She was also tall – five foot ten.

'Do you love dancing?' she asked Mona one session, when Mona was lingering behind, practising in the mirror while the other girls untied their shoes on the benches.

Mona nodded, looking up at the elegant woman who towered over her.

'Then if you love it the most, you have to practice the most,' Ms Lake said, 'You have to practice more than anyone else. It's not fair, I know, but that's just the way it is. You might not have been born a dancer, but that doesn't mean you can't become one. That's what I did.'

So that's what Mona did. At university she made a point of working harder than all the other girls in her class, not out of a sense of competition with them, but because she felt she needed to in order to keep up. She went in each day more than an hour before her classes began; the caretaker left the key to a studio for her on a hook in the corridor so she could practice in the space before anyone arrived. Once, one of her teachers, Zoe, who wasn't much older than she was, found out about these early starts and tried to persuade her to come in a little later. But Mona had been insistent. Eventually they came to a compromise. Instead of coming in at seven every morning, for the rest of her time at dance school Mona arrived at 7.15.

Mona has been practising and pushing herself for over a decade and finally she has got a break. The job is perfect – it's what she has been hoping for but didn't quite believe she could pull off, especially not at this stage in her career and in her life. And yet she doesn't feel the all-consuming happiness that she knows she should. She wipes behind the coffee bar, scrubbing at some spilt coffee grounds and wishing that things were different.

2.00 P.M.

MONA

Eleanor is busy serving a large group of office workers, splitting the bill between the ten or so of them, so when Mona spots the group of older women looking in her direction, politely raising their heads and eyebrows as though trying to get her attention without disturbing her, she leaves the counter and heads across the café.

'Sorry for the delay,' she says, 'Are you ready to pay?'

'Yes, we are, thank you love,' says one of the women, who wears a checked shirt and jeans and reaches into a bright yellow shopping bag for her purse. Before she can draw it out, one of the other women, in a navy striped top with a pearl necklace resting on her collarbones, puts a hand out and grabs her arm.

'No, Joan, I'm getting this.'

The first woman shakes her head and struggles to reach into her bag again.

'No, Cynthia, let me.'

'Oh, hold on there a minute,' says the third woman, her hair dyed bright pink and her expression mock stern, 'No you don't, this is on me!'

The three women look back and forth at each other, all reaching for their purses.

'I can split it three ways if you like?' offers Mona.

'That would be—' begins Cynthia, but the woman with the pink hair interrupts, thrusting her card towards Mona.

'Quick! Take it!'

She bats away the two other women and Mona smiles and accepts the card, slotting it into the machine.

'Wait …' says Cynthia.

'But …!' says Joan.

'Too late!' says the pink-haired lady, punching her pin into the machine with such vigour that Mona has to grip it with two hands.

'Oh, thank you Barbara.'

'Barbara, you shouldn't have.'

'My pleasure,' says Barbara, brushing a strand of pink hair away from her face and briskly returning her card to her purse.

'There,' she says, 'I'm glad that's all settled then. Such a fuss!'

The women turn back to Mona now and smile.

'Lovely coffee, thank you, dear,' says Joan. Mona doesn't tell her that it was probably Eleanor who made her coffee, or that if it was her, she made it in such a daze that she has no idea if it really was any good.

'And tell your chef the Eggs Royale were top notch,' adds Cynthia, 'In so many places nowadays they don't know how to properly poach an egg. But this was perfect, nice and runny. No point in a poached egg that isn't runny, is there? You might as well go hard-boiled!'

She laughs slightly as she says this and her two friends meet eyes and each raise an eyebrow.

'She's prone to hysterics, our Cynthia,' says Barbara.

'Gets all boiled up over a poached egg,' adds Joan.

The three of them look at each other and this time they all laugh.

'This young woman must think we're mad!' says Joan, wiping her eyes.

'She'd be right there,' says Barbara.

Despite her mood, Mona finds herself smiling at these three women. They make her think of elderly sisters, bickering and joking with each other, although they look much too dissimilar to be related. As she ponders how they know each other, they stand, shrugging coats onto their shoulders and lifting handbags.

'Until next week!' says the woman with the pink hair.

Mona lifts a hand in a wave as the three women turn for the door.

Knowing they will be back makes Mona smile, but then she stops. She might not be here next week. The thought jolts her and she finds her eyes wandering up to Ernest the bear, meeting his familiar glassy stare. There have been many times over the years when she has wished she wasn't coming back to the café, and that she could spend all day doing the thing she loves instead of making coffees and wiping tables. But she is pragmatic, too and has always understood that the coffees are what allow her the time and freedom to dance. And this job is so much better than others she did in the past when she was younger. There was a stint as a receptionist at an architecture firm when she was twenty-one, but she left when one of the directors forcibly kissed her in the lift one evening. She had been working late and he followed her into the lift and pushed his body against hers so quickly she didn't have time to react, his wedding ring glinting in the glare of the lights as he pressed his hands on either side of her. He was well-liked in the company, a mentor to many of the younger members of staff, and she hadn't worked there long. She knew they wouldn't believe her. So she left. She tried another receptionist job but found sitting down all day made her restless – her feet tapped beneath the desk and her limbs grew stiff and heavy. At least at the café she can spend most of the time standing. Although it can be tiring it is worth it; she feels better when she is moving and during each shift she crosses the café so many times that she loses count.

Mona scoops up the coins left as a tip on the women's table and returns to the counter. As she does so she notices for the first time the yellow Post-it note attached to the top of the till. Seeing Hannah's looped handwriting, she feels a jolt of emotion, but she tries to shake it off as she reads on.

MONA, keep a lookout for a young (20ish?) man, longish blond hair, slight beard, green hoody, large rucksack. IMPORTANT envelope for him in lost property. Love, H x

Mona crouches and reaches for the lost property box. It is a mess of assorted items, including the single glove she remembers finding on the floor yesterday and a set of keys that she has spent many idle moments wondering about. She spots a large brown envelope and picks it up, curious to see what is inside, but it is sealed. She gives it a shake (it feels like a book) then returns it to the box.

Her phone buzzes in her apron pocket and she checks quickly that no customers are waiting before reaching for it.

'Have you told Hannah?' reads the message from Poppy.

She sighs without meaning to, the earlier argument replaying in her mind. '*Bonne fucking chance*,' she hears Hannah saying loudly as she turns and walks away, her face damp with tears.

'Yes,' replies Mona, 'She didn't take it well.'

She doesn't feel in the mood to elaborate.

'You guys will work it out,' replies Poppy, 'You two are like that.' At the end of the message is a crossed-fingers emoji. Not for the first time, Mona thinks back to moving in to the house in Bounds Green with Poppy, Hannah and the others, and wonders if Poppy ever minded how quickly she and Hannah became inseparable. She knows that they did invite her to dinners and cinema trips together to begin with, but she also remembers it quite quickly becoming just the two of them. Hannah and Mona. As their rooms were opposite each other's they spent a lot of time in and out of each other's rooms, talking and giving each other encouragement and advice about upcoming auditions or jobs. Did Poppy ever feel left out? If she did, she never showed it. Mona suddenly feels even more grateful to her for letting her stay with her in Paris.

Knowing she has a sofa to sleep on and at least one friend in the city makes the upcoming move more manageable.

'Not so sure,' replies Mona, 'It was a bad fight.'

Will they work things out? And does she even want to? Mona still isn't sure, her head still spinning from the words that Hannah threw at her and that she shouted in response.

A series of dots blink on the screen, indicating that Poppy is typing. But then they disappear. Mona guesses that Poppy doesn't know what to say and isn't surprised – Mona doesn't know how to fix things either.

She returns her phone to her pocket and reads the Post-it note one last time, fixing the description of the young man in her head so that she will recognise him if he comes in. She gives a cursory look around the café, looking out for a flash of green, but he is not here. Instead her eyes fall on the woman with the engagement ring who is still sat by the window, flicking through her scrapbook absentmindedly. Mona catches glimpses of flowers, cakes and bunting.

Mona stands beneath the shadow of Ernest the bear, looking around at the pictures she knows as well as if they hung in her own home. In the kitchen she can hear Aleksander talking to himself in a low stream of Polish – a habit of his that she is so used to by now that it is almost comforting. It joins the other noises of the café that she knows so well. A pan sizzling, a customer laughing and *The Breakfast Club* soundtrack on the speakers above switching to 'We Are Not Alone'.

As she listens to the song her heart aches. Because she knows what it feels like to feel alone, even when she is with her closest friend. Over the past year she has learnt that's the kind of loneliness that hurts the most.

*

She wants to like Jaheim, she really does. At least that's what Mona tells herself.

When Hannah and Jaheim first start dating, Mona enjoys hearing about the dates and helping Hannah construct replies to his messages ('Don't reply straight away, keep it cool.') They laugh at each other for obsessing so much, but they do it anyway. She presses Hannah for more details when she describes their first kiss – she wants to know everything. But very quickly, something changes. Jaheim starts appearing in the flat more, his large brogues placed neatly by the front mat letting Mona know when he is there, and when not to charge straight into Hannah's room if the door is closed. When he is over, the door is closed much more often than it is open. Hannah becomes distracted when she and Mona spend time together, as though she is not always really listening to what Mona is saying. Hannah stops talking to Mona quite so much about her work, the thing that they used to spend hours discussing together, and instead talks mainly about Jaheim and their plans together. The change surprises Mona – she has always thought of Hannah as incredibly independent and self-sufficient. And Hannah has talked to Mona about her past relationship with Sam; Mona is surprised that this experience hasn't made her more guarded. But with Jaheim Hannah doesn't seem at all guarded, instead she gives all of herself to him readily. Perhaps it's this power imbalance that makes Mona so uncomfortable; although Jaheim is sweet and affectionate with Hannah, Mona gets the impression that Hannah needs him far more than he needs her. She is worried about her friend and where this might be heading but doesn't feel she can say anything. The not-saying sits as an empty space between them, unsaid words pulling them slowly a little further apart.

One evening about two months after Hannah and Jaheim have started dating, Mona invites Hannah to a show she has been rehearsing for and there is Jaheim too, sat next to Hannah on one of the small fold-out chairs in the community theatre. Afterwards, the three of them go for beers in a nearby pub and as she watches Hannah and Jaheim sitting close together in the booth opposite her, Mona tries to remember whether she'd invited Jaheim herself. She can't remember but hopes that she did. Of course she should have invited him, she thinks, it just doesn't come naturally yet – her first thought leaps to Hannah (as long as she is there, it doesn't matter how small an audience is) but she hasn't adjusted to factoring him in too. She is so used to it just being the two of them.

Later that evening, when Hannah and Mona are alone again (Jaheim has an early start at work so has returned to his own flat, which is much closer to his office) Mona pours them both a cup of tea, which they drink on the floor of Hannah's room, leant against her bed. They are both wearing their pyjamas; Mona has wiped the stage make-up from her face and has her hair tied up in a messy bun, a headband pushing loose strands away from her forehead. Beside her, Hannah plays with a bracelet on her wrist.

'I hope you don't mind that Jaheim came,' says Hannah after a while.

Mona turns to her quickly. So she didn't invite him, then. She curses herself silently, wishing she'd remembered and that it wasn't such an effort to try to remember.

'Of course it was OK,' says Mona, trying to sound cheerful, 'You know he's always welcome.'

Hannah looks down at her tea.

'Is he?' she says, 'Only, sometimes I feel like you don't like him.'

Mona feels her stomach dropping. She thought she had hidden her feelings well – she always tries to make an effort to chat to Jaheim about his work when he visits and to ask after him. But sometimes she forgets, still not used to him. She is not used to his brogues by the front door, or to seeing Hannah's bedroom door closed, or to the way Hannah often looks at her phone now when they are talking, as though she isn't entirely there – a part of her always being with him. And although Jaheim is perfectly nice – chatty, smiley and good looking – there is something about him that makes Mona uneasy. Hannah has so quickly become obsessed by him and there's something that makes Mona think he enjoys this – that he likes the devotion.

'I do like him!' Mona says quickly, realising she sounds defensive without meaning to.

'It doesn't always seem that way.' Hannah holds her tea in one hand; with the other she wraps a long lock of her hair around her finger and twists it round and round – a habit that Mona knows comes out when she is nervous.

'I'm sorry you feel that way,' Mona replies, trying to make her voice sound calm, 'Because I do like him. And I'm just so happy that you're happy.'

They are silent for a moment.

It seems too petty to admit that, aged twenty-nine, she is jealous. But she is, it's a feeling she hadn't expected and can't control. She is not jealous because of Jaheim (perhaps fortunately, Hannah and Mona share many things but not a taste in men) but of how much time he spends with Hannah, time that used to be hers – theirs. Two or three nights a week Hannah stays at Jaheim's, meaning Mona has the flat to herself. At first she enjoyed the freedom – on those nights she walked around in her underwear and had a bath with the door open, her laptop propped on a stool in the doorway while she binge-watched her favourite German dramas on catch-up until the water turned cold. But the tiny flat quickly came to seem too big without Hannah there. She knows that this time was bound to come – that one of them would find a boyfriend eventually, especially when so many of their other friends are already married – but she had enjoyed things the way they were, the two of them single and pursuing similar careers, sharing setbacks and spurring each other on. That had been the dynamic of their home, but now things have changed.

'Well I am happy,' says Hannah, finishing her tea and placing the mug on the floor, stretching her arms out in front of her, 'I don't think I've ever been this happy.'

Mona flinches. What about the surprise party that she threw for Hannah's twenty-eighth birthday? Their friends hid in the dark in their flat and when the lights came on Hannah stepped back in shock as she saw them all wearing masks that Mona *had got printed of her face: a whole crowd of Hannahs dressed in rainbow shades in honour of their friend. Or the time they stayed late at a pub after one of Hannah's gigs, getting locked in with the bar staff until the early hours of the morning: impromptu karaoke and Mona relenting and tap dancing giddily on the bar to the sound of Hannah's delighted cheers. A summer day trip to Hampstead Heath when they both had a day off and where they swam in the murky Kenwood Ladies' Pond beneath the trees and then lay in the meadow among groups of female friends, sunbathing topless and reading magazines. Falling asleep to the sound of splashing and quiet conversation, saying sleepily to each other that nothing in life could get much better than this.*

She knows it's different – that being in love is different to anything else in the world, but the reduction of all their shared memories as something 'before' this new happiness still sends an ache shooting across Mona's stomach and up towards her chest.

'If you're happy, I'm happy,' she says.

'OK,' says Hannah.

They say goodnight and Mona pads back to her own room, shutting the door and listening to the quiet shuffle and creak as Hannah climbs into bed.

*

The more intense Hannah's relationship with Jaheim became, the more Mona felt the distance growing between her and her friend. Many times she tried to bring it up, but she felt petty and embarrassed to express her feelings and besides, Hannah was so absorbed by Jaheim and her new love for him that Mona didn't think Hannah would hear her if she did say anything. Mona was used to Hannah being late and usually turned up late for dinners with her too, knowing Hannah would never be on time. But one evening when they'd planned to have dinner together at a favourite restaurant of theirs close to their flat, Hannah turned up an hour late, saying simply that she and Jaheim had lost track of the time. She had been apologetic and had bought dinner for the both of them, but she didn't promise it wouldn't happen again. Mona also noticed that since Jaheim had been on the scene, Hannah was spending less time practising her guitar and singing – something she used to do every day. It worried Mona, knowing how much music meant to Hannah. Could she really be happy without it? Mona couldn't help but feel that the giddy state of bliss Hannah seemed to be in since meeting Jaheim couldn't last, and wasn't a healthy kind of happiness, because it meant changing and suppressing parts of herself, like her drive and her passion for her career.

Over the months there had been moments when it felt like how it used to be between them. Like the New Year's Eve party that Hannah and Mona threw together. They invited their old housemates and mutual friends and the flat was bright and warm with laughter and energy. Jaheim was there too but left early as it was his best friend's birthday and he had another party to go to. Hannah had wanted to leave with him, but by then she was tipsy and he insisted that she stay in the flat. Hannah had sulked for a while after he left, but eventually she seemed to forget about him and instead got caught up in the music and the atmosphere. She and Mona danced together with their old friends, smiling and giggling and cheering in the new year, hugging each other tightly. In that moment it had felt to Mona as though she'd got her friend back. But the next day things had changed.

Mona had woken up in Hannah's bed where she had collapsed the night before, too drunk and tired to go to her own room. She woke to see Hannah slipping out of bed to take a phone call. Mona had thought it was Jaheim, but it wasn't. It was Hannah's mother, calling to tell her that Hannah's grandmother had died. Mona remembers how Hannah broke down in tears as soon as she was off the phone. Mona immediately rushed to hug her, a hangover pounding her head and nausea making her want to wobble but her arms tight and strong around her friend. She made tea and cooked them both bacon sandwiches for breakfast. She listened as Hannah half talked and half sobbed, telling Mona stories about her grandmother. She chose Disney films for them to watch in bed together and carried snacks into Hannah's room that she arranged on the duvet.

Later, in the afternoon, Mona left Hannah in front of the screen and headed into the kitchen to call Stella and tell her what had happened. She didn't want Hannah to have to worry about work. Stella told her Hannah could have all the time off that she needed.

'And I expect you'll want to go to the funeral too?' she said. Mona didn't even think before replying.

'Yes, of course.' Stella agreed to let her have time off too as soon as she knew the date of the funeral.

As Mona had stepped back into the room she saw Hannah

out on the balcony, talking on the phone. She couldn't hear her through the glass so sat back on the bed and waited, until Hannah eventually hung up the phone and stepped back inside, bringing a rush of cold air in with her.

'That was Jaheim,' she said. '*Finally,*' Mona wanted to say, but she didn't. He hadn't replied to Hannah's text or calls and she had been checking her phone obsessively all day, so much so that Mona had wanted to take her phone away from her. Instead of asking why Jaheim had left it so late to call, Mona told Hannah about the conversation she'd had with Stella. But it seemed that she had been too hasty in saying that of course she would go to the funeral. Because Hannah didn't want her there in the end. She wanted Jaheim instead. Perhaps it shouldn't have come as a surprise, but it had, because up until then the two of them had been each other's support. And Mona felt sad for her friend – she wanted to be there for her and to help her through it. Not being able to support her made her feel at a loss, like she wasn't needed or wanted any more. Mona realised in one crushing moment that the feelings she had experienced at the party had been misplaced. Hannah hadn't come back to her. In fact, she'd never been further away.

Back in the café Mona shudders slightly, remembering. Throughout the months that Jaheim and Hannah dated, Mona never thought that Hannah noticed the distance growing between them. When she and Jaheim broke up three weeks ago, Mona had wondered if things would change – whether Hannah would suddenly realise the way she had acted and the strain it had put on their friendship and say something

241

to Mona – apologise even. But Mona felt as though she had instead simply brushed things under the carpet, covering up their problems by being overly cheerful and pretending things were as they had always been. Maybe that's what Mona should do too but she suddenly finds that she can't – the hurt that has been caused over the past year has left its mark and the argument earlier has only made things even worse.

In the café, conversation drifts around Mona like snow but doesn't settle on her. She watches unnoticed, separate from the customers and their shared looks and words that she will never really be privy to, lives she will never really fully understand. And in turn, she thinks how little they know about the turmoil going on inside of her.

It hits her that soon she won't even work here any more, but these conversations, these cheesy songs and everything else in this café will carry on without her as though she never existed. And with a stab of pain she suddenly wonders whether Hannah will do the same.

SONJA

She takes another sip from her milkshake, imagining the fat bubbling up to her face. *Let it*, she thinks as she drinks. The coffee machine hisses at the bar, but behind the noise she suddenly hears a familiar tune. She sits up slightly, as though this will somehow quieten the noise of the machine and tries to pick out the words. For a moment it is a vague blur of hissing and chatter and a voice that she can't make out but that sparks something inside of her. Then the machine stops and she hears Van Morrison singing 'Have I told you lately . . .'

She immediately thinks of her mum and dad. It's their favourite song. Even her dad, a gruff former builder with tough hands but a soft heart, hums along when he hears it, his eyes growing misty. She remembers coming down the stairs one night when she was a child and couldn't sleep, and seeing her parents dancing to the song in the living room. They held each other tightly, her mother's head resting on her father's chest, his arms around her waist, hers around his shoulders. She watched them for a while, thinking that they would soon spot her by the door and ask her why she was up so late and whether she was OK. They might make her a cup of hot milk and carry her up to bed. But they didn't. They didn't notice her at all.

As she watched them dancing to the song a thought came suddenly into her head: that her parents existed before she came into the world. That there had been a time when she wasn't even as much as a wish, and they existed happily like this: just the two of them. At the time, the thought frightened her and she tiptoed back up the stairs and tucked herself silently into bed. But as she grew older and listened to more and more friends talk about their parents' divorces, she looked back fondly on that scene. She realised how lucky she was to have grown up as a witness to love like that.

When she and Timur told her parents they were engaged, both her parents welled up. Her father stood up to head to the nearest shop to buy champagne. Timur went with him, offering to keep him company and also to drive (her dad's hands were shaking).

243

While they were gone, Sonja's mother moved next to her on the sofa and took Sonja's hands, holding them and placing them on her lap.

'I hope marriage brings you everything it has given me,' she said to her, 'You have chosen a kind man. We are both lucky to have kind men. Just remember to always be kind to each other and everything will be OK. That's all that matters. I'm so proud of you, sweetheart.'

And her mum had hugged her tightly and Sonja had felt suddenly part of a club where the only rule was kindness. Nothing else mattered.

Sonja looks down at a small puddle of water on the table and realises she is crying. She can feel her make-up dripping down her cheeks, but she is smiling. She laughs a little, oblivious to the people at the table next to her giving her a strange look.

Wiping her face, she reaches for her phone and dials the number she knows by heart. When the phone is answered she speaks quickly and confidently. She has made up her mind.

'Mum, how many people do you think you can fit in the conservatory? And where do you think we can get eighty pairs of wellies?'

MONA

'Looks like the rain has stopped,' Mona says as she waits for the card machine to print a receipt for the woman with the scrapbook. She gestures out the café window where a small glimmer of sunshine breaks through the purple clouds and glints on the office buildings. It has been a strange day – rainy, then cloudy, then sunny, as though the weather can't make up its mind. The turbulent, changing skies match Mona's mood.

'Oh, I'm sure it will be back soon,' says the woman, her empty milkshake glass catching in the light. She smiles when she says it, though, and Mona notices how much happier she looks now than when she first came in the café.

'I'm getting married this weekend,' she adds as Mona returns her card, and the receipt. She looks up at Mona, smiling.

'Oh, congratulations,' says Mona, 'I hope the weather improves for you!'

The woman shakes her head and stands, hanging her coat over her arm.

'I don't think it will,' she says, 'But that doesn't really matter, does it?'

The woman's calm surprises Mona. She remembers friends going nearly mad planning their weddings, putting so much pressure on themselves to create the perfect day that when their wedding photos came back, they looked pinched and tense against a backdrop of laughing, drunken guests.

'Yes, I suppose you're right,' she replies, 'Have a great day, anyway.'

With a light step the woman turns and leaves, swinging her umbrella slightly by her side as she turns down Liverpool Street and Mona loses the shape of her in the crowd. Mona smiles and for a very brief moment she forgets everything else, warmed by the stranger's happiness.

3.00 P.M.

MONA

The lunchtime rush finally over, the café is now quiet. Several freelancers, identifiable by their shining MacBooks and the coffees that they drink very slowly, sit alone at tables throughout the café.

'What's the Wi-Fi password?' asks one, a man in his thirties with floppy black hair and black glasses, a mustard yellow corduroy shirt open over a white T-shirt. Mona directs him to the back of the menu where the code is printed in a small box. The sound of tapping keyboards merges with the music and the noise of the coffee machine: the café's soundtrack.

Otherwise, the café is nearly empty and as she glances outside, Mona notices the street is quiet too, workers having returned to their offices.

Eleanor finishes clearing a table and joins Mona at the

counter – it is the first moment they have had to properly speak to one another since Mona arrived on her shift. She feels suddenly awkward, embarrassed by the fight earlier and unsure what to say to the younger member of staff. They don't know each other well, despite sharing shifts together. They are usually too busy working alongside one another to properly chat. But Eleanor is smiling at her.

'Well done about the job,' she says, twisting a cloth in her hand.

'Thanks,' replies Mona, 'I didn't mean for you to find out that way. But you saw how Hannah reacted.'

She realises she sounds defensive but doesn't know how to stop herself – she doesn't want to admit to Eleanor how upset she feels.

'It sounds like a great opportunity,' continues Eleanor. 'I've always wanted to live in Paris.'

'I still can't quite believe it really,' Mona admits, softening a little, 'It's all so sudden. I only found out this morning – I haven't even told my family yet ...'

She trails off, wondering what her parents will say when she eventually manages to get hold of them. It's been several weeks, maybe a month since she last spoke to either of them on the phone. She can't remember exactly.

Eleanor looks up at the clock and then back at Mona.

'Sofia should be here soon to take over from me. Why don't you take a quick break before she gets here so you can call them?'

Mona blinks quickly, surprised and touched by Eleanor's gesture.

'Are you sure that's OK?' she says, warily, unsure whether she should leave Eleanor alone in the café. 'I wouldn't be long.'

'Yeah, it's fine,' replies Eleanor, 'It's quiet now, anyway. I can manage.'

Mona nods, says another thank you and then slips into the storeroom at the back, shutting out the sounds of the café behind her. The small, messy space always makes her stressed – there are boxes everywhere and she wishes that Stella would instil some sense of order in the room, or at least let Mona do it for her. She has offered many times, but Stella always tells her it's not something for her to worry about. But it is, when she feels that the boxes might tumble down on her and it adds to her overall feelings of anxiety. She sits down on the chair in the middle of the room, kicking away a dropped tissue on the floor and pushing a few boxes aside so she feels like she has a little more room to breathe. Then she takes her phone out to call her parents.

Her mother doesn't answer. Mona leaves a message, asking her to call her back. The phone rings for a long time before her father picks up.

'Hi Mona,' he says, the sound of fingers typing in the background, 'How are you honey?'

The typing continues and Mona pictures her father in his office in their apartment in Buenos Aries, the phone on speaker phone on the table or pressed against his ear as he types an email to a colleague. She can see the late morning sunlight streaming through the window, catching on the glass of the framed photographs of Matías and Camila, Mona's stepmother, that cover his office wall.

'I'm good thanks, Dad,' she says, her voice cool. With her foot she pushes a box that had been jutting out at an angle, straightening it.

'I've got some news,' she says.

'Thanks, sweetheart,' her father replies.

'Thanks for what?' Mona asks, her eyebrows meeting in a frown.

'Not you, honey,' her father says, the typing continuing again, 'I was talking to Camila, she just brought me a cup of tea – she's working from home today too. She's got a big pitch coming up – new potential clients – it could be a real game changer for her business.'

'That's great,' says Mona. 'Wish her luck from me. What I was going to say though, Dad …'

She tries to ignore the sound of typing in the background and the feeling that her father isn't really listening to what she has to say.

'Did I tell you that Matías has a try-out for the first team?' her father interrupts. 'There's a local junior scout. His coach thinks he has real potential. Ever since he was a baby I've said he's been a natural with a ball. Well, maybe not a baby but a toddler …'

'That's great, Dad,' Mona says again, taking deep breaths. She knows it shouldn't bother her, but her father has never described her as a natural dancer and the casualness of the words hit her in a deeply buried place within her. This is why she hasn't spoken to her father in a month. Because the conversations always go like this and she finds herself growing angry without meaning to, her hands clenching and unclenching on her lap.

'Well, the thing is,' she perseveres, 'I had this big audition for a job with a dance company in Paris. It's a really amazing opportunity and they offered me the job so I'm going to be moving to Paris in a couple of weeks. I know Camila's never been to Paris before so if you ever wanted to come over ... I mean, I'm going to be sharing with friends to begin with and then I'll probably only have a tiny room or apartment, but I could certainly show you around ...'

She trails off, ashamed at the hesitance in her voice. This is not her, she thinks as she hears her own words ringing in her head. She is calm and composed and self-reliant. She is thirty years old, has lived independently since she was eighteen and has just secured her dream job. And yet she is also a gangly eleven-year-old in a ballet outfit, deciding she wants to be a dancer and desperately seeking her parents' approval. Dancing harder and practising longer in the vain hope that the grades, the shows and the awards might make her parents proud and might stop them fighting. Perhaps if she could make them proud enough, they might remember that they loved her, and each other.

Mona swallows hard, remembering. Things have changed now, she tells herself. She is grown up. And yet she still listens to the brief silence on the end of the phone, waiting for the words she doubts she will hear but has not quite stopped hoping for.

'A dance job!' says her father, 'Wow! I was asking Camila just the other day when she thought the cut-off point for dancers was – you know, you don't see so many forty-year-old ballerinas, do you? Not sure we'll be able to make it to Paris though, honey, it's a really busy time for Camila's business, and the university has me teaching extra classes, and with Matías maybe getting his big break ...'

Mona breathes deeply, wondering whether a thirteen-year-old can really get a 'big break'. She is thirty years old and has been waiting for this break her whole life.

'But you'll come here next summer, won't you?' says her father.

As Mona looks around the messy storeroom and listens to the tapping of her father's keyboard, she sees herself through fresh eyes – about to agree to a trip she does every couple of years out of a sense of duty, but that never makes her happy. Why has she spent so much of her limited time and money on trips to Argentina, when she long ago realised any connection she'd once had to her father had long since broken? She should have been going on adventures – taking those weekend trips to Europe that she always dreamt of. And why is she still waiting for her parents to tell her they are proud of her?

As she thinks it, she remembers the fight with Hannah and how desperately she wanted her to congratulate her and tell her she was proud. Since they have been friends, Hannah has always been understanding about Mona's less than perfect relationship with her parents, listening to her and letting her rant after a particularly difficult phone conversation or after returning from a disappointing visit. She might not have always understood completely, her parents having been together all her life, but she always listened and always, always had Mona's corner.

And Mona suddenly realises why she needed the reassurance

251

of her friend so much – because over the years Hannah has become not just like a friend, but like family. The family that Mona has chosen for herself.

'I'm not sure I'll have time actually this year, what with the new job,' says Mona, 'Anyway, I've got to go now.'

And for the first time, she hangs up the phone, not waiting for a reply. In the storeroom she breathes out deeply and drops the phone into her apron pocket. Then she stands up and starts to tidy. Carefully, she straightens the boxes that are scattered on the floor until they are stacked in neat piles, a bigger space cleared around the two chairs in the middle of the room. She moves boxes of food and drink (spare sauces, coffee beans) to one side of the room, and puts extra paper cups and lids, napkins and receipt rolls on the other. Everything is done quickly; she hauls boxes that make her arms ache and frantically wipes the dusty surface of the shelf on one side of the room with the corner of her apron. Once the room is in some sort of order and she is out of breath from the sudden burst of activity, she pauses, resting her hands on the back of a chair. Her thoughts on her family, she suddenly thinks how much she has sacrificed to get to this point. She has always felt it is partly her fault that she doesn't have a closer relationship with her parents, because she chose to move so far away. Her father left for Argentina first, of course, but she could have split her time between the two countries, spending more holidays in Argentina and watching Matías grow up. Although she saves up and visits every two years, she can never afford to stay for long and has never formed a close relationship with her half-brother. And her mother ... She checks her phone again but there are no messages or missed calls, no acknowledgement that she has received Mona's message. Mona tells herself that she is teaching and can't get to her phone. Whether it's the truth or not, Mona blames herself for the distance between her and her family, because she has always put the pursuit of her career above everything else.

And that's when she thinks of Lucas. It has been a long time since she last thought about him, but suddenly he is there in the stuffy storeroom, the sound of his voice, last heard twelve years ago, remembered as clearly as if he were standing next to her.

He was her first boyfriend, and even though there have been plenty of fleeting encounters since, she knows that he is the only man she has ever really loved. He was the son of a friend of her mother's in Singapore. They started dating when they were fifteen and stayed together until Mona left for London. Thinking of him now, memories come back in snippets like flashes of sunlight through a crack in a wall. Tiny slivers of wood shavings caught in the thick hair in his forearms (he was training to be a carpenter); his older sister's twenty-first birthday party, how she let Mona get ready with her in her room, lending her a lipstick the colour of squashed berries; the wooden box he made her for their two-year anniversary and filled with her favourite things – her favourite sweets, a pair of cashmere socks she had wanted, a limited-edition copy of her favourite book.

Mona suddenly wonders what happened to that box. She didn't take it with her to London and tries to think what her mother might have done to it when she left Singapore for

Germany. She likes to think her mother might have kept it, but even as she thinks it she knows it isn't true.

*

'Don't you love me?' says Lucas, his knees tucked under his chin as they sit side by side beneath the window in his bedroom, the blinds pulled down against the heat, a thin sliver of sunbeam falling in a line between them. It is a week before Mona is due to leave for London, her place at dance college confirmed, her accommodation organised, her bags nearly packed. She looks around the room, taking in every detail. She knows the specific messy order of his room well, like a periodic table learnt by heart: on first view completely disorientating, but on learning its details, making complete sense.

A desk covered in tools and half-finished pieces of woodwork, seemingly haphazardly scattered, but actually arranged by project, the tools and materials for each one separated in individual piles. Makeshift bedside table formed from a pile of stacked books (The Time of the Hero; The Motorcycle Diaries; Lord of the Rings; Star Wars: Complete Locations; Modern Carpentry: A Practical Journal)*, an Anglepoise lamp resting on top. Bed with sheets unmade, the colourful blanket made by his grandmother half trailing onto the floor (Mona recalls kicking it off their feet in the night many times, too warm from the heat and from each other). Clothes flung over the end of the bed but arranged by item: T-shirts and shirts in one pile, shorts and trousers in another.*

'Of course I love you,' she says. She wants to reach for his hand but they are held tightly together across his knees.

'Then why are you leaving?' he says.

It is a conversation they have had many times before, ever since Mona told him her dream was to study dance in London and to perform in the West End. She has heard stories of it from her mother, who lived there for a while before she was married, and her dance teacher, who danced there when she was young. It is something she has wanted for a long time, so they have been having this conversation throughout the duration of their relationship. But it always seemed something distant, unbelievable somehow. Sometimes in the past he had even teased her about it, whispering to her that she would never really be able to leave him, as he touched her beneath the sheets in his bed, a pillow between her teeth to keep from making any noise and their ears both alert to the sound of the front door clicking and his mother returning home from the market.

But then time seemed to speed up and suddenly she is leaving next week, and the conversation has become serious and desperate.

'You know this,' she says gently, 'We've talked about it so many times. This is what I have to do. It's what I've always wanted to do. It's my dream.'

She can feel the warmth of him next to her although they are not touching – the heat of their bodies reaching out to each other where nothing else can. She looks straight ahead but can see every detail of him without looking.

'I know,' he says after a while, the noises of the apartment (cooking in the kitchen, his sisters shouting at each other) filling their pauses, 'I just wish your dream involved me.'

When the day actually comes, she doesn't know how she will

leave him. Once she has said that final goodbye, she has decided she will just have to walk away and not turn around to look back. If she looks back at him, she might not go. And she has to leave. Even though her heart aches as badly as throbbing toothache at the thought of leaving him, she knows she cannot stay here. She could still dance here, but there is more to it than that: she needs to go out on her own, to do something entirely for herself. She loves Lucas, but if she stays she knows she will live his life, not hers.

'You're going to make someone an amazing husband one day,' she says quietly. Because even though he is only eighteen, still a boy really, she knows him, and she knows the man he is going to become. A quick temper but a soft heart. A tendency to withdraw inside himself when he is truly upset, focusing all his energy on his woodworking, and needing to be coaxed with the offer of affection and home-made food in order to be brought back to himself again. Fiercely protective of his family, with a particular softness for his youngest sister, which he tries to hide but which is obvious to the whole family. This softness will be the same softness he shows for his own children. He will cry at their school performances and cheer louder than any of the other parents. Handmade beds and bookshelves; a garage on the side of the house converted into a carpenter's workshop. Thoughtful, handcrafted gifts for every anniversary.

'I wish it could be with you,' he says.

'So do I', she wants to say, but she can't, because she does and she doesn't and it is too hard to explain.

Instead silence, and then the sudden crash as one of his sisters slams their bedroom door. Footsteps, and soft attempts *at apology and reconciliation against a keyhole. The smell of cooking rice rising from the kitchen. Sunlight catching a curled flake of wood on the floor, making it flash bright white.*

'I'm going to miss you,' she says, leaning her head against his shoulder. He doesn't move her away.

She will miss lying with her head on his stomach in the shade of his room as they both read; meeting him after college and riding back to his house on the back of his scooter, her arms wrapped tightly against his stomach; eating dinner with his family, everyone talking over everyone and leaning to reach for the water or the salad and bickering with her as though she is part of the family; sitting in his room exactly like this, side by side but completely tuned to each other, somehow in sync without having to talk.

'I won't ever love anyone else like I love you,' he says quietly.

She says nothing. Because she knows he will. And it breaks her heart. But despite it all, she cannot resist the calling to get away and to build her own life. It is louder than anything, even the sound of his breath catching as he starts to cry, even her own sob as she breaks down and cries too, even the sound of their lips meeting as they kiss, even the crazed beating of her heart that echoes in her ears.

*

Mona steadies herself against the back of the chair, surrounded by boxes and silence. She has never told Hannah, but this is one of the reasons why Hannah's obsession with Jaheim was so hard for Mona to understand. Because Mona knows what it feels like to be in love, but she also knows that the choice she made back when she was eighteen was the right one, however hard it felt at the time. Perhaps it has made her selfish, she thinks to herself, but her dream is more important than anything else. She has always known that if she wants it to come true, that's just the way it has to be. When she first met Hannah, she thought that she understood that too. She listened to the way Hannah spoke about singing and thought she heard an echo of her own passion, and it was a relief, meeting someone who she felt understood her. It made her feel less alone.

But when she was with Jaheim, Hannah eventually put him above everything else – above her friendships, her career, above herself. Now, Mona is not so sure that she knows her friend as well as she thought she did. The thought makes her feel suddenly lonely again. She wants to talk to Hannah about the conversation with her father, but she knows she can't. Mona stands in the cluttered storeroom, feeling overwhelmed by emotions but refusing to let herself cry. Instead, she stands up straight, tucks her hair behind her ears, lifts her chin and steps back out into the café.

'Did you get through to them?' Eleanor asks from the counter. Mona spots Sofia at her side; it looks as though they were just deep in conversation and the image makes her think with a sharp pang of her and Hannah.

'Yes,' she says calmly, 'Thanks for letting me make that call. You should get home now, your shift's over. Hi, Sofia.'

Sofia nods in reply as Mona unwinds her apron. She wonders whether Eleanor has told Sofia about the fight and the fact she will be leaving, but if she has, Sofia has chosen not to mention it. Mona focuses hard on composing herself.

Eleanor says goodbye and leaves, holding the door open for a woman with a buggy as she goes. Mona looks up and the first thing she notices is a pair of small yellow-socked feet poking out the bottom of the buggy, a sheepskin blanket draped over the top. The little boy in the buggy looks about two years old and is fast asleep, one arm wrapped protectively over a soft-toy duck. The woman pushing the buggy is around her age, wearing a black and white polka-dot wrap dress that hugs the shape of her heavily pregnant stomach. As Eleanor holds the door, two other women follow just behind, both with prams. All Mona can see inside are little bundles of blankets, the faces hidden by the hoods of the prams. Eleanor waves briefly and then turns away down the street.

Inside, the woman in the polka-dot dress guides her buggy expertly into the centre of the room. The two women behind seem a little more hesitant than their friend, bumping their prams into tables as they manoeuvre inside the café.

'Can we sit wherever?' says the first woman, looking around the café.

'Yes, of course,' replies Mona.

'Girls, shall we go over there?' says the woman, gesturing to a table in the corner, 'There's space for the prams and we won't be in anyone's way.'

'Good idea,' says one of the other women, in exercise gear and a padded jacket with a fluffy hood, and the three of them push their babies to the corner and settle in, taking off coats, checking on the sleeping bodies in the prams and consulting the menus.

One of the prams makes a noise and the third woman, in glasses and with a colourful headband pushed up against the thick curls of her short afro, reaches quickly inside, pulling out a small bundle.

'It's OK, pickle,' she says as she rocks the baby, rearranging him so he is resting against her chest, his small head peering over her shoulder beneath an indigo blue hat. The baby makes a final small cry and then settles quietly against his mother's chest, wide black eyes facing out into the café. The woman's friends lean forward, one resting a finger against the baby's cheek, the other gently patting his back.

Mona is about to head over to the table but Sofia is there first; Mona knows she loves babies so she will always jump at a chance to serve a table of mothers, or the occasional father who comes in with a pram and a laptop and sets up in a corner of the café. Before long, Sofia is cooing over the prams, asking questions as she hands out menus.

As she watches the group, Mona feels a buzz in her apron pocket. She has two new messages. The first is from her mother.

'Got your message but can't talk,' it reads. **'Is it urgent?'**

Mona thinks about it. Her news feels monumental to her – she has just secured her dream job, will be leaving the city she has lived in for over a decade and has fallen out with her closest friend in the process. She is leaving everything she knows and is embarking on a new chapter in her life, doing something she loves and has worked for tirelessly for years. But is it urgent that her mother knows that? No. Right now there are things that Mona cares about far more than telling her mother about the job, like thinking how to break the news to Stella that she is quitting and how to untangle the mess that she and Hannah have found themselves in. What will Mona say to Hannah when she returns to their flat tonight? What will the atmosphere be like in their small apartment, and will they be able to find a way through their problems?

'No,' Mona types to her mother, 'It's not urgent. Talk soon, have a good day.'

The other message is from Stella, and as Mona reads, her heart starts to race, thinking again about what she will say to her boss and how she will react.

'Hope all's well in the café,' reads Stella's message, 'I'll be popping in this evening, see you then.'

Mona wonders if she should say something to prepare her but knows that quitting via text message is not at all professional, and not something she would like to do to Stella, someone she has come to admire over the years.

'No problem,' she replies instead, 'See you later.'

Mona looks up, her head spinning, and spots a couple in their sixties pausing outside the café door, two suitcases on the pavement behind them. Sofia is still serving the customers with the babies and she can hear Aleksander moving around in the kitchen. Outside the city buzzes with the sounds and movements of millions of strangers living alongside one another. But at the coffee counter in Stella's Mona feels isolated, the weight of her worries, thoughts and anxieties hers and hers alone to carry. She thinks suddenly that this is probably why we need friends – because however self-reliant and composed we may seem, none of us are quite strong enough to get through life shouldering these weights on our own.

4.00 P.M.

MARTHA AND HARRY

Harry holds the door open for Martha, placing a hand on the small of her back as she steps inside the café. He lifts their suitcases up the step and closes the door behind them.

'Where shall we sit, darling?' he asks, looking around the café and taking in the unusual decor.

Martha smiles. She likes that he asks her opinion on even simple things like this, and that he cares about her response. She looks around the café too, making her decision more carefully than she would if she were on her own. In one corner sit three women with prams and at a table nearby them a couple a similar age to Martha and Harry, who are just folding up their newspapers and standing to leave. A very elderly man sits in another corner, wearing a shirt and braces and eating fish and chips alone.

A waitress with dark hair leans against the coffee bar. Behind her is a large stuffed bear wearing a top hat that makes Martha jump for a second but then smile. Outside, the *Big Issue* seller calls cheerily at passers-by who walk to and from Liverpool Street station. Martha watches them for a moment, wondering where they are all going, where they live and what they do when they are not here on this street.

'How about a table by the window?' she says in a considered voice.

'Good idea!' replies Harry, leading her towards a table for two and pulling a chair out for her. He tucks their suitcases under the table and sits down opposite, giving her the chair with the view.

Martha and Harry are both sixty-five, although they feel much younger. It's something they have discussed before, in bed with a glass of red wine on each of their bedside tables. Harry says he stopped getting older on the inside at thirty; for Martha she feels no older than twenty-five. Strange for them both then, when they catch glimpses of themselves and realise that time has sped ahead, leaving its mark on their bodies but not on their interior worlds.

Martha wears a pale green summer dress over white leggings, a white jumper over the top and white trainers with green laces on her feet. She has folded her raincoat neatly over the back of her chair. Dressing earlier that morning she thought about layers: it is still cool and rainy in London and she remembered her last journey on a plane and how cold she had been, the vents stirring stale air around the cabin. But she imagined stepping out at the other side and being hit by a wall of heat. It made her feel warmer just thinking about it.

Harry is dressed in what looks like a linen suit but is actually a special non-crease fabric from Marks and Spencer. Worn with navy boat shoes and a straw hat with a navy trim, which he removes now and hangs on the handle of his suitcase.

'The start of our adventure,' he says as he reaches across the table for her hand, their matching gold bands catching in the morning light.

MONA

'Have you decided what you'd like?' she asks the couple by the window. They talk softly to each other and could be alone in the café for the way they appear so self-contained, so focused on each other. They break their gaze only to look out the window every now and then, the woman pointing and the man turning around in his chair to follow her gaze. The woman laughs suddenly, a loud, teenage sort of laugh. She covers her mouth with her hand as Mona approaches the table, controlling her laughter to a small giggle.

'Yes, we have,' replies the man, who then gestures to the woman who Mona assumes is his wife. She collects herself and looks briefly at the menu, nods to herself as though confirming her decision, then looks up at Mona.

'May I have a slice of red velvet cake and a pot of Earl Grey,' she says. She closes the menu and places it carefully on the table.

'And a brownie and an Americano for me,' says the man.

Mona nods and takes the menus from them. She is about to

turn back to the bar but notices the man is smiling up at her as though he is about to say something. She pauses.

'We're waiting for the Stansted Express,' he says, 'We got here early and thought we'd have some cake first. Any excuse for cake.'

He turns to his wife and the pair smile at each other.

'It's our honeymoon,' he adds.

'Congratulations!' says Mona, trying to hide the surprise in her voice. By their ease with each other and, she admits to herself, their age, she assumed they were long-married. There's something about them that makes her stay a little longer at their table. She realises they remind her of Hannah's parents, whom she has stayed with several times at their home in Wales and who have always been incredibly welcoming towards her. The thought brings a pain to her chest.

'Where are you going?' she asks to distract herself.

'Morocco,' says the woman, her cheeks slightly flushed.

'And then we're flying down to Tanzania via Dubai – we're going on a safari,' says her husband, 'We've always wanted to go on one, haven't we, sweetheart?'

His wife nods.

'Oh, I've always wanted to go on a safari,' she says, 'Since I was a little girl it's been a dream of mine to see an elephant in the wild. But my first husband didn't want to go. He was more of a Costa del Sol kind of man if you know what I mean. He knew what he liked.'

Mona glances quickly around the café. Sofia is making a takeaway order for an elderly woman who holds the lead of an incredibly fluffy labradoodle. The dog sits, looking adoringly up at the woman, who reaches into her pocket and drops the dog a treat in a swift, nearly unnoticeable movement. There are no other customers waiting, so Mona lingers a little longer.

'Oh really?' she says, 'Well I hope you find your elephant.'

'Do you know, we've known each other for ten years?' says the man, 'Ten years! And we only married two weeks ago! Martha worked with my ex-wife and we had dinners together sometimes. I also became friendly with Martha's ex-husband Chris when I started going to his gym. Of course, I only ever saw Martha at dinner parties where all four of us were there. No funny business, I assure you, I was married! But I did think she had the most beautiful eyes.'

He turns to his wife again and smiles. For a moment it's as though Mona is no longer there, and she turns as if to leave but the woman looks up at her now and continues talking.

'When Chris and I separated, Harry here,' and she places a hand on her husband's as she says this, 'was so wonderful. I didn't think I'd be lucky enough to get a second chance at love, but here we are!'

'Here we are,' says her husband.

'Well, congratulations,' Mona says, 'Your orders will be with you soon.'

They don't seem to hear her this time.

'Here we are,' the man says again as Mona turns away, still thinking about Hannah's parents. She realises that Hannah will probably have told her parents about the argument by now and will no doubt have only told her one side of the story. It pains Mona more than she could have imagined to think of Hannah's parents thinking badly of her. She thinks in particular of Hannah's mother, who stayed up late talking with her on one visit that Mona joined Hannah for. Mona couldn't sleep, not being used to the pitch darkness and the quiet. She missed the sound of traffic and the constant glow of street lamps. Hannah's mother, who Mona knew from Hannah struggled with sleep, made them both decaf tea and asked her endless intelligent questions about dancing and her career, questions that neither of her own parents had ever thought to ask.

Back at the counter, Mona checks her phone for a missed call or text from Hannah, or another message from Poppy, but there is nothing. Instead, she spots an email from the dance company, her new employer. It includes a series of forms she needs to complete and as she scans quickly through them she pauses on one particular page. A small phrase jumps out at her and she stops, suddenly staring at the words 'emergency contact'. For the past five years, Hannah has been her emergency contact and she remembers with a start the time she had to use her as one.

*

As Mona lands, her ankle buckles underneath her and with a shoot of pain she realises something is very wrong. This is not a usual trip or fall where she can shake it off and continue dancing a few minutes later, this feels different. Very carefully, she lowers herself to a sitting position, careful not to move her ankle too much.

By now the other dancers have stopped and are crowded round her.

They are in a dance studio in South London, learning the routine for an upcoming commercial gig where the group of them will be dancing in the background of an advert. It is a good job – not because she finds the steps particularly inspiring or challenging, but because it pays well and that is so rare. As she thinks it she realises with a drop of her stomach that, from the throbbing coming from her ankle, she won't be able to do the job any more, meaning she won't get paid. She curses herself for having tripped. The steps are not hard but they have been practising for five hours already without a break. Last night she worked a late shift at the café and only had three hours sleep before heading to rehearsals.

'Are you OK?' asks the choreographer, leaving the front of the studio where he had been watching and coming towards her.

The other dancers shuffle around her, sharing sympathetic noises.

'Does it hurt a lot?'

'Someone should get some ice.'

'This is a dance studio, there isn't any ice.'

'Can you put any weight on it?'

Mona shifts, wincing even at the slight movement, and tries to place the ball of her foot on the ground but as soon as her toes touch the floor, a pain so sharp shoots up her foot and ankle that she feels nauseous. Not wanting to let her colleagues see her cry, she bites her lip and shakes her head.

'Oh, you poor thing,' says one of the dancers, the others nodding in agreement. It sounds sincere, but Mona knows that they must also all be sighing in relief, grateful that it's not them who tripped and that they will still get paid for their time.

Another wave of pain rolls through her and she feels suddenly as though she might be sick.

'I think it's best if I lie down,' she says, sinking slowly to the floor, her legs stretched out in front of her.

The choreographer suddenly leaps into action.

'Yes, of course, don't move,' he says. 'Frankie, can you get Mona some water. Kelly, can you find a jumper or something to make a pillow for her foot. Mona, I'm going to call your emergency contact. Do you know their number or do you want me to look it up on our system?'

'Yes, Hannah,' says Mona, her voice woozy and strained with pain, 'I can call her . . .'

She moves as if to sit up but feels suddenly dizzy, the slight movement causing another burst of pain.

'You stay where you are,' says the choreographer, 'Just tell me her number and I'll call her. Then if she can get here soon she can take you to the hospital – I'll book you both a taxi. If she's busy one of us will come with you. Is that OK?'

Mona nods gently and closes her eyes. She is aware of a buzz of movement around her, voices blurring as she focuses on the pain and on breathing as steadily as she can. After a few moments hands gently lift her ankle and rest it on something soft. She hears shuffling and the tapping of feet and assumes the other dancers have continued practising either around her or on the other side of the studio. She doesn't open her eyes to check, instead she squeezes them tightly shut and concentrates on not crying and not being sick.

She is not sure how much time passes, but eventually she hears a door slam and the urgent sound of a voice she recognises.

'Mona!'

Mona opens her eyes and sees Hannah standing over her, still dressed in her work uniform, her apron tied around her waist. She reaches down for Mona's hand and Mona takes it.

'You poor thing,' *says Hannah, her red hair frizzing around her face, her eyes soft with concern.*

'You've got ketchup on your face,' *Mona says, because she feels slightly delirious and because she suddenly notices a blob of red on Hannah's cheek.*

'I came straight from the café,' *Hannah says, wiping her face,* 'Sofia said she'd be fine on her own and I called Stella – she's going to head over there in a bit too. But now we need to get you to hospital.'

With a lot of effort, Hannah, the choreographer and a couple of the dancers help Mona to her feet. Or foot – she is only able to stand on one leg and half hops, is half carried outside, where an Uber is waiting.

'Are you sure you two will be OK?' *asks the choreographer as they gently bundle Mona into the car, the driver giving a worried look at Mona's pale, clammy face. She thinks he is probably more worried about his car than about her, but she feels a little better now after lying down, her ankle still throbbing but her nausea subsiding.*

'We'll be fine,' *says Hannah, following Mona into the back of the car,* 'Thanks for calling me, I've got her now.'

And the car pulls away, the choreographer and dancers watching for a moment before turning and walking back into the studio. Mona doesn't expect she will see them again.

Hannah holds Mona's hand throughout the whole journey,

not seeming to mind when Mona squeezes suddenly tighter as they go over speed bumps and her foot jogs and throbs.

'Not long now,' Hannah keeps saying, and eventually they do arrive.

'This is A and E?' asks Hannah as the taxi stops outside the hospital building. She can't see any signs but the driver nods and points.

'Yes, yes, A and E,' he says, 'This is where I stop. I can't stop anywhere else.'

Once they are on the pavement, Mona standing on one leg and leaning against the wall, Hannah stops a pedestrian carrying a bunch of flowers and asks if they know where A & E is.

'It's round the other side of the building, love,' he says, pointing and then walking away quickly.

Mona and Hannah look at each other. Under normal circumstances, the other side of the building would be just a short walk away, but on one leg and with her ankle burning with pain it feels suddenly impossible.

'Right,' says Hannah.

'I can hop,' says Mona determinedly, gritting her teeth. She sets off, hopping awkwardly, Hannah standing close beside her for support. But after just a few paces she is exhausted and has to stop to rest, leaning against the wall of the hospital building. They set off again, but this time she makes it an even shorter distance before having to stop. The pain in her ankle is growing stronger and she feels faint.

'OK,' says Hannah, stopping in front of Mona, 'I'll have to carry you.'

Mona attempts a laugh but is in so much pain that it comes out as more of a grunt.

'But you're the same size as me,' she says, 'There's no way you can carry me.'

'It'll be fine,' says Hannah, turning around and crouching slightly, offering Mona her arms to loop her legs through. Mona is too tired to keep going so reluctantly she lets Hannah lift her slowly into a piggy-back.

Together, they walk a little closer towards A & E. Hannah walks slowly, her breathing heavy. Once they have gone a little way she pauses to rest, before continuing. Mona holds her arms around her friend's neck.

'I can see it!' Hannah says eventually, 'The sign for A and E, it's just there.'

She is walking even more slowly now, struggling to take even the smallest of steps.

'I'm going to need to go to A and E too after this,' she wheezes and suddenly they are both laughing, in spite of the pain they are in.

'Stop!' gasps Hannah, 'I can't laugh and carry you!'

Slowly, with many stops on the way, tears streaming down both their faces as they laugh and groan and Mona's foot burns as though it is on fire, they make it to the doors of the accident and emergency department. Hannah sets Mona carefully down on the ground and takes a few deep breaths, her face flushed and damp with sweat.

'OK, you wait here,' she says, stretching her back and then walking into the hospital. A few moments later she returns, pushing a wheelchair.

'Your chariot,' she says, and Mona flops heavily into the seat. Hannah pushes her through the doors. She stays with her during the two-hour wait, during the consultation and the scan where a doctor tells Mona she has badly sprained her ankle, and together with a newly acquired pair of crutches, they head home again together that evening, Hannah still wearing her café apron. Mona's ankle might still ache with pain, but she smiles because when she'd needed her, her friend was there. And when she thought she couldn't go on, Hannah had carried her.

'Thank you so much,' she says to Hannah when they arrive home, both of them understanding that it is meant for today but also for so much more.

*

In the café Mona stares at the forms, remembering her injury and the several weeks it took to recover. Throughout it Hannah was incredibly supportive, doing her food shopping for her to save her struggling to the shops and buying frozen peas for her to rest on her ankle to reduce the swelling. When the injury happened, she had been so relieved to hear Hannah's voice as she lay on the floor in the dance studio and to feel her hand reaching down for hers. Thinking of it now she feels so softened by the memory that she suddenly considers calling Hannah just to hear her voice and to try and work things out. But she hesitates. She thinks back to all the times Hannah has taken their friendship for granted this year and hurt Mona with her carelessness. She remembers the harshness of Hannah's voice earlier and her failure to be proud of her like Mona so desperately needed her to be. She recalls the slamming of the café door and the customers staring at them in surprise and so her phone stays in her pocket.

She reads the form again, supposing that Poppy will be her new emergency contact. As she thinks this, it is as though something changes and she has just taken one big step away from her life and her home here in London. She feels a shifting, a readjusting of things that both excites and saddens her in equal measures.

Her eyes return to the couple in their sixties who are on their honeymoon. They sit in companionable silence, smiling at one another. Looking beyond them and out the window, Mona spots John the *Big Issue* seller again. She goes to wave, but he is facing away from her, his eyes fixed on the busy street. She watches for a moment, taking in the details of the view she knows so well and trying to fully comprehend the fact that she will soon be leaving, that her life is changing, until the café door opens again and the demands of drinks to make and orders to pass through to Aleksander return her to the counter, her back to the street and her mind, for now, focused on nothing but the act of making coffee. The crunch and grind of the coffee beans, the cough and splutter of the milk steamer.

5.00 P.M.

HARRY

He takes a sip of his coffee and settles into his chair, his fingers linked through Martha's. It feels strange to see their new wedding bands shining on their fingers – bright and fresh, unlike the ones they used to wear that had both grown dull by the time they met, much like their marriages.

Harry had loved Jennifer, but he didn't know how to love her the right way to keep her happy. Over time he realised that perhaps it was simply impossible.

When they were first married they lived in a tiny one-bedroom flat in Whitechapel behind the Royal London Hospital. They took showers together in the evening and had breakfast together each morning even though their differing commutes and office start times meant they left the flat an hour apart. They talked about their childhoods and their jobs (they came to know each other's colleagues as well as if they were family, even though they had never met them) and where they would go on holiday if they had the money, and what they wanted to achieve in their lives and later, what to cook for dinner and whose turn it was to pick up toilet roll and bin bags on the way home.

He couldn't say exactly when it happened, but things changed. Over time he felt Jennifer drifting away from him, as though she had looked at him one morning and suddenly found his existence an irritation. It started with small remarks, so lightly said that Harry only realised he was allowed to be hurt by them after many years.

'Is that really what you're wearing?' 'Don't put that there, you fool.' 'You know, my mother told me I shouldn't marry you.' (Harry: 'I thought your mother liked me?') 'Do you know that Maggie's husband just bought her a Tiffany ring? Tiffany! Of course, this bracelet is nice too ...'

He had noticed her make the odd cutting remark when they were dating – telling a waitress calmly but clearly exactly what was wrong with their food or speaking to her sister on the phone and telling her that it was time she got her life together. But at the time he hadn't minded. The food *had* been bad, her sister *had* needed pushing to leave home and get on with her life. When they were young, it was Harry whom Jennifer turned to with gentleness when her flashes of anger at the rest of the world subsided. But as the years passed, increasingly he became the sole outlet for her anger. He sometimes thought the irritation seemed to increase with each new son (they stopped at three) and each slightly larger flat, then house, as if their expanding lives were somehow shrinking Jennifer's affection for him. He often wished they were back in that flat in Whitechapel, which only on looking back did he remember Jennifer complaining about, but which seemed to him their happiest home.

It became hardest to bear when Jennifer involved the children in her criticism of him.

'Isn't Daddy silly?' 'Daddy's burnt the toast again, looks like it's cereal for breakfast today, poppets.' 'I'm sorry I married your father – you'd be doing much better at school if I'd married someone smarter.'

At first the children were too young to understand, but as they grew older Harry assumed they chose to ignore it, or that perhaps they thought their family dynamic was normal. Perhaps all fathers were fools. He could understand why the boys might turn away from their mother's nastier side and instead shelter themselves against the parts of her that were vivacious, and often (with the children, at least) warm-hearted. On Friday nights she bought ice cream and filled three small buckets with sweets for the boys, letting them take it in turns to choose their favourite film. When they were ill she took the day off work and made them beans on toast and jelly and ice cream and read to them until they fell asleep, when she settled herself on the floor by their beds and continued reading to herself, making sure she was there when they woke up. Harry remembers coming home from work one day when Jonathan was off sick and seeing Jennifer sat on the floor looking at their son with such love that Harry locked himself in the ensuite and cried. He felt immediately guilty and ashamed – of course a mother should be devoted to her son. He just hadn't been looked at like that by her in a very long time, possibly never.

That night he read Jonathan the extra chapter he asked for and hugged him until he squirmed out of his arms and reached for the toy dinosaur at the end of his bed to hold as he fell asleep. Back in their room, Harry kissed Jennifer more fiercely than usual, but her eyes had a faraway look to them. *Come back to me*, he thought.

Increasingly, Harry felt a constant, numb sort of loneliness when he was at home. He carried it with him to work and knew it made him appear more withdrawn than he would have liked, but it was hard to shake. Most of Harry and Jennifer's friends were Jennifer's really, so even at their dinner parties where he was surrounded by people he felt himself floating separately from them all, watching the conversations and nodding and saying the occasional comment but not truly engaging.

'Why don't you make an effort with our friends, Harry?' said Jennifer.

'I'm sorry darling, I'm just tired.'

'Well, next time can you not be tired when we have company. It makes us look incredibly rude.'

Martha and her husband Chris were some of Jennifer's friends who came over for dinner every now and then. Of all the people they had round, Martha was the one person who could sometimes make Harry laugh like he hadn't laughed in a long time. But he always felt nervous about it and would quickly withdraw inside himself again, anxious about sparking Jennifer's anger without meaning to.

Harry's life had become increasingly unpredictable.

Jennifer's moods seemed to have worsened – her anger was more easily sparked. Perhaps through guilt (he liked to think she felt guilty about the way she treated him, although he couldn't be sure), she became more lavishly affectionate with the children. There were new bikes and cinema trips *'Just with Mum and her boys'* and sleepovers with their friends.

One night all three boys were staying with friends and Harry and Jennifer had the house to themselves for the first time in a long time. Jennifer was working late so Harry decided to cook dinner for when she arrived home, hoping the smells of the tacos they used to make together in the Whitechapel flat would soften her, would make her happy. He cooked carefully and cleaned up after himself, wiping the surfaces and loading the dishwasher. He waited for her in the kitchen, reading the paper with a bottle of red wine on the table, letting it breathe.

When she arrived home he could tell she was angry before he even saw her. She closed the front door firmly and threw her keys on the sideboard with a rattle. When she appeared in the kitchen, her coat still on, her face looked pale.

'Bad day at work, honey?' Harry said, reaching to pour the wine into a glass for her.

'Every fucking day is a bad day at work,' she said.

Despite their early, detailed conversations about their jobs (what projects they were working on, who was going for a promotion, how they felt about their team leader's managerial style, how they might do it differently one day) as time went on, Jennifer talked to him about work less and less. He assumed she was happy there – she had worked in the same company for the past fifteen years and had worked her way up.

He didn't know what to say so he handed her a glass of wine. She put it down on the table, next to a cold mug of tea that he had been drinking while he was cooking, but which he had forgotten about.

'Can't you put your things away?' she said, picking the mug up and pouring the tea down the sink, 'You're as bad as the boys sometimes.'

She opened the dishwasher and pulled out the top drawer. She paused, her hand and the mug raised above the dishwasher shelf.

'For fuck's sake Harry,' she said, slamming the mug down on the counter, 'I've told you a million times not to put any plates on the top shelf, things don't get washed properly when you do that. And then they have to be cleaned all over again, and it's a total waste of time. I've told you so many times. Why can't you get it right? Why can't it be right?'

She was shouting, her hands gripping the edges of the dishwasher. Suddenly she pulled the entire drawer out, lifted it and threw it towards Harry. Mugs and glasses lifted out of their slots, Harry leapt out of the way and the drawer came crashing down at his feet with a terrible splintering sound as crockery and glass smashed across the floor. He felt his head spinning, fear that he hadn't felt since he was a child rushing through him. He looked down at the smashed mess, thinking what could have happened if he hadn't moved in time. Jennifer stood by the dishwasher, staring at the floor. She started to cry quietly.

'It's OK,' he said, even though he wasn't OK, his whole body was shaking and he felt nauseous, 'It's OK. I'm sorry.'

She stared at the floor for a moment longer and then turned

and left the room, her footsteps climbing the stairs and disappearing into the bathroom. Once she was gone, he stood surrounded by broken glassware and china and started to cry too. Tears slid down his face and his body shook. He thought about his parents – about how much he wished he could call them or get in a car and drive to them and let himself be held like they held him when he was a child. But his father didn't believe that men should cry, and the thought of him knowing what just happened and understanding the sheer terror that Harry felt while it did so filled him with shame. He had been frightened of his wife for a long time, he realised, although she had never done anything like this before. Admitting the thought even to himself felt like too much – he couldn't imagine ever telling anyone else. Men don't cry, and men are not afraid of their wives.

He quietly cleared up the mess, rescuing the few pieces of crockery that weren't broken and wrapping the rest in newspaper and throwing it in a bin bag. He spotted a smashed china bowl by the sink, one that Ben had painted and given to him when he was six or seven, and nursed the pieces in his hands, putting it aside in case he would be able to fix it (although deep down he knew it was hopeless). Then he took the bin bag filled with crockery and newspaper-wrapped glass straight outside, not wanting to leave it in the house where it would remind him of what had happened. He didn't want the boys to see that bag, even if they wouldn't understand what was inside or why. He made a mental note to go to IKEA next week to pick up new glassware and plates and then he sat and ate dinner alone while he listened to the sound of the bath filling upstairs.

Later that night as he climbed the stairs, he heard Jennifer talking on the phone in their bedroom. The door was ajar and he paused on the stairs, listening. He wasn't sure who she was talking to, perhaps her sister, or a friend.

'I hate my life,' he heard her say, 'Is this really what it's all about? Doing a job you despise, day in day out, sleeping with the same person forever, looking after three children who completely consume your life? Sometimes I think I hate them too.'

He walked quietly down the stairs again so that she could finish her phone conversation undisturbed. He had heard enough.

Harry started going to the gym. First, he went just once a week, but before long he went there most nights, either on the way home from work or much later in the evening when the boys had gone to bed – he would say goodnight to them and then silently collect his gym bag and leave. He found it strange that these solo visits made him feel less lonely than he did at home. He loved running on the treadmills and hearing the thud and puffs of the runners around him, feeling like they were all in the same race, even if their machines were set to different paces. In exercise he found a comfort and a way to exhaust his body so that daily life was somehow more manageable.

'Daddy's started "working out",' said Jennifer to the boys, putting air quotations around the term 'working out'. It was true that Harry had never really exercised before in his life and didn't exactly look like a gym-goer when he first started. He didn't even really own exercise gear – only a pair of old trainers he used for gardening, a pair of tracksuit bottoms that were for the same purpose, and a T-shirt he usually wore in summer.

'It's because he's having a mid-life crisis,' added Jennifer, 'We'd better keep an eye on Daddy – he might buy a sports car next!'

Harry had wondered whether Jennifer was right. Maybe he was having a mid-life crisis. But his crisis had been going on for many years. A 'crisis' sounded like a tipping point or a singular, dramatic event. His was just life.

The second time he visited the gym, he bumped into Chris. They were a little awkward together at first, having only ever spoken with their wives present. But then one day Chris asked Harry to join him for a cup of tea in the leisure centre café after they'd finished. Harry happily accepted. They gave each other updates about their jobs (Chris was an estate agent), their wives and their children. They discussed in detail the benefits and drawbacks of the leisure centre gym and their favourite equipment.

Thinking about Chris now as he holds Martha's hand and looks at the new wedding band that encircles her fourth finger, Harry knows he should feel guilty. Chris had started as just an acquaintance, more Jennifer's friend than his, but at the gym they formed their own friendship too. Harry has never had many friends, but for a while he would have counted Chris as one of his closest. So he knows he should feel sorry that he ended up marrying his wife. But he can't. Happiness, he has found, has a miraculous way of rubbing out the unsavoury parts.

When Harry finally decided to leave his wife – or, more

accurately, decided to act on the decision he had made years ago – things happened strangely quickly. Word got out among the group of his and Jennifer's friends that their marriage was ending. A few weeks later, Martha called. Harry picked up the phone and assumed she was calling for Jennifer. He was still living in the house – Jennifer had said he could stay for as long as it took him to find an apartment and organise his things, an act that he found unusually generous but that made him feel constantly on edge as though something terrible would be coming in exchange any moment.

'I'll just get Jennifer,' said Harry, but Martha interrupted him quickly.

'No, no, I actually wanted to speak to you. Can you talk?'

Jennifer was upstairs and Ben, their youngest, had moved out just two months ago, leaving Harry and Jennifer on their own.

'Yes, I can,' Harry replied.

Martha hurriedly told Harry that she had heard his marriage was ending, but instead of giving her sympathy she asked if he might meet her to talk sometime.

'You see,' she said, 'I think my marriage is over too. And, well, it would be good to talk to someone else about it. Someone who is going through the same thing. I haven't told Chris yet, or any of my friends. I didn't know who else to talk to.'

Harry agreed to meet her for a coffee the following evening. They met near Harry's office in west London, far enough away from Martha's work to have no chance of bumping into Jennifer. Harry chose a Caffè Nero near the office – it felt impersonal enough for a meeting with a woman he had never spent time with outside of their dinner party foursome. When he arrived she was already there, her almond eyes darting around the café. When they landed on his face she broke into a smile that made him feel warmer than he had in a long time.

With Martha, he found that conversation flowed easily. At their dinner parties he usually spoke mainly with Chris, leaving the two women to talk about gossip at work or the plans that the new CEO had just unveiled, dissecting them in detail and sharing their opinions in a heated but affectionate manner. But in the café his entire attention was given to her. She spoke in a low but determined voice, each sentence seeming considered, peppered with pauses where she scrunched her eyebrows as though searching for a moment for the perfect words to express herself exactly. He didn't mind these breaks in conversation – silence seemed just as easy as talk with her – and when she did find the words she was after they often surprised Harry by their astuteness, by their way of perfectly conveying her feelings. He then felt immediately guilty for being surprised and for overlooking this woman for so many years.

She spoke about Chris's affairs, saying matter-of-factly that she had of course known about them for years, but that the most recent one – a fling with a friend of their twenty-year-old daughter Annabelle – had finally signalled to Martha the end of their marriage.

'I know I should be feeling sorry for myself,' she said, 'But strangely this time I simply pity him. That girl has made him a fool – of course for her it was just a frivolous fling. She ended it a month ago, but he won't leave her alone. He says he is in love with her. He has made himself ridiculous, and despite all the hurt he has caused me over the years, it's this that has made me finally decide to leave him. I simply cannot continue to be married to a man whom I pity.'

Martha told him that Annabelle didn't know about this affair, or any of the previous ones, and she was doing her best to keep it that way. She had even visited Phoebe, Annabelle's friend and Chris's now former lover, to calmly explain that Annabelle should be kept out of it all, and that if Phoebe did that, Martha would do her best to get Chris to stop contacting her.

Harry watched Martha and saw the strength in this gentle-looking woman and felt something inside himself relaxing. They decided to meet again the next evening, and then the next. On their third meeting Harry told Martha about Jennifer, finding himself admitting for the first time the truth of his marriage and his constant state of fear. She listened so intently that he felt himself speaking more freely than he ever had – her serious expression somehow legitimised every fear he had felt over the past decades.

'She does her best to hide it at work, but I think she's a very unhappy woman,' Martha said after Harry had finished speaking and once she had taken one of her long pauses. 'I expect one day she will look back and deeply regret the way that she has treated you. But you cannot live the rest of your life wondering if or when that might happen. Life is frankly too short.'

Harry has never known how Jennifer found out about their meetings, but when he came home that night he found a suitcase and two overnight bags packed and piled by the front door. Jennifer was waiting for him, sat on the stairs.

'So, you've been having an affair with that bitch from Accounts then?' she said.

Harry stood in the doorway, not taking off his coat.

'I don't know what you mean,' he said, 'Who are you talking about?'

'Martha Wright!' Jennifer shouted, 'I should have known! I saw the way you look at her when she's here for dinner. How could I have been so stupid. Right under my nose, over all these years!'

'I have been for coffee with Martha three times,' Harry said, trying to stay calm, 'Three times, all after you and I *both* decided this marriage was over. I have not been having an affair.'

'I don't believe you,' shouted Jennifer, 'You're a liar and I want you out of my house.'

Harry found he simply didn't have the energy to argue, so he left. He checked into a Travelodge and stayed there until he found a flat two weeks later, back in Whitechapel. He and Martha continued to see each other, and eventually, a year later, she moved in.

By that point, Harry hadn't seen his sons in months. Jennifer convinced them, and all her and Harry's friends, that Harry had been having an affair. Harry has tried phoning his sons, now all living away from home, to persuade them their mother wasn't telling the truth. But they don't want to speak to him.

His life now includes only Martha. One evening shortly after she had moved in they were sharing the dregs of a bottle of prosecco, her legs draped over his on the sofa.

'You know, Harry,' she said softly, 'I don't believe Jennifer ever really thought you and I were having an affair.'

Harry had tucked a strand of her grey-blonde hair behind her ear as she continued talking.

'I really don't. But it gave her something to legitimise her behaviour, to make her feel less of a bad wife, and a bad mother. I expect she couldn't bear the thought of you telling the boys what she was really like. Our made-up affair saved her.'

Harry had felt anger rising inside of him. He had lost his sons, his friends, his home, everyone, all to protect Jennifer's own vision of herself.

As though Martha could sense his rising rage she had kissed him softly on the forehead and then rested hers against his.

'But it doesn't matter now, does it darling?' she said quietly, 'Because you and I have saved each other.'

As Harry looks across at her in the café, this woman who has brought so much happiness to the later part of his life, he remembers her words and smiles from that night. He doesn't need his old friends. He doesn't need anyone. All he needs is her.

MONA

'Can I get you anything else?' Mona asks the couple by the door. They are still sat together with their suitcases; their plates now empty apart from a few crumbs.

'What do you think?' asks the woman, 'We've still got a bit of time.'

At this she turns to Mona.

'It's just like Harry to get us here several hours early for our train to the airport!'

She shakes her head and rolls her eyes but in an affectionate way. Harry smiles and pats her knee.

'We wanted a leisurely afternoon though, didn't we, Martha? Start the honeymoon early. And any chance for a nice bit of cake and some people-watching is worth taking, I think!'

'Maybe another Earl Grey then, please,' says Martha, 'And another coffee for Harry.'

Mona returns a few moments later with the drinks, steam drifting above the mugs as she places them down. She watches them both for a moment. Their warmth and affection with one another is something she always desperately wished for between her own parents when they were still together.

She smiles at them and then heads back to the counter, joining Sofia as office workers wait for the coffee that acts like a bookend to every working day. A man loosens his tie and checks his phone. Next to him, a woman in a smart shift dress and trainers looks intently at the cakes in the glass stand. Mona serves her and when the queue is at a more manageable level Sofia returns to waiting on the tables, leaving Mona at the counter facing the door.

'What would you like?' she says, reaching the final customer in the queue, a young woman with a tired face and a heavy-looking laptop bag slung over one shoulder. She wants a macchiato and Mona turns to the machine, her back to the room. When the drink is made and she swivels round to hand the coffee over, she nearly drops the cup. Because behind the customer the café door is opening and Mona immediately recognises the man stepping hesitantly inside.

'Here's your coffee,' she says, trying to hide the shake in her voice and in her hand. She will not let him see her shake or falter.

The customer turns to leave, the man stepping out of her way to let her past, his eyes fixed on Mona.

'What the hell are you doing here?' she says sharply when he reaches the counter. She folds her arms across her chest and is aware that Sofia has turned to look at her. Mona nods at her, indicating she has things under control – she hopes that she has, for now at least. She turns back to the man, who is holding his hands up in front of him.

'I don't want to fight, Mona,' says Jaheim, his cheeks flushed, his brown eyes full of concern that makes Mona feel nauseous, 'I just want to speak to Hannah. I thought she might be working today.'

'Well, she's not,' replies Mona. She can't believe the cheek of him, coming in here after everything that happened. What would he have done if Hannah was working here? Cornered her in public and at her workplace so she was forced to speak to him? Made her upset in front of customers, in front of her colleagues? Mona feels rage burning inside her. Before Jaheim came along, Hannah was focused on her career and she and Mona were closer. Before him, everything was fine.

'She won't answer my calls,' says Jaheim sheepishly, looking at the floor and then up at Mona, his hair flopping in front of an eye. His face has a boyish look to it that she knows Hannah found endearing but Mona finds sickening. She notices that although Sofia is still serving the tables she is also looking up frequently, looking at Jaheim closely, clearly listening to the conversation.

'Of course she won't answer your calls,' replies Mona, 'You're a thief.'

She says this bit louder on purpose. She doesn't care if the customers hear – she wants them to hear. A few do look up and throw glances towards the counter, some confused, others intrigued. Mona's eyes fall on the older couple by the window, they look concerned and for some reason this makes her even more angry – the fact that Jaheim would interrupt the calm afternoon of these gentle customers. That he would have the nerve to come here at all ... She plants her feet firmly on the ground, straightening to her full height. She is taller than Jaheim and suddenly this matters.

'I just want to talk to her,' he says quietly, hands now in his pockets, 'I just want to say sorry and to try and explain. When we broke up I didn't get to say everything I meant to ... She has to understand why it happened, that I never meant to hurt her.'

'There's nothing to understand,' Mona says, her voice fierce and strong, 'You lied to her, you stole from her, in her home, in *our* home. She is better off without you – she is *happy* that you've gone.'

Mona knows that this isn't strictly true – although Hannah has at least now got up and out of bed and has been trying to hide her feelings, she knows that she is still reeling from the break-up. She feels a stab of sympathy for Hannah before she remembers how Hannah has treated her recently. The accusations she made, the distance she let grow. Her anger towards Jaheim is partly towards Hannah too.

'I miss her,' perseveres Jaheim, 'I'm sure she misses me too. If I could just talk to her ...'

But Mona interrupts.

'I think you should leave now,' she says.

As she says it, she feels movement behind her and turns to see Aleksander stepping out of the kitchen and notices Sofia weaving through the tables until she is by her side, standing behind the counter with her arms folded too. Mona feels relief and another surge of anger as she finds her strength – she is not alone. Aleksander doesn't say anything but stands by the door to the kitchen, staring forcefully at Jaheim, his hands on his hips.

'You heard what Mona said,' says Sofia, to Mona's surprise, 'You should leave. Go on, fuck off.'

The anger in Sofia's voice surprises Mona. She has always been so quiet. But now her voice is strong and determined, her posture mirroring Mona's.

Jaheim looks at the three of them, clearly faltering. He stares at Aleksander for the longest. Aleksander says nothing but stays where he is, unmoving and unflinching. The whole café is looking at Jaheim now too and he suddenly seems to shrink under their gaze. He might have controlled Hannah and charmed her so successfully that she was oblivious to his lies, but he has not charmed or controlled this room. Mona feels her heart pounding in her chest.

'It sounds like you're not wanted here, mate,' says a customer who is sat close to where Jaheim is standing.

Mona doesn't say anything else, she doesn't need to. Jaheim pauses for a moment but then gives in and turns to leave.

'And don't fucking come back,' says Aleksander suddenly. For a second Jaheim pauses, looking back at the café and at Mona. Their eyes meet for a moment and Mona thinks she sees in his face a look of acceptance. She feels sure it will be the last time she sees him and hopes and believes it will be the last time he enters this café.

As he leaves, the customer who spoke earlier gives a little cheer.

'Sorry about that,' says Mona to the room, and within a few moments normal conversation has resumed in the café, the customers returning to each other and their drinks.

'Are you OK?' asks Sofia, placing a hand on Mona's arm. Mona nods.

'Thank you,' she says to the other waitress, 'Thanks for helping.'

Sofia shrugs and then heads back to the café floor, taking the order of a young couple in one of the booths. Mona lets herself relax a little, trying to calm down and rid her body of the anger. She suddenly notices that Aleksander is still stood in the kitchen doorway.

'Thanks, Aleksander,' she says with a smile. He shrugs.

'Who was that?' he says, gesturing towards the door where Jaheim just left. 'A boyfriend?'

Mona laughs bitterly.

'Not mine,' she says, wondering for a moment if Aleksander almost smiles as she says it, 'an ex of Hannah's. They broke up three weeks ago.'

Aleksander nods and pauses, and for a moment Mona wonders if he is going to say something else, but instead he returns to the kitchen and calm returns to the café. Except Mona can't calm down. Instead she is stuck in the past, remembering a moment she has tried hard to forget but that seeing Jaheim has brought back vividly. Of everything that has happened over the past few months, this is the one thing that stays with her like a pebble lodged in her throat. It is a cold, hard memory that is always there. As she serves the few customers in the café she relives it one more time.

*

Things between Hannah and Mona have grown steadily more stilted and distanced, but Hannah doesn't seem to notice. When they are in the flat together or are sharing shifts in the café Hannah is often distracted, looking at her phone or watching the clock, waiting, Mona assumes, for the seconds to pass and bring her closer to seeing Jaheim. She spends more time at his flat, heading there straight after shifts in the café.

But often she is light and breezy too as though nothing has changed. She buys flowers and places them in a jug in the hallway. One evening when Mona gets home from work she finds a bunch of gerbera in her bedroom too, on the bedside table. They watch her as she sleeps and although Mona used to love these flowers they suddenly seem to her falsely cheerful.

Mona focuses on auditions and dance practice and her shifts in the café. It's during a shift with Hannah early one morning that it happens. As they refill salt and pepper shakers, Hannah asks a question that can never be taken back.

'Mona, are you OK for cash at the moment?'

It comes as such a surprise that for a while Mona can only stare at Hannah blankly. The café is quiet, the only customer an elderly regular who listens to music on an old iPod, tapping his fingers on the table.

'What do you mean?' she says when she realises what Hannah has said, and that she is waiting for her to reply.

For both of them money has always been something to be acutely aware of. A good tip week can mean feeling more settled, perhaps a takeaway or a dinner out, but there are more troubling weeks too when a glance at her bank account is enough to make Mona feel vaguely ill. She often finds herself dipping into her savings account to keep things in order. Over the years she has become used to it though, this constant juggling. It is part of her life that she has come to accept. It's something she knows Hannah experiences too, but it's not something they talk about. They don't need to: if one of them catches the other eating beans on toast for dinner or calling Stella and asking for extra shifts, they understand immediately without needing to explain. It's the first time Hannah has asked her so directly about money.

Hannah takes a breath and talks quickly, 'It's just my purse is short twenty pounds and I've noticed it a few other times too recently when I could have sworn I had more in there. It's not a big deal, you know I don't mind lending you money if it's a tight month, you've just got to ask, that's all.'

Mona feels her stomach drop. She wonders if she has misheard Hannah, or at least misinterpreted the words. But there's surely no other way to take this question? Hannah looks down at the floor but then glances at her quickly as though checking something. Her face wavers slightly as she catches Mona's eye.

'So, did you?' she asks quietly.

Opening her mouth as though to speak, Mona finds there are no words in her throat. She watches her best friend and the implication of what she has just said burns her with a fierce heat. She knew things had become strained between them over the past months, but surely things couldn't have got this bad? She has worked hard to keep her feelings about Jaheim and Hannah's relationship with him to herself and despite the recent troubles, the two of them have been friends for years – surely she has done nothing to deserve this suspicion from her flatmate and closest friend? Her ears ring as she looks at Hannah and suddenly sees a stranger.

'I can't believe you'd think I'd steal from you,' she says eventually. Even speaking the words aloud is painful and as they pass her lips she listens back to them, not quite believing they are real. Not one to cry usually, she feels herself blinking back tears of anger, hurt and confusion.

'Not stealing,' Hannah says hurriedly, 'I can just see how it might have happened, you know, if you were short on rent or something ...'

She trails off and looks down again. The way she avoids Mona's eyes hurts almost as much as what she is saying and what it implies. Because although she says 'not stealing', there is no other way for Mona to interpret her words. The language might be softer, but she knows she is being accused just as clearly as if she were standing before a judge.

Mona wants to ask Hannah how she could possibly ask this of her and at what point in their friendship she changed in her mind from her best friend to a potential thief. Or has she never truly trusted her? Throughout all the years they have lived together, all the times they have laughed together and cried together and shared takeaways and gossip and shifts in this café – was Hannah always holding something back from her? If Hannah truly believes that Mona would ever steal from her then she has never really thought of her as a best friend, or any kind of friend at all. Mona thinks about the times she considered Hannah to be something like a sister – part of the family she has chosen for herself to make up for her real family's shortcomings. If this is what Hannah really thinks of her, then they are simply flatmates and colleagues, nothing more.

'No, Hannah,' she says instead, working hard to control her emotions and not to cry, 'I haven't taken any money from you.'

Hannah frowns slightly, but like a cloud passing away from the sun she then laughs lightly, smiling and shrugging her shoulders.

'Oh, I'm sorry, it's probably just me being clumsy,' she says brightly, 'I probably dropped a twenty getting money out at the cash machine, that's happened before. Just forget I said anything, OK?'

Hannah returns to the salt and pepper shakers, focusing on pouring salt from a large box into the small glass bottles. Mona watches her, trying to work out what she is thinking and whether some explanation or further apology is on its way. When nothing comes she picks up the box of pepper and reaches for another set of bottles, not looking at Hannah.

'Sure,' she says. But she doesn't forget.

It was the day after that conversation that Mona sent in her application for the job in Paris. She had spotted it a week before and felt disappointed that a job that suited her so much had to be in another city. Despite it being perfect, when she first saw it she didn't even consider applying. But the day after Hannah's accusations about the money she was scrolling through Instagram on the bus back from a dance class when she paused on a picture of Poppy and Antoine, the image reminding her of the job advert for the dance company in Paris. She looked at the smiling face of her friend and for the first time imagined what it would be like to leave London. She had never even visited Paris before but something inside her suddenly stirred – the start of an idea unfurling.

When she arrived home that evening the flat was empty and quiet. Dropping her keys on the table by the door she spotted a Post-it attached to the mirror there. 'At Jaheim's for the night. H x'. With the flat to herself, Mona wandered in and out of the rooms, noting the mould in the bathroom that had grown steadily darker over the years, the peeling paintwork on the kitchen ceiling and the scrap of tinsel in a ceiling corner in the hallway that had got stuck there a couple of years ago and that neither of them had ever bothered to pull down. Despite the tattiness of the flat and its cramped size, for the past few years it had felt like home. But standing alone in the hallway with the pain of Hannah's words from the night before still fresh, as though they were tattooed into her skin, Mona felt as though she had wandered somewhere she no longer belonged.

Almost as though she had returned to a former childhood home only to find a new family living there with new furniture and photographs on the walls, she felt suddenly out of place in the flat. It was still her flat, but it no longer felt like home.

She wrote the application that evening, sending it before she could change her mind. She told herself that it wasn't just out of anger: it was a good job and if she was as serious about her career as she'd always thought she was, she should have applied anyway. But really, she hadn't thought about it too much after sending it. She didn't expect to hear back.

In the café, Mona looks around at the quietly talking customers and at Sofia whom she now sees in a new light and feels a new sense of warmth towards. She watches the space where Jaheim just stood, her anger cooling slightly now that he is gone but never truly going away.

6.00 P.M.

MARTHA

As they drink, Martha finds her attention wandering to the other people in the café. There was an argument earlier that had caused Martha to look over in concern, watching the dark-haired waitress shouting at a young man with floppy hair and slightly protruding ears. She didn't trust him just from looking at him, the way he squirmed and looked contrite but in a way Martha didn't believe was truly authentic. She has a way of seeing the truth of people, something that she didn't have when she was younger (if she did, perhaps she would never have married Chris) but which has grown more attuned and precise over the years.

Now though, things are back to normal and the café buzzes with the sound of workers stopping for a coffee before heading home. The street outside is busy, reminding Martha that it is

300

nearly time to cross the road and catch their train to the airport. She teased Harry for arriving so early but really this is one of her favourite things to do: to sit for several hours in a café with him and watch the world go by outside the window. He knows that, of course, which is why her teasing was affectionate.

A harried-looking woman eyes up the cake stand, orders an orange juice to go, and then changes her mind and asks for a caramel shortbread before paying. The waitress places the shortbread carefully inside a paper bag and as the woman pays a dark stain creeps through the paper. The woman punches in her pin number while eyeing the spreading grease stain. When the waitress hands her the bag and the juice she shoves the bag quickly inside her handbag. Next in the queue are a man and a woman who order two Americanos to go. They look down at their phones as the waitress makes the drinks.

'Did you remember to renew the car insurance?' says the woman without looking up.

'Yes,' says the man next to her.

'And you've booked next Friday afternoon off work for Rachel's assembly?'

'Yes,' replies the man.

The woman nods. They are handed their drinks and then they turn towards the door in silence.

Martha puts down her now-empty cup of tea and reaches for Harry's hand. She thinks back to the earlier argument between the young man and the waitress and how grateful it made Martha feel for Harry's honesty and gentleness.

'I'm so glad I'm here with you,' she says.

'What, here specifically?' he replies, 'You should have told me you'd be happy with just a café and we could have cancelled the honeymoon!'

She laughs. Although their trip has cost them both a large chunk of their savings, she knows he is looking forward to this holiday as much as she is. It feels appropriate to mark a new start with a journey. Her first honeymoon didn't feel as significant somehow. It felt almost too much after the indulgence of the wedding – a much bigger affair than her second. A church wedding and a country house reception – she and Chris rented the whole house for the weekend. There was a cake the size of a small child, lots of dancing, and speeches that went on longer than Martha would have liked. Her cheeks ached from smiling but she didn't feel as happy as she knew she should.

By the time they set off in a rented vintage car for the airport she felt exhausted, although of course she didn't admit it at the time. Mauritius had been Chris's choice – stunningly beautiful and what he thought of as a 'perfect' honeymoon destination (he might have read it in a newspaper somewhere), but she had felt bored after a few days. The hotel resort was full of other newly married couples. She watched them all at breakfast, lunch, then dinner, noticing how after a few days old habits emerged out of the post-wedding glow. Couples snapped at each other – gently, but still enough to be noticed – and interrupted one another and failed to laugh quite sincerely enough at each other's jokes. As she watched she felt her chest tightening. Were they like that? She wanted to escape the resort for an afternoon and go on a very long walk on her own. It took her thirty-five years to realise the trapped feeling she felt in their honeymoon suite above the water was not just newly-wed nerves.

Her first partnership lasted thirty-five years and produced two daughters – now grown up – but this new one already seems to Martha like her true marriage. As if the first was a test run preparing her for this. On bad days she thinks of all those years that she could have been with Harry and her heart aches. She never tells her children about this sense of regret, but sometimes it sneaks up on her and grips her tightly. But other days she thinks that at least now she is truly ready for this. She knows what it means to be married. She has thirty-five years of experience to bring to this new marriage.

But why did she wait ten years between meeting Harry and breaking things off with Chris? She knew it wasn't right with Chris early on. And then came the first affair, his guilt, both their tears and their agreement to work things out. But then came another. And another. And then she met Harry – this good-natured, funny man who made her laugh across the dinner table in a way that made both Jennifer and Chris clearly uncomfortable, but which she couldn't help, couldn't bring herself to stop. What was it, then, that held her back from walking out of her home as soon as she met Harry and saw in him something she had never seen in her husband? Her daughters, her darling daughters, yes. They were still young then and their cries when they tripped over or fell out with friends were enough to make her want to rip out her own heart and hand it to them if only it would make them happy. She couldn't bear to cause them pain herself – because she knew that leaving their father would cause them huge pain.

She worked hard to shelter them from their problems, sending them to their grandparents or her sister for the weekend so that she and Chris could spend entire weekends screaming at each other or instead ignoring each other as fiercely as they could, spending the two days in separate parts of the house, only crossing each other for brief moments in the kitchen. Her children had no idea how alone she felt in her marriage, perhaps hadn't really even considered that she had feelings of her own outside of her love for them. She couldn't do that to them. But it was also more than that – it was fear. It took ten years to scale the height of her fear.

'We should probably head off soon,' says Harry, and Martha's eyes flick to the clock above the counter. Her mind returns to thoughts of their upcoming honeymoon. She pictures the suite that she will happily shut herself in with Harry for several days, but also wonders what shade of blue the sky will be in Morocco and how warm the air will feel draped around her shoulders. She can't wait to find out and to share these discoveries with Harry. She thinks of the safari in Tanzania and what it would be like to actually see an elephant – to finally have one of her childhood dreams realised after so long. Despite the years of waiting, she is glad that it will be Harry by her side when it finally happens. This has been worth the wait, she thinks, he has been worth the wait.

MONA

The couple by the window, Harry and Martha, Mona remembers them calling each other, wave as they head to the café door with their suitcases. As they leave, Mona wonders if they will find their elephant.

At the counter a man in a well-fitted suit orders a latte; a man in a suit that hangs off him and that looks even shabbier next to his companion's orders an Americano.

'Any plans for the evening?'

'Oh, just the usual ...'

Behind them a mother links arms with her grown-up daughter, the pair instantly recognisable as family. They hold shopping bags in their free hands. The daughter looks up at the menu, the mother looks at her daughter.

'It's been so nice to spend the day with you,' she says. Mona isn't sure whether the daughter hears.

'A cappuccino please,' she says, 'Mum, what do you want? I'll get this.'

The bell in the kitchen rings. As she fetches the food (fish and chips for a family in the corner who speak a language Mona doesn't recognise), she catches Aleksander's eye. He is looking at her in a strange, intense sort of way.

'Everything OK?' she says, balancing the plates on her hands and in the crook of her elbow.

He nods and turns back to the oven, stirring something vigorously on the hob. Mona and Hannah have both tried to coax conversation out of him over the years but he is resolutely quiet, apart from when no one is watching when he mutters to himself in a steady stream of Polish. Mona wonders at his life outside of the café: she doesn't even know where he lives or who with. At the end of shifts she often tries to ask him his plans but he usually shrugs on his leather jacket and leaves quickly. Perhaps, like her, this is not his dream job and maybe that's what makes him always in a hurry to leave.

'OK then,' she says, turning back to the café.

Mona's eyes flick to the clock, wondering when Stella will be arriving and how their conversation about her leaving will go. Mona might not be someone who would do anything to avoid conflict like Hannah is (or was, before her sudden, unexpected outburst earlier) but even she has had far too much for one day. She feels exhausted by arguing and by the thoughts fighting inside her head, and by the hours spent on her feet, right after her audition yesterday and the double shift the night before that. She suddenly wants to lie down in a dark room. For a moment she even considers escaping again to the storeroom for a breather, but then she pictures the mess in there. It might be tidier after her flurry of activity there this morning, but it is still too cramped to be truly calming.

Her phone buzzes. It is another message from Poppy.

'Any word from Hannah?' the message says, followed by a long series of kisses.

Mona sighs. At points throughout the day she has wondered if Hannah will send her a message, but she hasn't. She thinks again to what they will say to each other when she arrives back at their flat tonight. In a flat as small as theirs, it is impossible to avoid each other for long. They will have to talk – they will have to continue the argument they started earlier. Mona wonders what else there is left to say. She thinks about Jaheim's visit to the café just now and wonders whether she should tell Hannah he was here but decides quickly that she won't. Mona might be angry with her friend, but she still can't shake the deeply-rooted instinct to want to keep her from being unnecessarily hurt. Knowing that Jaheim came to try and see her would only confuse and upset her.

Thinking about Jaheim makes Mona's body tense again. His visit to the café just now wasn't their first argument. As she busies herself tidying behind the counter she remembers that other confrontation several months ago.

*

When Mona opens the door to the flat she is greeted by the sound of the shower running and Hannah's voice as she sings snatches of a song. She closes the front door gently and crosses the hallway – it has been a long day and she is in need of a glass of wine. Before she reaches the kitchen, she glances into Hannah's room. The door is slightly ajar and she sees movement. She spots the back of Jaheim's body and notices he is leant over something. Mona steps a little closer and nudges the door slightly with her foot. As she does, Jaheim turns his body slightly and Mona sees what he is huddled over. It's a navy-blue handbag she knows well – she has seen it abandoned on Hannah's bedroom floor or slung over her arm countless times. In his hand Mona spots a flash of pink. Jaheim flinches and drops what he is holding so quickly that Mona can't see it clearly, but she doesn't need to.

She knows that Hannah's wallet is bright pink. Jaheim drops the handbag on the bed and turns fully around to face her.

'Mona!' he says, a smile fixed on his face. She notices he is dressed smartly and that there is an open bottle of wine and two glasses on Hannah's dresser.

'We're just getting ready to go out. Hannah's running late of course – you know what she's like. She asked me to bring her lipstick from her bag but it's like a teenager's bedroom in there. Which isn't surprising of course.'

He gestures around the room as though inviting her to comment on the mess. He is still smiling.

Mona stares at him. Her heart beats fast and she feels her hands clenching into fists without her realising. Jaheim doesn't seem to notice.

'Do you want some wine?' he says, walking towards the dresser and picking up the bottle, 'I can go get you a glass?'

'The money,' Mona says.

'What money?' Jaheim replies quickly, pouring himself a glass of wine, his hand steady.

From the bathroom Mona can hear Hannah singing 'Don't You Forget About Me', one of the regulars at the café that they both often get stuck in their heads after a shift.

'Don't do that,' she says, trying hard to keep her voice low, 'I just saw you.'

He takes a sip of wine. Mona wants to slap the glass out of his hand, or to pick it up and pour it down the front of his pale blue shirt. Her body starts to shake, her anger betraying her. As much as she would like to, she has already decided that she mustn't shout – not yet.

'You didn't see anything,' he says, 'You saw me trying to find Hannah's lipstick, and failing, I might add.'

He even laughs, a short laugh that doesn't go anywhere but instead hangs and then fizzes out like air let out of a balloon. But it is still a laugh. His calmness is infuriating and it takes all of Mona's strength not to scream. The only thing stopping her is Hannah. She thinks about the way her face softens when she gets a text and glances down and Mona immediately knows it's from Jaheim. She pictures Hannah sitting next to Jaheim at their tiny dinner table propped up in her room, looking at him with wide eyes and a hand placed over his as he tells a story about his day at work that is very similar to a story he has told before. If she were to tell her what she just saw – or more what she thought she saw (although she is convinced of it now, convinced in a way that is like coming up from a darkened cellar into a brightly-lit room) she wouldn't believe her. She wouldn't want to believe her. Mona is certain of this, because there are only two people who have such easy access to Hannah's purse and whom she would trust enough not to suspect anything, or at least not for a while. And of those two people she chose to confront the person she had lived with for four years – her closest friend.

'She's noticed it missing,' she says, 'She says it's been happening for a while.'

At this Jaheim's smile dips very slightly. He puts the wine down on the dresser. At his hesitation Mona continues before he can say anything else.

'She even asked me if I'd taken it. I told her she was mad to think I would, of course, but if she's asked me it's only so long until she asks you too.'

Jaheim watches her carefully, his arms crossed over his chest as he leans against the dresser. Despite his relaxed stance, he is very, very still, reminding Mona of a cat watching a bird. The sound of the shower running and Hannah singing to herself fills the silence between them until Mona continues.

'God, it's so obvious now. She's never lost money before and she suddenly finds herself "misplacing" a load of cash over the past few months – the same amount of time that she's been with you.'

'Are you going to tell her?' Jaheim says suddenly. He is not smiling now. 'Are you going to tell her what you saw – what you thought you saw?'

He is still leaning against the dresser but he has straightened slightly. He looks at her closely.

'No,' she says, sighing quietly, forcing herself to uncurl the fists that are still clenched by her side, 'Right now she's too loved up to see what's right in front of her. To admit to herself that it could be you. I could try and tell her the truth, but she isn't ready to hear it. I honestly don't think she'd believe me.'

They stare at each other: two players at a stalemate. It's Mona who makes the next move.

'But one day she's going to open her eyes and confront you about this,' she says, louder now, forcefully, 'And when she does, you are going to tell her the truth. And if you don't pay her back every penny I swear to god I will do whatever I can to fuck your life up. I will come to your office and tell them exactly what you are like. I'll tell your friends. I'll phone your mum – I know Hannah has her number on her phone. I'll do whatever I can. Understand?'

Hannah changes song: suddenly she is singing in the rain. Her sweet, gentle voice is muffled slightly by the bathroom door but is still clear enough to fill the space between Jaheim and Mona. And perhaps it's her voice and the glorious feeling she is singing about, or maybe Jaheim has simply found himself at a dead end. But his head droops and his shoulders slump forward, his whole body crumpling. He looks at Mona with wide, boyish eyes.

'Mona,' he says quietly, 'I honestly didn't mean for any of this to happen. It just got out of control. I love her, I really do.'

His voice trembles slightly – something she is not used to. Usually, he is all laughter and confidence and affection. And after his composure earlier she wasn't expecting this. Somehow this attempt at honesty angers her even more than his indifference. How dare he feel sorry for himself.

'I don't fucking care,' she says, 'I just want you out of our lives. You know, I never trusted you.'

The water stops, and a moment later Hannah is in the doorway, a pink towel wrapped around her body and tucked in at the front, her slippers on her feet and another towel crowning her head. Her long legs poke out beneath the towel, her tattoo stark against her pale skin.

'You're here!' she says to Jaheim, tiptoeing over and kissing him.

'Hope he hasn't been boring you, Mona,' she says affectionately, holding her towel with one arm and wrapping the other around his waist. He pulls her towards him and Mona watches as she snuggles into his armpit. Mona doesn't take her eyes off Jaheim, who is suddenly avoiding making eye contact.

'Not at all,' says Mona, 'We've been just fine.'

'Oh, I'm glad!' says Hannah, her voice breezy as she turns back to Jaheim, 'I'll just get dressed and then shall we go?'

She kisses Jaheim again and Mona turns and leaves the room. The sound of Hannah's giggles follow her into her own room, where she shuts the door and sits on the edge of her bed for a long time, staring at nothing.

*

Mona has never told Hannah about what she saw, or about that conversation with Jaheim. There were many times over the weeks that followed that she very nearly did.

When she caught Hannah rummaging through her handbag on the way out of the flat, looking flustered. When she heard her speaking on the phone to Jaheim in her room and wanted to grab it and shout at her that she was dating a liar and a thief. Thinking of it now, she wonders if it was wrong to lie to her friend like that – there was a time when she could never have imagined keeping anything from her, let alone something this big. But even now that it has all come out and Hannah and Jaheim have broken up, Mona is certain that Hannah wouldn't have believed her. She had to come to the realisation on her own.

Over the past year, that's the hardest lesson Mona has had to learn. That however close you think you are to someone, you are still ultimately on your own. You might have been walking comfortably down the same path together, but at any point that path can diverge. You won't know who will veer off in what direction, or whether it will be possible to follow. And for Mona the biggest question of all is whether their two paths will come back together further down the road.

The café door suddenly shuts firmly and Mona looks up. A petite woman stands just inside the café, her hair blonde at the tips but dark at the roots and sticking out from her head in a mess of curls. She wears a trench coat and jeans and looks around the café for a moment before deciding on a table at the back, far from the window.

The woman flicks through the menu and Mona looks across at Sofia, but she is busy serving another customer on the other side of the café. So Mona picks up her pad and crosses the room, pushing thoughts of Hannah and Jaheim from her mind.

'What can I get you?' she asks the woman, noticing grey circles around her eyes and a pale stain on the collar of her coat. The woman orders a cappuccino and returns to staring at her phone, which is placed in front of her next to a pair of keys and her wallet. When Mona brings her the drink she doesn't look up, instead she looks down at her mug as though searching for something there. Mona pauses for a moment before stepping away, leaving the woman alone with her thoughts.

As she moves back to the counter she suddenly spots a flash of yellow on the floor next to a table in the corner – she wanders over and picks up a soft toy duck, its fur plush.

She hasn't noticed it before and thinks back through the day, trying to picture which small child might have dropped it. She places it in the lost property box, next to the keys, the business card holder, the lonely glove and the large brown envelope intended for the young man in the green hoody who hasn't appeared. She picks it up for a moment, holding the envelope and considering tearing it open just to find out what is inside. But instead she remembers the coffee order she has to make and places it back in the box among the pile of forgotten things.

7.00 P.M.

MONIQUE

The chocolate flakes on her cappuccino sink slowly into the froth. Monique watches them closely, each brown spot melting and then disappearing into the white like snow thawing in the morning sun. She lifts the spoon from the table and stirs, carefully making patterns in the foam before destroying them. A star, a heart, a cloud – all created and then stirred back into nothing.

The froth is disappearing now, the bubbles popping and leaving the liquid flat. She tries to draw another shape in the surface but nothing sticks.

Monique turns to look around her. Until last night (or this morning: when she looked up at the clock on the wall it had shown just after 4 a.m.), she had never visited this café before. Coming here hadn't been her plan when she dressed in the early hours of the morning, taking her husband's jumper and a pair of her tracksuit bottoms from the chair next to their bed to save opening and closing the drawers.

It had surprised her how easy it had been to leave her husband's sleeping body in their bed. It used to be when she felt most flooded with love for him: watching his face plump with sleep, all worry fallen away, him looking almost like a child. He tucked one hand under his face when he slept, squashing one cheek into his sleeping eye. Sometimes she used to try and stay awake longer than him just so she could watch him for a while before she too fell asleep.

But not even his face can reach her now.

Padding through the quiet flat she had found her coat and shoes by the front door and put them on. Her keys rested in a bowl on the table and she put them in her pocket. Before heading out she turned back, crossing the landing to a door at the end. She opened it gently and peered inside. The room was dark apart from the green glow of the light on a baby monitor. As she edged further into the room it cast just enough light for her to make out the shape of the small baby in the cot. She crouched down until her face was level with the sleeping body, its chest rising and falling gently with its breaths. Tiny arms were flung out to each side as the baby lay on its back in a pose of complete trust, its face tilted slightly to one side and its small cheeks glowing pink.

After a moment Monique stood up, closed the door again and went swiftly out the front of the flat. She made her way down the stairs softly and then she was out into the street, the cold flooding her and making her feel alive for a moment.

The street was quiet and dark; the windows had their eyes shut. Plump bin bags crowded the pavement, ready for the bin lorry that would be along in a few hours. As she stepped onto the street, she saw a cyclist riding by – a surprising flash of wheels. She caught a glimpse of him as he passed: joy on his face, cheeks flushed from the cold. He pedalled fast down the empty street and around the corner. She imagined what that must feel like, wheeling away to somewhere, or maybe to nowhere. To freedom. The wind cold on your face as you cycled towards the stars and the moon.

She started walking again, following her feet as if they were an impatient dog taking a sleepy owner on a walk. Above her streetlights glowed, obscuring the stars.

At the end of the road she turned right and kept walking, passing a night bus and a short row of shops with their shutters pulled down like blankets. On the corner of the street she paused, unsure whether to turn right or left. She opted for right, which took her onto a wider street with more shops, mostly dark, some with a few lights on – for security she supposed. Outside one, a furniture shop, she stood close up to the window, her breath fogging the glass as she looked inside at the neat beds piled with cushions and the desks arranged with just the right number of books and pen pots. If she could have melted through the glass and into the perfect interior she would have done. Taken her shoes off, placed them neatly on the rug and curled up in the middle of the pristine, impersonal living room set. Devoid of any detritus of life: a blank, a new start.

Instead she turned and walked on until she reached

another bus stop. A night bus was just pulling up. She felt for her Oyster card in the coat pocket where she always left it and hopped onto the front of the bus, tapping her card and avoiding the eyes of the driver. She made her way to the back of the bus, although there were only two other passengers. A woman reading a novel and a man wearing a woolly hat and headphones, nodding his head to a steady silent beat.

She watched the city rolling past the window – quiet at that time of morning but never as quiet as she expected. Dark shop fronts and empty office blocks, but cars still tearing down the street and all-night convenience shops where shopkeepers leant against the fruit and veg crates and talked together in the night. And then she saw the sign for Stella's glowing brightly above a large window and she buzzed to stop the bus. She had never noticed it before, the 24-hour café which, on stepping inside, had the feel of an American diner crossed with an old-fashioned British 'caff'.

At 4 a.m. this café had felt like a refuge. She sank into the quiet as though into soft pillows on a hotel bed. But then that woman had come in and yelled for no reason and it had brought Monique back to reality. She could no longer ignore her phone that had been buzzing for a long time and had picked up, listening to her husband's voice on the other end. He had sounded angry but scared too and Monique could hear the sound of a baby screaming in the background. She had told him she had just popped out and would be back soon. And she had left.

He was angry, of course, when she arrived home. He was carrying the baby in his arms, her face hot with tears. When she came in through the door he thrust the screaming child at her.

'Where *were* you?' Mike said, 'She's hungry. You're her *mother* for Christ's sake.'

Monique had held the baby and listened to the screams that had dulled slightly but still surprised Monique by their force – how such a small thing could make that noise. As she listened to the screaming she wanted to recognise the sound, to feel a pain somewhere in her heart. But all she heard was noise. Where there should have been feeling there was nothing but emptiness.

She fed the baby and together they put her back to bed. She didn't tell her husband where she had really been, although she wanted to describe the bear in the top hat to him, and the strange comfort of the near-empty café that was open when the rest of the city was asleep.

Now, the baby is with Monique's mother and a bottle of expressed milk in their flat. Monique had asked her to come round earlier this afternoon, saying she just needed watching until Mike was home from work, that she had chores to do. She didn't give details and her mother didn't ask; instead she scooped the baby up in her arms and smiled a huge smile.

'Take as long as you need,' she had said, 'we'll be just fine.'

Monique wasn't exactly sure why she headed back to the café, but as soon as she left the flat that's where she came. Despite the many decorations and pictures adorning the walls, it feels impersonal somehow too. An in-between place, a waiting room, a space where she is not a mother or a wife. Here, she is no one.

Monique turns back to her table, picks up her coffee cup, brings it near her mouth and then puts it down again. She picks up the spoon and stirs the liquid, then puts both the cup and the spoon back. Her elbow comes to rest on the table and she sits her chin in the cradle of her hand. With her free hand she uses her thumb to push her wedding ring up and down her finger. When she first started wearing it she couldn't get used to the feel of it or the look of it shining gold on her finger. She didn't like how brightly it glowed, how her skin was still tanned underneath it. She wanted a pale line of flesh around her finger, marking the years of her commitment – like her parents.

'I want to be married to you for a hundred years and until my ring is scratched and stuck on my fat finger,' she told him back then, covering his neck with frantic kisses. In the café she twists the ring round and round until it slips off her finger. She places it on the table next to her now-cold cup of coffee.

MONA

The café is quiet now and Sofia joins Mona at the counter. Mona sees her looking up at the clock; it is not long until her shift is over.

'Not long now,' Mona says with a smile, trying not to feel a stab of resentment that she is not finishing soon too. She is thankful really for the double shift – there are lots of costs associated with moving and it will be at least a month until she receives her first pay cheque, so she needs the money. But her whole body aches.

'Yes, not too long for you either,' says Sofia. Mona smiles at her, thankful to Sofia for trying to cheer her up, even though right now she feels sombre and the remaining hours seem to stretch endlessly in front of her. She is torn – she is exhausted and wants to sleep, but she is also anxious about returning to the flat and to Hannah.

'That guy that came in earlier...' says Sofia.

'Hannah's ex,' replies Mona to the question that hadn't been asked but was there in her voice.

'And you said he'd been stealing?'

Mona nods.

'He'd been doing it for months,' she says, 'Hannah had no idea.'

Sofia shakes her head.

'He sounds just like my ex.'

Mona looks at her, frowning, surprised.

'Oh, he never stole from me,' continues Sofia, 'But he lied constantly.'

'Why did you stay with him?' asks Mona, leaning against the counter, watching Sofia carefully.

Sofia shrugs, running a hand through her hair.

'He was a master manipulator,' she says, 'He had me totally under his control. He did it subtly at first, just charming me and seeming totally devoted to me. But then he slowly took over my life. He didn't like it if I went out so I stopped going. He said he missed me too much when we were apart, so I stopped seeing my friends. I didn't mind at the time – I was happy to spend time with him – but looking back I real-ise he isolated me on purpose. When I eventually started

321

questioning his lies he made me feel as though I was going mad and I had no one around me to back me up. When that guy came in earlier, I thought he seemed just like him, just like my ex.'

It's the first time Sofia has opened up to Mona like this and she feels shocked, because she never knew her story and because it sounds so similar to Hannah's. Hannah might never have seen it herself, but from the start Mona thought there was something not quite healthy about their relationship, about the way it quickly took over Hannah's life and Jaheim seemed happy about the situation.

'That does sound like Hannah and Jaheim,' Mona says slowly, lost in thought.

'Eleanor told me about the fight between you and Hannah earlier, and that you're leaving,' Sofia says suddenly, making Mona return quickly to the café. So, Sofia did know, she just didn't mention it. Mona feels surprisingly grateful – she didn't feel ready to talk much more about it all when Sofia arrived on her shift.

'Congratulations on the job by the way,' adds Sofia.

Mona attempts a smile but she is still feeling distracted, thinking about how Sofia described her relationship and about everything that happened with Hannah and Jaheim.

'Thanks,' says Mona eventually, 'It's a bit of a mess really though. I mean, I'm so happy about the job. But things with Hannah ... We've been friends for years but it seems to have totally fallen apart.'

'And do you want to put it back together?' asks Sofia.

Mona thinks about it. Does she? She thinks about all the

hurt that Hannah has caused her over the past year, and how angry she still feels at her.

'I'm not sure,' Mona admits, 'She was pretty unkind to me when she and Jaheim were together. She forgot my thirtieth birthday.'

It's the thing she hasn't said aloud because she feels so hurt by it, and petty for feeling so hurt. Her birthday was just over three weeks ago, just before Hannah and Jaheim broke up. Ever since Mona left home, she has never really celebrated her birthday. She doesn't like the attention and it brings back too many memories of unhappy childhood birthday parties, her parents arguing and making all the guests uncomfortable. Each birthday is also another reminder that the years are passing and she is still a waitress, not doing the thing she loves every day. Only her very closest friends even know the date of her birthday – she has made a point of never putting it on Facebook and never has a party or even a group meal. But since they've been friends, she and Hannah have always done something together, the two of them. One year they went to a speakeasy cocktail bar and got so drunk so quickly that they ended up coming home at 9 p.m., ordering takeaway and eating in their pyjamas. Another year Hannah bought her tickets to a show at Sadler's Wells. Another they cooked a special meal together, making all the Argentinian food that Mona sometimes craved.

But this year, Hannah forgot. Hannah had turned thirty earlier that year, celebrating with a big meal at one of her favourite restaurants, Jaheim, Mona and her other friends seated around a long table. Hannah had asked Mona then if she might like to do a similar thing for her own birthday, but

Mona had been adamant she didn't want a fuss. She didn't want to admit how daunted she felt about turning thirty – it felt significant and yet she didn't want to acknowledge it as such. It was just another year, she told herself, not any kind of turning point. When the date rolled round she picked up the birthday cards from her mother and father from the doormat, realising as she entered the hallway that Hannah hadn't returned home that evening. She checked her phone for messages from her but there were none. Mona assumed that Hannah had stayed the night at Jaheim's, and that she would be home that evening. But she never came home. Mona waited up, unsure whether to cook a meal for herself in case Hannah had a reservation for them somewhere. She considered calling her but didn't want to have to remind her friend – it felt embarrassing and painful. At ten o'clock she made herself beans on toast and then went to bed. The next evening when she returned home from work Hannah was in the flat, but she was shut in her room underneath her duvet. She and Jaheim had broken up, she told Mona through her tears.

The days went by and Mona wondered if Hannah was going to remember, but she didn't. And then Mona went to Paris and spent the weekend with Poppy and Antoine, where she auditioned for a job that she suddenly wanted even more than when she'd first applied.

Mona swallows back tears, trying to keep her chin high and her face unreadable, but she can't help it. Her eyes are damp, her vision suddenly blurred.

Sofia reaches out and places a hand gently on her arm.

'That must hurt,' she says, her voice soft, her expression

concerned, 'But honestly, when I was with my ex I did so many hurtful things to my friends. I missed the christening of one friend's first baby because my ex didn't want me to be away for the weekend, and he didn't want to come with me.'

Sofia winces as though in pain, shaking her head.

'I know it wasn't an excuse, but I was so totally blinded that I couldn't even see it. It didn't mean I stopped caring about my friends, though; he just made me careless with them.'

Mona can't quite believe that Sofia is opening up to her this much. She looks around briefly to check there are no new customers, but the café is still quiet.

'What happened with those friends?' asks Mona, wiping her eyes, 'I mean, are you still friends with them?'

She feels rude asking, but she wants to know, she has to know.

Sofia suddenly looks very sad. She slips her hands into her apron pockets, her shoulders slumped.

'Some of them – no,' she says, 'Others I'm still working on, trying hard to get back what we once had. But my very closest friends – they are still in my life. They told me that however badly I'd behaved, there was still enough good stuff that they remembered about me and about our friendship before it all happened, that they thought it was worth trying to fix things.'

Mona's mind is racing, her heart beating fast. Sofia looks intently at her.

'I suppose for you and Hannah you just need to decide if there was enough of the good stuff. Whether she's worth holding on to or whether you want to let go.'

Mona breathes deeply, Sofia's words settling in her mind

and causing thoughts to shift around uncertainly. Suddenly Sofia looks up at the clock again.

'Time for me to go,' she says, unwinding her apron, 'I hope things work out for you. I'll see you before you leave, right?'

Mona nods silently.

'Thank you,' she says eventually, as Sofia reaches for her jacket and handbag, 'For earlier with Jaheim, and ... Just thanks.'

Sofia gives her a quick but firm hug. Then she waves and turns for the door, leaving Mona alone, replaying Sofia's words over and over in her mind. Was there enough of the good stuff? Was her friendship with Hannah worth holding onto, despite how upset and angry she feels towards her?

Before she can think about it more, her eyes fall on the customer with the messy hair who sits at a table alone. Mona notices that her coffee cup is empty and the woman looks up and meets her eye.

'Can I get you anything else?' asks Mona. The customer stares up at her as though she has just come up from being underwater, before ordering another drink. Mona nods and makes the stranger a fresh cappuccino, all the time thinking about Sofia's words and the decision that she must make.

8.00 P.M.

MONIQUE

'Here's your coffee,' says the waitress, placing the cup on the table and removing the empty one. She pauses by the table for a moment, frowning and tilting her head.

'Are you OK?'

Monique stares back. Then she shakes herself a little and replies.

'Yes, I'm fine. Thank you for the coffee.'

The waitress nods and turns away. Monique watches her as she makes her way through the café. Two new customers have just arrived: two men who Monique guesses are in their fifties and who sit opposite each other in one of the booths. One is dressed in tracksuit trousers and a white polo shirt, the other in jeans and a T-shirt. They both have beards, one short and scruffy, the other full, reminding Monique of photos of her grandfather. They speak in strong East London accents. Between them on the table are two plates: a slice of Victoria sponge on one and a slab of carrot cake on the other.

Monique returns to her phone, opens Facebook and starts scrolling. Someone has had a promotion and celebrates with a photograph of champagne and smiles. It is someone's birthday and their wall is covered with messages: 'Happy birthday mate,' 'HB x'... One of her friends is on holiday and has posted a picture of a sunset over the edge of a balcony, two glasses of wine resting on a table just in front. Then there is her dad, who has changed his profile picture to one of him in the hospital, cradling his new granddaughter. The post has sixty-three likes and a stream of comments from old friends. He has replied to all of them.

She looks closely at the two of them in the photo. He looks old, or maybe it's just that the baby is so young – only a few hours of breath in her body, her tiny hand clasped around his seemingly giant thumb. Her father might be older than Monique likes to think (he will always be her dad, lifting her up on his shoulders and winning a toy unicorn for her at the carnival with his expert shot) but there is light in his eyes, pride glowing as he looks at his granddaughter – her daughter.

'She looks just like you,' her father had said when he first met her, his eyes filled with tears – Monique had never seen him cry before.

'Yes, I suppose she does,' she replied, forcing herself to smile. But she had peered at the squashed face in her arms and seen a stranger.

When they left the hospital her husband squeezed her tightly with one arm, the carrier held carefully in the other. He looked ahead but she stopped to look over her shoulder, expecting to see the nurses running after her. They were stealing a baby; how could no one be chasing them? But no one came; they let them carry the bundle of blankets and soft, crinkled flesh out the hospital doors and to the taxi rank outside.

Ella. Her name is Ella. Monique's mother cried when she told her they had chosen her name for their daughter.

'My darling daughter,' she said, kissing her cheek, 'And now my darling granddaughter. Thank you.'

Monique closes Facebook and opens her messages. She pauses, her hand hovering over the keypad. Since Ella was born Monique has half-written texts to her mum so many times but never sent them. 'Mum, I'm not coping.' She types it into her phone again now just to stare at the words she hasn't let herself say out loud and can't imagine ever saying to her mother's face. She reads the words over and over again.

Monique always wanted a baby. When she was a little girl she pushed toy dolls in prams like her friends, but her desire didn't go away when most of her friends moved on to other interests: travelling and men who made excellent lovers but would be terrible husbands. Monique carried the yearning for a baby inside her, keeping it quiet when it didn't feel appropriate. It felt like a dirty secret when she talked with her friends about careers and ambitions – she didn't dare tell them that one of hers was not new or pushing boundaries, but thousands of years old and tightly woven into the fabric of her body.

She expected her first moment with her daughter not to be a meeting, but to feel like a reunion. She imagined she would know the small face, the tiny fingers and toes, instantly and almost as well as her own body. This was the shadow that had followed her whole life, the being she had carried for nine months – the wish she had held for much longer.

When she came face to face with a stranger it rocked her. This was not how it was supposed to be. In her lifelong imaginings it had never occurred to her that maternal love might not come to her as easily as breathing. She took it completely for granted that she would love her child. North is north and south is south, the sun rises and always sets, and mothers love their children.

Monique drinks her coffee and looks around the café. She stares up at the stuffed bear in the top hat and wonders if he has a name. She imagines it would be something old fashioned and noble. Beside her, customers sit in booths and at bar stools sipping coffee, but she barely registers their faces.

She pictures her mother at home with Ella, holding her in her strong arms and rocking her to sleep. After a while she picks up her phone again and types one more time the words: 'Mum, I'm not coping.'

Her finger hovers over the 'send' button as buses pull up and move away outside the window and workers disappear into the belly of Liverpool Street station.

MONA

'Is that your daughter?' Mona asks. As she cleans tables around the customer with the curly hair she can't help but notice the photograph.

The woman looks up, startled. Mona gestures at the key ring attached to a bunch of keys placed on the table. Inside the small plastic frame is a photo of a new-born baby wearing a pink knitted hat.

'She's very cute,' says Mona, placing a jug of water and a cup on the woman's table and wiping the one beside it.

The woman looks at the photograph and studies it closely, as though trying to work something out.

'Yes, I suppose she is,' she says.

'Lots of sleepless nights then?' says Mona, working her way to the next table but turning back to listen for the woman's response.

'You could say that,' replies the woman. She is silent after that and Mona, not wanting to push it, smiles and nods.

'Just shout if you want anything else, OK?' she says. As she turns to leave she notices the woman type something on her phone and hears the small noise indicating she has just sent a message. As she puts her phone down her shoulders sink and Mona notices a very slight smile on her face, but it looks grim, not happy.

'Can we pay our bill?' says a voice and Mona looks up – it is one of the two men sat at the booth. They have been here a while, eating cake and talking.

'Of course!' says Mona, hurrying over with the card machine. As the two men pay (they split the bill fifty-fifty) she notices that they both have the same tattoo on their forearms: a small anchor.

'Thanks,' says one of the two men, pulling on a grey hooded jumper, the tattoo disappearing under its sleeve. At the door, Mona watches as the two men hug each other, holding one another firmly. They stay like that for a moment then pat each other hard on the shoulders before parting.

'Let's not leave it this long next time,' says one of the men.

'We say that every time,' says the other.

'Isn't that what being an adult is?' says the other, 'Saying "it's been ages" on repeat until you die?'

They both laugh, and shake hands, before opening the door and stepping outside. They turn in opposite directions down the street and then are gone. At the table on the other side of the room the woman with the photograph of her baby in a key ring stands, drops a handful of coins onto the table and looks around once more before leaving.

'Good evening, good evening,' comes a distinctive female voice a few moments later. Mona looks up at the elegant woman in her seventies who is stepping inside, grey hair set in curls as usual, dressed in the retro style she always favours. Tonight, it is a pair of high-waisted black jeans, a red and white top and a silk scarf around her neck. Mona smiles at Stella, the café's owner, trying to calm her breathing and her heartbeat which has suddenly started to race as she tries to work out how to break her news to her. Stella is one of those people who has what Mona's dance teachers would have called 'presence'.

Despite her age and her petite stature she fills the room with simply the sense of her.

'Quiet tonight?' Stella says, looking around at the tables which are empty apart from an elderly man drinking a cup of tea in one corner, and a quiet couple who sit near the back of the café, not talking to one another. Mona follows Stella's gaze around the room.

'It was busier earlier,' she says. *And there were also two full-blown arguments here today*, Mona thinks but does not say. She feels ashamed suddenly about the outbursts, imagining what Stella would think if she'd overheard them and seen the customers turning to look at the spectacle.

Stella wipes a hand over one of the tables. Her fingernails are painted red, silver bangles jangling on her slim wrist.

'I'm thinking of redecorating in here,' she says, casting her eyes around the signs, the lamps, and up at Ernest the bear.

'Really?' says Mona, surprised. The café feels like an extension of Stella herself; Mona knows that she personally picked out everything in here, some pictures coming from her own home when she first opened the café many years ago and had little money to decorate. The pictures stayed, and over the years more and more things have joined them too, adding to the busy, eclectic nature of the place. It is not to everyone's taste, Mona knows that, but it is Stella's. It's her name above the door and her place inside too.

'Oh. I don't know though,' Stella says, walking between the tables until she reaches the bar, where she slips gracefully onto one of the stools. 'I probably never will.' By now the café must seem too familiar to change; Mona assumes it will stay exactly the way it is as long as Stella is here to run it. There is no question of her ever retiring.

Mona pauses, knowing she has to tell Stella that she is leaving but wanting to stay talking about decorating instead.

'Anything to report from today then?' says Stella, 'Tricky customers? Running low on anything? Everything OK with the food?'

Stella does most of her ordering and admin from her home but pops in regularly to check up on things. She has no children to take over from her, but even if she did, Mona doubts she would give up control that easily. Stella looks at Mona, her hands neatly folded on the table, waiting for Mona's reply.

'It's all been fine,' Mona says, her mouth dry, 'Just a typical day really.'

She feels the words catching in her throat. It hasn't been a typical day, not for her. It's a day when everything has changed, when her life and its direction has altered completely.

Stella nods, happy with Mona's answer.

'So how are you then?' she asks.

Mona looks at Stella, her boss of five years who has always been so fair and considered, who has let her have the flexibility she so needs in order to support her other life. And with a great surge of feeling she realises she has let her down.

'I'm leaving,' she says suddenly, blurting out the words she knows she should have said the moment Stella arrived. 'I had an audition for a role with a contemporary dance company and I should have told you but I never expected I'd get it. The job is in Paris, it starts in two weeks, but I'd really like to leave sooner so I can pack and get everything ready. I know that gives you hardly any notice though, I'm so sorry.'

She stops, breathless. Stella is frowning, her red-painted lips pursed. She pauses for a long time before saying anything and Mona watches her, desperate to hear what she will say, feeling terrible.

'Hmm,' Stella says eventually, 'It's going to be tough to find a new member of staff at such short notice. Especially someone like you, of course. I'll have to speak to Hannah, Eleanor and Sofia about picking up extra shifts.'

Mona shifts uncomfortably on the spot.

'I'm honestly so sorry to let you down,' she says, 'I wish I could say that I could stay longer, or that I didn't have to go, but ...'

'Oh, you *must* go!' says Stella suddenly, her tone changing, her eyes meeting Mona's, 'Yes, it's a loss for us and it means things to sort out, but it's wonderful for you. Of course you must go. Congratulations, Mona.'

Stella smiles now and Mona smiles too, only realising she'd been holding her breath as it escapes from her in a sigh. She still feels guilty but Stella's enthusiasm, and her understanding, come as a relief.

Stella pauses for a moment, gazing around the café. Mona scans the room too, checking to see if either of the tables need anything, but they are both quiet and seem content, and don't catch Mona's eye when she looks in their direction. Stella's eyes have a somewhat faraway look to them, and as she turns back to Mona they seem suddenly to sparkle.

'You know,' Stella says in a soft voice, 'I used to be a dancer too.'

Mona raises her eyebrows; she had no idea. Looking at Stella now she can suddenly see it though: her petite, slender frame, the elegance to her movements.

'You never said anything!' Mona says. She has worked for Stella for five years and has often told her about auditions and shows that she needs to change shifts to accommodate. And yet Stella has never once mentioned that she shares her passion.

'Oh, it was a very long time ago now,' says Stella, looking up at Ernest the bear before turning her eyes back to Mona, 'I stopped decades ago, when I was just a little older than you.'

'What made you stop?' asks Mona. She tries to picture Stella at her age, dancing on a stage, and finds it surprisingly easy to do. Mona can tell she must have been a wonderful dancer – it's that presence that she had always noticed. But she can't believe she had never before guessed that Stella was once a performer. It makes complete sense now.

Stella's face suddenly grows serious as she considers the question. Eventually she answers.

'I grew tired of waiting to see my name in lights,' she says.

Mona thinks of the sign that hangs outside above the café door: 'Stella's' written in large, glowing letters. As though knowing exactly where Mona's thoughts have gone, Stella laughs quietly.

'I do love it here,' she says, looking around again at the café that she has created and that Mona thinks has so much of her on the walls, in the atmosphere. 'It started as a new chapter to my life that I never expected. But over time it has become the main story in my life. I have now run this café for far longer than I ever danced. I'm happy, and I like that I've made somewhere that people can come whatever the time of day or night. Where they can get pancakes at midnight. I like the possibility of it all – that the city might be dark and cold but we are always here, ready to serve coffee and cake and to be a meeting point for lovers, for friends, for colleagues. To me, it's a bit like the city itself – lives brushing up against one another, always something happening somewhere.'

Stella pauses again.

'But to say I have no regrets would not be true. I always wondered what would have happened if I'd kept going just a little bit longer. Perhaps my big break was just around the corner but I never reached it, I stopped trying before I got there.'

She looks at Mona and as Mona looks back she sees her own desires and dreams reflected in the older woman's eyes.

'So you *must* go,' says Stella, fiercely this time, passionately, 'You must do what you are meant to do.'

Mona feels her blood pounding inside her, her skin tingling with the feeling she has tried so hard to hold on to over the years – that anything is possible.

'Thank you,' she says, hoping her voice conveys how much she means it, 'I really am sorry to let you down. But thank you for being so understanding.'

Stella shrugs and shakes her head slightly.

'We'll manage,' she says. She glances around again and then stands up.

'Well, given that it's so quiet here I think I'll go,' she says, 'I just wanted to check in really, and now I need to start looking for a new waitress.'

Stella brushes the counter lightly with one hand and then nods at Mona.

'If you do your shifts on Sunday and Monday, and then don't worry about coming in after that,' she says. Mona thanks her again and Stella nods.

'I might not see you before you leave, then,' she says. 'But good luck in Paris.'

Mona is out from behind the counter now, Stella standing a little stiffly in front of her. Mona overcomes her own awkwardness and does what she knows she should do – she reaches out and hugs her. She feels the warmth of Stella's body and smells her perfume – she can't tell the exact scent but it is classic and has a strength to it, just like Stella. Then the two women step apart, Mona returning to the counter and Stella walking through the café before stepping out onto the street where her name shines above her in bright red letters.

338

9.00 P.M.

MONA

The door opens on a couple who look a few years younger than Mona. They are both dressed in jeans that are ripped at the knees, old-looking T-shirts and leather jackets. The woman is slightly taller than the man and has a large yellow scarf wrapped around her neck; her partner has a closely shaved head and the bluest eyes Mona has ever seen. Mona would describe them as edgy but in a sort of wholesome way – they look like the sort of couple who attend rock gigs in underground clubs and have friends who own tattoo parlours and bars, but who also shop at Whole Foods and possibly own a dog. They are both smiling but look tired as they sit down heavily at a table close to the door. Aside from them there are only a few other occupied tables: a man in a crumpled suit has ordered fish and chips and types on a laptop; a woman with purple hair who wears a Carphone Warehouse uniform scrolls on her phone and a tall man in a floral dress and red lipstick sits at one of the high tables and orders pancakes.

The young couple glance briefly at the man in the dress and then return to looking at their menus. Mona loves this about the city – it is so full of people that nothing is really that unusual.

'Do you know what you'd like to order?' says Mona once the couple have had time to read the menu and she has checked on the other customers. The pair lean back in their chairs, leather jackets hung over the backs and their legs stretched out, feet intertwined under the table.

'We're starving,' says the man, his blue eyes sparkling as he looks up at Mona, 'Aren't we, cabbage?'

He turns to his girlfriend, who smiles at him.

'*So* hungry,' says the woman, a southern lilt to her voice, 'We've been packing all day. Packing and packing and then we realised we'd only gone and packed away all the plates and kitchen stuff. So we thought we'd come out.'

The couple talk as though Mona has asked them many questions, or as though they are old friends. Mona says nothing, simply holds her pad and listens, nodding every now and then. She feels distracted, thinking about Stella and her former life as a dancer, and about Sofia's words which she has replayed in her mind over and over but hasn't fully confronted yet.

'It's our last night in London,' says the man, 'We're moving to Bristol tomorrow – found a nice little place down there. It's even got a tumble dryer.'

Mona can't help but smile this time. She can't imagine this man in the scruffy ripped jeans using a tumble dryer.

'Oh, really?' she says. He grins widely, clearly taking this as an invitation to continue talking.

'Yeah! And a dishwasher! Just a small one, mind, no good for your big pans and that, but great for the everyday stuff, you know?'

'So what's made you move?' says Mona, getting into the swing of things. She finds it actually feels good, this mindless chat, it calms all the other things that are spinning around her head. 'New jobs?'

The woman shakes her head.

'No,' she says, 'Well, we do both have new jobs, but that's not why we're leaving. We're just sick to death of London.'

'Oh, really?' Mona says again, not knowing what else to say. Although she might have fallen for Paris herself, she can't imagine that she'll ever stop loving London. It has been her home for twelve years and although it has grown so familiar that she doesn't always notice everything about it any more, she still loves it. She thinks that she probably always will. And as she thinks it, it hits her again that she will be leaving. She'd been so excited about the new start and so desperate to get away from the stress and unhappiness that had grown over the months in the flat, that she hadn't thought in detail about saying goodbye to the city she calls home.

'Yeah!' says the man, even more enthusiastically, 'The rent prices!'

'The underground,' adds the woman.

'The pollution,' adds the man.

'All them fucking pigeons.'

'Leicester Square.'

They don't seem to be fully aware of Mona any more, and instead throw different things they hate about the city back and forth between them like shuttlecocks tapped over a net. As they go on, the list becomes more specific.

'When a bus driver announces that "the destination of this bus has changed" midway through your journey without telling you where it's changed to. Fucking *what*?'

'Oh, oh, those restaurants where you can't book a table so instead you have to queue and sometimes people even stand out in the rain and queue for *hours*.'

Mona tries to interject. *What about the view over Waterloo Bridge?* she thinks. Even after all this time, whenever she catches a bus across it she puts down her phone to properly appreciate it, looking left and right to take in the view in either direction: the Houses of Parliament, Big Ben and the London Eye in one direction, and St Paul's, the OXO building and the soaring skyscrapers of the City in the other. She likes it best at sunset when Big Ben is silhouetted against a peach sky, the buildings are washed in gold and the lights from windows reflect on the river. What about the fountains at Somerset House and Granary Square where children run through the water, screaming and laughing, their parents watching from the side with dry clothes, complete strangers beaming at the joyful, innocent sound? What about Broadway Market, which comes alive every Saturday with food stalls, the smell of Thai curry and fresh doughnuts wafting into the air as people push bikes through the crowds and buskers (really good ones, too) sing and strum on guitars? The fact that you can wear anything you like and be whoever you want to be here without judgement, she thinks, glancing again at the male customer in the dress. And the theatres – the big ones of course but also all the tiny ones crammed into stuffy rooms above pubs where you can often catch an amazing new show for a tenner. But the couple are on a roll.

'The Circle Line!' says the man.

'Oh god yes, the Circle Line!' says the woman.

They both start laughing.

Mona tries to find a laugh too but suddenly finds that she can't.

'What can I get you to eat?' she says, perhaps a little more forcefully than she intends.

The couple look up at her, back at each other and then down at the menu.

'Bangers and mash!' says the man, folding the menu and handing it to her.

'Umm, scrambled eggs on toast!' says the woman.

'OK,' says Mona, turning towards the kitchen.

As she leaves, she hears the man continuing the conversation.

'Oh, what about the way people with backpacks don't take them off when they're on the Tube and so you end up getting knocked in the face by their bag.'

'Oh yeah, and also …'

Mona loses the sound of their voices as she approaches the kitchen, Aleksander's radio taking over instead. She leans for a moment against the doorway. Her heart is pounding again. The couple are right of course; all the things they mentioned are things that Mona finds frustrating about her city too. But despite it all, she realises it has become what she had been looking for when she left Singapore when she was eighteen: a home. She has chosen to leave, and yet the impending reality of it all has only really just hit her. She had been so excited about the new start that she forgot that all beginnings are also endings.

'Pound for the thoughts?' says Aleksander and Mona looks up.

'Sorry,' she says, 'I've got some orders for you.'

She passes him the order sheet and he nods, turning back to the kitchen. Mona stays where she is as he starts to prepare the food.

'What is it?' he says after a while.

Mona looks up again, startled. Aleksander usually keeps himself to himself – when she and Hannah chat about what's going on in their lives and try to ask him questions too, he usually shrugs and returns to the stove.

'It's nothing,' she says.

'Not nothing,' he says as he cracks eggs into a bowl, 'You look sad.'

Mona laughs a little. Does she really look that bad? Evidently, if even Aleksander has noticed. She rubs her face, as though it might be possible to wipe away exhaustion and sadness.

'I should have told you earlier,' she says, 'But ...'

'You're leaving,' he says matter-of-factly.

'How did you know?' she says.

He shrugs and starts whisking the eggs ferociously.

'Too good for here.'

Mona feels herself blushing.

'And also, Pablo told me. He overheard your argument with Hannah.'

Mona feels herself growing hot. She thinks back to the fight with Hannah and recalls looking up and finding a café full of customers staring at her. Although she was surrounded by people, she'd never felt more alone.

'So you're not happy about the new job?' Aleksander says, moving from the eggs to an onion gravy that he stirs on the hob. Mona turns briefly to check on the café but there are no new customers and everyone seems content enough. The couple have stopped talking now and are looking at their phones. The man in the floral dress selects a book from the telephone box library and starts to read.

'I am happy,' she says, turning back to face Aleksander, who grinds pepper with a flourish into the gravy, 'It just hit me that I'm really going to be leaving. I've lived in London for so long. I feel at home here. And I know it's expensive and polluted and crowded, and that I have *chosen* to leave, but I do love it too.'

Aleksander doesn't look up from the gravy, but he nods as she talks.

'It's where I've grown up, it's where I've built my life,' she says, 'And I love it. I love that I know the way on the underground without having to look at a map. The metro map in Paris is so confusing. I bet I'm going to end up getting lost. I love the way people change in the summer and suddenly become lighter and happier. I love the old-fashioned terraced houses with lots of little chimneys ...'

Aleksander nods again.

'I just know it so well, you know?' she says.

The pan suddenly hisses and bubbles dramatically as

Aleksander fries the sausages, pushing them back and forth with a spatula, oil spitting in beads. Mona takes a deep breath. She can feel her eyes filling and she blinks quickly, desperate not to let herself cry. The move to Paris had felt like the right choice, but what if it doesn't work out? She has only spent a weekend there, and now she is moving her entire life there. What if she hates it, or struggles to find her place?

'You know,' says Aleksander, 'When I first moved to London from Krakow, I hated it.'

Mona raises an eyebrow, surprised to hear him offering up such a personal piece of information. The most she knows about his personal life is that he supports Arsenal, like Pablo. Aleksander continues looking at the pan as he speaks.

'So grey! People always in a rush. No manners. Tesco – full of different foods and not my favourite things. Lonely all the time, no friends, living in a small flat with three other men, two from Poland, one from Russia.'

Mona listens carefully, absorbing each new piece of information and trying to use it to paint a picture of Aleksander's life that she has never seen before. He turns down the heat on the sausages and fetches a new pan for the eggs.

'But then it got better,' he says, 'I found Polish supermarket near my flat – so many of my favourite stuff and like I was home again. And the local Wetherspoon's – my flatmates met there every weekend and I came too and met new people. Still go there for the football, for beers ... I have local pub and a better flat and now I am happy. Same thing for you when you move to new city.'

It is the most Mona has ever heard Aleksander say. She is

346

glad that he is focused on the food because she knows she would struggle to hide her surprise. For someone who has said so little to her in the past, he has managed to find the exact words she needs to hear.

'I guess you're right,' she says.

He hands her the two plates: bangers and mash and scrambled eggs on toast. Then he turns away, as though signalling that the conversation is over and that he has better things to be doing. Mona watches for a moment as he turns up the radio and noisily starts unloading the dishwasher. Then she carries the steaming plates through to the couple in matching jeans, thinking about what Aleksander has just said.

'Thanks,' says the woman as Mona places down the plate.

'Rudeness!' says the young man loudly, raising his hand as though answering a question and nearly knocking the second plate out of Mona's hand, 'That's another thing I won't miss about London.'

He doesn't look at Mona as she places his plate on the table; instead he picks up his knife and fork and starts eating immediately.

ALEKSANDER

'You're never going to be one of life's shouters,' he remembers his mother saying to him when he was a child. 'You're just a quiet person, not a chatter. That's just who you are.'

He'd hoped that as he grew older he might prove his mother wrong. But he hadn't. She had put him in a box at the age of ten and he had never managed to climb out of it. Over time he had instead grown to fit it exactly.

As he cooks, he thinks with embarrassment back to the earlier conversation with Mona – the longest conversation they'd had, probably, since they'd been working together. When he speaks to her he feels like he is fishing for words but catching only silence. He feels foolish, which is why he usually chooses to say nothing instead.

It isn't helped by the fact that he is in love with her. He has been in love with her since they started working together. She joined the café two weeks after him and until he met her he never thought it was possible to fall in love with someone straight away. But when she walked through the door, her long dark plait resting on her shoulder and her body moving with such ... He searches for the word and eventually finds it. Grace. She moved with grace. He knew straight away what was happening because two words were screaming at him inside his head: '*Oh fuck.*'

He knew straight away that he loved her but he also knew straight away that it was impossible. Just like he knows he isn't a chatter, he also knows he isn't a lover. He has never had a proper girlfriend. He still lives with his two Polish friends, now in a better flat (the Russian has since moved in with a girlfriend) and when he isn't working he spends most of his time playing computer games with his flatmates, reading and watching videos on YouTube. He doesn't know many girls. He doesn't understand them. Sometimes he listens in on Mona and Hannah's long conversations with each other and has no idea what they are talking about (and by now his understanding of English is pretty good). They sometimes probe him for comments or advice but he says nothing because he can think of absolutely nothing to say. Eventually they turn back to each other and he turns back to his kitchen, taking comfort in the fact that at least here he knows what to do. He isn't even sure that he particularly likes cooking – he certainly doesn't *love* it – but at least in the kitchen he feels safe and in control.

Carefully, he pours the batter into the pan and watches patiently, waiting for exactly the right moment to flip the pancakes, when bubbles are starting to form on the surface, but not too many. Flip, wait, flip. Then he plates them up and brings them to the front for Mona.

'Table three,' he says.

'Thanks,' she replies with that smile, but he has already spun around and returned to his kitchen.

As he clears up and starts on the next order he thinks about the conversation again. He isn't quite sure why he snapped today and actually spoke to her. Perhaps because she is leaving, so it doesn't really matter any more if he makes a fool of himself. Or maybe because she looked so sad, sadder than he had ever seen her, and it made him feel like his heart was being squeezed. And even if he knew he was likely to choose the wrong words, he suddenly, desperately, wanted at least to try to find some.

She had looked so surprised that he knew immediately that he had said the wrong thing. He persevered anyway, because, having started, he found it hard to stop. And now here he is again, alone in his kitchen thinking of her and loving her.

Mona hadn't even noticed him arriving today. He stood

in the café, waiting to say hello to her but she was staring so fixedly into space – her dark eyebrows scrunched in one of her many expressions he knew so well – that he gave up and headed straight into the kitchen instead. That's when Pablo told him about the argument, and that Mona was leaving. Aleksander suspected Pablo had long ago guessed how he felt, because he placed a hand on Aleksander's shoulder and patted him.

Mona is leaving. The fact hits him again and he blinks quickly, telling himself it is just the pepper he has been adding to a macaroni cheese. He tries to comprehend it – what the café will be without her. He knows he will still see her everywhere, hear her soft voice with its unusual accent – almost American but not quite. To him, the café *is* Mona. But there is also a part of him that is pleased – a bittersweet sort of pleased – because loving her means he wants her to be happy. And he knows that dancing makes her happy: you just have to look at her as she walks between the tables or stretches to dust the pictures or holds the door open for a customer, to know that she is not a waitress, she is a dancer.

He suddenly curses to himself, a steady stream of Polish swearwords. The ironic thing is, although he finds it so hard to talk to other people (particularly women, particularly Mona), often he catches himself talking to himself. It's as though each human has a certain number of words they need to use up each day, and as his are not dispensed on conversations with other people, he has to get them out somehow and this is the only way. Mona has caught him at it before and he knows she must think him mad because of it. He thinks he is mad because of it.

He forces himself to stop talking to himself and chances a

peek out the kitchen window, wondering if Mona has heard him. But she is facing away, serving a young man and a woman Aleksander assumes is his girlfriend. She hands them two coffees and then returns to the counter, leaning against it and looking out across the café. Aleksander knows that both Hannah and Mona spend a lot of their shifts watching the customers that come in. Sometimes he catches them talking about some of them in the brief moments when the café is completely empty. As Mona watches the customers, Aleksander watches Mona.

MONA

The man in the floral dress has been joined by an old woman in a yellow beret that she has not removed despite the warmth of the café. Mona isn't sure whether they know each other (his mother, perhaps?) or have just happened to start talking, but they seem intent in conversation and every now and then they both laugh. Their laughter joins that of the women who just arrived and now sit in a large group, two tables pushed together. They speak in a language Mona guesses is Scandinavian, although she couldn't say which language exactly. Nearby, an Asian couple hold hands across their table. The woman has a large birthmark on her cheek and Mona spots an engagement ring sparkling on her hand.

Suddenly, everywhere Mona looks she seems to see love. Sometimes the café is dominated by anger as a couple have a heated argument or one customer bumps into the other and spills their coffee. Other days there seems to be such a mix of emotions that it is impossible to pick out one over another. But right now as Mona sees it, the feeling is love. It takes different shapes – the interlocked hands of the couple, the loud conversation of the group of friends – but it is there. And as she watches, she comes to a sudden realisation. She may not have a boyfriend but it is not true that she hasn't had a partner, or that she has never experienced love. It's just that the great love story of her life so far hasn't been a romance – it's been a friendship. She is hit with a sudden sharp pain as she accepts that it might be over. The pain cuts through her as sharply as grief, a sense of loss rocking her. She grips the coffee bar tightly, holding herself up, holding herself together.

10.00 P.M.

DAN

The warmth of the café welcomes him as he opens the door and steps back inside. It is much busier than when he left this morning (although the morning seems a long time ago), but he spots a table near the back and sits down, taking off his backpack and tucking it under the chair. He nods up at the stuffed bear, prepared this time for his staring eyes and out-stretched claws.

The red-headed waitress is not here; instead Dan spots the dark-haired one whom he remembers seeing when he first arrived early this morning. Her hair hangs in a plait and she stands behind the counter, holding on to it with both hands. Also in the café are a couple a little older than him who sit opposite each other at a small table, a man in a floral dress who talks to an old woman wearing a yellow beret, a group of women in their thirties who talk loudly to one another in what Dan guesses is a Scandinavian language, and an Asian man in what looks like some sort of security guard uniform who holds the hand across the table of a pretty woman with a large birthmark on her cheek.

Suddenly too warm, he unzips his green hoody and folds it on top of his bag, stretching out his legs beneath the table.

In class this afternoon he received his grade for the first assignment he had completed. He had been nervous all day, but when he was handed back his paper he saw that he had done well, really well. He held the paper to his chest and thought immediately of his mum.

Dan still hasn't worked out where he is going to stay tonight. He has sent messages to a few old friends, but they are people he hasn't spoken to in a long time and so far he hasn't heard back. He isn't sure he can face another night of forcing himself to try and stay awake in the café, but the alternative seems much worse, so when the library closed he headed here again.

The waitress hasn't spotted him so he walks up to the bar.

'What can I get you?' she says with a smile.

'A cappuccino please,' says Dan. He looks into the Cadbury's counter at the array of cakes: there is a carrot and walnut, a red velvet and a dark chocolate cake.

'Anything else?' says the waitress.

'No, just that. I'm sat over there.'

'I'll bring it over. You can pay later.'

Dan returns to the table and pulls his textbooks out of his bag.

MONA

The young couple who are moving to Bristol pay their bill. Mona notices their feet nudging each other under the table as they hand over their cards.

'We won't miss London prices either!' says the man with a smile. Mona simply nods as she deals with the payments. As they stand and prepare to leave she is hit by a sense of the transient nature of the city she lives in. Looking out the window at the street that is busy even at this time, she wonders how many people are coming and how many going. Who is a local and who is just passing through? A car screeches to a halt to miss a woman who has dropped her handbag in the road and is reaching to collect it. She grabs the bag, the driver punches his horn and then swerves away, skipping a red light. Further down the street a young woman in a yellow tracksuit drags a huge suitcase quickly down the pavement, a couple in their seventies sidestepping out of her way as she tears past them. They watch her for a moment and then link arms, continuing at a leisurely pace. The pavements are dusty and marked with the dark patches of chewing gum long since trodden into the ground.

Mona thinks about moving to London for the first time. She landed in a drizzle of rain, the air not as cold as she had expected as she stepped off the plane but damp and dull – the meteorological equivalent of being welcomed by an indifferent glance. The city didn't care one bit about her arrival.

At first, she wondered why she had travelled so far for such an anti-climactic greeting. Was this really what she left her family for? All this grey? But over time she found a way to slot into the puzzle of the city and learnt to appreciate its own kind of beauty. She moved between houseshares, she made friends on her course, including with Poppy, the first real friend she made in London. The cheerful, chestnut-haired young woman had approached her after a dance class one day and asked simply if Mona wanted to get lunch with her. Over lunch she asked a dazzling number of questions, showing genuine enthusiasm for every detail of Mona's life. Poppy had stopped mid-conversation, resting her chin in her hands and saying, 'Gosh, it sounds like I'm interviewing you, doesn't it?' She had then switched to telling Mona about her life: about her family in Manchester and her dog Tyler – a beagle. Poppy referred to her parents as 'Mummy and Daddy' and at first it embarrassed Mona, making her flinch slightly every time she heard the words, but over time she came to find it endearing.

Thinking of Poppy makes Mona feel a little less sad about leaving London – she is looking forward to spending time with her again. As she thinks about Poppy her mind also turns to Hannah again, and the Halloween party when they first met.

The message from Poppy about the party came out of the blue when Mona was just about to head out for a shift in the nightclub where she was working at the time.

'MONA! HALLOWEEN PARTY AT MINE!' read the message (Poppy always texts how she speaks, in capital letters), 'COSTUMES ESSENTIAL. xxxxx'.

Mona very nearly didn't go. As she read the message she recalled other parties at Poppy's house in Bounds Green. The parties were always heaving and for once Mona couldn't imagine facing a crowd of dancers and reciting her current CV to them, as the inevitable questions would be asked about what she was currently working on and what she'd done since they last saw each other.

How close she came to staying at home, Mona reflects as she watches the café and thinks about that time in her life. On the day of the party she was still undecided. She picked up a costume but it hung in her wardrobe, the labels still attached in case she decided to return it. She can't even remember what made her finally decide to go. Perhaps she couldn't face the thought of a night alone with Netflix. Or maybe she didn't even think about it, but just found herself reaching for her costume as though some force outside of herself was moving for her, pushing her out the flat and towards the party that would alter the direction of her life.

*

It is a long way to Poppy's house and as she walks to the Tube she feels uncomfortable, very aware of her costume and the blonde wig that sits on her head. But as she rides the Piccadilly Line into the centre of the city she notices more and more gruesome characters getting on and off. A man wrapped head to toe in bandages sits and looks at his phone. A group of girls dressed as skeletons stand by the doors and chat to each other, a bottle of wine badly hidden in a plastic bag and passed around the group every now and then. When they spot Mona watching them they smile and wave at her. As she passes through the most central stations – Piccadilly Circus, Leicester Square, Covent Garden – the train carriage heaves, everyone dressed up somehow, either in going-out clothes (short dresses and high heels, suit jackets and gelled hair) or in Halloween costumes. The train has a noisy, carnival feel to it as groups clearly already softened by drink laugh and joke, even chatting with strangers who stand near them. It cheers Mona, even as the train heads further east and the carriages empty. When she gets off at Bounds Green she thinks she is the only one until she spots someone walking a little ahead of her down the platform towards the escalator. Looking closer, she notices the woman is dressed as Wilma Flintstone. Too shy to run and catch her up, Mona is still grateful for this costumed woman who walks a little ahead of her, guiding her all the way to Poppy's house.

As expected, the party is heaving. Poppy and her housemates have decorated all the rooms and Mona has to duck under trails of toilet roll, bin liners and cobwebs as she follows a few guests into the living room. She spots Poppy immediately – Cruella De Vil dancing in a showering of silver stars given off by the glitter ball.

'Mona!' Poppy says, rushing over to hug her. They chat for a moment, but then the doorbell rings and Poppy dashes off, leaving Mona in the middle of the room surrounded by people who, in their costumes, she struggles to recognise. She heads for the kitchen, thinking that a drink will ease her in to the party, help loosen her and shield herself from the inevitable questions about her career.

The kitchen is already a mess, the floor sticky from spilt drinks. In the centre of the room is a table littered with bottles – most half-empty – and the sink is filled with ice and cans of beer. Mona rummages for an empty cup, rinses it in the sink just in case and opens a beer, pouring it into the cup. She drinks half the cup in a few sips. Taking another long drink, she prepares herself for returning to the party. She thinks about what she will say in response to the questions and sets her face in a calm expression, tilting her chin.

She turns to leave at the exact same moment that a red-headed woman dressed in a patchwork dress and painted in green walks quickly into the room. Before Mona can step out of the way they are colliding with each other and the rest of her beer has launched itself out of the cup and onto the floor.

'I'm so sorry!' says the woman, steadying herself on the table. She is a similar height to her, Mona notices, and her face and arms are covered in black seams, her mouth extended into a wide, eerie smile. But beneath the make-up she looks concerned. The contrast makes Mona smile.

'No, it's my fault,' says Mona, 'I'm sorry!'

The woman with the red hair and the green face reaches for some kitchen roll from the top of the fridge, leaning to wipe the floor.

'Thanks,' says Mona, 'It really was my fault though, I should have moved out of your way.'

'Wow,' says the woman, standing up, 'We don't really make great evil characters, do we?'

Mona smiles. She notices an accent – it has taken her a while to get to know all the different British accents, but she thinks this woman's is Welsh. She is smiling back at Mona and there is something about her face, despite all the make-up, that makes Mona feel comfortable immediately.

'No, I guess we don't,' she says eventually, 'I'm Mona by the way, the rest of the time.'

'I'm Hannah.'

Mona learns that Hannah is one of Poppy's housemates, although she has only lived there for a few weeks. Hannah mentions there is a spare room going in their house and it sparks a thought in Mona's mind – her current flat share is with two women who seem to like to live in filth and whom she can't stand. She has been desperate to move out but has been struggling to find somewhere. She files the thought and continues listening to Hannah. She is working as a part-time receptionist and Mona notices how she spins this in a positive way as though it's exactly how she planned things to go. She doesn't mention it, but it makes her smile – this language of positivity that she is so used to as well. Listening to Hannah talk so excitedly about singing and music, she feels a renewed sense of enthusiasm for her own career. This woman painted in green reminds her what it feels like – that drive, that hunger – because she can tell immediately that she shares it too. It makes her feel an immediate warmth towards her.

Hannah laughs easily and her smile is so wide that the painted grin on her face isn't too much of an exaggeration. As they chat people come and go, looking for drinks, but Mona and Hannah barely seem to notice them.

'So why dancing?' Hannah asks after a while.

Mona pauses. She has been dancing for so much of her life that it has become part of who she is. She thinks of herself first and foremost as a dancer, even though at the moment she spends more of her time working in a nightclub, her shoes sticking to the floor and leering comments from drunken customers reaching her across the bar like slaps. Her love of dancing is something that has informed the most important decisions of her life, and yet she can't remember ever really stepping back and thinking why exactly this is. To her, it makes so much sense that it doesn't even need explaining. It is her, it is what she is meant to do.

She isn't really aware of what she is saying when she answers. Hannah watches her closely, nodding. As she speaks, Mona feels that well-known yearning inside her that she feels every day and every time she thinks about all the things she wants to achieve. Sometimes she feels she has to hide it or at least dull the strength of her ambition. But with Hannah, she senses she can be honest. It is a relief to speak like this. It makes her feel like herself – like a dancer, not a bartender.

When she finishes speaking she feels slightly dazed.

'Does that sound mad?' she says.

'Not at all!' replies Hannah, 'I know exactly what you mean.'

Mona smiles. Because she gets the sense that this smiley, red-headed woman does understand her, and that with her she doesn't have to be anyone other than herself.

In the living room the music continues to boom and the glitter ball sends stars around the walls and ceiling. Mona catches the voice of Poppy somewhere in the house and the sound of laughing. She thinks about returning to the rest of the party, but instead she pours another drink for her and Hannah. They still have so much more to talk about. They talk quickly and animatedly, gesturing with hands and nodding at each other.

The drink and the rush of such an instant connection go to her head, making her forget for a moment the stresses that wait for her back in her flat and her part-time office job.

I think we're going to be friends, *thinks Mona to herself as Hannah talks. She is suddenly very glad she came to this party – she thinks it might be one that she will remember.*

*

Remembering their meeting, Mona thinks for the first time how similar it felt to falling in love. The same rush, the same sense of excitement, just different motivations. Mona feels an ache as she realises she still needs to confront what Sofia said earlier and decide whether there is anything worth salvaging in her friendship with Hannah – if it is worth fighting for. She glances to the clock again and it is as though time has suddenly sped up, pulling her closer to her return to the flat and to the words she knows she must say to Hannah but hasn't found yet.

Suddenly a blast of cold air rouses her from her thoughts as two of the women in the group stand and step outside for a cigarette. Mona looks up and as the door shuts behind the women she notices for the first time the only other person in the café who, like her, is alone. The young man who ordered the cappuccino and who is now reaching for a jumper from the rucksack that she notices for the first time is stashed under his chair. Long blond hair falls over his unshaven face as he zips up his green hoody.

DAN

'It's you!' says the waitress. She is looking directly at him but Dan still turns around.

'It's you!' she says again. She is holding a Post-it note in her hand.

'Young – twenty-ish – man,' she reads, looking up at him and then back at the Post-it note, 'Longish blond hair, slight beard, green hoody, large rucksack. That sounds like you.'

Dan frowns, his heartbeat rising. Had he done something wrong? Maybe the waitress had spotted him sleeping last night and had written a note for her colleague, telling her not to let him in if he came back. But the waitress's voice sounds cheerful. He is completely confused.

'Um ...' he says, but the waitress is already turning back to the counter. She returns a second later, holding out a large brown envelope.

'Here,' she says, 'This was left for you earlier. I've been looking out for you all day. I'm so glad you came back.'

Dan can't help but smile – relief, but also an unusual feeling of being welcome, wanted even. The waitress is still smiling at him, holding out the envelope.

'What is it?' he says.

'Don't know,' she says. 'It's yours though. Here.'

After a small pause he reaches for it. The waitress stands by him for a moment, perhaps waiting for him to open it but then she does a little nod and returns to the counter.

Dan is left on his own again, staring at the large envelope

in his hand. It is quite light and flat, but whatever is inside feels solid – he feels sharp corners as he runs his thumb over the edges. Carefully, he opens it and slides his hand inside. He pulls out a book, and as he turns it over he realises it is the crossword book. He thinks immediately of the writer, the man in the Pink Floyd T-shirt and the shirt with the red button, who talked with him and bought him pancakes and a strawberry milkshake. Dan feels his face softening into a smile.

At the table next to him the woman with the birthmark and her boyfriend stand up, knocking the table slightly. A drink spills and the waitress is suddenly there again, mopping at the pool of liquid.

'I'm so sorry,' says the man, leaning forward to help. The waitress waves him away.

'Don't worry. You two have a nice evening.'

The couple give her one last glance, nod, and then head for the door, the man stepping aside to let his girlfriend out first. Dan glances briefly at the waitress as she finishes wiping the table. She catches his eye and peers at the book in his hand, laughing as she does so.

'I can't believe I got so worked up over a crossword book,' she says, 'Honestly, I was jumping every time I saw someone in green.'

She straightens the table and returns to the coffee counter.

Dan decides to have a go at one of the crosswords and reaches down to find a pen in his rucksack. As he reaches, his arm accidentally knocks the book and it falls onto the ground, an envelope and a folded sheet of paper slipping out from between the pages as it falls. Dan stoops and picks up the book, the envelope and the paper and sits back on his chair. The envelope is not sealed. He feels inside and pulls out two fifty-pound notes and two twenties. He stares at them. The fifties are crisp and smooth but the twenties are slightly more worn and crumpled. He runs his fingers over each note.

With hands that have started to shake slightly, he unfolds the piece of paper that fell out alongside the envelope. It is a handwritten note, made out in slanted writing and a black biro, and he starts to read.

To my crossword companion,

Over the years as a writer, I have developed a habit of guessing at people's stories. Sometimes I get it wrong, sometimes I get it right, but I can't help but think about what is going on, what kind of journey someone has been on and what their life is like.

If I have correctly guessed your story, or at least parts of it, then I hope that this will help you a little while you try to get back on your feet, and that you will see it not as charity, but as a selfish act — a father getting a kick out of helping a stranger when he is struggling so much to help his own son.

If I have guessed wrongly, then please enjoy this as a random act of kindness — perhaps to be spent on a deserved night out after all your studying.

In either case, I wish you all the best. You have been dealt a hand that would not be wished on anyone, and unfortunately only time can start to heal your pain. I hope that time will bring you peace, new horizons, and a fantastic and well-earned job as an engineer.

Yours in friendship,

A crossword-loving insomniac

Dan reads the note twice, only realising at the end of the second reading that he is crying. Tears stream down his face and drip onto the fabric of his green hoody. He cries from shock, for the kindness of a stranger, and he cries for his mum.

Trying to stifle his tears, Dan slips the money and the note inside the envelope and reaches down for his rucksack. For a few moments he digs around inside, searching for something right at the bottom. Eventually he finds it, and out from a pile of clothes and books he pulls a large glass jar. The jar is filled with coins – coppers and silvers and golden pound coins, some dull, some glinting in the glare of the café lights. A pair of socks is rolled up on top, Dan's solution to prevent the jar from rattling too much. It is heavy and just looking at the jar his shoulders give a twinge of pain. On the front of the jar is a label. In neat handwriting that he will forever remember as his mother's are the words, 'Orient Express'.

Dan carefully opens the jar, removes the socks and places the envelope with the cash inside.

Since his mum died, he has resisted spending the money in there. Even when he has skipped meals and desperately scrolled through the contacts list on his phone, thinking who might let him stay with them, the Orient Express jar has remained stuffed at the bottom of his backpack. But as he neatly stows it back in his bag he makes a decision. His mum would want him to use it. He will find a hostel – he has enough for a few nights, maybe even a few weeks. Tomorrow he will push through his pride and go to the students' union at his university. He will tell them about his situation and he will ask them if they can help. And as he makes the decision and realises that he needs help and is ready to ask for it, he starts to cry even harder.

'Oh!' comes a voice, and he looks up. Through his tears he spots the dark-haired waitress again, moving quickly towards him across the café. When she reaches him, without pausing she bends down and wraps her arms around him, pulling him into a tight hug.

'It's OK,' says the waitress, and even though she doesn't know him, and he knows that it isn't OK, not really, not yet, he lets himself be hugged.

After a while the waitress pulls back and stands up.

'I'm sorry,' she says quickly, 'I know that probably wasn't very professional. I just can't stand seeing people cry.'

Dan wipes his face and tries a weak smile, shaking his head in an attempt to tell her that he didn't mind – that he was grateful for it. She watches him for a moment as he tries to compose himself.

'Do you really hate crosswords that much?' she says.

And despite it all, Dan laughs.

11.00 P.M.

MONA

Once the boy in the green hoody has stopped crying, he orders pancakes with bacon and maple syrup and a side of chocolate cake. Mona occasionally glances over, checking on him. She had wanted to ask why he was crying, but despite the tears he seemed like he was OK, or as though he was going to be. She watches as he uses the last bite of pancake to mop up the last drop of maple syrup before moving on to the chocolate cake. She doesn't know his story, but she feels pleased that the café is here for him and she was at least able to bring him cakes, despite the fact it is the last hour of her shift and she feels exhausted.

Her mind is a tangle of thoughts. Snippets of her argument with Hannah replay in her mind. She pictures Jaheim standing in the café and Sofia and Aleksander supporting her as she asked him to leave. She thinks of Stella, who used to be a dancer but kept her past a secret for all these years. She thinks of Poppy in Paris and of Hannah at home in their flat, perhaps asleep, perhaps waiting up to speak to her. She pictures her thirtieth birthday that she spent eating beans on toast alone.

The table of Scandinavian women ask Mona to take a photograph of them all, and she holds an iPhone for them and tells the women to move a little closer so they will all fit in the frame. Mona learns that it is one of the women's fortieth birthday and as she has always wanted to visit London they have come over, from Sweden, it turns out, for a long weekend. On the back of their receipt Mona writes down a few places she thinks they should visit. Borough Market, Harrods just for the food court, Battersea Park, Portobello Road, Little Venice. She points them in the direction of Shoreditch, where they are continuing their evening, and they leave her a large tip which she slips into her apron pocket.

The man in the dress and his companion have left now too, linking arms and laughing at a joke that only they know. In the booth a couple who arrived earlier are finishing their drinks, a red-haired woman wiping a splash of coffee with a folded napkin. A strand of hair falls in front of her face and the man sat next to her reaches and tucks it back behind her ear.

In the windows, Mona can see the interior of the café reflected in the glass. The red telephone box, the pictures, the lampshade, and above them all the face of Ernest the bear who watches over everything, regardless of the time of day or day of the week. Mona adjusts her eyes and looks out at the street. The pavements are busy, people crossing from the station towards the café before they will turn away down a side street towards Brick Lane or continue walking down the main road towards Shoreditch and its many bars and nightclubs. Three young women in a similar uniform of jeans, heeled boots and leather jackets in varying shades link arms and share a laugh as they pass by the window. A cyclist tears past, whizzing through a red light. A bus pauses as it waits for the lights to change, and Mona can see inside to the passengers on the lower deck, some standing, some sitting and looking at phones, ears covered with headphones. One young woman, a baby strapped in a carrier to her chest, is staring intently out the window. Mona catches her eye, smiles, and then the bus pulls away. The movement returns Mona to the café, which is now completely empty, the couple and the young man in the green hoody having left, cash tucked beneath a mug and a plate on their tables.

Deserted, the café looks strange and sad. Empty seats wait for customers in need of caffeine to perk them up, comfort food to make them nostalgic and somewhere warm to sit with a friend and pass gossip like salt and pepper across the table. The coffee machine stands silent, tables and chairs reflected in its surface. Aleksander is quiet and Mona realises she will miss the sound of him talking to himself in the kitchen. She will miss Pablo and the photos of Rosa that he shares with such pride. She will miss Stella, whom she feels like she has only just come to really understand. She will miss the customers that walk in at all times of the day and night carrying stories like heavy bags on their shoulders. She will miss the view from the café window and the city that spreads around it, its twists and turns impossible to fully master, but that all the same has become her home.

Alone in the café, Mona finally returns to Sofia's question, this time truly confronting it. In two weeks she will be leaving London for Paris, but as well as leaving her flat and this job, will she also be leaving her friendship? For a moment she puts aside the unhappy memories and all the times Hannah has hurt her over the past year. Instead, she asks herself the question that Sofia posed to her a few hours ago. If she thinks back over her friendship with Hannah, is there enough of the good stuff? Is there enough to hold on to?

Suddenly, Mona's mind is filled with memories from their friendship.

The day Mona moved into the house in Bounds Green, and how Hannah spent hours helping her unpack, ordering them both a takeaway when they realised it had got late and they were too tired to cook. Evenings spent watching films together in one of their rooms. The time they found out that their housemate Lily had been keeping her illness a secret for so long, and the fact that Hannah and Mona both took some small comfort in the fact they knew they would always look after each other. Hannah in the audience at every dance show Mona has ever performed in since they met. Hannah might be late for everything else and may have kept Mona waiting in restaurants and bars many times over the years, but she has never once been late to one of Mona's performances. The Christmas that Mona spent with Hannah and Hannah's parents when she couldn't afford flights to Argentina and when her mother was spending the holidays catching some sun in

Australia with her boyfriend. A home-made stocking from Hannah's mother, despite the fact Mona was twenty-seven at the time, and tickets to an upcoming dance show that she had been wanting to go to but couldn't quite afford, from Hannah (who, she admitted, had saved her tips for months to be able to buy them). Hannah leaving work early because Mona had locked herself out of the flat, arriving with her key and a smile instead of annoyance. The time Hannah washed her hair when Mona was sick and missed out on their planned trip to Paris to take care of her. The hospital trip for Mona's sprained ankle, where Hannah carried her to A & E. The fact that Hannah often buys flowers and leaves them in a vase in Mona's room for no reason. Hannah's arm around her shoulders on one of the rare occasions when Mona has let herself cry after a phone conversation with one of her parents, frustrated and pained by their broken relationship. Hannah's unwavering belief in her – the many, many times she has told Mona that she is absolutely certain that Mona is going to make it. The messages Hannah often sends her with links to silly YouTube videos and photos that are simply intended to make Mona laugh. The hundreds and hundreds of times that Hannah has made Mona smile and laugh so hard she cries.

In the café, the sound of a new song comes through the speakers. It is 'Tutti Frutti', the song that always gets Hannah and Mona dancing together, however tired they feel, whatever else is going on in their lives.

Mona suddenly decides that when she gets home she will talk to Hannah and try and work things out. Because in the emptiness of the café the words of their earlier argument seem to fade, the pain she has carried for months dulling just enough for her to want to hear Hannah's familiar voice. The hurt is not gone, and she knows that there is still so much to talk about, so much to try and fix. She needs to tell Hannah about the pain she has caused and show her the marks that her actions have left. But she finds that she wants to at least try to fix things. Because Hannah might have hurt her, but over the past five years she has also made her laugh, and smile, and helped her when she felt lost and looked after her when she felt sick. There might have been bad bits, but there was also so much good. Mona thinks about leaving for Paris and how much she will miss about London, and realises that she will also miss her imperfect, at times careless but at times kind and wonderful friend. She looks up at the clock, watching as the minutes tick past, bringing her closer to the end of her shift when she can return to the flat and try to speak to Hannah. In the same thought she wills the clock to turn faster and also wishes it to slow down, not knowing yet what she will say to Hannah and what her friend will say to her in return.

ONE YEAR LATER

12.00 A.M.

HANNAH

As she approaches Stella's, it surprises and relieves her how little it has changed. She spots the glowing light as soon as she steps out of Liverpool Street station, the bright windows standing out from the dark shop fronts along most of the rest of the street. She waits at the pedestrian crossing, caught up in a crowd of people who look dressed for a night out. A man holds tightly onto the lamp post, singing a song that Hannah cannot make out through the slur of his words. The lights change and Hannah walks across, breaking free from the noisy group as they continue down the main street and she veers off towards the café.

For a moment she stands outside the window, looking inside at the room she knows so well. Although there are only a few customers, it is relatively busy for this time of night, and she

377

feels pleased. The black and white linoleum looks a little worn but is still clean and bright. She notices that the tables have been rearranged slightly and she tries to remember exactly what the old layout was like but can't. She decides she likes it like this – the café seems less crowded somehow, but still cosy. The lampshade has been reupholstered but the pictures on the walls are the same. And there is Ernest, still watching over things, still wearing his top hat. She takes a breath and pushes open the door.

The young man at the counter looks up.

'Hi!' he says. He has sandy blond hair and green eyes and wears a polo shirt and jeans, a black and red apron tied round his waist.

'What can I get you?' he says in a soft voice. The voice seems familiar, as do his bright green eyes. She frowns slightly, trying to place him, but she can't.

'I'll have a cappuccino,' she says, and, finding she is surprisingly hungry and knowing she is in the one place where to be hungry at midnight is OK, she adds, 'And some pancakes with berries please.'

Looking around, she spots a table in the corner, where she will have a good view of the rest of the café.

'I'll bring it over,' says the waiter as she makes her way to the table.

Once seated, she looks around at the other customers. At one of the booths sit two familiar-looking young men, coffee mugs in front of them, their hands held tightly across the table. In the middle of the café are a man and a woman who look dressed up for the night, the man in a navy shirt and black jeans, the woman in a red dress, blonde hair that looks recently highlighted resting in neat curls on her shoulders. Their cheeks are flushed and they smile at each other as they talk in low tones, leaning closely together. At a table by the window sits a man in his sixties, drinking a cup of coffee alone.

'Here we go,' says the waiter, placing the cappuccino on the table.

'Thanks,' she says, reaching for the mug and wrapping her hands around its warmth.

The waiter looks at her for a moment, as though about to say something, but then nods and turns away.

It feels strange for Hannah to be a customer. She quit nearly a year ago now, not long after Mona left. Thinking back to that time she remembers Jaheim for a moment and is surprised and relieved to realise it has been a long time since she last thought of him. The thought enters her mind for a second but then drifts away again like a scrap of litter carried on the wind down the street and disappearing out of sight.

She notices a splash of milk on the table and wipes it carefully with a napkin. Then she leans back in her chair, takes a sip from her coffee, and waits.

JOE AND HAZIQ

They hold hands across the table, their coffees growing cold beside them.

'A year ago today,' says Haziq with a smile. They are both dressed smartly, Haziq in a white shirt and black jeans, Joe in pale blue and chinos. They have been out for dinner in one of their favourite restaurants but decided to end their evening with coffee here.

'A year ago today,' repeats Joe. He squeezes Haziq's hand and Haziq squeezes back.

The engagement had been more complicated than they had expected. Despite proposing, Haziq had been forced to return to Indonesia anyway. It was several months before he was granted a visa to return. For both of them, the separation had been even harder than they'd imagined. Since becoming engaged, the need to be together had grown even stronger and each of them slept curled up on 'their' side of the bed, thousands of miles apart but still making room for each other. A month after saying goodbye at Heathrow airport they met in Portugal, renting a whitewashed house for a week where the sun blazed outside but they barely left the shade of their room. At the end of the holiday, saying goodbye for a second time had been painful, especially as they still weren't sure when Haziq would be able to return.

But eventually the paperwork had arrived. They will be married in three weeks, in Stoke Newington Town Hall with a reception at the pub opposite afterwards. The hall and the pub are a ten-minute walk from the flat they now share together, grey pinstripe sheets on their bed, a mustard yellow beanbag in their living room and plants on every spare surface. Haziq's parents won't be there at the wedding, but Joe's will. Joe's mother will walk Haziq down the aisle to marry her son.

Joe withdraws his hand for a moment and looks down at his coffee cup.

'It's getting close now,' he says.

'It is,' replies Haziq.

Joe stares intently at the dregs of coffee coated to the bottom of the cup. Despite the music in the background the café suddenly seems quiet as all the things Joe wants to say buzz in his head. He talks quickly before he can change his mind.

'I just wanted to check you're absolutely sure this is what you want,' he says, 'I mean, I know we've done all the paperwork and we've booked everything, but I want to know that you don't think I forced you into this. That you're still absolutely sure this is what you want.'

With all his strength, Joe forces himself to look up. His eyes meet Haziq's and as he looks at him he feels that same rush he felt when he first met him years ago. In Haziq's dark eyes he sees the sacrifices they have both made to get to this point. He sees a life woven together despite the odds and the life that he hopes lies ahead of them.

Haziq reaches out a hand and places it on Joe's cheek.

'It's what I want,' he says firmly, his fingers soft against Joe's face, 'You, Joe Walsh, are what I want.'

And he leans forwards and kisses his fiancé firmly on the mouth.

DAN

He knew immediately that the woman at the table in the corner was one of the old waitresses. She is hard to miss, with her bright red hair that nearly reaches her waist. She sits alone,

381

drinking her cappuccino and glancing up at the door every now and then. Perhaps he will say something later, he thinks, or perhaps he will leave her to her thoughts.

He glances around the café, checking to see if anyone needs anything but everyone seems content, and no one is looking up for his attention. Carefully, he wipes the glass of the Cadbury's counter. Then he turns to the machine, making an espresso and carrying it through into the kitchen.

'I thought you might want this,' he says to Aleksander, who is preparing to leave, his coat half on. Pablo is making pancakes, and also stirring a pot on the hob, having arrived for his shift not long after Dan. The kitchen is filled with the quiet sound of the pancakes bubbling and the music coming from the radio.

'You're off to see Erika then?' Dan says, passing the espresso to Aleksander, who takes it and nods his thanks. He drinks it in one go, placing the empty cup on the counter. Since he started dating Erika, Aleksander hasn't been able to stop talking. He seems to like to talk to Pablo and Dan about her: about her small, slightly pointed nose, about the bar she works at nearby, about the fact her favourite food is macaroni cheese, about the flat they will live in together one day.

'Yes,' he says, doing up the buttons on his coat, 'She finishes work now too. Thought about going out, but no. Takeaway and film at home. Best thing about this city – always someone to make your food for you!'

With a flourish he hangs up his apron. Dan laughs and then remembers the other reason he came into the kitchen.

'Oh, I think your old colleague is here,' says Dan, 'The red-headed waitress. The pancakes are for her.'

Aleksander and Pablo look at each other.

'Hannah!' they say at the same time.

Pablo plates up the pancakes, scattering them with berries, and hands Dan the spatula he was using to stir the other pot, still on the hob.

'Do you mind taking over for a minute?' he asks.

'Of course,' replies Dan, 'You go and say hello.'

As he stirs the pan he listens to the sound of laughter and voices as the two chefs greet the former waitress who sits alone in the corner of the café. It makes Dan smile. This is one of his favourite parts of his job: listening to old friends meeting each other. He likes to watch them from the coffee bar, unnoticed but sharing in the happiness of their moment.

After the day with the envelope, he had headed back to the café many times in the evening, hoping to bump into the insomniac writer to thank him. But he never saw him again. Instead, he spotted a notice saying the café was in need of waiting staff. He had read it carefully, imagining how working in the 24-hour café could fit well alongside his studies, and how the cash would help to top up his student loan. And now that he had a fixed address – a room that the students' union had helped him to find, he could apply. So he did.

He likes his job here. He likes the order of it, how in control he feels when he makes a complicated coffee order and gets it right. He likes the quiet but friendly chat with Aleksander and hearing about Rosa, Pablo's granddaughter. Over time he has come to recognise regular customers and to know the *Big*

Issue seller, John, and the scruffy dog who a few months ago started to sit at his feet. The dog is called Lucky and on warm days Dan brings her a bowl of water. When he does so, John beams at him as though the bowl is filled with gold and calls him a 'true gent'.

'OK, give me back my pan,' says Pablo, returning to the kitchen and rubbing his hands on his trousers before taking the spatula from Dan.

'Thanks,' Pablo says as they swap places, 'That was a blast from the past.'

Dan nods, thinking how much there is about his past that his workmates don't know, and wondering if the same can be said for them. Although he is friendly with his colleagues he also holds something of himself back. He sometimes worries that his reluctance to talk about his mum makes it seem as though he is ashamed of her. But he guards his memories of her protectively, as though holding them tightly against his chest will keep them fresh and alive for longer. He cannot bear to think about the day when the sound of her voice and the smell of the pancakes she cooked for him are gone completely.

He blinks quickly, nods and heads for the doorway, returning to his domain and leaving Pablo in his.

MONA

She has only been back in London for two hours, but already she feels home again. The black taxis, the red buses, the sounds and smells of the city. As she heads out of Liverpool Street station she feels it again – that rush of familiarity.

Mona has lived in Paris for nearly a year. After a month of sleeping on Poppy and Antoine's sofa bed she found a tiny rented apartment for herself, on the outskirts of Paris. It is so small that there is only room for a mini-fridge: last winter she kept most of her food in a box on the tiny balcony. During the summer she mainly ate out, happy to escape the sweltering heat of the one-room flat. The size and lack of decent cooking facilities don't bother her too much though, as she is rarely in the flat. The dance company keeps her busy; she has never worked so hard in her life and yet she feels a new sense of calm, too. In her limited time off she hangs out with Poppy and Antoine and a few new friends from the dance company, and she walks. She has walked so far across the city that a map of its streets is now imprinted in her mind. This is one of the things she loves most about Paris – it is smaller than London, which means it is much easier to get about on foot. She has learnt the streets as well as the names of her favourite pastries in her local boulangerie and the name of the shopkeeper at her local fruit and vegetable store. She has come to notice and love certain unique touches in the city, like the queues of grand-parents and grandchildren at the bakeries just after school closing time and the rich Parisian women with their tiny dogs who seem to her just as much a part of the fabric of the city as the ornate Metro signs and the brasseries on every street.

And yet it is still not home, and she isn't sure if it ever will be. Since she has been away her concept of home has become hazy: if she doesn't feel it where she lives does it even exist?

But standing on the pavement of Liverpool Street she remembers suddenly what it means. She has walked these pavements hundreds of times, so frequently that she still knows where to sidestep the loose paving stone. The people who mill around her are different but also the same. The street at night has the same sound and smell, as groups head to bars and clubs in the area and buses kick up dust and litter in the street. And there among it all is the glowing sign for Stella's. When she worked there she thought of it as a necessity – the job that facilitated what felt to her as her 'true' life as a dancer. She never would have imagined that seeing the café again could feel so much like coming home.

MONIQUE

Without meaning to, she finds herself touching the ends of her hair, curling strands around her finger. Every now and then she catches her reflection in the glass and hardly recognises herself. It makes her blush to admit to herself that it looks good – she looks good. The red lipstick she put on to match her red dress has faded slightly, from the dinner they ate earlier, from the coffee cup, and from kissing her husband.

He watches her closely, a smile tickling the corners of his mouth. He has made an effort tonight too, his face cleanly shaven, his clothes neat and ironed – free from any signs of Ella and the mess that follows her like a shadow. Tonight and tomorrow Ella is staying with Monique's parents, the first weekend she and her husband have had truly to themselves since Ella was born. She had been anxious leaving her, they both had, but they knew it was a step they needed to take. As Monique leant down to kiss her baby goodbye she had felt overwhelmed by love, a love that to her felt even stronger for being something she had been forced to learn. She knows that others might not understand this – that despite having been diagnosed with post-natal depression and been told time and time again by her doctor that it was an illness, not a personality trait, that some people might still see her as a bad mother for having had to learn how to love her baby. But she knows they are wrong. Finally, after a lot of support from her doctor, her husband and her family, she knows that while she is not perfect, she is not a bad mother.

She tugs at her red dress – it feels tight after dinner, and after so long opting for comfortable, practical clothes over anything smarter. Her husband notices and reaches a hand out for hers.

'You look beautiful,' he says.

She looks up, caught off guard. As she looks at him she feels her love for him overwhelming her too. Over the past year it has been tested; she thinks with a sudden sharp pain of the months after Ella was born when things were at their worst. She knows that her depression has challenged them both. In her darkest moments she doubted that they would make it through. She still isn't sure what lies ahead for them, or how their life and their love will change as Ella grows older and new obstacles are thrown in their way. But they are here.

'Shall we go home now?' her husband says, squeezing her hand.

'Yes,' she replies with a smile, 'Yes please.'

As they leave she glances back at the café, remembering sitting there alone in the middle of the night. She thinks about how lost and lonely she felt then, how terrified she felt about her own feelings and about the future. She still feels frightened, she thinks as they step outside, but she also knows that's OK. Being frightened, she has learnt, is just part of being a parent. Together, they shut the door on Stella's and walk hand in hand towards the bus stop, towards home.

HANNAH

As the door opens she looks up. But the face she sees is that of a stranger: a middle-aged man with a bottle of vodka poking out of the pocket of his large coat, who orders a takeaway bacon sandwich from the counter. Hannah looks down again, trying to calm her heartbeat that raced at the sound of the opening door.

She doesn't know what she will do when she sees Mona's face. It has been a long time but she can still picture it clearly, trying to forget the look of anger there when they fought in the café a year ago and instead remembering it painted with a warm smile.

When Mona left, something inside Hannah broke. It was as though her friend leaving was the final thing after several years of gradually building and unaddressed stresses and anxieties that pushed her until she toppled over. She felt as though she couldn't keep going any more – not with her career but also with the simplest of tasks. She went home because

London suddenly felt too big for her, everything felt too much to manage.

She arrived in Wales with a small suitcase, intending only to stay a couple of weeks. She stayed for six months. For the first few days she stayed in bed, finding herself unable to move. She felt exhausted and yet she couldn't sleep. Instead she lay under the covers in a half-awake state, darkness surrounding her and thoughts rising like tentacles from the deep to pull her under. *I'm a failure. What am I going to do with the rest of my life? I've messed everything up. I can't do this any more. I'm useless, I'm worthless, I'm nothing.*

Her parents drove to London after a few weeks and packed up the rest of her things, helping her deal with the landlord who, in the end, was understanding and let both Hannah and Mona end their contract early. It was Hannah's parents who passed on the details to Mona. So many times, Hannah wanted to call Mona but guilt and hurt and sheer raging-hot embarrassment held her back. She knew she had treated Mona badly when she was with Jaheim and afterwards too, but she felt too ashamed to admit it and too overwhelmed to make it right. Everything suddenly felt too much, and although she hated herself for it, she just didn't have the energy to fix things with Mona, not back then. Part of her still wanted to get on a train though and head back to London, catching Mona before she left and telling her all the things she felt deeply inside her – that she was proud of her and that she cared about her. But in her half-awake, half-asleep state the thought of getting on a train made her sweat. She had never felt that way before, but suddenly even the thought of leaving the house made her panic. And most of all, she felt convinced that Mona wouldn't want to see her. She hated the thought of being turned away by her friend so it felt safer to stay in bed, missing her silently and fiercely but not picking up the phone. Thinking back to that time, now nearly a year ago, Hannah realises she now understands what people mean when they describe someone having a 'breakdown'. That's what it had felt like to her – as though she had been travelling along a road for a long time, gradually running out of fuel but keeping going, spluttering along as much as she could until eventually she came to a grinding halt.

And then her mum had got sick. She found a lump in her left breast that she thought was nothing but wanted to get checked out anyway. But it wasn't nothing. Everything happened very quickly after that: operations, chemotherapy. Hannah quickly forgot about her own problems because this was so much more important – she suddenly managed to hold things together because she had to, for her mum.

Back then, she thought about calling Mona. She knew how much Mona cared about her mum and Hannah also desperately needed a friend. But everything was suddenly so urgent and all Hannah's attention was devoted to the only thing that suddenly mattered – keeping her mother alive. She drove her and her father to hospital appointments, her mother too unwell to drive, her father too upset. She cooked for them and cleaned the house and kept her parents' friends informed. Her guitar lay untouched in the spare room that she had been sleeping in, along with all the other thoughts she had chosen to push aside in order to focus on her family.

Slowly, gradually, things started to improve. In the end, her mother lost her breasts but kept her life. Hannah knows that her mother will always have to have regular check-ups, and that there is a chance that the cancer might come back. But for now, things are OK. She still has her mum.

Hannah moved back to London six months ago, when her mother was starting to get better and her father said he could manage on his own again. She still goes back to visit regularly but has tried to rebuild her life here after her time away.

The waiter hands the customer on the other side of the room a bacon sandwich and Hannah suddenly realises she has seen him before. He is the young man whose money she nearly stole from the inside pages of a crossword book. She blushes at the memory: it is one of many of which she is not proud. Although she fixed it in the end, like so many other times her first instinct was not the right one, she knows that now. She wishes she could go back and change things, undoing the decisions she made back then as though she is unpicking tight knots.

She smoothes her dress: green silk that slips snugly over her slim hips. She has come here straight from work – a new steady gig at a hotel, a different one this time, one where her traditional style works for them. She only sings there two nights a week and the money isn't great but it feels like something to finally feel proud of. It is a nice hotel and the guests sometimes come up and speak to her at the end of a set, often older couples who tell her these jazz songs remind them of their youth. She always smiles at this, wondering what specific memory her singing must have sparked in these grey-haired men and women. The rest of the time she now spends giving singing lessons to children and sometimes their parents – adults who crave the feeling of letting their inhibitions go and surrounding themselves with music. Hannah knows that feeling well; in fact it's teaching that has brought her back to it, reminding her when she sees the joy on the faces of her pupils just how freeing music can be. She never imagined she would enjoy teaching so much but has found that at thirty-one, she has discovered a new passion.

She looks up at the clock: Mona's train would have arrived at St Pancras a couple of hours ago, but she said she wanted to head to her hotel first to drop her bags and change. They would meet at midnight, that time between night and day that they used to share so often in this café, gossiping quietly about the customers amid the sound of *The Breakfast Club* playlist and the smell of coffee and fried food. To others it might seem an unusual meeting time, but to them it felt just right.

Hannah had been nervous about contacting Mona after so long, but when she heard from Bemi that Mona would also be attending her and Anya's wedding at Islington Town Hall that weekend, she sent her a message before she could change her mind, asking if she wanted to meet before the ceremony. She hated the thought of their first meeting in a year being among a crowd of people, canapés and glasses of prosecco thrust between them and no quiet moment to talk, to finally say the things that have stayed unsaid this past year. Because as she waits in the café for her old friend, Hannah realises that is what she wants. She needs to apologise and to try to put into words her breakdown and everything that happened afterwards with her mum. Not as an excuse for her behaviour, but just to say

392

it, to fill the space between them with the words she knows she should have said months ago.

Over the past year she has felt the absence of Mona as a physical pain akin to grief. Their stories used to be so closely woven together: tearing that apart left Hannah's life gaping, loose threads hanging, frayed around the edges. When she broke down and then when her mother was sick, she missed her friend fiercely.

She knows she should have got in touch sooner but her emotions, and then her life got in the way. Then, when she got back to London she realised how long it had been and it suddenly seemed hard to pick up the phone. The longer it went on, the harder it felt.

She worried Mona wouldn't want to talk to her and she didn't know what to say, how to pick up their friendship. Instead, she focused on getting herself back together and starting a life of her own, without her friend. Back in London, she threw herself into her singing again – practising, writing songs and sending her CD out to hotels and restaurants. She tried not to think about Mona, but there were moments when she was hit so suddenly and forcefully by thoughts of her friend that she found it hard to breathe. A song playing on the radio, a dark-haired woman walking across the road and the day she heard back from the hotel saying they wanted to hire her, and her first thought was how much she wanted to tell Mona.

If she could go back in time and do things differently, she would. She would never have dated Jaheim, for one thing. She would have been more honest with Mona about how truly terrified she felt about her future, instead of letting th feelings build up to the point that they made her obsessive and irrational and eventually pushed her to breaking point. She would have appreciated the support of her friend instead of starting to take it for granted. She would have thrown her a wonderful party for her thirtieth birthday instead of spending it in bed, crying over Jaheim. She would have come to wave her goodbye at the station. She would have told her that despite their arguments she loved her and was proud of her. And then she would have called. And called and called and called. She would never have cut the thread of their friendship, she would have held on tightly, never letting go. Her life might now be more settled, but she still carries this regret and the pain of her lost friend. Her career may never have reached the heights she dreamed of when she was younger – she doesn't have a record deal, she has never been on tour, she is not able to support herself financially by singing alone – and yet this doesn't seem to matter so much any more. The biggest regret of her life so far has been the breakdown of her friendship with Mona.

She shuffles in her seat, pushing her knife and fork onto her now empty plate and looking anxiously out the window, searching the anonymous faces for a glimpse of brown eyes and long, dark plaited hair. Her heart beats quickly inside her chest. Maybe they can never go back to how it was before, but she wa‍ explain everything that has happened since they l‍ ‍ther, and how hard it made it for her to reach ‍ting to. She wants to say how sorry she is. She ‍irst step back towards her old friend.

MONA

And yet something holds her back from opening the door. She stands a little way down the street from the café, looking towards it but frozen on the spot.

She hasn't seen Hannah in a year. She thinks back to that night a year ago when she arrived home from her shift ready to try and fix things with Hannah but was met with an empty flat and a note taped to the mirror in the hallway that said Hannah had gone home for a few weeks to stay with her parents. She wouldn't be back before Mona left, the note said. Despite the note, on the day of her train to Paris Mona lingered a little longer than she meant to in the flat, wondering if Hannah would turn up at the last moment to say goodbye. The flat felt bigger now that it was empty of her things: some in storage, most sold or given away, and the rest piled into the two large suitcases that stood by the front door. She wandered through the apartment, running her fingers across the walls and over the peeling posters and standing for a few minutes in her empty room. Before leaving she went into Hannah's too and sat on the edge of her friend's mattress. She looked at the framed photo of them both that still stood on her bedside table. She picked up a dress from the floor and folded it over the end of the bed. Then she closed the door, reached for her suitcases and left the flat for the last time, posting her keys through the letterbox.

In Paris, it was easier to shut out thoughts of her friend. Everything was new and different and exciting. Poppy and

Antoine met her at the Gare du Nord and they shared a taxi back to their apartment, Poppy chattering the whole way while Mona looked out the window, watching her new city flash past her and trying her best to take in every detail. She caught Antoine's eye and he smiled at her.

'You'll get used to it,' he had said. And over time, she did.

Whenever her thoughts turned to Hannah, as they often did despite her best efforts, she considered picking up the phone and calling her. But there was always something to do instead – a rehearsal to attend with her new company, or a party to go to with Poppy and Antoine, or a brunch with her new colleagues. She distracted herself in order to push out the painful memories of the breakdown of their friendship. She distracted herself for nearly a year.

When she received the wedding invite from Bemi and Anya, one of her first thoughts had been whether Hannah would be there. And yet it still came as a surprise when her phone buzzed and she saw Hannah's name there. It had been so long since they had spoken that it felt strange to see her name, even if not too long ago she was the person who texted her most frequently. It was a short message asking if she wanted to meet in the café before the wedding. Mona stared at the message for a while before replying. Did she want to meet her? She considered for a moment how awkward it might be to meet for the first time at the wedding, but how safe too – among the crowds of wedding guests and in the glow of Bemi and Anya's special day there would be no chance for honest words or explanations. It's this that finally made her reply to Hannah's text with a simple answer: **'Yes, let's meet.'** Her own reaction to the message had surprised her, but she realised that after so long shutting out thoughts of their friendship she was ready to confront it again. She wanted to talk to her, she wanted to see her. She couldn't explain why exactly, because she still felt a twist of anger knotted inside her when she thought of Hannah, but something pulled her back towards her too. Their shared history, and all the happier memories.

But as she pauses on the street next to the café, she suddenly isn't so sure if it was a good idea. She doesn't know what she will say to her, or whether she wants to hear whatever words Hannah has to offer in exchange. She thinks of her friend when they were at their closest – living together and working together and sharing every detail of their lives. She realises she is terrified of opening the door and seeing a stranger. She hesitates on the pavement.

A couple with hands entwined brush past her and veer off down a side street. Mona stands alone, looking up at the familiar sign of the café and wondering if she wants to see her friend again. The thought of her hotel room enters her mind: cool and safe and impersonal. She thinks about Hannah and whether there is anything left from their old life together for them to hold onto. Are there any words left to say, any new chapters to add to their story, or is what it has become all that it can ever be – two women with two separate lives, in two separate cities, two separate worlds?

Mona stands on the pavement, the cold beginning to bite at her as she pauses between decisions, between paths, between anger and forgiveness.

HARRY

The sound of something crashing in the kitchen rouses him; he looks around the café, suddenly remembering where he is. He takes in the café, the place he has visited often in recent weeks. As he does a memory comes back to him as it always does when he is here – of Martha and himself here before their honeymoon a year ago. The memory seems a very long time ago now even though in reality it is not so old. It belongs to another time, a time before.

Harry grips his coffee cup, now cold, so tightly that he fears he might break it. But it remains intact – the only breaking is happening inside him.

He had six months of being married to Martha before she died. A heart attack, completely unexpected, completely un-believable at first. They had only just finished putting their wedding and honeymoon photos into albums. Harry and Martha cutting a cake, Harry and Martha dancing together, Harry and Martha leaning out of a safari truck, an enormous elephant towering in the background. He had only just got used to being married again, to calling Martha his wife, to seeing the new wedding band shining on his finger.

At first, he had raged against her death – against the unfair-ness of it all, against the horror and the suddenness. He was consumed by anger, turning to drink instead of his friends, instead of the sons he hadn't spoken to since he left Jennifer. He barely left the flat, pacing and shouting during the day and at night lying in bed and staring at her wedding ring on the bedside table, her pyjamas still folded on the pillow.

Then his anger had turned to something different: a numbness, an inability to feel anything at all. He couldn't imagine ever being happy again, but he didn't feel sad exactly either. He felt nothing, a nothingness that was all-consuming. He stopped drinking so much then, no longer needing the alcohol in order to feel numb. He stopped eating too.

Tonight, he couldn't face the emptiness of his bed again, so without realising what he was doing, he had dressed again and come here, to the café that reminds him of Martha and their honeymoon where they saw an elephant and she had laughed so hard she had cried. He recalls it again – the sound of Martha's laughter. He remembers it so clearly that it is as though she is there next to him, holding his hand and looking out the window, pointing things out to him and talking to him. She is wearing her green summer dress with the carefully selected layers over the top – so like her to think everything through like that. Their suitcases sit under the table, neatly packed, waiting for them to carry them to the coach and then the airport. They are both excited, looking forward to their honeymoon, to the prospect of seeing an elephant, but also to the whole rest of their lives together.

'I'm so glad I'm here with you,' she says, in that voice that Harry knows so well.

And although when he looks up to reply he realises that she is not here, that he is alone, Harry is glad too. Glad for her voice, for her laugh, for the way she smiled, and glad for the time he had with her, even though it was too short. Their time together was full of happiness, a happiness he had never known was really possible, not for him, not any more. He had waited ten years of knowing her for two years together, two perfect years. As he sits and thinks of her, remembering her so much his whole body aches with grief, he realises something. That he would have waited a whole lifetime for just one day with her.

DAN

He stands at the counter, watching the man who sits alone in the middle of the café. Sadness is painted on his face and Dan wants to go over to him, to say something, but he pauses, sensing that right now this man would prefer to be alone. Instead, Dan focuses hard on sending him happiness, hoping that just by thinking it and wishing it for him, some of it might land on the man's drooped shoulders.

The rest of the customers have gone by now, apart from the red-haired former waitress who sits in the corner. She has been here for nearly an hour without moving, her eyes fixed on the door. She has drunk a cappuccino and eaten a plate of pancakes while she has been here, the whole time looking outside. She is so focused on the window that Dan leaves her alone, staying at the counter.

Eventually the old man stands very slowly and walks to the door, leaving a pile of coins on his table. He takes one last look back inside, as though he has forgotten something. His eyes search the café. But he must not be able to find what he is looking for, because then he turns and is gone.

Dan starts to slowly clear up, removing empty cups and

wiping tables, making the most of this brief moment with no new customers and no new orders to make. But strangely, as he works and stares out the window into the night, he doesn't feel quite so alone any more. He is an island in the dark, the city moving around outside the window. As he looks out at the street he spots other islands – a woman waiting for a bus, an unexpected night cyclist whizzing past – and realises all over the city must be people like him, passing time, carrying sadness and worries but a tiny whisper of hope too. The people he sits next to on the bus and who visit the café have their own stories, some with words and chapters that read just like his. He lives alongside them, their lives brushing up against each other for brief moments, before moving on. He might not know them, but he knows they are there and that however different they might be, at times they feel things that he has felt before and will likely feel again. As long as this is true, and as long as they exist, he will never truly be alone.

HANNAH

The clock on the wall edges closer to one and she shifts on her seat, her body growing numb. A cold cup of tea stands on the table in front of her. She looks out into the night and realises that it is probably time to leave.

She is the only customer left now and the chairs sit empty, waiting. The waiter leans against the counter, a book open in his hand and a look of relaxed contentment on his face. Hannah reads the book cover: *The Hobbit*. Above him, Ernest the bear watches the café and the street beyond, his stern eyes peering down from beneath the top hat.

Hannah wonders if she will come back here again. It seems too strange now – a part of a previous life. Her heart aches as she realises that the friendship that was once so important to her is truly over. She has lost the friend who for years felt like a sister. The woman she lived with, worked alongside and shared her dreams and ambitions. The woman who spurred her on and who supported her, but whom she ultimately pushed away without truly meaning to. She feels the sharp pain of regret and most of all she misses her friend. She misses the moments that are now memories and the moments she had hoped they would one day share together. Weddings perhaps, where they would watch each other marry and feel a huge happiness for one another; children they might meet, feeling astounded that their friend had managed to create a whole, wonderful person; parents' funerals where they would cry for each other and hug each other fiercely, hoping that friendship might help heal wounds and nurse broken hearts. Hannah pictures these moments and sees them disappearing, knowing that they will never happen now, that she will no longer be a part of her friend's life. She reaches for her jacket on the back of her chair and her handbag on the floor.

As she is reaching down, she notices the sound of the café door opening. She grips her bag tightly as she hears a voice she recognises.

'Hello,' says the voice.

Hannah turns around in her chair, looking up at the new customer standing in the middle of Stella's. Through the tears that are suddenly falling down her cheeks, she sees a face that she knows well. For a moment it is set in a frown and Hannah's heart beats fast, her feet rooted to the spot. But then the face opposite her breaks into the start of a smile. And in an instant the two women are crossing the space of the café, stepping through the distance of a year and hundreds of unspoken words. When they reach one another, Hannah wraps her arms around her old friend. This time she won't let go, she thinks as Mona hugs her back. For the past year, Hannah has felt stuck at an ending. But in the quiet of the café, hugging her friend, she feels as though she has just found a beginning.

ACKNOWLEDGEMENTS

Although Hannah and Mona may have their ups and downs, the starting point for this book was wanting to write about the importance of female friendships – about the strength, the support, the laughter, the love. So, in these acknowledgements it feels fitting to firstly thank my wonderful friends. My school friends Alice, Harriet and Janaissa, who knew me as a dorky, awkward teenager and still wanted to hang out with me. It feels so special to still have you in my life. Juliette, my 'French sister' - your letters dropping on my doormat always make me smile. My London friends: Lucy (the first friend I made in the city) and 'diosas' Kitty and Marie who helped me find my place and took me to shows and jazz bars. Kim, Dee and Shalini who started as work friends but soon became *friend* friends, with a special thank you for all the *food* we have shared together. Frankey, my Ladies Pond swimming buddy. Sharon and Juno, for the trips to the zoo / park / story centre that always brighten my day. Alex, who as well as being my sister is the very best of friends. To friends unnamed but who each bring their own type of happiness to my life. And to friendships that may have now run their course but that still brought so much at a particular time in my life.

Thank you, Mum and BK, for your constant love and support. I feel so lucky to have you both as parents. Thank you Sally and Michael for turning up to so many of my book events and seeming to never grow sick of hearing me speak – your support means so much. Thank you to my Grandpa, Fred, for all the ways you've supported me and cheered me on over the years.

Writing this book was somewhat different to writing *The Lido*. This time round I was fortunate enough to dedicate all my time to it rather than sneaking in moments at my laptop around a full-time job. And I was cheered on and encouraged by actual, real, *lovely* readers. So a HUGE thank you to every single person who supported my first book – to all the book sellers, bloggers, journalists and librarians who championed it and to every reader who read it, recommended it, came along to an event or listened to the audiobook. Thank you.

Thank you to my brilliant agent Robert Caskie for being the best champion and supporter, and to Liza De Block for all your hard work too. Thank you to the whole team at Orion, for your endless enthusiasm and brilliant work. Clare Hey, for your fantastic editorial eye and in particular for allowing me the freedom to write the book I wanted to write. Virginia

Woolstencroft for all your work promoting this book and for coming along to support at events. Cait Davies – whose creativity knows no bounds. A big thank you also to Sarah Benton, Katie Espiner, Britt Sankey, Olivia Barber, Harriet Bourton, Paul Stark, Rabab Adams, Jen Wilson, Barbara Ronan, Esther Waters, Victoria Laws, Francis Doyle, Ruth Sharvell and Sally Partington.

And last but not least, thank you Bruno for everything else. For talking me round whenever I doubt myself, for putting up with my moods when I'm struggling to get the words down on the page, for making me laugh and for simply being home. I'm so lucky to call you my husband.

CREDITS

Libby Page and Orion Fiction would like to thank everyone at Orion who worked on the publication of *The 24-Hour Café* in the UK.

Editorial
Clare Hey
Harriet Bourton
Olivia Barber

Copy editor
Sally Partington

Proof reader
Laetitia Grant

Audio
Paul Stark
Amber Bates

Contracts
Anne Goddard
Paul Bulos
Jake Alderson

Design
Rabab Adams
Joanna Ridley
Nick May

Editorial Management
Charlie Panayiotou
Jane Hughes
Alice Davis

Finance
Jasdip Nandra
Afeera Ahmed
Elizabeth Beaumont
Sue Baker

Production
Ruth Sharvell

Marketing
Cait Davies

Publicity
Virginia Woolstencroft

Sales
Jen Wilson
Esther Waters
Victoria Laws
Rachael Hum
Ellie Kyrke-Smith
Frances Doyle
Georgina Cutler

Operations
Jo Jacobs
Sharon Willis
Lisa Pryde
Lucy Brem

If you loved *The 24-Hour Café,* you'll adore the new uplifting novel from *Sunday Times* bestseller Libby Page

Lorna's world is small but safe.

She loves her daughter, and the two of them is all that matters. But after nearly twenty years, she and Ella are suddenly leaving London for the Isle of Kip, the tiny remote Scottish island where Lorna grew up.

Alice's world is tiny but full.

She loves the community on Kip, her yoga classes drawing women across the tiny island together. Now Lorna's arrival might help their family finally mend itself – even if forgiveness means returning to the past . . .

So with two decades, hundreds of miles and a lifetime's worth of secrets between Lorna and the island, can coming home mean starting again?

Read on for a sneak peek of this feel-good story of friendship, community and finding where you truly belong . . .

LORNA

Euston station, 8.30 p.m. It's midsummer and London sweats and steams, clutched in the middle of a heatwave. The after-work crowds have thinned but the concourse is still busy, figures in damp, crumpled suits staring at the announcement boards where times and destinations flash in orange letters. Families huddle in groups, mothers fanning young children and handing out water bottles as they wait, perched on piles of luggage. A surprising scent of coconut wafts from the glowing doorway of The Body Shop, mingling with the sourer human smells of hundreds of hot passengers leaving and arriving, carrying bags and their own secret burdens. A few discarded evening newspapers litter the floor, trampled underfoot by rushing commuters and holidaymakers. A police officer patrols the perimeter of the station, an Alsatian sniffing the air at the end of a short lead. Occasionally the officer pauses on his route to wipe beads of sweat from his forehead.

We are early. The 9.20 train to Fort William is up there on the board but there's no platform yet. Beside me my daughter Ella pulls her new pink suitcase as though it's empty, her steps light. My own case feels much heavier as it drags behind me. Partly because this whole trip was Ella's idea really, not mine.

I glance across at her, my teenage daughter on the cusp of turning fourteen in just a few weeks' time, as she pauses, staring eagerly up at the clock. Her pale cheeks are flushed with excitement and the warmth of this summer evening and her auburn hair hangs loose, for once in natural curls rather than the poker-straight style she spends nearly an hour achieving each morning. When Ella asked for hair straighteners for Christmas, I refused at first. I've always loved her curls, ever since she was a baby and the soft ringlets first started to grow. I'll always remember the sweet, talcum-powder scent of her head when she was a baby and the feeling of her hair tickling my face when she struggled to sleep as a toddler and shared my bed. Back then I'd often wake with Ella's face pressed against my cheek. Her reddish-brown curls would be the first thing I'd see when I opened my eyes. The thought of her singeing them makes me wince. And yet she was insistent about those straighteners, pleading with me for the first time in her life. So I bought them. When she opened them she nearly knocked over the small Christmas tree in our flat as she leapt over to thank me with an eager hug. That's partly why I agreed to this trip: it's only the second time she's ever truly asked anything of me.

My hair is the same shade as Ella's but even wilder – I long ago gave up trying to control my own curls and today they're pulled off my face in a messy bun, the nape of my neck damp from the heat and the rucksack on my back. How is it so hot? Surely it should be cooler this late in the day, but the heat clings to me.

'Shall we grab some food while we wait?'

Ella glances across at my question. There's wariness in her eyes. We've always been so close: the two of us against the world. But these past few days have tested us like nothing else. I can feel my emotions simmering beneath the surface – anger, fear, grief – but I push them down like clothes stuffed into an overfull suitcase. I may have my reservations about being here but here we are. In the end I agreed to this trip for my daughter's sake. And perhaps for my own too. After all these years, maybe it's finally time to go back to the place I once escaped and to face everything that I left behind.

'Leon?' I suggest, knowing, of course, that it's her favourite. Her lips part into a broad smile and there it is, one of those surging swells of love that so often take me off guard, a love that fills up every cell in my body and makes me feel as though I could levitate. For a second, I forget the reason why we are here and everything that awaits us at the end of our long journey and link my arm through my daughter's.

'Good idea, Mum,' she replies.

Ella waits with the bags while I queue for our food. Ahead of me in the line is a family – two grandparents, a grown-up daughter and three children, one in a buggy, one on the mother's hip and one holding the hand of his grandfather. My stomach twists as I watch them.

'You all have what you like,' the grandfather says, reaching for his wallet.

'Thanks Dad,' replies his daughter, smiling wearily but gratefully.

I look away, blinking quickly.

'Next please!' calls the server and I return my attention to the menu, choosing two halloumi wraps and the waffle fries Ella loves. A few seconds later I'm holding the steaming foil parcels and returning to our table outside where Ella is wiping a debris of discarded food and litter into a paper napkin. On a neighbouring table a pigeon with one gnarled pink foot hops among a scattering of leftovers. From up here we have a view of the concourse below as well as the platform boards. I can hear the hum of the street outside, the buses pulling up in front of the station and the Friday night traffic crawling down the Euston Road. Even inside, the air feels heavy with fumes and dust: the hot, heavy fug of the city that I have grown used to over the past twenty-two years.

I moved here as a teenager, arriving with a stolen suitcase and a head full of dreams. I quickly learnt how brutal the city can be though, especially when you are alone with nothing but a few hundred pounds in coins and rolled-up notes stuffed in your rucksack. I took whatever jobs I could find. Temp jobs and then years of bar work. It was only when I fell pregnant with Ella at twenty-six that I decided I needed a proper career and trained as a teacher, helped out by a hefty student loan and the council flat I managed to get for us both in a sixties block on the Isle of Dogs, that not-quite island encircled by the muddy River Thames where the shining tower blocks of Canary Wharf glint garishly on the horizon. Over the years I managed to save just enough money to buy our flat from the council, although each month I still feel the same panic that I might not be able to meet my mortgage payment. I always do manage it but the fear is still there, as familiar by now as the sound of my own breath. I've always been anxious about money. Because if something happens – if I get sick or the boiler breaks or I suddenly need something important for Ella, there's no one to bail us out. I know this well because all of those things and plenty more have happened over the years. And each time I've had to find some way to make ends meet by myself.

Ella's phone chirps and she looks down, her hair falling slightly in front of her face. She smiles and types a reply, her thumbs tapping at incredible speed on the screen.

'Ruby and Farah?' I ask. The two girls have been Ella's best friends since primary school. I'm used to seeing them at our flat, preparing snacks for the three of them and hearing their laughter spilling out of Ella's bedroom. I know it makes me a terrible mother to admit it, but many times over the years that noise has caused an involuntary pang of jealousy in my gut. Being envious of your own daughter does not feature on the 'ways to be a good mum' list. But I do envy Ella's closeness with her friends. I lost touch with the ones I used to have and have struggled to make them ever since. Making friends means answering too many questions and revealing too much about yourself and your past. It's simpler to keep to myself, devoting my life to Ella and my job. Mostly I've got used to it over the years but sometimes the loneliness catches me like a splinter.

'No,' Ella replies, not looking up, 'Molly.'

At the mention of the name the reality of the nature of this trip hits me again, throwing me off balance. Is it too late to turn around and head home? We could catch the tube and then the DLR and be back at our flat in less than an hour. Then we could spend the summer how we'd originally planned – visiting galleries and ice-cream shops and reading magazines together in the parks. Just me and Ella, the way it's always been.

My own phone pings and I reach for it in my pocket, the familiar motion distracting me. It's Cheryl.

'Have a safe journey,' the message reads, 'Let me know when you get there. xxx'

The message calms me slightly. If I say that Cheryl is my closest friend it's only really a half-truth. The full truth is that she is my only friend. We first met five years ago when she started as a teaching assistant at the school where I was then a year head and am now deputy head. I remember spotting her on playground duty that first day, playing football with the kids, her large gold hoop earrings swinging as she ran and the children chased her, her smiling mouth painted in bright red. Her laughter rose high and loud above the background din of the playground and I remember feeling an instant need to get to know her – this woman who could make herself heard over a rabble of children. She caught my eye and waved, pausing in the game for a moment and coming over to introduce herself. I'm not sure if we'd ever have become friends if she hadn't been so persistent though, chatting cheerfully to me every day at school and inviting me to go for a drink together after work. At first, she did most of the talking, but over time and as we grew closer she gently coaxed out details of my past. She's the only person who knows at least parts of my story, parts I've

416

always glossed over with other colleagues or with the mums of Ella's friends who've at times made unsuccessful attempts to draw me into their groups.

Cheryl is ten years younger than me and sometimes it shows – when she tries to talk to me about what songs are in the charts and celebrity gossip and I just nod and smile blankly. But mostly the age gap between us doesn't matter. We've grown close over the years and we each know enough about what it means to work at an inner-city primary school run by a chauvinist to understand one another well.

'Thanks,' I type back, 'End of term, hurrah! No more Dave the creep for six weeks! xx'

Dave, or Mr Phillips to the children, is our head and my boss. He's always made me somewhat uneasy, but ever since he appointed me as his deputy six months ago his inappropriate comments have become worse. If I knew it was going to be like this then perhaps I might have turned down the job. But I needed the extra money. And after ten years of teaching at the same school it felt like the recognition I'd been craving for so long. The recognition I *deserved*. Now I'm not even sure I truly earned the job or whether I was appointed for some other reason entirely. It's a depressing thought.

'I'm already on to my third glass of wine,' Cheryl replies. I smile, picturing my friend in the flat I've come to know so well. For my fortieth birthday last year instead of a big party Ella and I spent it at Cheryl's with her husband Mike and their two-year-old Frankie. Cheryl cooked for us while Mike dutifully topped up our wine glasses, pouring a splash for Ella to try too. It was a good evening and I wouldn't have wanted to spend it any differently. But there's still a part of me that imagined something bigger and noisier, if only I lived a bigger and noisier life. It's a thought that has visited regularly over the years – at birthdays, Christmases and New Years when Ella and I have celebrated alone in our flat again. We have our traditions: matching pyjamas at Christmas and watching the fireworks from our window at New Year with mugs of hot chocolate towering with marshmallows. But after we've said our goodnights I always stay awake, wondering if I've let Ella down by not being able to give her more than this – more than me.

Another message arrives from Cheryl and I know that she has seen through my joking tone. Of course she has; she knows me well.

I hope you're doing OK though. It must be so hard. I bet you're feeling nervous. I'm here whenever you need me. Just text or call, any time. xxx

A lump rises in my throat. I picture the black dress folded at the bottom of my suitcase and all the miles and all those years that stand between this station and our final destination.

'Platform one' says Ella suddenly, her voice high-pitched with excitement. I glance up at the board; is it really that time already? My pulse quickens. This is it. It's too late to turn back now and besides, I made a promise to my daughter. I can't let her down.

We gather our things and move through the station, passing a stand where baguettes sweat behind glass and another where a florist struggles to keep rainbow bouquets from wilting in the heat. Above us dozens of other possible destinations glow in amber, reminding me of all the other places we could be heading. Notices advise us to be alert to anything suspicious and adverts blink and flash in bright lights. And my daughter and I roll our suitcases behind us, weaving in and out of other passengers.

The Caledonian Sleeper waits at the platform, bottle green with an emblem of a stag on the side of each carriage.

'Is it your first time travelling with us?' asks a pink-faced man in a green uniform with a thick Glaswegian accent. He clutches a clipboard and pulls briefly at the collar of his shirt.

'Yes!' Ella says.

'No,' I say at the exact same moment.

This train might look slightly more modern than the one I caught to London when I was eighteen, but I still remember it well. The man in the uniform looks at us both, frowning for a second before regaining his charming customer-service smile.

'Well here is a brochure about your journey,' he says, handing it to Ella, 'You'll find a card in your room, if you could write down your preferences for breakfast. You're in coach G, right down the other end. Just keep walking.'

'Perhaps we're walking to Scotland,' Ella jokes as we head further and further down the platform. I don't laugh though; suddenly I can't even find a smile.

Finally, we find coach G and another staff member ticks our names off a list and helps us carry our luggage on board. The train's corridors are so narrow that we have to walk to our berth single file. If we met someone coming the other way we'd have to back up like cars reversing on a country lane. Luckily the carriage is empty for now.

Ella opens the door onto a room not much larger than an airing cupboard.

'This is so cool!'

My daughter has always been an optimist. The room contains a sink, a narrow set of bunkbeds and a small window. Ella dumps her suitcase on the floor and clambers straight up the ladder onto the top bunk. There's just enough space for me to step inside and close the door. As Ella tests out her bed, I stow my suitcase under the bottom bunk and lift Ella's onto the rack above the sink.

The train is mostly as I remember it, with its tiny corridors and long windows. But it's my first time inside one of the cabins. When I took the sleeper train all those years ago I spent the night in the seated carriage. All the saved tips from my job at the local pub hadn't been enough to cover a cabin, especially as I knew I'd need to keep money for when I arrived in London. I didn't sleep all night. Instead I sat wide awake, running my fingers over a pebble stowed in my coat pocket and staring out the window into the darkness.

At 9.25 p.m. I feel a jolt in my stomach as the train pulls away from the station.

'We're moving!' Ella says from her top bunk. She's already changed into her pyjamas and is lying on her bed. Her voice brims with anticipation.

Standing by the window, I watch as the train eases away from the station and rolls through the city. The sky is a dark lavender washed with peach, city lights starting to glow as evening draws in. Endless office blocks and rows of terraced houses hug the railway line, bricks stained black from pollution. A few lone workers are still visible inside one office while in another I spot a cleaner pushing a hoover steadily between empty desks. I look up at the tower blocks not dissimilar to our own, lives cramped side by side and on top of one another. I wonder if any of the people inside these blocks know their neighbours, or whether it's just me who has lived alongside strangers for most of my life. Some of the blocks we pass are sleek and modern, geometric shapes cut out of steel and glass. But squashed right up close too are buildings with boarded-up windows, supermarkets housed in ugly squat buildings, car parks and junk yards and building sites where cranes make a mess of the skyline. I picture the city stretching beyond the boundaries of what I can see, rolling out in a sprawling mass of buildings and streets, parks and stamp-sized gardens, the backbone of the River Thames arching through its centre. Millions of lives rubbing up alongside one another, crossing over and converging in the sounds of neighbours shouting and the smell of cooking seeping through ceilings and walls.

I can't help but think of our flat, dark and empty now. The collection of stones and smoothed glass on the kitchen windowsill, collected from my daily runs alongside the river. The small living room with photos of Ella on the walls and a few of the two of us, and the growing patch of damp in the corner that I really need to get sorted. And Ella's bedroom, the bed neatly made and a soft-toy puffin named Dora resting on her pillow. Whenever I step inside my daughter's room I dread seeing that Dora has been relegated from the bed. It will happen one day, just like so many things I fear about my daughter getting older. But each time I see that floppy, faded puffin there I thank god it's not today.

Outside the train window the city continues to flash by. This city has been my home for over twenty years but as the train edges towards the suburbs and then out into open countryside it's as though a thread linking me to London strains and then snaps. In its place I feel the tug of a much older connection, one I've tried to ignore for years but that I feel now pulsing under my skin. It's a connection that pulls me north. I picture mountains and black lochs, sheep and sunburnt bracken. Large, sweeping skies and teal sea. Something a bit like terror and something like excitement flutters uncontrolled inside. I gave everything to escape the place where I grew up. And I have resisted making this journey back ever since. I fought against it, ran away from it, hid from it. But despite it all, there is a part of me that longs to see a mountain again.

The Island is available in hardback, eBook and audio in summer 2021